Rogue
Mistress

Shadow Lane Volume Twelve

A Novel of Sex, Spanking and Fetish Romance

by
Eve Howard

CCB Publishing
British Columbia, Canada

Rogue Mistress Shadow Lane Volume Twelve:
A Novel of Sex, Spanking and Fetish Romance

Copyright ©2015 by Eve Howard
ISBN-13 978-1-77143-207-8
First Edition

Library and Archives Canada Cataloguing in Publication
Howard, Eve, 1953-, author
Rogue mistress shadow lane volume twelve :
a novel of sex, spanking and fetish romance / by Eve Howard. -- First edition.
Issued in print and electronic formats.
ISBN 978-1-77143-207-8 (pbk.).--ISBN 978-1-77143-208-5 (pdf)
Additional cataloguing data available from Library and Archives Canada

Cover artwork by Tarsis: www.briantarsis.com

Disclaimer: This is a work of fiction. The characters, incidents and dialogues are products of the author's imagination and are not to be construed as real. Any resemblance to actual events or persons living or dead is entirely coincidental.

Extreme care has been taken by the author to ensure that all information presented in this book is accurate and up to date at the time of publishing. Neither the author nor the publisher can be held responsible for any errors or omissions. Additionally, neither is any liability assumed for damages resulting from the use of the information contained herein.

Publisher: CCB Publishing
              British Columbia, Canada
              www.ccbpublishing.com

Contents

Part One: July

Part Two: August

Part One: July

Chapter One

Colby and Amanda go to Europe

At the beginning of July Amanda Sands, still eighteen for a few months yet, and her boyfriend Colby Hodge, nineteen, began their European holiday in Rome. On the morning of their arrival, the two soon-to-be Harvard sophomores checked into their snug, 3 star hotel, admired the velvety wall paper, showered in the beautifully designed Italian bathroom, made love on the narrow bed, which was in any case, wide enough for their two slim bodies and took a small nap, before going downstairs for a pasta lunch in the hotel dining room. Amanda exhorted Colby to fill up, remembering that Italian restaurants and cafes tended to close between two and six. Colby always listened to Amanda's advice because she was good at thinking ahead, and made sure to buy chocolates. She pointed out that his foil wrapped truffles selections would quickly melt in the current heat, so they ate the rich bonbons immediately before proceeding to the Pantheon.

Lean and fair-haired, clad in khaki shorts and white shirts, the young tourists looked exactly like the fresh and pampered American children that they were. Her straight blonde hair was even a bit shorter than his, but she was in every other aspect so classically feminine that the pixie cut merely served to counterpoint her womanly charms. Colby, not normally overly protective of his beauty, nor often instantaneously jealous of other men, could not fail to notice that as soon as they hit the street, the men looked at Amanda with a vulgar lasciviousness that American men might reserve for lap dance clubs.

1

Accordingly, he took Amanda's hand and did not let it go anywhere they went, glowering at any man or boy who seemed disposed to grossly feast his eyes on the generous curves of his girlfriend's high, full bosom and lush, round bottom.

At the Castle St. Angelo, the placards set about the monument, which detailed the violent history of that papal adjunct, chilled Amanda. One told them that the walkway upon which they trod had afforded the last glimpse of the outside world to the prisoners arriving at the castle, before they were led to the dungeons, from which they would never emerge. Inside the ancient pile, they passed by straw lined chambers where captives were chained, tortured, starved and left to die. Colby was less interested in the plight of these unfortunate enemies of Rome than in the good Italian beer served in the rooftop café.

Late in the afternoon, they visited the Vatican and immediately became enraptured by the pink, brown and gold veined marble floors and astonishing art. Amanda saw a figure in a painting that reminded her of RanXerox, a comic character in a graphic novel of the same name, created by the Italian artist Liberatori, in the 1980's. Colby was familiar with the character and agreed that the figure in the Vatican mural must indeed have served as the model for the bullet-headed, girl-paddling, cyber punk.

While strolling the cobbled streets of Vatican City, they found a small tiled coffee bar with the best small cups of coffee with cream they had ever had.

As the afternoon waned, Amanda insisted upon doing some shoe shopping. The first shop they found was conveniently located next door to an internet café, in which Colby decided to wait. She was a fast shopper and appeared beside him in ten minutes, carrying a small bag containing one pair of burgundy leather, high heeled, ankle-bootie sandals. Finding a seat available beside her lover, Amanda fed a number of Euros into the computer station and logged into her email.

"This is strange," Amanda said to Colby.

"What, babe?"

"I just got an email from my mother. She says Eddie pulled a Rodney Yee on her and that she's leaving him."

"Who's Eddie?"

"My stepfather."

"Who's Ronnie Yee?"

"Rodney Yee. He's a famous yoga instructor."

"Hold on," said Colby, finding a web browser and doing a search. "I've got his wiki page up. Okay, it's says here the so-called "stud muffin" broke up his twenty five year marriage to pursue an affair with one of his pretty young disciples, whom he subsequently married."

"Really? Rodney Yee did that?" Amanda replied in amazement. "Oh no, this is terrible!"

She sent her mother a quick reply and she and Colby walked out of the café.

"I like your mom. She's super cute," said Colby.

"I just can't believe it. They've been together since I was two."

The next day, Amanda and Colby toured the Coliseum and the Forum, where friendly cats beset them. It was all extremely interesting to Amanda, but she was distracted by the email her mother had sent her the previous day and felt a great sense of disquiet at the situation developing in San Francisco, where her mother had owned a psychic emporium and head shop, alongside her step father's yoga studio and health food store, for nearly twenty years. How could Cassandra leave Eddie? Where would she go, what would she do?

The next email Amanda got from her mother answered these questions succinctly. It simply read: "Going to Random Point. I'll see you there when you get back in August."

The next day they were on the train to Florence, comfortable in first class. Staring out the window at the receding aqueducts of Rome, Amanda lamented her mother's decision to return to Random Point with some anxiety.

"I don't understand, babe," Colby said, "I thought you liked hanging out with your mom."

"I do, of course I do. But don't you see, Hugo just married Laura. If my mother suddenly shows up it might ...I don't know, confuse them all."

"You think she might be wanting to get back together with Hugo?" asked Colby, who knew and liked Amanda's natural father, Hugo Sands.

"How could she not?" Amanda sighed.

"Your mom is no home wrecker," Colby assured her.

"I know she wouldn't mean to be. She knows how long and hard Hugo worked at courting Laura. But how can Hugo resist her once she's in the village? She's very magnetic, you know."

"I know I think she's cute as hell. She's in the scene too, right?"

"She used to be, when she was with Hugo. And then afterwards, she dabbled in mistressing."

"Well, if she ever wants to play with a younger man, I volunteer."

"Colby, don't be perverse, we're talking about my mother."

Colby saw she was more amused than angry at the suggestion and kissed her.

The men on the streets of Florence were worse than the Romans with regard to groping backsides, as Amanda discovered the instant she let go of Colby's arm or wandered off even a few feet by herself. Simply walking to and from the nearest Cathedral to their hotel, she was provoked enough to at least try to slap one rude bottom clutcher across the face, but he dodged the blow and darted away into the crowd laughing. Meanwhile, Colby vigorously pushed another insolent pincher off the pavement and into the street, amazed that these aggressively lecherous idlers had nothing better to do with their time than annoy American girls cultured enough to choose to spend their tourist dollars here. The economist in him wondered at this ingratitude.

While repelled and frightened by the hungry eyed men in the streets, Amanda found herself anything but indifferent to the handsome and modestly blushing young waiter who brought them their pasta that night. She was looking every inch the junior model in the new high-heeled sandals she had bought in Rome and a clinging, sleeveless, burgundy jersey halter dress to match.

"What are you doing, Amanda?" Colby asked sharply, as soon as the waiter went away for the third time. "Do you want a good spanking when we get home?"

Amanda looked down, realizing she had been well and truly caught and murmured, "Sorry!"

"You know our agreement."

"What agreement?" she asked, dipping some very good Italian bread in olive oil and nibbling at it.

"To play with other couples if we like them, but no one else!"

"I didn't realize we had made an official agreement like that," said Amanda.

"I mean, it's been an unspoken agreement, since that night we spent in Boston with Pamela and Dru. Hasn't it?"

"Well, yes and no," mused Amanda. "After all, I did bring you in on that scene with Pamela and me where you got to play doctor with her."

"That was generous of you," Colby acknowledged. "But that doesn't get you a free pass to have sex with another guy."

"How about the fact that you recently had sex with that older woman in Boston?"

"That was long after you had sex with Pamela's husband. Granted that happened before they were married and as part of a paid session, but you know you enjoyed it. And I'm pretty sure you also gave it up to that photographer who's so hot for you, though you won't admit it," Colby shrewdly pronounced.

In all fairness, Amanda conceded that she had taken more liberties with her vows of love and fidelity to Colby than he had to her and taking his hand, earnestly pledged not to flirt with any other men or boys during their current sojourn in Europe.

"I'm still going to spank you later," he threatened before completely downing a large glass of excellent red table wine.

Chapter Two

Cassandra Returns to Random Point

It was a drizzly, muggy morning in early July when Cassandra Campi drove her brand new, small but luxurious compact into the village of Random Point and parked it outside Margaret Alexander's bookshop. A slim, athletic brunette of small and graceful proportions, the former resident of the coastal village just a few miles from the tip of the Cape still wore her wavy hair very long, but today it was pulled back to the nape of her neck in a tortoise shell barrette to fully set off her agreeable features and her smooth, slightly olive toned, slightly peach toned skin. She was not recognizably Amanda's mother, for the daughter was much taller, even more slender, much more bosomy and with pale, ash blonde hair. But the poised self-possession of the daughter was very like her mother's and Amanda had also inherited Cassandra habit of intuitive thinking, which traits made them both wonderful and exasperating to their admirers. And the mother and daughter did have many admirers, both being beautiful and generous creatures, made for love and esoteric sex, as long as it was practiced with good taste.

She was wearing a pale pink print, halter pencil dress with a small turquoise and rose flower design under a beige trench coat and taupe peep toe high vamp sandals that set off her shapely legs to advantage. The outfit, like the car, was just purchased and each was perhaps slightly richer than the former head shop proprietor was accustomed to parading about in. But that lady had decided it was time to alter, upgrade or enhance several aspects of her day-to-day existence in her new life away from her longtime partner, and the element of style seemed somehow more important than it had previously been. She'd been wont, in years past, to not hide, but to more or less play down her attractions and had rarely sported overtly provocative apparel to display the lean contours of her yoga-trained, vegetable nurtured body. But now she seemed to feel a need to change her image from one of modest introspection to one more freewheeling and overtly adventurous.

Cassandra walked directly into the coffee bar within the galleried bookshop and sat at the counter, behind which Hope Spencer Lawrence, the premiere blonde belle of the village, had served as barista and snack server for over four years. The beautiful Hope had recently made an investment in and had become a partner in the bookshop and as a result, wore her crimson apron over her plain white shirt and jeans with a new pride and enthusiasm for her work.

Hope stood before her pretty new guest and asked her what she wished to order with her full, smiling attention. Cassandra said she would drink espresso with cream on the side and also selected a large, fresh baking powder biscuit from a case of cakes, breads and pastries under glass to one side of the coffee bar.

"I think you know my daughter," said Cassandra, stretching out her small, delicate hand to shake Hope's. "She's often spoken of the beauty at the bookstore, Hope Lawrence."

"Who is your daughter?" asked Hope, taking Cassandra's hand in both of her own.

"Amanda Sands."

"Oh, I love Amanda!" said Hope, squeezing Cassandra's hand affectionately. "How lovely to meet you…"

"Cassandra," said the brunette, smiling back at Hope.

"I don't see the resemblance, and yet I do," said Hope, preparing her guest's espresso.

"She takes after Hugo," said Cassandra.

"She certainly does," Hope agreed. "They're both so tall and fair. But what brings you to Random Point after all these years? You're practically a legend, you know. Though you don't look like a legend. You look very young to be Amanda's mother."

"You're sweet," said Cassandra, with a becoming blush at the compliment. "What brings me to Random Point is that my relationship just broke up and as a consequence, I'm thinking of moving back to the Cape. Amanda will be in Cambridge for the next three years and I'd like to be in closer hailing distance to her than San Francisco."

"Don't you own a shop there?"

"I did until last week. But I'm tired of being a shop keeper and I've let my ex-partner buy me out of both the shop and the house we shared."

"Wow. That's huge. What are you going to do here?"

"I have a plan but I'm not sure it's going to work out yet. But I will gladly share all the details with you after I've had a few meetings with key people. William Random, for example. Is he in town this summer?"

"Yes, I saw him just the other day."

"What about Anthony Newton? You know he sent me a ring for the Venus Club."

"I know for a fact he is in town," said Hope of the New York composer, for she was on intimate terms of friendship with both Newton and his younger girlfriend, Susan Ross and was a frequent summer visitor at the Cliff house to avail herself of the pool and tennis court. She had been swimming up there over the weekend and she and her husband David Lawrence, a teacher at the local prep school, had even dined with Anthony and Susan.

Before leaving the shop Cassandra went out into the main room and finding the card section purchased a blank note card with a reproduction of the Botticelli Venus on the cover. She went back into the coffee bar with the card and getting out a pen sat at the counter for a moment to write a note.

"Do you happen to have Anthony Newton's address?" Cassandra asked Hope.

"Yes, he has an account with us," said Hope, checking her computer.

"Write it on the envelope for me?" Cassandra asked, quickly reviewing her note to the wealthy and artistic patron who was famous in the scene for showering his largesse on spankable girls and ladies. Hope copied Anthony Newton's address from her screen onto the envelope and handed it back to Cassandra.

The Bone and Feather Inn had of course been remodeled many times since its initial opening, but had stood on the same spot in the village for over a hundred and fifty years, and Cassandra remembered it well from her residence in Random Point twenty years before. She had in fact taken care to dress as smartly as she could in the knowledge that upon checking in she would walk by the pub room and dining room and possibly chance to see or be seen by someone she had known long ago. As it happened, the only guest sitting in the pub was Ambrose Bartlett, the owner of Bartlett's Department Store in the neighboring village of Woodbridge. He was a person well known to her daughter Amanda and subsequently spoken of by Amanda to her mother. But at this point, Cassandra had no way of connecting the attractive not quite middle aged businessman sitting at the bar drinking a red wine to the colorful individual who had hired Amanda several times to walk in his store fashion shows and who was also married to Amanda's best friend, Pamela. But Mr. Bartlett did look up and take note of Cassandra as she passed by the door on the way to the stairs leading up to the rooms. First of all, her body was light and graceful, which two traits he greatly admired, secondly, she had beautiful, sexy shoes on and thirdly, her face was charming.

"Who's that?" Bartlett asked Connie, the innkeeper who poured the random drink required of a midafternoon.

"I'll find out," Connie told her perpetual customer agreeably, going out to the reception desk to discover Cassandra's name from her assistant. The name meant nothing to herself or to Ambrose Bartlett when he heard it, yet there was something about the slim lady that seemed familiar to him, even though he had glimpsed her for but a moment.

Cassandra climbed to one of the third floor chambers and had only to wait a few moments before the check in clerk brought up her luggage. She had engaged to stay at the inn for at least the next week as she decided where in the village or near it she would eventually move. Rain began to patter and splash against the mullioned panes of her pleasant, rustic room as she exchanged her tight sundress and heels for walking shoes and socks, a pair of denim capris and a white cotton shirt. Thus attired for comfort, she took her umbrella and raincoat and walked out into the village, towards the street where she had once kept shop.

She stopped at the village post office to mail her card to Anthony Newton then continued on her way.

The Pearl still stood almost exactly as she had left it, the only shop of its kind in the village and as stuffed full of candles, incense, rolling papers and magical books as it had ever been. She'd just detached herself from a similar store in San Francisco and felt not the slightest urge to go and ask the present owner what he or she wanted for the entity. However, just looking in the window, Cassandra was reminded that she had no recreational supplies with her, having traveled by plane and realized that she could put off a visit to the antiques shop no longer.

It was a three block walk back to Shadow Lane, where Marguerite Alexander's bookstore and Hugo Sands Antiques shop occupied opposite corners of the small, cobbled cross street. Cassandra's heart pounded and her face flushed as she went through the front door and the familiar bell tinkled. The first time she'd walked into that shop Hugo had only just bought the property and opened the business. She was one local business owner welcoming another. He had come to her shop first, to buy rolling papers and incense. Then she had returned the visit, bringing him LSD. It had been an unconventional relationship from the start, with Cassandra instantly recognizing Hugo's powers of seduction and yielding to them with the enthusiasm of a student or a gifted apprentice. Now she only feared that his new bride would be present at this first meeting since her return to the village, which would be awkward before she'd had a chance to explain how things stood with her. She had every reason to believe that she and Laura would grow to be the truest of friends, but it would take some time to gain that lady's confidence and convince her that she, Cassandra, had not returned to Random Point to steal her husband. For Hugo was the father of Cassandra's beloved only child and the bond between the three of them, although they had never been together, all at once, was growing stronger all the time.

She had only sent Amanda to Hugo for the first time the previous autumn, just before the girl's first term at Harvard commenced. She had kept Amanda's existence a secret for 18 years, only allowing their child to enter Hugo's life after she had come of legal age. Now she wondered why. It was something to do with pride, certainly. He had never asked her to marry him during their two happy years together and she knew he wasn't particularly fond of children. When she became pregnant, she knew that if she told him, he would do the proper thing, but feared he might feel trapped and resentful, while doing so. He had loved her with warmth and affection, but without intellectual respect. He wholly discredited astrology, which was her hobby and expertise. She had always given readings as a sideline and as a result had been able to pamper Amanda with lessons, camps, European holidays, high tech toys, a large wardrobe and many other luxuries. Hugo had no patience with superstition and believed her to be as gullible as her followers, in spite of her explaining to him on more than one occasion that her talents were clearly of an intuitive nature rather than a psychic nature.

"Why couldn't he have just been nice about it?" Cassandra asked herself as she looked around the familiar front room of Hugo's shop, which was well arranged, nicely dusted and included some of the best and rarest vintage pieces in his collection. It was, as usual empty, but this was absolutely to be expected on a rainy day, even in high season. At the tinkle of the bell, Hugo got up from behind his computer monitor in his editorial office behind the shop and hurried out front to greet his possible customer. He appeared first behind the back counter and as she came forward into his line of vision, his face broke into a smile.

"You? Here in my shop?" he cried, coming around from behind the counter to embrace her. Then he held her away from him. "Why?"

"I need some weed, of course," she laughed.

"Sure, come into the back and I'll hook you up right away. Did you just get into town?"

"Yes, via Boston yesterday," explained Cassandra, following him into the back. "Is your wife around?"

"She's at home."

"When can I meet her?"

"Whenever you like. Come for dinner tomorrow."

"Really? She won't mind?"

"Not at all, she was fine with Anthony sending you the ring. Even though she knew it would bring you back."

"I like her for that. But that's not why I came back."

"No?"

"My partner of seventeen years has been seeing a younger woman, one of his students. He wants to marry her. It's been going on some time. So it's ended between him and me. I sold him my shop and decided to come back here. I always liked it here. It is all right with you?"

Hugo handed her a pouch and a pipe and led her out a back door into a small garden patio behind the shop, which flanked the familiar Random Point brook. "I think it's a very smart idea," said Hugo, handing her a lighter.

"I knew you'd be nice about it," Cassandra smiled.

"Amanda will be happy. She's missed you. And maybe you can do better than I have keeping her out of trouble."

"I thought we were all trusting Colby Hodge to do that at the moment," Cassandra grinned.

"Maybe yes, maybe no on that one. She's got him wrapped around her little finger."

"Even so, he's a good man," said Cassandra.

"I kind of led her a little astray, I think," Hugo admitted, "encouraging her to make those little video clips and do some other crazy things. I hope I didn't do wrong."

"You didn't. Amanda's is nearly irresistible when she sets her mind on doing something or having something, she showed up here wanting to do all that before you gave her one referral."

"I can't get over how sophisticated girls have gotten. Well, have you thought about where you're going to live and what you're going to do?"

"I'm going to ask William Random's advice on where to live. As to what I'm going to do, I have sufficient income to coast for a bit while I consider my options."

"I'm so glad you're moving back," Hugo said. "You never should have gone away. But you stayed away so long that I had to finally marry someone else. Of course, I still love you, so it's going to be awkward at times. But we'll get through it. You have a way of smoothing people out and I'm sure you'll easily work your spell on Laura."

The rain had become a light mist as Cassandra walked across the village to the Damaris dress shop. Within the small boutique, a very pretty petite brunette in a charming outfit stood behind the back counter drawing on a tablet. Damaris looked up with a smile as her attractive customer entered.

"Hello. May I help you with anything in particular?" Damaris asked. She was in her early 30's and as sleekly well groomed as a dress designer might be expected to be.

"Hi. I'm Cassandra. You know my daughter, Amanda," said Cassandra, extending her hand.

"Oh, how lovely to meet you!" Damaris said. "Amanda did such a wonderful job for us this year," the dressmaker said, for Amanda had appeared in the spring ad campaign for her shop, which had included a billboard on Harvard Square.

"I'm moving back to Random Point, so I hope we can be friends," said Cassandra, showing Damaris her Venus Club ring. "Look, Anthony Newton sent me this and made me an honorary member."

"Cool!" Damaris clicked her own Venus Club ring lightly against Cassandra's.

"I'm going to meet Anthony Newton for the first time this week and I want to buy a new outfit. Can you help me? Do you know his taste?"

"Yes! Go in the fitting room, I'll bring you some things to try on. You're a four, right?"

Cassandra grinned. Damaris knew her shapes. Cassandra had no sooner entered the plush dressing chamber with its triple mirrors then Damaris came in with an armful of dainty, fitted dresses in neutral solid colors, with nipped waists and well-tailored seam work. "The more feminine and retro the better for Anthony," said Damaris, unzipping the frocks for Cassandra to try on. "But we have to be careful not to overwhelm you with material," the designer wisely decided, taking away the crinoline lined dresses. "You're very slender. We'll stick to forms that cling to your slim curves."

Cassandra choose three new sundresses dresses, all of which emphasized her small waist, rounded bosom and shapely buttocks while drawing additional attention to her long thigh line. While Damaris carefully arranged them in a hanging bag Cassandra's eyes were drawn to the geometrically precise stacks of lingerie arrayed in glass cases along one side of the shop. These silk teddies, camisoles, panties and chemises were imported from Europe and of the highest quality.

"If you could pick just one of these dainties for your own personal wardrobe, which would it be?" Cassandra asked her pretty new friend.

Damaris thought a moment then said, "Instead of spending one fifty on a satin slip, let me show you something sexy that just came in." Damaris went into the stockroom and came back a moment later with a sleeveless, cherry red, leather zip dress over her arm. "It's $275 but you'll keep it forever. And you can lend it to Amanda once in a while."

"That's just what I need," agreed Cassandra. Damaris put the leather sheath into a separate hanging bag.

"I used to know your husband a very long time ago," said Cassandra, putting away her credit card. "I wonder if he remembers me."

"Of course he does. I have all the back issues of Hugo's magazine and one of the first numbers has a photo set with you and William. So cute!"

"Do you think he could help me find some property around here?" Cassandra asked.

"Yes, he could do that very easily. Here's his numbers," said Damaris, writing them on the back of a shop card. "He's at his office regular hours. But let's you and I have lunch someday soon, okay?"

"Thank you, that sounds lovely. I'll call you later in the week," Cassandra promised before leaving with her new garments.

After depositing her new clothes at the Inn, Cassandra took herself to Polyxena Guzman's gym and spa to purchase a membership, do a yoga class and go for a swim. As the beautiful Dutch immigrant gym owner processed Cassandra's paperwork, the newest gym member reminded Polyxena that they had met before.

"I remember meeting you at the London Rubber Ball about ten years ago," said Cassandra. "You were working at Club Doma at that time. I remember you being dressed in a sheer, pale latex gown and you looked stunning."

Polyxena looked at Cassandra with deepening interest, not quite remembering her from the Rubber Ball but noticing something familiar about the brunette. After learning that Cassandra was in the scene, Polyxena was even friendlier to her new member, inviting Cassandra to have dinner with her at her earliest convenience, so that they might learn each other's histories. Cassandra of course had heard about the white-blonde siren from Amanda, who had given her mother a detailed account of every lady who had attended the Venus Club dinner several months before. And Amanda had a remarkable mind for detail. Amanda had told her mother that there were three goddesses in Random Point, Hope Spencer Lawrence, Marguerite Alexander and Polyxena Guzman. So far Cassandra agreed with her daughter. The final goddess, Marguerite Alexander, was even more special, for she had been Hugo's last protégée and was therefore rather like a sister Cassandra had yet to meet.

As she was just leaving the gym early that evening, Cassandra once again crossed paths with Ambrose Bartlett. He was still in his well-tailored business suit, having just left the department store. They made eye contact in the lobby as he was coming in and she was going out. She half smiled, which was enough encouragement for him to stop and say, "Have we met? I seem to recognize you, but can't remember from where."

"I don't think so. Who are you?" she asked. Ambrose Bartlett introduced himself.

"Oh, you're Ambrose Bartlett!" Cassandra smiled.

"You do know me, then?"

"My daughter has worked for you," Cassandra said. "Amanda Sands. She's modeled for you a few times at the store."

"You're Amanda's mother?" Ambrose flushed while shaking Cassandra's small hand. "Yes."

"That's so interesting. You want to get a drink?"

"I thought you were going to work out?"

"That's true," he agreed, "but I want to talk to you!"

"We'll do that. I'm going to be living in Random Point from now on, I think."

"Is that so? Well, come visit me at the store some day this week. I'll give you lunch."

"That's very nice of you," said Cassandra.

Chapter Three

Cassandra's Proposition

The next day, Dennis brought Anthony his mail with Hope's hand addressed card on top and Anthony read with interest the following note:

"Dear Mr. Newton,

Thank you for the Venus Club ring. It meant the world to me. I am presently in Random Point and beg to be permitted to pay my compliments to you in person. May I visit you sometime soon? I'm at The Ball and Feather.

Yours truly,

Cassandra Campi"

"Dennis run over to the Ball and Feather and bring Amanda's mother back here, would you?" Anthony said, handing his personal assistant Cassandra's note. "Tell her I can't wait to meet her."

It was just going on eleven when Dennis arrived at the inn driving Newton's Bentley. Cassandra was out in the village but innkeeper Connie told Dennis that her guest would doubtless be back within the hour. Dennis went into the pub and drank a beer while watching soccer on the bar TV. Within the half hour Connie alerted the English boy that Ms. Campi had just come in. Dennis ran out to the lobby and intercepted Cassandra, who had only been out for a walk.

"Ms. Campi? I'm Dennis Cowper, Mr. Newton's driver. Mr. Newton sent me to bring you back to the house, if it's convenient," said the attractive young man in his soft English accent.

"Really? He got my note that fast?" Cassandra was more impressed with Random Point by the moment. She looked at herself in the lobby mirror and was happy she had thought to wear the white, V-neck sundress with its nipped, belted waist and the 3" high, white, peep-toe, stack-heeled pumps. Out of the corner of her eye Cassandra caught Dennis stealing a look at her small, dainty feet, as does a connoisseur. Her tiny toenails were varnished clear, as were her tapered fingernails.

Cassandra resisted sitting all by herself in the back of the large sedan and asked to sit up front next to Dennis, but he urged her to sit in the back like a proper passenger and allow herself to be chauffeured to the house on the cliff where Mr. Newton awaited her arrival.

Customarily during the summer, Anthony's girlfriend Susan Ross spent the week in New York City working at the ad agency where she was an illustrator and the weekends on Cape Cod with Newton in the small mansion to which Cassandra was now being conducted. It was a weekday, so Newton received Cassandra alone, in the dining room, where two places had been set for lunch. When Cassandra arrived, savory aromas hung in the rarified air of the quietly luxurious room.

Anthony Newton was instantly recognizable to Cassandra, as she had seen his musicals on Broadway and owned all of his recordings. He was an athletically trim, good looking man in his late forties, clean cut, well groomed and dressed in a light summer suit with a white shirt and no tie. Amanda had described Newton to her mother as "sunny and affable" and her host seemed ready to live up to the testament as he clasped her hand warmly in his.

"Hello! Thank you for coming directly to me," he said. "Sit down and tell me what you'd like to drink."

Cassandra sat at the table at his right hand and said she'd like some iced tea. Anthony poured her a glass from a jug on the table.

"Should I call you Mr. Newton?"

"Anthony is fine," he said. "I'm so happy to meet you."

"I don't know what I did to merit your attention, but something made you send me that Venus Club ring. What was it?" Cassandra asked.

"Well, Hugo and I have been friends a long time, though I don't go as far back as you do," Newton began. "He introduced me to Susan Ross, who's been my girlfriend for the last eight years. Hugo just married her sister Laura. So we're more or less brother-in-laws. Then, last year, out of the clear blue sky autumn sky, drops Amanda, the daughter Hugo didn't know he had. What a secret to keep for that long. We were all agog. Especially when she turned out to be in the scene. And not just a little, a lot. It made Susan and I wonder how she got that way."

"I didn't have anything to do with that," Cassandra claimed. "She just took to it naturally. She did grow up in San Francisco."

"And of course, she read Hugo's magazines."

"They were on the top shelf of the bookcase. She noticed them at around age 12."

"I think you wanted her to find them," Anthony suggested.

"I didn't try to keep them from her but I didn't tell her to read them. She was attracted to them in a way that she wasn't to the other erotica I had up on that shelf. She was the one who told me that. And at the same time, she was experimenting with boyfriends. There was no stopping her from developing just as she did. I used to hear her playing spanking games in her room with her high school boyfriend."

"Which begs the question, why did you ever take her away from Random Point? Why didn't you just stay here and let Hugo know you were going to have his baby?"

Cassandra looked down, then said, "Do you think I did wrong?"

"I think you raised her very nicely. I can see she gets her poise from you."

A young male chef, black haired, white skinned, pink faced with shyness and clad in an apron over his black trousers and white shirt, brought in bowls of well garnished, beautifully seasoned mushroom bisque soup.

Newton said, "He and his little girl partner are culinary students who will be feeding us all summer. I've tested their cooking and they're great. I told them you're a vegetarian, by the way."

"How do you know all these things?" Cassandra asked.

"Amanda talks about you. She and Susan have become extremely good friends, as you know. Amanda told Susan you're adorable and this made me even more interested to meet you."

"The Venus Club. Was that whole thing your idea?"

"Oh no, I mean, not exactly. I was talking to Marguerite Alexander one day and she expressed an interest in starting a scene girls' club for

19

dinners and lunches, since there are so many ladies in the village who play. I offered to underwrite the first dinner and get rings made up for the members."

"Beautiful rings too. Thank you again for mine."

"You're welcome. Your story is very romantic. It's captured my imagination. I'm glad you came back to us. But what made you do so exactly at this time? It can't just be because of the ring."

Cassandra told Anthony the story of how her long relationship with her partner Eddie had just come to an end. The composer listened with interest. They enjoyed the delicious soup and agreed that the youngsters in the kitchen were brilliant. Then the female half of the cooking crew, as equally shy and blushing as her male partner, brought in a bottle of cold white wine along with small watercress sandwiches, a cauliflower puree and a spicy pickled carrot slaw.

"Well, if I can be of service to you in any way, you'll let me know?" Anthony asked, well satisfied with Cassandra, as she sat, slim and calm in her pretty white dress, nibbling her dainty food.

"Yes, I think you can. I have a proposal for a project I'd like to work on that requires some financing."

"Really? What sort of project?"

"I want to have a house, that is, a spanking club."

Anthony was genuinely surprised and a smile came into his eyes.

"Tell me about your idea," he encouraged her.

"Well, it came to me as Amanda described the Venus Club dinner. She has an almost photographic memory and she recounted everything each lady said. It made me realize that practically everyone at that dinner had switched partners at least once in the last five to seven years. Damaris started out with Michael, but ended up with William. Laura started out with William but ended up with Hugo. Paula started out with Ambrose, but ended up with Sloan. Pamela started out with Sloan but ended up with Ambrose. Alison started out with David, who was, incidentally, cheating on Hope, but wound up with Freddie Johanson. David also seduced Paula, who eventually wound up with Sloan. Michael started out with Damaris but wound up with Marguerite. Even Phoebe Casper, who started out with Pascal Robbins, went off track a few months ago with ... well, you."

"How in the world do you know about that?" Anthony asked.

"Because it coincided with Pascal Robbins running after Amanda and he complained to her about what was going on between you and his wife."

"You're well informed," said Newton, without heat.

"Amanda tells me things because I'm not judgmental."

"In any case, continue on about the Venus Club," said Newton, not embarrassed or put off by Cassandra's intimate knowledge of his most recent adventure.

"Well, it struck me forcibly that if there was ever a town that needed a club for people to go and let off steam, it's Random Point. The men need somewhere to go play that won't jeopardize their relationships and some of these girls need to work off some of their energy with sessions on the side. At the very least, they all need dungeon space they can go off to and play in with each other."

"You make some very good points," Anthony said, loving the thought of a local club, right in the village.

"My sister Carola has been working in Boston BDSM for the last twenty years. She'll bring me girls and can also visit. And then of course, Hugo knows a lot of girls who would love to work in an exclusive dungeon."

"So, you see me bankrolling this club?"

"Who else?"

"We'd have to find just the right place," Anthony said.

"And plan it out to the last detail," she agreed. "I expect William Random could find us the perfect location and fit it up."

"Yes. I'm sure he could."

They sat sipping wine and looking at each other for a few minutes.

"You've been patronizing scene girls for years. It's your hobby. Isn't it?" Cassandra asked.

"Yes."

"A club would suit your interests, amuse your friends and offer opportunities to new talent. It would serve you and it would serve the scene."

Anthony thought about how convenient it would be to have such a place in which to occasionally rendezvous with Phoebe Casper. He didn't have many secrets from Susan, but he trusted that his passion for the married contralto was still one of them. Also, he had promised Phoebe's husband Pascal Robbins that he would give Phoebe up. But he really did not wish to completely give her up. A private destination, well fitted out for play, would suit his interests even better than Cassandra presently knew.

"It would cost a mint of money to do correctly," he observed.

"I know. And I can't guarantee it'll ever be profitable beyond its own maintenance. And even that may take a few years."

"H'm," he agreed, then said, "Would you like to see the beach?"

"Oh yes!" she cried.

Anthony called Dennis on the house phone and his assistant soon appeared. "Dennis," Newton said, "go and find a pair of flats or sandals for Cassandra in Susan's closet. We're going down the steps." He looked at Cassandra's feet and said, "You look about the same size as Susan. About a 6?"

"Yes, that's right," Cassandra said. Dennis instantly departed on his mission and while they waited Anthony told her she should let the English boy help her on and off with her shoes as she would be making a customer for herself for her future club.

Cassandra did not tell Newton she had already noticed Dennis eyeing her feet, but smiled her assent and when Dennis returned, she begged him to do her the favor of strapping on the little rose colored sandals he brought her. Dennis knelt to Cassandra and quickly changed her shoes for her, without removing his eyes from her feet for a moment.

"I'm feeling very pampered," Cassandra smiled at Newton over Dennis' head.

Once she was properly shod for walking, Newton conducted her out the back door of the kitchen, past the dark haired, rosy skinned boy and girl who had prepared their lunch, through the back garden to the long stone staircase that led down to the cove. It was now high noon of a warm and balmy day and blue sky met blue waves in the picture perfect vista that shimmered before them as they descended the many scores of steps down to the beach.

Anthony waited to speak again until the beige sand was beneath their feet on the narrow strip of beach where they began walking up and down while regarding the gently lapping waves. Then he surprised her greatly by saying, "I'm finding you very attractive and you pretty much had me at spanking club. When I find a thing I like to do, I tend to commit to it. But it's the idea of you coming along with the club that's interesting me the most."

Cassandra instantly blushed, but it was useless to pretend that she hadn't noticed the warmth of his gaze. Something about her stirred him and she had a nice enough sense of her own worth not to question the added element of sexual romance that had suddenly introduced itself into her future career plan. She had expected Newton to mainly be interested in the notion of new talent constantly flowing into his realm, not in the conduit of the same.

"From what I've heard and what I see, there's no one I'd rather belong to," she replied, placing her hands together in front of her in Namaste position and bowing her head to him with a Cheshire cat smile.

"You probably know I'm a top. The day that dungeon is finished, I'll have you over a spanking bench," he promised.

"Why wait until then?" she asked, stretching her slim arms up lazily to lift her small, round bosom even higher and accentuate her flat stomach. "I've just been cut loose by my man of 17 years. We enjoyed a high-minded, politically tantric sex life that was multi-orgasmic but at the same time somehow flat. I haven't had an exciting love affair since Hugo introduced me to the scene. You're a top, you're handsome, you were charming to my daughter without trying to seduce her and I love your music. Everything about you turns me on. "

"I would never come on to Amanda. She's too tall. I like petite ladies," said Newton, pulling Cassandra towards him by her small waist and hugging her against his own lean torso. "I like you," he said against her ear, with its tiny stud earring and velvet ear lobe for him to nibble on. "But today is too soon. I'll let you get to know me a little first," he said. Now she wrapped her arms around his waist and pressed her head against his chest.

"Don't wait too long," she said, looking up at him. "Summer

makes me feel restless and I'm all alone at the inn."

"Oh about that," he said, letting her go as they resumed their walking up and down the beach, "you should come and stay here with me until you find a suitable place of your own."

"Wouldn't that be a great intrusion?"

"Not at all. You see I have those kids coming to cook for just Dennis and me every day. That's a crime. Susan's not even coming out to the Cape for a few more weeks, she's going on a vacation to Europe with her girlfriend. I've been completely abandoned and am in need of a companion. And we can work on the plans for the club."

"Nothing would be more pleasant to me than staying here with you for a little while," Cassandra replied. "But are you sure Susan won't take any of this amiss?"

"She'll love the idea of a local BDSM parlor being in our possession. Think of all the models she could use for her next graphic novel. And she certainly would have no objection to you staying here at the house. All the girls stay here sooner or later. But of course, we'll be discreet. I doubt my being attracted to you will occur to her at all."

William Random was behind his desk in his office at his construction company that Thursday afternoon when his secretary announced that his three o'clock appointment had arrived. The architect-owner of Random Construction had been apprised by his wife, Damaris, that Cassandra Campi had returned to Random Point and would be getting in touch with him regarding the purchase or rental of property and he had greatly looked forward to seeing this friend whom he had not seen in so long. What he did not expect was for her to enter his office with Anthony Newton in tow.

"Well, hello!" William said, rising to greet Cassandra with a hug. "I can't believe it's been almost twenty years. You look wonderful. Hi Anthony."

Anthony said hello and took a seat opposite the big desk, behind which a large window looked out on the woods.

"Thank you, so do you," said Cassandra. "I see you're still working out."

"Sit down," William said, smiling at them both. "And tell me how

I can help you. I understand you need a place to live."

"That too, but it's a secondary location we came to talk to you about today," said Cassandra.

"Oh? Are you looking to open another shop?" asked William.

"We want to open a club," said Anthony. "And we want you to design it for us."

"What kind of club?" William asked, not understanding at once.

"A spanking club," said Anthony. "With dungeons for people to play in and girls to work in. Cassandra is going to run it. And I've agreed to underwrite the entire project."

"Are you serious? A dungeon, here?" William cried, as this was the very last thing he expected.

"A dream dungeon," said Newton. "With everything bang on perfect. Now, we'll need a nice, private location, a little off the beaten track, if possible, with plenty of room inside. I've got a little list here of the requirements."

Anthony passed a piece of printed paper to William who looked at it and read aloud, "Two or three chambers furnished for bondage and corporal punishment, a school room, an examining room, bedrooms, a lounge with pool table and bar, a sitting room, a library, a finished basement with video lighting installed for shoots and out back, some sort of stable, barn or loft. Needless to say, we'll need multiple state of the art bathrooms and discreet parking for guests." William looked up at them, adjusted his horn-rimmed glasses on his nose and added, "Wow. Sounds like it'll be a great place."

"We might think of other things," said Newton, "but those are the basic requirements. I'm looking to buy rather than rent the property."

"Are you going to… advertise?" William asked.

Anthony and Cassandra looked at each other.

"Are we going to advertise?" he asked.

"Yes, I think we should, but only on Hugo's website and in his magazine," she replied. "And it must be a membership only club with a mystique of exclusivity."

"No walk-ins," Newton agreed. "Unless they're locals. Locals will get preferential treatment and their membership fees will be waived."

"What is your budget?" William asked Newton, who shrugged.

"Whatever it takes to make it perfect," Anthony replied.

"Believe it or not, I've just finished renovating a property around here that might be retrofitted to your requirements very quickly," said William, who flipped many more properties than he built from scratch. "It's a fairly plain, unadorned, modernistic house from the late 60's that was built to withstand a nuclear attack. Nice and big too, about 8,000 square feet, with a loft alongside. I just put in planked floors, Scandinavian bathrooms and re-painted all the rooms Tuscan style. We can go look at it right now if you like. It's actually on the same road as Michael Flagg's house. There are woods behind it too."

"Yes, we'll go now," said Newton, eager to set the interesting plan in motion. "We'll follow you in our car."

William jumped into one of his trucks and led them back through Random Point and then out the other side of the village onto a wooded road that led to the neighborhood of Michael Flagg's house, which William had remodeled and sold to the pub keeper several years before. Anthony and Cassandra were both enchanted with the house, which so recently refinished, gleamingly fresh and handsomely painted seemed perfectly suitable for the salon they envisioned.

"How long would it take to custom fit the dungeons with furniture?" Anthony asked.

"Well," said William, "if you're thinking of three dungeons, that's a hell of a lot of bondage beds, X frames, whipping posts and spanking benches to construct. I wouldn't want to put my entire crew on that project. I have a couple of guys I can trust to be discreet and I'll help them out myself. I'd say at least a month for the furniture that has to be hand built. The medical suite we can furnish from an online supplier, same goes for the black board and school desks. Fastest way to get bedroom and parlor furniture is to go to Bartlett's in Woodbridge."

"Yes, that's a good idea," said Anthony. "He'll be one of your best customers."

"So, you want the house? It'll be about three altogether, not including the dungeon furniture I'll be building for you."

Anthony understood that William meant three million. For the location and beauty of the recently restored house, the price seemed reasonable and the property an excellent investment.

"Draw up all the papers and I'll have my accountant settle with you next week," said Anthony. "You'll have to come with me to see him," said Newton to Cassandra, "so we can figure out how to get the club in your name. My matinee ladies can never find out that I own a B&D club. For your protection also, Cassandra, we'll classify it as a social club, so it's not looking like a brothel on paper. In addition, once it starts to make money, you'll have to keep good books and pay withholdings for the girls and yourself. I'll get my accountant to advise you on that."

Cassandra put her hand on Anthony's arm, saying, "Are you sure you want to go through with this?"

"I'm sure," he said reassuringly. "And my accountant is always advising me to buy more real estate."

Chapter Four

Dinner with Hugo and Laura

Laura Sands arrived home at five thirty, having spent the afternoon in the art studio at her sister Susan's house on the graveyard side of the village. Laura and Susan had been collaborating on graphic novels and comic strips for years and had many loyal fans. Laura had been writing and lettering the talk balloons of a particular chapter for the past few hours and entered Hugo's house with an excellent appetite for dinner than was further piqued by the aroma of garlic and shallots in the air. She went directly into the kitchen and found Hugo chopping vegetables.

"You started dinner all ready?" she asked, for it was unusual to see her new husband at the house so early. Usually he didn't close the shop until six and then stopped at Michael Flagg's tavern for his first glass of wine of the night on the way home. There he would catch up on the news of the village, catch a few innings of the baseball game and chat to any friends who happened in.

"Cassandra's coming over for dinner tonight," said Hugo, measuring dry spices into his shaker with teaspoon, half and quarter teaspoon measures.

"Ah, so I'm finally going to meet my sister wife."

"Laura, don't be like that," said Hugo.

"She's come back to Random Point. Not just for a visit. Really come back. And you know that you still love each other," said Laura, almost carelessly. Inwardly, however, her heart had begun to pound the moment he mentioned the name of the mother of his child.

"Laura, no one will come between us," he promised, in all sincerity. "I worked too many years to get you. Now do me a favor and set the table for four. She said she's bringing a friend for moral support. You see, she's terrified of meeting you."

"Set it in here or the dining room?"

"Here is fine," Hugo said, always preferring the big wooden kitchen table to the more formal dining room.

A few minutes later the doorbell rang and Laura ran to open it to Cassandra and Anthony.

"Hi Laura," said Anthony, embracing his almost-sister-in-law, "this is Cassandra. Cassandra, Laura."

"Hello," said Laura, extending her hand to the other brunette.

"Hi," said Cassandra, holding Laura's hand for a moment and smiling.

"You?" Laura looked at Anthony quizzically.

"Cassandra is staying with me up at the house until she finds a place," Newton explained as Laura led them into the kitchen. Nor did Laura fail to notice that Anthony led Cassandra by the hand in a proprietary manner while Cassandra blushed becomingly. Everything about Newton's easy, comfortable body language communicated the fact that he had taken Hugo's former lover under his protection. Laura didn't quite understand how Cassandra Campi had managed to win Anthony Newton's affection so quickly or so completely, and yet there was no denying that this was the case. Laura's shoulders untensed and her stomach unknotted. Even her heartbeat slowed.

Cassandra and Anthony were invited to sit at the table and Hugo poured wine for them all, raising his glass first to Cassandra. "Welcome home, honey," he said and drank half a glass of good merlot in a swallow. "Welcome home," echoed Laura and Anthony. Now Cassandra drank her wine and smiled back at them. How easy Anthony Newton was making everything for her, she thought, looking at him.

"So, Anthony is going to help me start a new business here in town," said Cassandra to Hugo.

"Really? What kind of one?"

"A spanking club," said Newton. "Can you believe it? Cassandra thought of the idea but I've agreed to be her silent partner."

"What's this you're saying now," said Hugo, "a B&D club?"

"Tell them why, honey," said Newton to Cassandra.

"I think this town needs a place for all its players to let off steam," Cassandra explained. "Instead of everyone cheating on each other all the time and having to break up their relationships and reform them with each other's spouses, everyone can just have play dates at the dungeon."

"And you can do shoots there, it'll be all set up for that," said Newton to Hugo. "And you and Susan can find models for your cartoons and inspiration for your stories among the girls," he said to Laura.

"And people like Mr. Ambrose Bartlett can be as hard as he likes on the more experienced girls," said Cassandra, remembering how that department store owner had ill-used Amanda upon their first encounter. This made Hugo remember Amanda and he suddenly felt a sense of unease about the proposed dungeon.

"What about Amanda?" he asked. "She's going to ask to be allowed to work there. You know she will."

"No, she won't!" Cassandra replied. "Not as long as she's dating Colby Hodge. He'd never let her and she's too in love with him to want to be manhandled by strangers right now. But she can be permitted to shoot there if she wishes."

"It's quite an idea," said Hugo.

"William has already found us a house," said Newton.

Hugo apologized for his back but said he had to return to cooking at the moment. Within fifteen minutes he had served an eggplant curry with basmati rice and a coconut chili salad. They sat around the wooden table eating the savory food and drinking the good wine with appreciation.

After dinner, Hugo took Cassandra around the house to show her the changes he'd made since she'd last been there. Newton and Laura walked out into the back garden, accompanied by several cats, finishing the last of the bottle of wine.

"I just realized something," said Anthony, "you and Susan can contribute some art to the new club, can't you?"

"Yes, anything you like," said Laura. "What about some murals in the dungeons? And then, you can have those framed cartoon panels we have up in our studio as well."

"Isn't it a fun idea?" Anthony asked. "Our own club. So many ways to show off all the talent we have here in the village."

"It is a fun idea," Laura agreed, for she could really think of nothing against it. It was just the sort of place that Hugo would surely let her sneak off to now and then to misbehave on a whim. And of course, he would use it often himself, to shoot stills for the magazine he still continued to publish and no doubt to play in. They had agreed while on their honeymoon that they would set no unrealistic limits for each other, since they both had a long history of sexual adventurism, but that they would always put each other first and love each other best, as that was the entire purpose of getting married.

Now that they had been married a few months and had indeed for all intents and purposes, been living together for a few years, Laura had found Hugo Sands to have evolved greatly from the implacable tyrant he had been or had pretended to be when she had first met him. After how hard won she had been, he had no intention of testing her with rules, discipline or punishments. He didn't want her keeping secrets from him because she was afraid of him. That was fine for a video or short story, a TV sitcom or screwball comedy, but not for actual life.

"Laura," said Anthony, as they went back into the house, "do me a favor and don't tell Susan I have a crush on Cassandra."

"Do you?"

"I do."

Laura herself had a romantic history with her not quite brother in law and was disposed to keep any secret he shared with her. Anthony had been her interested benefactor since her divorce from William nearly six years before, always allowing her to live in his house and until her recent marriage to Hugo, paying all of her expenses and maintaining a caressingly intimate relationship with her based on his admiration for her attractions, talent and amiable disposition. But while she was delighted to find Newton instead of Hugo concerning himself with Cassandra's needs and future career, she felt a twinge of concern on her sister Susan's behalf. Not that there was the slightest chance of Anthony throwing Susan over for Cassandra. He obviously just wanted a new plaything that summer, seeing as his affair with

Phoebe Casper had temporarily come to a halt and Susan was out of town anyway. But between Phoebe and now Cassandra, Laura wondered if Susan's feelings would not begin to feel hurt if her sister discovered her older lover's latest attachment. And that it was an attachment there could be no doubt. When they departed for the evening, Newton had gained possession of Cassandra's small hand and did not seem to care to let it go. Everything about his demeanor fortified the impression that Amanda's mother had captivated him.

Chapter Five

Summer Evening in Random Point

The next day Hugo did make his regular after work stop at Michael's tavern to sit over a glass of wine and chat with the proprietor. At 6:15 the bar was already filling up with summer tourists as well as townies, all calling for beer. But the former Boston detective had an excellent barmaid named Carmen, a competent local girl, who could fill, carry and deliver a heavy tray of mugs in under a minute. So the 6'3", lean and muscular Flagg, had ample time to pour wine for Hugo and trade tidbits, with Michael standing behind the bar and Hugo sitting on one of the stools.

Hugo quickly recapped the story of Amanda's mother returning to the village after twenty years away and somehow talking Anthony Newton into financing her new B&D club. Michael was naturally astonished and instantly intrigued. Now that he wasn't a police officer any longer, vice related subjects no longer filled him with confusion and distress. He also found Cassandra's concept of giving the locals a place to play entirely sensible.

"Sounds like a great place for Jane to work part time," Flagg surprised Hugo by saying.

"Jane Eliot?" Hugo asked, mentioning the full name of a young lady who some years ago was engaged to and jilted by Michael and who had subsequently come to work in the antiques shop for a short period before returning to the social work that was her true calling. While working with him at the shop, Jane had been taught by Hugo how to dress seductively and also how to take a good spanking. Formerly, a rather plain Jane, the girl who had been abandoned by Flagg blossomed into an alluring beauty simply by following Hugo's counsel to tightly wrap her slim curves in sheath dresses and slip her dainty feet into 4" heels. But Jane had, for some time now, been the significant other of Marnie Price, a tomboyish lesbian heiress, which was why Hugo evinced so much surprise at the mention of her name in connection with moonlighting at a play club.

"I don't know what's gotten into her lately," Flagg said.

Hugo smiled, knowing very well what had gotten into Jane, for Laura had told him that she'd seen Jane leaving Flagg's house early in the morning just the other day. Although married to Marguerite Alexander at last and residing in Marguerite's house on the edge of the village with that pretty lady, their infant daughter and the baby's young English nanny, Michael still kept his lodge-like house in the woods for a quiet retreat. And it was outside of this house that Laura had seen Jane Eliot kiss Flagg goodbye. But Hugo asked Michael to explain his remark all the same.

Michael sighed and confessed, "Marguerite would kill me if she knew, but I've been seeing Jane a little."

"Wow. How come?" asked Hugo, putting up his empty glass for a refill.

Michael poured and said, "I blame that silly Venus Club dinner. It seemed to awaken a lot of emotion in her and she came to me insisting that I...give her a baby."

"A baby?" Hugo was taken aback.

"Yes. Because her current boyfriend is a girl and she says she wants a baby now. And she feels as though it should be mine because we were engaged and she'd always wanted me to be the father of her children."

"So, you're not telling me you're trying to get Jane pregnant?"

"She's insisting."

"You're kidding me, right?"

"No. She says it's the least I can do."

"Jane seems to have developed a good sense of humor," said Hugo, not believing for a moment that Jane truly planned to conceive a child with Michael.

"Hugo, it's not funny," Michael protested. "Do you have any idea how awkward it's going to be when that baby is born?"

"Michael, there isn't going to be any baby. Jane's putting you on."

"Why would she do that?"

"Oh, she's probably just restless. It makes sense that Venus Club triggered it. I think you're right, she should work at the club."

"You really think she's putting me on with the baby stuff?" Michael asked, for this had never occurred to him before and the idea was pleasant, much more pleasant than the contemplation of seeing Jane Eliot through a pregnancy right there in the village under Marguerite's sharp eye. He once again shuddered at the thought of that excruciatingly awkward situation.

"Yes. Because it's too ridiculous a notion for a sensible girl like Jane to embrace."

"She stole my condom to have herself artificially inseminated with after our first bout of makeup sex," Michael revealed.

"Oh no," Hugo laughed. "Now I know she's just fucking with your head."

"Seriously?"

"She's being very naughty to tease you like this," said Hugo.

"That's an angle I hadn't considered," pondered Flagg.

That evening Cassandra returned to the Inn to sleep there for the last time before relocating to Anthony Newton's house. He had told her that Fridays, Saturdays and Sundays were busy days for him due to his directing and playing piano for a summer stock revival of Kiss Me Kate all through the month of July. But that night he had ample time to take her to dinner at an elegant roadside inn between Random Point and Provincetown to further discuss their plans for the club.

After choosing the wine to go with their meal Anthony began to enumerate the tasks that Cassandra would have to complete before the club could open.

"We're lucky we're dealing with William," he said, "because he'll start the carpentry work and let us start delivering furniture before the paperwork is done. I'm going to put you in touch with Susan's best friend, Diana Stratton. She's an interior decorator and can help you figure out some of the rooms. She'd enjoy outfitting the medical exam room. She understands that type of thing. I'll take you to Boston to buy the mirrors and a piano in a day or two. You might as well order the linen, china and silver from Bartlett's. We'll want the bedrooms to be particularly nice for any girls who may come in from out of town and need to stay over. You'll need to engage a cleaning crew to visit at least bi-weekly. I'll have Dennis arrange that for you through the agency we use. Visit the Raphael Price Gallery in the village, it has excellent art. And I'm going to order as many Ray Caesar prints as I can find for décor."

Cassandra's eyes widened at the litany of expensive accouterments Newton was suggesting she immediately begin to purchase. When she'd thought of him financing her in a club she'd envisioned a more modest investment of capital. She'd expected to rent an older house of perhaps five bedrooms and a parlor, clean but creaky, with an older infrastructure and narrow stairs. And as far as fitting it out, she'd expected to be kept to a strict budget and to have to raid the back rooms of Hugo's shop for sticks of appropriate furniture.

"I know," he smiled, as if reading her mind, "It's going to cost a large fortune. But I'll get my money's worth. I have a couple of young ladies in the scene I've been seeing for years on the side who will absolutely love coming out to Random Point and visiting your dungeon. And I'll enjoy that."

"As far as girls go, what are your thoughts on the type of ones we should invite to work for us?" she asked.

"Independent ones," said Anthony, "and no head cases."

"What about slaves? They can be problematical employees," said Cassandra.

"I find an excess of humility oppressive, and slaves are often needy too. Better to work with professionals, I think."

"I agree," Cassandra agreed.

"And obviously we want to avoid anyone connected with a psycho master."

"Yes."

"I don't want any cages at the club. Corporal punishment should be the predominant theme. It's a lot less complicated than S&M and it's what we know."

"Agreed!" said Cassandra, who hadn't the slightest desire to torture, pee on or penetrate anyone, though she was open to gently training cross dressers.

"Until we get you set up with a special credit card for the club, you can use my computer and my online accounts to order paddles, straps, floggers, canes, restraints, and a good selection of wooden brushes. You'll never find all that in one store," said Newton.

"That Raphael Price, with the gallery," said Cassandra, while enjoying a sublime polenta, "I believe he's one of Amanda's suitors."

"Oh, I wouldn't be surprised. He's a little old for her but he looks like a rock star."

"She made a big sale off Hugo's floor to him," Cassandra remembered.

"Then she brought me to his gallery that same night and I bought some art from him," Anthony said.

When Anthony reminded her that he expected her to come to him tomorrow, she agreed and wondered if it would be appropriate to give him a small kiss good night. They were in the back seat of the Bentley and Dennis was up front, ready to take his master home for the night. "Raphael Price will be all over you," Anthony surprised her by saying. "Too bad for him that you belong to me now."

Cassandra blushed at his teasing, wishing that she might return to the Cliff house with Newton that very evening instead of even waiting for the following day. For she had grown increasingly attracted to her new benefactor as the day progressed.

Before going up to her room she stopped into the office provided for guests and sent Amanda a new email.

Amanda and Colby had taken an early train to Milan and arrived mid-morning. The hotel they had chosen was one of Hugo's recommendations and in addition to its sleek, modern décor, it featured a delightful restaurant with just the sort of food Amanda loved. As usual, the bed was small by American standards, but the teenagers only enjoyed it the more for that. Amanda straddled Colby, with her cotton sundress dress pulled up to her waist. Colby reached up to unbutton the top of her dress and free her large, creamy breasts, then took her by her tiny waist and bounced her up and down. They were quickly restored to a sated contentment and after putting themselves back together, went down to the dining room where a perfect Milanese pizza was ordered.

Amanda went into the message center after the order had been placed and checked her email. There was another enigmatic message from her mother, reading:

"Have been adopted by Mr. Newton. Feel like Salander on that endless shopping spree after she embezzled the fortune. Don't forget my embroidered handkerchiefs in Venice."

When Amanda returned to Colby in the cool green and teak dining room, the exquisitely thin pizza was just arriving. Colby was drinking an Italian beer and glancing at a newspaper someone had left in the lobby.

"I could eat two of these all by myself," said Colby as they each began a slice.

"Mother says Mr. Newton has adopted her and she feels like Salander on that shopping spree."

"I remember that shopping spree," said Colby, who had read the Millennium Trilogy the previous winter, "it went on for pages. I wonder whether Steig Larsson got a kick back from Ikea, not that it matters now."

"Why would he adopt her?" Amanda wondered, securing for herself at least one additional slice of heavenly pie before Colby demolished the remainder.

"It's summer, Susan is out of town and he's bored," suggested Colby.

"Interesting though," said Amanda, "he seems to have intervened like some Deus ex machina to save Hugo from having to interest himself in mother's affairs. What a nice man! How lucky Hugo is to have him for a friend."

"Sounds like your mother should thank Eddie for what he did," said Colby.

Chapter Six

Plans, Visits and Conversations

Cassandra was thinking almost this exact thought the following afternoon when she arrived at the Cliff house to stay. Dennis took her bags up to a beautifully furnished suite with a private bath on the third floor. As they went up the broad, circular polished wooden staircase she could hear Anthony in the second floor music room practicing the brilliant Cole Porter score of Kiss Me Kate. As soon as she had put away her things she went back down to the second floor landing and sat outside the music room in a comfortable velvet chair, listening to the rehearsal with rarified pleasure. He played well and with such gusto. Then suddenly the music stopped and he strode out to the landing, stopping short with surprise when he saw her.

"How long have you been here?" he asked, taking her hands.

"About twenty minutes. I loved listening to you play. Can I come to the show tonight?"

"Oh yes, please do!" he smiled and let her hands go, as he was on his way downstairs. "I'm going down to get some coffee. Come with me," he said. They went down to the kitchen together and surprised the two young chefs prepping for their master's early dinner.

"Hi kids," Anthony said, "we'll need some coffee and maybe a bit of cake." Then he took Cassandra with him out to the back garden and through to the recently remodeled pool building, with its tropical landscaping, glass domed roof and full spa amenities, as she had not yet seen it. She did know, however, that the pool boy, Jaime, who was that very day tending the orchids and Bird of Paradise pots, had received certain favors from her daughter in that very pool the previous month. Amanda hadn't provided the exact details, but she had confided that she'd been especially naughty with the beautiful young man on a sexual whim, like a bad debutante in a 1960's bedroom farce. Looking at Jaime, Cassandra could understand her beautiful young daughter's fancy for the gardener, for this boy was manly, handsome, modest and wise. Cassandra smiled at him.

"Are you going into town to see that gallery today?" Anthony asked Cassandra when the coffee tray and almond raspberry torte arrived. They sat at a patio table and allowed the crop haired girl chef to pour their coffee for them before departing, blushing harder than ever. So far Mr. Newton had loved every morsel that she and her cooking partner had prepared for him, his assistant Dennis and his pretty guest, Ms. Cassandra. But the young girl dreaded the inevitable first slip up.

"I thought I would."

"Before you go open a file on my computer desktop called Venus Club. It's got a folder in there on the house. One of the files has the color scheme break down of all the rooms. William sent it this morning. Print that out and take it with you whenever you do any shopping for the house. It'll help."

"Thanks, you think of everything. When I came to you with the idea I didn't have any of these details in mind. You seem to have it all at your command. How are you doing that?" she asked.

"Well, it's simple, I'm very bossy and I have a genius for organization. But you still get credit for the idea. 100% credit."

"Is that what we're going to call it, The Venus Club?"

"I don't think we can call it anything else, do you?"

"No," she replied, appreciatively finishing her small but ambrosial fruit tart.

"Now don't forget what I said about Raphael Price," Anthony reminded her, jumping up to go back to his piano. "And that goes double for Ambrose Bartlett. I'm sure you'll be getting over to his store too. And he'll be making overtures to you before you leave the store. Especially when he finds out who you really are."

"He's already asked me to have a drink with him. He saw me at the gym."

"Stall him on that," said Anthony. "Make him wait until the club is open and then he can come and do a session with you. Eventually. But not until I say."

Cassandra flushed with pleasure even though she knew he was only teasing her.

"Where should I sit tonight?" she asked.

"Sixth row center. I'll arrange for that seat to be saved for you."

Then he squeezed her hand and was gone. Cassandra went to his office and printed out the color schemes for the Venus Club.

Raphael Price's gallery occupied three storefronts on a corner on the main street of Woodbridge, the neighboring village. The gallery was also in walking distance of large and luxurious Bartlett's Department store, where Anthony had directed Cassandra to go and shop for furnishings, china and linen for the house. She entered the shop in one of the form fitting sundresses Damaris had sold her and pretty flats suitable to a day of shopping. She asked for Raphael Price at the front counter of the corner store, the one with the best pieces. An attractive young female clerk in shorts and a tank top went into the back to retrieve the gallery owner, a handsome young man in his late twenties with long black hair, white skin, dark eyes and a gym honed torso. As Cassandra gazed at Raphael Price she remembered that in spite of Anthony's facetious warning to beware the lad's amatory advances, that this was one of Amanda's lovers and accordingly, she dropped her eyes lest she be tempted to smile at him too warmly.

"Hello, I'm Raphael," he said, "may I show you something?"

"Many things, I hope. I'm Cassandra Campi. Mr. Newton sent me over to look at some prints. He's hired me to decorate one of his properties and told me I might find things here."

"Oh yes, I've sold him prints before," said Raphael, now even happier to serve the attractive brunette before him. "Were you looking for anything in particular?"

"Yes, I am, but I won't know it until I see it."

"All right. Come with me," he said, leading her around the main room of the gallery and showing her his most arresting black and white photography and color illustrations. Cassandra used her small camera to photograph the pieces she liked and promised to call Raphael back in a few days with Mr. Newton's decisions.

"Do you live around here?" Raphael asked as he took her through the second gallery with the more commercial prints for sale.

"I just moved back to Random Point after twenty years away," said Cassandra. "And I might as well tell you, I'm Amanda's mother."

"Amanda Sands? My white goddess?" Raphael's face broke into an even wider smile. "Oh, how I love her!" he confided cheerfully. "But she has put me on the shelf for the moment, promising to dust me off again once in a while as the years unfold."

Cassandra relaxed, now certain that Raphael, with his memory full of Amanda, would not be making any advances to herself.

"It's something to look forward to," Cassandra smiled her encouragement.

"You should come over to my house one night and let me cook you dinner," said Raphael immediately.

"Should I?"

"Yes!"

"That's very nice of you," said Cassandra.

"So, are you married?"

"No," said Cassandra, wondering why her face was growing warm. It was exactly as Anthony had predicted, Raphael Price was coming onto her.

"We need to become friends," Raphael assured her. "I'm sure Amanda wouldn't disapprove."

"Oh no, probably not. I get along well with all her friends."

Cassandra promised to call Raphael as soon as she spoke to Anthony about the prints. He walked her to the door. "Where are you off to?" he asked her.

"Bartlett's. I have a lot of shopping to do."

"Sounds like fun. They have a lovely café on the third floor, you should have lunch there."

Cassandra walked the two blocks over to Bartlett's and looked up at the store that took up almost the whole block and a large, tree shaded parking lot behind it. Walking into the store through the perfume department, she became aware of the rarified air within at once. The most luxurious store on the Cape was paneled, tiled and painted in palatial style and even smelled expensive. This was the store where her daughter had walked in several in house fashion shows for which she had been rewarded with both cash and bonus wardrobe pieces. Not every model got to take home wardrobe, but Ambrose Bartlett made a habit of lavishing scene girls with dresses and coats. Amanda said that Pamela, her best friend and Bartlett's new bride, had told her that her husband liked dressing and undressing his women as though they were his dolls. He had been in retail all his life. Bartlett's was his family business. And he knew the effect clothing had on women. It worked like nothing else. In fact he had discovered that the surest way to get a woman to want to take off her clothes was to give her a different outfit to try on.

As Cassandra was consulting the directory of departments and trying to decide which to visit first, Damaris Random was entering the store by the employee entrance in back. She took the service elevator up to the top floor where her partner in her dress making business, Pamela Bartlett, had her own design studio, recently created for her by her husband, Ambrose Bartlett, in an effort to demonstrate to his bride how much he wanted her near him. Damaris found Pamela working at a machine while the two older Bartlett's seamstresses enjoyed coffee in the pleasant lounge that Pamela had insisted Ambrose provide for their use during the remodeling of their former dreary alterations attic into this stylish atelier.

Tall and willowy, with a shiny black Louise Brooks bob framing her charming oval face, Pamela was all that a fashionable young woman should be, from the perfect fit of her black and white checked mini dress to the elegance of her 4" high stack heeled pumps.

"Hi girl," said Pamela smiling up at her friend, "did you come to take me to lunch?"

"Yes and you won't believe whose just moved to town," said Damaris, extending her hand to pull Pamela out of the studio. "Let's go down to the café. I've been dreaming about the chicken pistachio sandwiches all morning."

"Someone interesting moved to town?" Pamela grabbed her purse and trotted behind Damaris towards the elevators.

"Amanda's mother!" Damaris cried.

"Amanda Sands?"

"Yes! And you'll never believe why. You'll be amazed when I tell you. It's going to have a huge impact on all of our lives from now on!" Damaris said dramatically. They exited on the third floor and made their way to the stylish little café that would soon be packed for lunch, but was now relatively empty. They found a booth at once and sat down.

"Amanda's mother?" Pamela was still trying to process exactly what that meant. Amanda was her new best friend. She had mentioned her mother often and of course Pamela had been intrigued about the woman Hugo had been seeing when he began his publishing career and came out with the first issues of his New Rod Quarterly.

"How old is she? What does she look like?" were Pamela's first questions. Damaris laughed.

"She's a cute little brunette. Neat proportions, slim, toned, smooth skin, nice hair, just what you'd expect. I sold her some dresses."

The waitress came by and Damaris ordered her favorite sandwich and an ice tea. Pamela ordered a Caesar salad and a white wine. Damaris called the waitress back and ordered a wine as well.

"Why did she come back here?" Pamela asked.

"She's going to open a dungeon."

"You mean a B&D salon?"

"Yes! A house. Anthony Newton is backing her and William's already found a house for them. She may be coming shopping here to Bartlett's any day now for furniture. William says he's going all out. It's going to have a schoolroom, a medical suite, bedrooms for girls to stay over, dungeons for couples to rent. And Cassandra is running it."

"I can't believe it," said Pamela, immediately thinking of her husband and his taste for ever newer, thinner, subbed out girls. "What a strange idea!"

"She's a pretty lady," said Damaris. "We should make her a perfect cat suit as a good luck gift."

"I wonder if Ambrose has seen her yet. Is she pretty enough for him to go after, do you think?"

Damaris was well acquainted with the concupiscence of Pamela's husband and of Pamela herself. She knew, for example, that Pamela was that very month, carrying on a love affair with a college boy who was home for the summer and devoted to the designer. While Pamela had also confided to Damaris of her husband's new interest in Polyxena Guzman, the owner of the gym and spa. Damaris and William, who had an infant to think about, as well as their respective businesses, were too busy to play anywhere other than in their own bedroom and with each other.

"She's good looking, but in a quiet way," said Damaris. "Her being Amanda's mom is what will make him look harder at her."

"Not to mention her being Hugo's scene lover from way back," Pamela mused, sipping the wine the moment it was delivered. "That's a platinum pedigree."

"But doesn't your husband prefer younger women?" Damaris asked.

"I always supposed he did. But I think he's mainly concerned that they be thin," said Pamela.

"Well, she's thin enough to fit an off the rack size 4 perfectly," said Damaris.

"And as you said, she's Amanda's mom," said Pamela. "That'll really resonate with him. He's absolutely crazy about Amanda."

"But Amanda defected from him to you. You took her and she belongs to you now," Damaris shrewdly observed. Pamela was proud of having conquered Amanda Sands. They had even had some adventures together, involving good-looking boys. Pamela had never had such a close and endearing female friend before and she was enjoying her precious possession.

"I wonder if she knows about any of these developments," Pamela mused, taking out her cell phone and texting Amanda, "Warn your mother about Ambrose. He might go after her."

"She won't get a text. She's in Italy."

"I'll send it to her email."

"I want dessert," said Damaris, picking up the menu and consulting it.

"That's crazy, you just had a huge sandwich and salad," Pamela admonished her petite partner, who had gotten her dainty curves back as quickly as it was possible to do so after having a baby and was always mindful of her figure.

"We'll both just have a nibble," said Damaris, motioning over their waitress and requesting one slice of the dark chocolate raspberry tart. Then Damaris said, "Did I mention to you that when she came into the shop to buy the dresses she hadn't met Anthony Newton yet and by the following afternoon he had bought her a three million dollar house?"

"Really?"

"Yes, she made a point to ask me what kind of clothes he liked to see ladies in. I didn't realize she was going to ask him to put her in business."

"Even though she'd never met him before," Pamela said thoughtfully. "That's one confident woman."

"She had a Venus Club ring. He had one made for her and sent to her."

"That's interesting," said Pamela. "That means Anthony Newton was thinking about her before she was thinking about him. But it was certainly no guarantee that he'd finance her in a business."

"No, but he's going to."

The chocolate tart arrived and the girls each took tiny bites until it was gone.

"Did you set her up with perfect dresses?" Pamela asked.

"She looked heavenly," Damaris replied. "I made her buy that red leather clubbing dress last minute. Now I realize why she was such an easy sell on that piece. It'll be a perfect hostess dress for the house."

"Is she going to be sessioning there herself? I mean, is she a top or a switch or what?" asked Pamela.

"I don't know. She never mentioned a word about a club when I saw her. It was William who found all of this out when she and Anthony came to see him about finding a property yesterday."

"I wonder if all of our men will be using the house," said Pamela. "I know mine will, but will yours?"

"I don't know," said Damaris. "But if he does and I find out about it, anything is liable to happen." The petite Puerto Rican girl grinned.

"You mean like you meeting your devastatingly handsome ex-husband in a dungeon?" Pamela asked, referring to Michael Flagg.

"That can never happen. He's married to Marguerite now and she would hurt me."

"For that matter, would I meet Sloan?" Pamela wondered aloud, referring to her own former fiancée.

"An afternoon rendezvous with an attractive former lover is an interesting idea," Damaris agreed, "but I would never initiate something like that. William would have to be completely and provably unfaithful to me before I would consider it. And he won't be. I don't think."

"You're right. Your man is very steady. Whereas mine is an alley cat," Pamela said. "But if this new crazy bitch in town distracts him away from that blonde slut at the gym, I'll be glad of it." Pamela was not a fan of Polyxena Guzman, though she had graciously accepted the fact that she was her husband's current plaything on the side. In exchange for her indulgence, she had received her beautiful new design studio, had been taken off the sales floor at Bartlett's and had been given leave to dally with a boy during the summer vacation.

"Why did you make me eat that?" Pamela asked Damaris as they left the dining room. "Now I'll have to go see the blonde bitch tonight at that hellish yoga class she conducts. Dutch people should never conduct yoga classes, they sound too much like Germans. I don't want to be told by Ilsa of the SS to lie in the ocean and lie in the sand. It feels wrong."

"Come on, Pamela, you know she isn't a bit harsh."

"She is to Ambrose. She's been personally training him for months and have you seen his abs? She forces him to do scores of sit-ups. She's even gotten him to quit smoking for good. I hate her so."

Chapter Seven

Friday

On Friday morning, after spending her first night in the beautiful suite Anthony had assigned to her, Cassandra put on a black bikini and went down to the pool for an early swim. Anthony was already in the water, finishing his laps.

"I didn't expect to see you so early," he said, as he got out of the water and she got in. "I didn't mean to disturb you," she said.

"I'll call and have our breakfast brought down here," he said gaily, going into the cabana to get a cotton robe. Cassandra had expected his torso to look good in swim trunks and was not disappointed. She did the backstroke for several laps and enjoyed looking up at the dark blue sky lightly dotted with a few clouds on the edges through the glass domed ceiling of the pool building. When she got out of the pool, the two culinary students, James and Josette, were attending Newton with a coffee service and a tray of fresh baked biscuits, butter and jam. James was tall and thin with jet-black hair combed forward on his forehead. Josette was a small girl, with the same shiny black hair, cropped short and parted on the side with an attractive sweeping bang going across her white brow. Both children were under twenty years of age and had dark, shoe button eyes and the whitest skin imaginable.

"Kids, don't need to worry about lunch today. But after the show tonight I'm having the cast and crew back for drinks and snacks, so I want you to think up something lovely for about twenty people," Anthony told the terrified duo before him. "I suggest some little sandwiches, a couple of salads and several desserts. We won't be back here until about eleven thirty. And Dennis will help."

James and Josette nodded and went off to plan the late night supper. Anthony went away to practice his piano and Cassandra went up to her room to shower and dress.

Putting on another of her new sundresses, Cassandra drove into the village to visit Marguerite Alexander's bookstore. This time she sought out the original owner, the redheaded Marguerite, whose statuesque beauty had been fully described to Cassandra by Amanda. Marguerite was clad in a beige pencil skirt and white shirt and a pair of smart beige and black high-heeled oxfords. The bookseller wore her luxuriant locks loose about her shoulders and tortoise shell glasses made her green eyes look even larger than they actually were.

"I've read all of your novels," said Cassandra, shaking Marguerite's hand warmly. "I love them."

"I can't believe I'm meeting you," said Marguerite. "Come into my office." The shapely Marguerite led the way back to her small office behind the shop, where she offered Cassandra a seat beside her on a sofa. "Shall I get Hope to bring us some coffee?"

"Could you?"

"Of course," said Marguerite, dialing the coffee bar on the store phone. "Hope, could you send Dru to my office with a couple of cappuccinos?" Marguerite asked.

"I'll tell you why I'm here today," said Cassandra. "I have a library full of empty shelves and I'm looking to stock it with erotic literature. I was hoping you could sell me those books."

"Of course, as many as you want," Marguerite smiled.

"I'll let you choose. And please don't feel constrained. Mr. Newton has authorized me to use his account for these purchases."

"Has he?" Marguerite's brows went up.

"Yes, I'm staying with him at the moment. To be absolutely frank, he appears to have adopted me."

"That's delightful," said Marguerite. "So you really do mean enough books for a library?"

"For a wall of a room in a house I'm in the process of decorating."

Dru Baxter, the blond, blue-eyed boy who was paying court to Pamela Bartlett that summer, always worked at the bookstore while on vacation from school. He generally helped Hope Lawrence run the coffee bar and today was no exception. Being an admirer (and one time lover) of Marguerite going back several seasons, the good looking Dru blushed as he delivered the hot cappuccinos in gold-rimmed white cups to Marguerite and Cassandra.

"Dru, this is Amanda's mother," said Marguerite, who knew that Dru knew Amanda, without knowing of Dru's decadent weekend in Boston with Amanda, Pamela and Colby the previous month. Dru had, on that occasion, been lucky enough to have been included in certain spanking and sex related antics, dreamed up on a whim by Amanda and Pamela together, at Hugo's Boston flat, to which Amanda had been awarded a key to use with permission from time to time.

"Oh, I love Amanda," said Dru, clasping Cassandra's hand for a moment. "She's the nicest girl in the world."

Cassandra grinned at him. She knew very well why Dru thought that. For even that bit of naughtiness had been confided to Cassandra by her daughter.

"I think she mentioned meeting you," Cassandra told him. "She said you were a very nice boy."

"Cassandra is going to live in Random Point now," Marguerite informed Dru, who was fascinated to learn this. Dru left them to return to Hope, amazed by what he had heard.

"Don't tell anyone who doesn't need to know, but this house that Mr. Newton is furnishing, is going to be a B&D salon and I'm going to run it," Cassandra disclosed to the suddenly wide-eyed Marguerite. "Yes," said Cassandra, "it is to be a club. In fact, it is to be the professional arm and after hours playground of the Venus Club. I'm almost as shocked as you that this is actually happening. I only proposed the idea to Mr. Newton the day before yesterday. But he moved on it immediately."

"Well, you really are back with a vengeance," Marguerite said with admiration. "I didn't realize you were quite so steeped in BDSM."

"I'm not in the slightest. I was only really starting to get into pro switching when I left Random Point. I'd done some sessions as a top and some as a bottom and some as both while I was still Hugo's girlfriend. He encouraged me to market my talents. I think he did the same with you. I did work in a dungeon in San Francisco until I was three months pregnant."

"Really! That explains why Amanda has always been into it,"

chuckled Marguerite.

"Mr. Newton agrees that the dungeon should be mainly corporal punishment oriented. So I'm not going to concern myself with areas I don't understand anyway. He wants a spanking club and that is what is in my ken."

"Tell me more!"

"It's going to have space for couples to rent and play in. After Amanda told me how many locals are cheating on each other with each other's mates, I realized that a well-equipped, by-the-hour make-out mansion could supply a great deal of much needed private playing space in this village."

"And will girls be brought in from the Czech Republic to staff it?"

"No, but certainly from Boston," smiled Cassandra. "And maybe from right here in Random Point."

"You certainly have a built in customer supply for the services of girls, from Boston or beyond," Marguerite mused, putting her husband, Michael Flagg, at the top of the list.

"Yes, that's another reason why the idea of having it here in the village made so much sense. By the way, the location is right down the lane from your husband's house."

"Oh my, is it really? Well, it's a wildly decadent idea and I'm not surprised Anthony is underwriting it. You apparently awoke the latent puppeteer in him. But if our various husbands stray to your club, will you tell us?" asked Marguerite, with her catlike smile.

Cassandra thought for a moment before replying, "That would be a betrayal of trust. But in your case, you could just walk over to the house and see if his car is parked there."

"May I ask you a personal question?" Marguerite asked.

"Of course. Anything."

"Has Anthony become your master?"

"Yes, but only in a playful sense, if I read him correctly. Though we haven't played yet. Is there anything I should know? I'd like him to be satisfied in exchange for all he's giving me."

"Oh, don't give that a thought. He likes a spankable lady he can take to bed, especially if she can entrance him like Scheherazade, with tales from his own personal bagnio. He's been collecting scene protégées for years. He's patronized artists, video girls, club girls, and writers. You're going to be the only club mistress in history who doesn't have to worry about making a monthly nut. Well played, my Lady," said Marguerite, bowing her coppery head to her guest.

Chapter Eight

Cassandra's New Lover

That night at the performance, Cassandra exchanged her sixth row center seats for second row left, so she could be as close to Anthony Newton as possible to watch him as he played the score on the piano. As always, he was dressed in an immaculate suit and his entire demeanor radiated ease and confidence. Cassandra barely looked at the stage, so charmed was she by her new benefactor's powerfully energetic aura. The music was exuberant and he played exuberantly, but still managed to notice at once that she was sitting close and focusing on him. He didn't take his eyes from the keys but smiled in such a way that she knew was meant for her.

After the performance they hurried back to the house to see if the culinary children were ready with a repast for the cast and crew. Dennis was calming the nerves of the young cooks, as they set out their buffet of pates, salads, sandwiches and petit fours in the downstairs dining room. Anthony and Cassandra tasted the dishes and he was happy to note that there were enough purely vegetarian options to enable her to make a proper meal. It touched her that with so much else on his mind, this concerned him. Anthony commended the cooks and Dennis went off to open the front door for the arriving guests.

At first it seemed to Cassandra that with so many people stopping by the house that evening that her host would be busy for hours with them. But she learned that Newton opened his house and larder to thank his talent with a good meal and as much wine and beer as they wished to drink, at least once a week, but didn't feel compelled to keep them company the whole time they were there. And in fact as soon as he saw everyone well provided for he told the junior chefs they might go to bed and leave the cleanup for the housekeepers the following morning. Dennis knew he was similarly relieved of duty, but he enjoyed partying with the players and ate and drank along with them for several hours more.

It was only just gone on midnight when Anthony asked her if she wanted to have a nightcap in his room. She loved this idea and asked him if she could change into something comfortable first. He told her where to locate him once she had changed and slipped away from his guests without bothering to separately say good night to anyone.

Cassandra went to her room and stripped naked, then slipped into a pale pink cotton wrapper and a pair of black velvet embroidered slippers. She found Anthony in his large suite on the third floor, already in his own tailored robe, opening the French doors to his balcony to let the warm, balmy summer night air into the room.

"I don't need anything more to drink," she said.

"Me either. Let's get into bed and relax," he said, pulling back the luxurious counterpane.

"Okay," she smiled, going around to the other side.

He took off his robe and climbed into bed nude. She untied the belt of her own robe and let it drop to the floor.

"Beautiful," he said, patting the bed beside him. She came to him and he turned her so her back fit against his front as they lay on their sides. Then he pulled up the covers to their waists and touched a button to extinguish all the lights in the room. It was a full moon night and also bright with stars and these illuminated the suite to perfection. "You know, you have a lovely waist," he commented, placing his hand over her flat stomach.

"So do you. You're very fit," she murmured, pressing her bottom back against his pelvic girdle and suddenly evident erection, which he nestled in the crease of her bottom.

"Have you thought about an assistant yet?" he surprised her by asking. She turned her head towards him over her shoulder. "You'll need a second, strong girl to serve as your lieutenant."

"No, I hadn't thought about that," said Cassandra. "But you seem to think of everything."

He stroked her hair and throat and gently turned her head back away from him.

"Just relax, honey," he said. "I can feel you're a little intimidated at the way I've jumped into this, and all the money I'm spending."

It was true! Cassandra had been feeling the awesome responsibility of the monetary commitment he was making just moments before.

"Yes," she confessed.

"Someone said, 'Luxury is the apotheosis of sensual pleasure' and I agree. So everything needs to be first rate. Now as far as your top girl, consider Hope Lawrence."

"That's right, Amanda said she used to work in a Hollywood club," Cassandra remembered.

"She's intensely knowledgeable and would be of invaluable assistance to you," said Newton, who had played with Hope a number of times, rewarding the charming blonde with ample allowance for her compliance.

"You're right. I have the right instincts, but I know practically nothing," agreed Cassandra, while her body noticed the way Anthony was drumming his ever so long and strong fingers against her public mound while nudging his ramrod hard penis between her smooth thighs from behind until it just began to graze her labia.

"It's been an exhausting day," he said, reaching into a bedside drawer for a condom; "I doubt I'll last a minute. No disrespect to your beauty is intended."

"I was watching you play tonight. You were so handsome and magnetic. I'm already wet," she said, positioning the quickly sheathed knob of his cock against her vagina, which was indeed somewhat slick and certainly well parted to receive him. He began to enter her and she encouraged him adeptly.

"I promise to give you the attention you truly deserve once the weekend is over," he said, slipping in deeper and feeling her squeeze him harder as he went. "If you keep that up it'll be more like thirty seconds," he told her. So she relaxed and just let him push through and continue to probe her with his pleasingly ample member. Her Eddie was not quite so well-endowed and Cassandra felt an extra thrill as her new lover began to possess her.

"I also promise to take the time to spank you after the weekend is over."

"Okay!" she replied breathlessly.

"Reach over to that drawer and get the lube," he told her. She had to stretch considerably but he kept hold of her waist and stayed anchored inside her until she passed him back the small bottle of lube. He withdrew, lubed both of them and then slipped back inside her so deeply and so quickly that she cried out. He pulled back a little. "That's better," he said, beginning to ply her steadily. "You're so tight. Relax more, honey." She obeyed him and then it went very well. Once he got a rhythm going, he proceeded to give the same hard, fast, pounding performance he had on the piano that night. In spite of his claims of exhaustion, his energy was equal to outlasting her orgasm, which he caused to occur by pressing his palm alternately against her lower abdomen, Venus Mound and swollen, throbbing clitoris simultaneous to filling her with his pile driving cock from behind.

After setting himself to rights, he got back in bed with her and hugged her to him.

"Are you sleepy?" she asked.

"I am but let's chat some more," he said, content that their first encounter had gone so effortlessly well.

"Tell me how many women in the village you've had sex with," said Cassandra, leaning up on her elbow to look at him in the moonlight. He laced his fingers behind his head and thought about this.

"Not that many. Marguerite a few times, Susan's not in the village but I met her here. Susan's sister Laura lived here for a couple of years after she and William got divorced and we've been together about a half dozen times. That tended to happen when Susan was away.

The girl Susan is currently traveling with, Diana Currie, the interior decorator, is a girl Susan met at Vassar and brought home to me to play with years ago. She was very submissive to Susan and then to me, and the entire situation was piquant. She met her husband, Plastridge Currie, the head of the ad agency where Susan works, at a B&D club in upper Manhattan, where she and Susan went one night. Susan's boss, Plastridge Currie, was there, waiting to do a session with one of the girls. But as soon as he saw Diana, he proposed she go in a dungeon with him. He's an ardent bondager and so is Diana. They've been together ever since. He married her right out of college and they have a toddler now. In fact, Diana has received permission from him to escape from her duties for ten days to travel with Susan in Europe on the express condition that Susan take beautiful bondage pictures of Diana and send them back to Currie for his amusement. That's why clubs are magical to me. Another couple who met in a B&D club is Hope and David. He found her working at The Keep in Hollywood while he was a teacher at Hollywood High. I know other stories besides."

"Go on telling me about your other lovers," Cassandra encouraged him.

"Let's see, I always had a girlfriend, even in junior high. I went to Julliard and then Yale on scholarships and of course, I met some lovely girls there. I hit early with my first show in my late twenties and found myself a wealthy man before age thirty, which naturally increased my popularity with women. I've had five wives," Anthony sighed, embarrassed to admit this.

"Whaaaa?" Cassandra laughed.

"They were all girls I met in the theatre. It was always their idea we get married and I could never say no to a lady. We always seemed to break up right after I finished a new show. So all of their settlements have come from my plays. None of the marriages lasted longer than a year. And the last one of those ended over ten years ago."

"Why did all of those marriages end?" Cassandra asked.

"Basic incompatibility. But I've been with Susan almost eight years and think of her as my one true wife. I even gave her a wedding ring and a Valentino wedding gown a few years back and we were all geared up to get married in Vegas the same weekend as Damaris married William. But Susan backed out at the last minute. She witnessed an argument between Marguerite and her first husband, Malcolm Branwell that led her to believe that husbands are less pleasant than lovers and she said I needn't marry her. Prior to this she had been longing to be married and I had held out because I'd done it so often before that it seemed silly to do it yet again. As it is, I've provided for her as though she were my wife and show her the same respect. So let's make sure she doesn't find out that you're my new pet if we can possibly help it."

"Keep affair secret from Susan, check," said Cassandra. "But I'm sure you haven't finished telling me about your scene girlfriends."

Anthony said, "There's my sweet Teresa Clifford, she's a cartoonist from L.A. who sessions with me whenever I get out there and whenever she gets to New York. Sometimes I bring her out for a few days and put her up at a hotel near my house. She's one of the out-of-town ladies you could have guest visit at the club. Oh and this is hardly worth mentioning, but before she was married, I played with my secretary Paige a little bit."

"What about your leading lady, Phoebe Casper? She looked ravishing in her corsets and velvets tonight."

"I love Phoebe," Anthony sighed, "but so does her husband and it isn't right for me to take advantage of her temporary infatuation with me to continue to cuckold him."

"He's not doing too badly. He got Amanda to give in to him."

"Ah, did he completely? I knew that he had made a pass at her and I used that as ammunition to shut him down when he came to see me as the righteously offended husband. 'See here, I told him, I know you're trying to get up to something with young Amanda Sands, but I won't tell Phoebe if you let her come to me, just once. She needs to get it out of her system.' He agreed, reluctantly, realizing that was the only way he would be able to hold onto the moral high ground when he confronted her about spending a night in Boston with me. Oh and by the way, he did more than confront her; he used a hairbrush on her and made her cry. But it was useless; she still persisted in being in love with me. Then Amanda did something smart, she let Phoebe see Pascal attending on her, his beautiful, 18 year old model, for just a minute, and it reminded Phoebe that she does love her husband best. So she has agreed, for now, to stop sleeping with me."

"Amanda says he takes very beautiful photos of her but that he's not really in the scene. He just knows how to work the scene to get what he wants from women in the scene," said Cassandra.

"That's interesting that he persisted until he actually got Amanda," Anthony observed. "Good for him. I'm sure that made him feel much better about the me and Phoebe thing."

"Ambrose Bartlett actually got Amanda too," said Cassandra. "But unlike Pascal Robbins, Mr. Bartlett apparently paid a good deal for the privilege."

"How do you feel about her doing that at her age?" Anthony asked.

"It doesn't disturb me. Mr. Bartlett is good looking and he courted her for months with dresses and coats and boots from the store. And most of this went on before Colby laid claim to her. The big session that he paid for, with the sex at the end, was a kiss and make up for the session they had just before Christmas when she traded taking a hard, fully nude spanking from him for permission to shoot videos in his store on Christmas day. Hugo had set that whole thing up for her, in innocence of Mr. Bartlett's demanding character, (and the fully nude part). Allegedly, Ambrose Bartlett always makes a submissive cry the first time he plays with her. On the second date, the one he himself proposed and paid Amanda five grand for, he was charming to her and didn't make her cry. At any rate, she's starting sophomore year at Harvard in the fall and her spanking boyfriend isn't likely to allow any more call girl related activity to distract her from her studies or himself."

Chapter Nine

At Bartlett's

On Saturday afternoon, Cassandra returned to Bartlett's to start buying some of the furnishings and household goods she'd selected on the previous day. That morning she'd forced Anthony to sit with her at the Bartlett's website and begin approving her purchases. "Honey, I don't have time for this," he said, after looking at several pages of products. "I trust your taste level. Just go in there and shop."

"All right," she agreed, enjoying his arm around her waist that morning as she stood beside his chair. "But if I talk to Mr. Bartlett today, should I let him know what kind of house I'm buying furniture for?"

"Sure, why not?"

"Well, you said you didn't want him to become interested in me. If I start talking about B&D salons to him, he's bound to."

"I don't mind if he becomes interested in you, just don't give into him."

"Oh, no, I wouldn't. He sounds frightfully severe. If playing is that much work, what's the point?" Cassandra asked.

"Did you like last night?" he asked, looking up at her.

"Yes, I even orgasmed. It was lovely."

"Be back from your shopping in time to have a little dinner with me before I go to the theatre," he told her. "Around four. The children did a splendid job last night, didn't they?"

"Wonderful!"

"You really should stay here with me for the rest of the summer and enjoy the cooking," he invited her.

"I would love to do that," she replied.

"Don't forget to talk to Hope today too," Anthony reminded her.

"Should I be offering her a salaried position?"

"I'd offer her 75% of every session she books instead of the standard fifty," he suggested. "That should be enough to tempt her over to us. Now that I think about it, her husband David is sure to object to her working there. That may be an insurmountable hurdle to getting Hope."

"Amanda mentioned playing with him when she first came out to Random Point."

"I like David. He tries to be conventional but he's often getting into trouble because his girl students develop huge crushes on him and the ones who happen to be in the scene are hard to keep at bay. Still, Hope will have to exert all her influence on him to get permission to work for us. He's possessive of her. In the end she always unearths some little bit of misbehavior he's engaged in, for leverage, but they might be even at the moment. Anyway, let's try for Hope."

Cassandra was thinking about how much she would appreciate Hope's company and counsel, especially during the first weeks and months of the new club's existence, when she strolled into Bartlett's bedroom furnishings department and hailed the first clerk she saw. She then proceeded to take the salesman's breath away by asking for the three smartest queen bedroom suites on the floor, complete with dressers, vanities and wardrobes, telling the associate to charge everything she selected to Anthony Newton's account.

One minute later the phone rang in Ambrose Bartlett's office and the owner of the store received a report about the lady in home furnishings. Ambrose looked at his bank of screens and located the department, then Cassandra standing and gazing at a wall of designer bed linens, comforters and counterpanes. Looking closer he recognized Amanda's mother. Bartlett told the clerk to ring up the sales and didn't question that Anthony Newton had authorized the purchases. He got out of his chair and thoughtfully made his way downstairs to greet Cassandra.

"Hello," he said, shaking her hand a moment after entering the department. "Has Anthony made you his personal shopper?" Ambrose asked. She paused for a moment before answering, thinking the suggestion was extremely convenient for avoiding a protracted conversation with this suave, handsome fellow who had laid siege to her daughter the previous winter and put that young lady through several ordeals to gratify his own ego and sexual sadism.

"Yes," Cassandra said. "He's bought a new house and I've been charged with furnishing it."

"Wonderful!"

"I'll be purchasing linens, silver and plate," she further delighted the storeowner by saying.

"Well, consider the head of each department at your disposal. If you don't see what you want on the floor, we've got catalogs you can browse," he told her.

"Thank you."

"Sounds like a big job that will take multiple visits to complete," he observed.

"I'm sure it will."

"Have lunch with me next time you come back?"

"All right. I'll check in with you next time I come back," she promised.

"Or come have coffee with me now," he said.

"Must I?" she asked reluctantly, like a schoolgirl being ordered to the Dean's office.

"Why do you say that? Don't you like me?"

Cassandra shrugged and looked straight into his dark eyes, which were looking quizzically back at her.

"Why?" he demanded.

"I don't like strict tops," she replied simply, leaving him momentarily speechless. So Amanda had told her mother everything, he thought, not a little peeved.

"Really? Does that mean you're in the scene as well? This is getting better and better!" he said with a grin, thinking how youthful and flirtatious Amanda's mother was. As for having a reputation as a hard top, he didn't think he minded that in the slightest. "Please don't be afraid of me," he said. "I'm getting better. I have a nicer side. I proved that to Amanda and she forgave me. She told me she did."

It was an indiscreet conversation to hold on the floor of a department store, but Mr. Bartlett's employees had tactfully withdrawn as far across the floor as possible to give their boss privacy.

"I know, but I'm more sensitive than Amanda," Cassandra replied frankly.

"Didn't you used to be Hugo's submissive?" Ambrose asked shrewdly, for he was a compulsive collector of spanking erotica and now remembered certain still photographs of Cassandra going back twenty years in the history of Hugo's magazine.

"Yes, but when I was with him he was much less demanding than his later image would suggest. The severity level in his magazine was market driven."

"Have you met my wife Pamela yet?" Ambrose lightly changed the subject with a smile.

"No."

"She's madly in love with Amanda."

"Amanda loves her too. She's the sophisticated older sister Amanda never had."

"But it's Amanda who dominates Pamela. She made her cut her hair."

"Amanda cut her own hair too," Cassandra pointed out. "In support."

"Yes. It made me furious. Come across to the pub and have a drink with me!" he insisted.

"No, I have to do my shopping now," she said, but not unkindly.

"Very well, I'll leave you to it. But don't forget to stop in and have lunch with me next time you're in the store," he told her, realizing he'd gotten as far as he could and nodding to the department head to come over and attend to Cassandra.

The moment he stepped out of bedroom furnishings and into the central foyer of the store he ran into Pamela, who was clicking across the floor on her long, slim legs, with a rapid step even in her 5" high heeled booties.

"Is that Amanda's mother?" Pamela asked, taking her husband's arm and casually tossing one searching look back into the bedrooms department to identify Cassandra.

"Yes! And she's furnishing a house for Anthony Newton. He sent her here. Nice of him! That'll double our July," Bartlett said, referring to the overall sales of his department store that month.

"Do you know what kind of a house?" Pamela asked, as the excitement of sharing this item with Ambrose slightly outweighed her anxiety about her husband pursuing additional erotic adventures outside their marriage.

"No. She didn't say anything about that," Bartlett replied.

"It's going to be a club," Pamela whispered, lest one of the sales girls or customers passing by on either side of them on that busy Saturday afternoon hear. "A BDSM club!"

"A what? Are you kidding me?" Ambrose was truly amazed while aware of his heart beating a little faster. For if there was one thing Bartlett truly enjoyed, it was spanking girls.

"Damaris told me Anthony and Cassandra came to William and asked him to find them a house and custom fit it for dungeons."

"Where is it going to be?"

"On Pine Tar Road."

"And Amanda's mother is going to run it?" Ambrose mused. "Is she qualified?"

"I don't know," said Pamela. "But it seems she's just broken up with her longtime partner, so she's free to do virtually any crazy thing."

"Not so crazy getting Anthony Newton to set her up in a plush lined new work place!" said Bartlett admiringly.

"I should go back and introduce myself," Pamela said, stopping to turn on her heel.

"Take her upstairs and sell her some clothes too," said Ambrose. "We just got in some silk teddies from Paris. Don't let her leave without one of those."

Chapter Ten

Saturday Matinee

"I successfully fended off Mr. Bartlett," Cassandra announced to Anthony across their late luncheon table on the terrace of his master suite that afternoon. "But he was ardent in his advances."

"I knew he'd be," said Anthony, beaming down at the perfect mushroom parmesan risotto Josette had just set before them. James uncorked and poured them white wine before disappearing as noiselessly as he had appeared. Josette still blushed furiously every time she entered Anthony's presence.

"Anthony, I've been doing some calculating and even if it did ten sessions a day seven days a week, the club would take fifteen years to make back what you're spending on it."

"Oh, I wasn't expecting it to," he assured her; patting her hand before taking the first rapturous bite of the truffle infused risotto. "When you came to me asking me to back you in a club you probably visualized a much humbler location than the one William found for us."

"Exactly!" Cassandra said.

"Well, stop thinking about paying me back. Whatever profits the club makes will be for you and the girls who work there."

"What would qualify someone for membership?" Cassandra asked, loving the risotto, the balmy breeze rolling up off the ocean below and the light, crisp pinot grigio.

"A referral from someone we know or at the very least, a willingness to allow us to copy his drivers' license. This place is going to be as beloved to us as our home. We can't have strangers walking in off the street. If someone doesn't trust us enough to tell us who he really is, we can't trust him enough to be locked in a room with one of our girls. Know what I mean?"

"It's a good plan," agreed Cassandra, "but won't all this exclusivity severely limit our clientele?"

"Even if it does, you and the girls will make enough to make it worth your while."

"Regarding my sessions," said Cassandra, "what do you think of me subbing?"

"Usually the owner manager plays as a top," Anthony observed. "Don't you think you can handle that?"

Cassandra smiled, "I don't know. I was hoping to. But inevitably some of the clients will ask me to switch or sub to them."

"I think that you should pick and choose your sessions based on your own inclinations."

"Thanks, I agree. Now, about the girls," Cassandra began.

"Yes, tell me your ideas!"

"I just remembered, Amanda has a close friend named Thalia who is putting herself through college doing sessions. Hugo even scolded her for taking too many risks and chances. He may have spanked her too. She's the first one we need to get out for an interview, I think."

"I like the idea of interviews," he grinned.

"I pictured you interviewing all the girls. But you really should adopt a much sterner demeanor when you do."

"We'll have to get as many out over the summer as possible. As soon as Autumn comes I have to go back to New York and after that I only get out to Random Point about once a season," he said regretfully.

"Oh, that's sad. Just when I'll be falling passionately in love with you, you'll be going away," she predicted.

"Silly. We have all July and August, that's more than enough time for the maddest infatuation to flare up and wear itself out," he informed her, inwardly hoping that this was the case with his other new lover, Phoebe Robbins. For Phoebe had grown passionate enough about him the previous month to threaten to dissolve her own marriage to Pascal over it. Only seeing Pascal flirting with Amanda had brought the young wife to her senses and caused her to give Pascal the promise that she would cease to love the composer who had given her so much work as well as thoroughly charming her. The Phoebe romance, while exciting and gratifying to Newton, was also problematical. He couldn't have a luscious little diva obviously in love with him without Susan ultimately noticing and taking exception to the relationship. For years he had balanced the freedom and liberality of his long affair with Susan Ross with discretion and respect. When Susan brought him home a girl, he naturally enjoyed her, as Susan had intended he should, but when he obtained sexual companions in his off time, he tended to conceal rather than flaunt them before his girlfriend. He was aware that she practiced the same courtesy with regard to whatever young lovers she had found in school or at work over the years. She was a good deal younger than he was and he never set out to limit her experiences, but each cared too much about the feelings and sensitivities of the other to risk giving them pain. "You are much too sensible to actually fall in love with me, though, aren't you?" he asked earnestly.

"No," she replied, taking his hand and kissing it. "I love my new master already."

As on every Saturday at the coffee bar, by five-thirty p.m., that café's beautiful blonde manager was completely exhausted. She had arrived at the bookshop at eight a.m. and had been running back and forth behind the counter almost non-stop all day. Her assistant that summer, Dru Baxter, was an excellent busboy and barista, quiet, reliable and tireless. But the popularity of the coffee bar, so greatly increased in the summer, had caused Hope's workload there to become overwhelming. She had resolved to hire more help the following day, even if it meant sacrificing her own salary and tips by 50%.

At a quarter to six, Cassandra walked in and took a seat at the counter.

"Are you almost done?" Cassandra asked Hope, who was wiping down the wooden counter for the last time that evening.

"I am," said Hope, glad to see her new friend again.

"Wanna take a little walk with me and get high?" Cassandra asked.

"Absolutely!" Hope grinned. "But I have to count my drawer and close down. I'll be another twenty to twenty five minutes. Why don't you browse in the bookstore for a bit? It's closing in a few minutes but

Sloan will let you hang out and wait for me."

Cassandra went into the bookshop and bought the large coffee table book of Pascal Robbins' photography featuring Pamela and sat in the enclosed outdoor patio that was an extension of the coffee bar to look at it.

It was a warm and pleasant early evening and the sound of the rushing Random Point brook, visible through the openwork patio wall was serenely ambient. Cassandra had missed the brook more than any other physical aspect of the village.

When Hope joined her they walked out the back gate of the bookstore garden and began to stroll alongside the brook, passing a pipe as they went.

"I am beat," said Hope, stretching her lithe, slender body in pleasure at finally being liberated from work.

It was the perfect moment for Cassandra to make Hope Anthony's offer, which both stunned and delighted Hope. To work in a smart, luxurious spanking club owned by Anthony Newton and get to keep 75% of her earnings sounded like paradise compared with the ten hour day, six day a week schedule she had maintained almost since starting work at the coffee bar of Marguerite and Sloan's bookshop three years before. Not quite thirty yet, Hope had been judicious during her marriage to David Lawrence and had saved most of her earnings, which she had then invested in adding the outdoor patio to the coffee bar, which had in turn allowed her to become one of the partners in the bookstore. Hope was now pocketing all the profits from the snacks and coffee served at the bar, less her overhead and the pay of a few local busboys and counter girls she had in to assist her throughout the week, but the physical hours of toil the management of such a business demanded was taking the joy out of her life. With her cheerful and gregarious personality, being fixed in the center of the village, meeting and chatting with everyone who lived there or visited, had suited Hope's temperament. But the nature of the work was far below her unique capabilities, her artistic capacity and her remarkable physical attractions. Not just pretty, Hope Spencer Lawrence was the kind of beauty you didn't want to tear your eyes away from. All of these assets were marketable at a higher price than the tips on muffin and coffee orders could ever equal and after far less effort. She remembered her days and nights of sessioning at The Keep in Hollywood fondly.

They stopped and sat on some large, flat rocks, continuing to smoke and look at the brook. Hope was dressed as usual for work in jeans, sensible shoes and a white three quarter sleeved button down shirt. Over this outfit she had worn her iconic red chef's apron for what had now stretched into years. She imagined opening people's eyes in glove tight club wear again and smiled. It wasn't as though she didn't get enough attention. Her charming and affable demeanor brought her that. But there was in Hope a tendency toward exhibitionism, which as a barista she had generally underplayed, to save herself from vulgar ogling. To be set as a gem in a jewel box of a club, created by her favorite millionaire, would bring her beauty to the notice of just the sort of handpicked connoisseurs she liked to meet. She would get off her feet, relax, and enjoy being pampered with allowance and gifts and spankings that lasted for an hour behind a thick closed door.

"David will say no and we'll have a terrible row," Hope predicted with a sigh. "He can be so unreasonable about things like that."

"Anthony wants me to have you," said Cassandra.

"Oh, I love him for that!" Hope cried.

"Do you think you'd make as much as you are the book store?"

"I'd only have to work two days a week to do that if the old days are anything to go by," Hope said. "Of course, I'm a few years older now. But in B&D years, 29 is still almost a teen."

"What about forty five?" Cassandra asked honestly. She had forbore expressing any insecurities about her age to Anthony, always having been advised that confidence was sexier than self-doubt, but Hope was going to be like a sister to her and was, even in spite of being so much younger, much more experienced in the world of salons than she.

"You? You shouldn't admit to be older than thirty-two," Hope smiled. "By the way, exactly what are you going to do at the club?"

"Spank guys. I know a little tying too."

"They're going to want to spank you. You realize that, right?"

"Anthony thinks that will be fine, if I feel like it."

"He's so lovely. Maybe I'll tell David the same thing, that I'm only going to spank men."

"Will he believe you?"

"It's believable. You'll need lady spankers, I can tell you that."

"We'll do a lot of doubles, I hope. So you can teach me what I need to know," said Cassandra.

"It sounds divine!"

They walked back to the shop and departed from Main Street each in her own car. Cassandra proceeded to the gym while Hope went home to Cobweb Cottage to discuss Cassandra's proposition with her husband.

The cottage, a property they had been renting from William Random since arriving in Random Point, was really too small for the two professionals, consisting of only a living room, bedroom and kitchen with dining room and pantry. But on balance, it was set atop a scenic cove, quite the only house commanding that particular view, with a garden behind it and woods behind that. Both the bedroom and sitting room had its own small fireplace and there were several niches between the rooms that held each of their desks, with bookshelves above. Had it not been for the inlet ocean view and the fireplaces, Hope would have suggested their finding a larger house long since, but both of them adored the romantic cottage, its proximity to the village and the long history of scene people who had been its occupants, bestowing upon it a certain sense of enchantment. Cassandra herself had inhabited Cobweb Cottage twenty-one years before, when Hugo Sands had first come to Random Point to open his antiques shop and simultaneously begin publishing his New Rod Quarterly magazine.

That evening Hope found her handsome husband in the kitchen, with his sleeves rolled up, chopping vegetables for a salad. She knew he had been at Braemar that afternoon, teaching summer school classes. During the regular school year, the exclusive prep school groomed upper middle class to wealthy college bound students for the Ivy League, as it had done since its inception in the 1950's. David always juggled second jobs in the summer, also teaching courses at the local community college from July to September.

"Hi Honey," he said. "I started the salad. And I stopped and got us some steaks."

"Thanks, I'm dead tired," said Hope, falling into a kitchen chair and gratefully pouring herself a glass of Syrah from a bottle he had just opened. "That job is wearing me out."

"Oh, honey, I'm sorry," he said, looking up from chopping cucumbers.

"I thought when I bought into the shop I'd feel like a savvy and successful business woman but I'm working longer hours than before and after all of my overhead, I'm making pennies more for ten times the aggravation."

"You cut your own salary. That wasn't very smart," David observed.

"I had no choice if I wanted to keep on a full time busboy plus extra help during the season."

David looked sympathetically at her. She never got up from the chair for the next half hour, with her elbows on the table and her face between her hands as she lazily watched him expertly pan grill their rib eyes. He refilled her glass and nodded with approval as she drank. "At least you have tomorrow off," he said, clearing off their plates when they had finished. Hope was about the raise the subject of the club, but she forced herself to put off the unpleasant conversation for a few more hours, highly unwilling to spoil the splendid meal with a quarrel.

After dinner they went for a walk, then returned to the cottage where David worked for a while on his lesson plans for the following week and Hope watched some fashion competition shows she had recorded.

When they were finally ready for bed, Hope changed from her street clothes into a gossamer thin white cotton nightie and sat in front of her vanity brushing out her long, fine, wavy, pale blonde hair. David had as usual put on his tailored cotton pajamas to get into bed, though he would characteristically shed them minutes later, and took up a book of Bryon's poems to read until she put out the light.

"I've had an offer of a better job today," she said, looking at him in the mirror.

"Seriously? You're really thinking of leaving the book shop?"

"I told you it's killing me," she said. "I'm tired of waiting on people and being on my feet all day long six days a week."

"So what kind of offer did you get?" David put down his book.

"There's a club opening in Random Point soon, a BDSM club. And I've been invited to be the co-manager."

"Are you serious?"

"Anthony Newton is going to be the owner and it's being run by Amanda Sands' mother. She just moved back to the village for that reason."

"That's the craziest thing I ever heard. And of course you can't work there."

"Why not? It's going to be the dreamiest club ever, with everything in the best of taste and a private membership."

"Hope, I'm a teacher at Braemar. You know there would be a scandal if anyone found out you were doing that."

"No one is going to find out. The boys are much too young to find their way to a place like that and the only staff members likely to discover its existence are Freddie Johanson and Paula Taylor, both of whom are in the scene."

"And what if someone on the board of directors were to find out?"

"Anthony Newton is on the board of directors by dint of all the money he's donated to the Braemar music department over the years."

"This is outlandish. You think I'm going to let you go back to working in a club where any man can come in and own you for an hour at a time?"

Hope smiled at her husband's continued ardent and possessive affection for her.

"Oh, you'd rather me be a scullery maid, a Cinderella, always running back into the pantry for milk and cream, churning out my millionth latte? I'm sick of it, I tell you!"

"All right, I understand that. But there are more than two choices of careers. It's not barista or B&D slut with nothing in between."

"David, I need a complete change. I'm burned out on waitressing. I can make as much money working three days a week at a club as I can in six exhausting myself at the shop as I try to figure out how to beat my overhead."

"Hope, since I got promoted to head the English department, people are paying more attention to me and you than ever."

"Well, I'll have more time and energy to attend academic functions if I'm not at the bookstore six days a week. At a club I'll have the most flexible schedule imaginable. I'm always pouring coffee and mopping up counters, even when I'm visiting with my friends. I want to live like a yuppie for once, not a peon."

"I'll never consent to you working at a BDSM club again. I know the sort of antics you'll get up to!" he bristled, his eyes flicking towards the hairbrush in her hand.

She noticed this and but said with quiet determination. "You're doing exactly what you want to do, David. You teach the brightest students from the wealthiest families, in the prettiest prep school in the commonwealth. You're not an overworked drudge. You don't have to serve the public. You're respected and obeyed at work and also here at home. You've had me now for over four years as your wife. If you want to keep living with Hope, you'll stop eyeing this hairbrush and admit that this is an argument you don't deserve to win."

"You never used to think of disobeying me," he observed wistfully.

"Yes, I did. I very much wanted to disobey you about working at Michael's bar part time. I realize now that you were right about that, but for the wrong reasons. That would have been a step sideways."

"And what direction does working in a parlor take you? Other than bent over something."

"Right now that sounds a lot more restful and pleasant than running back and forth behind a counter for fifty-four hours a week."

David hadn't realized his wife was so exhausted by her job.

"But you just bought into the business. You were climbing to a different level," he pointed out.

"That turned out to be an illusion. The more business that comes in, the more help I have to hire and pay insurance for and file withholdings on. After all is said and done, I was just as exhausted – but less stressed – when I was on regular salary myself. This profit sharing idea is swell in theory but the overhead is killing me!"

"I didn't realize."

"I'm ready to walk away from it and Marguerite and Sloan can pay me back the money I put into the patio in easy installments over the next twenty years. I don't even care about that. I want my life back. I want whole days a week when I can just go and walk on the beach, shop, have lunch with my friends, read, write. I'll be able to do all that with this new job."

Anger at her defiance surged through David and his chin came up as he thought of what to say or do next. She sat watching him warily but still maintained the cool determination she had evinced throughout their discussion. He really hadn't realized she was so unhappy with her job. But the more details she filled in, the clearer the picture became and he felt uncomfortable at the contrast she had painted between their current professional lives. It was true that when he had met her she was a happy go lucky club girl who occasionally did a fetish video, lived modestly in a Hollywood walk up but enjoyed an abundance of free time to play with her friends. At twenty nine she was still the most beautiful and sexually alluring woman he had ever met, and amiable into the bargain. This was the first time she had ever complained about working at the bookstore, which was the social hub of the village and of which she had become a principal attraction. And yet, how could he possibly bear for her to go off to play in a B&D club with strange men, even for only three days a week?

"So I'm supposed to share my wife with anyone who can pay for her… services?"

"There won't be any walk-ins off the street or ads in the Free Press if that's what you mean. It's going to cost a lot to play in this club and there will be a screening process. And the other thing is that I'm going to be co-manager of it. That means I'll be doing mostly top sessions."

"Oh? Is that so?" he asked doubtfully.

"Of course it is."

"Hope, what if you went back to school and finished your degree? You could look for a real job then. With the promotion and my second job at the college, you don't need to work anymore."

"Is that what you want?" she asked.

"Yes!"

"But it's not what I want!"

"Now you're being unreasonable," he said. "You said you're tired of working at the bookstore. I understand that. So quit. Dump the job. And just let me support you from now on. You'll have all the freedom you want. You can go back to school or settle down to write your memoirs. Just don't say you're going back to work in B&D!"

Hope knew as surely as she knew anything that before the night was over she was going to end up over David's knee and the inevitable happened less than ten seconds later. He had made what he thought an immensely generous offer and she was stubbornly clinging to this obscene and insolent notion of going back to being a club girl, right there in Random Point, for any of their friends, not to mention strangers, to possess for a price. It was simply untenable to a husband who had hitherto been unchallenged in his supremacy except for on the rare occasions when Hope had learned of David's own sexual indiscretions.

He took her off the bench, drew her down across his lap and wresting the brush from her grasp, laid it onto her bottom through the thin cotton of her nightgown.

"I told you I don't want you working at a club," he reiterated, bringing the back of the polished wooden oval brush down at least a dozen times on either shapely cheek hard and fast. She cried out in pain at every swat and kicked her slim legs up so high that he had to duck to avoid a battering from her velvet-slippered feet.

"Let me go, you brute. I won't be bullied into submission this time," she cried, putting her hand back to protect her bottom and having her wrist instantly pinned to her waist.

"Don't make me lock those legs," he threatened, causing Hope to momentarily cease her kicking, for if there was a thing she feared it was the leg lock of a strong male thigh across the back of her knees.

"How dare you?" she said, thrashing to escape his smacking. "This isn't some domestic discipline fantasy. This is my life, you male chauvinist beast!"

"You call me that?" he was amazed and hurt, and it caused him to pause in spanking her. She tried to look at him over her shoulder, showing him her beautiful profile with her long blonde hair swept behind her framing her face.

"Yes, I call you that! You've been tyrannizing over me for years with these corporal punishment moves and getting away with murder," she quite fairly pointed out. He reluctantly let her go. She sprang off his lap, her hands pressed to her bottom, which was hot and stinging from the dozen or fifteen swats he had managed to deliver.

David sighed, "When do you start?"

After a yoga class, a swim and a transformative massage from Dieter Brandt at the gym, Cassandra, fairly melting with relaxation, slipped into the red leather dress she had bought from Damaris, and a pair of high heeled black booties and took herself to Michael Flagg's tavern for the first time. She knew that Amanda had been there once to shoot a photo set for Hugo's magazine along with her friend, Thalia. Cassandra also remembered that Michael Flagg was the husband of Marguerite Alexander, the co-owner of the bookstore, who was about to be deprived of her jewel, Hope Lawrence, as she and Anthony lured Hope away to their perfect club in the woods. Complicating the politics was the fact that the house they had chosen was just down the road from Michael's, with no house in between.

Cassandra recognized Michael Flagg from his description at once. 6'3", fair haired, muscular and possessed of a perfect V-shaped torso, her host was an arresting figure and when he came to take her order at the bar, his smiling face irresistibly attractive.

"Hello," she said, putting out her hand to shake his. "I'm Cassandra, Amanda's mother."

"Hello!" he said enthusiastically. "I'd heard you were back in Random Point."

"Did you hear why?"

"Yes! What a great idea. Put me down for the first membership."

"Thought you'd be interested," she grinned. "Mr. Newton told me to ask you about putting in a security system for us as soon as possible."

"I'd love to. Meanwhile, what can I get you?"

"Some nice merlot."

Michael opened a bottle and set it aside for a few moments. Cassandra settled comfortably on her barstool, looking around the room, which was filled with summer visitors and locals. She was lucky to have found one seat at the bar. A Psychedelic Furs song was playing on the jukebox and a few young couples were lazily dancing.

"Finally I catch you alone," said a voice from behind Cassandra. Reflected in the bar mirror before her was Ambrose Bartlett's well groomed image, his toned form impeccably dressed in one of the designer suits from his own store. Magically a bar stool opened up beside her and Bartlett took it. "Can I have a martini?" he asked Michael, who began preparing it in a shaker.

"Oh, hello," she said.

"Well, aren't you the sly boots with your own B&D club! Why didn't you tell me that at the store?"

"Who did tell you?"

"Pamela."

"Did she also tell you she sold me two silk teddies?"

"Yes, I suggested that. You have the kind of body that looks fantastic in bias cut silk satin," he observed.

"Mr. Bartlett, please stop flirting with me," she advised. "I can tell you right now that I'm never going to play with you."

"What? Why not? How can you say that? And call me Ambrose," he said, downing his first martini quickly and gesturing to Michael to start another.

"Because Amanda told me what you are like and how you made her cry. Do you think I'm going to let you make me cry?" she asked, sipping her nice merlot while looking at him thoughtfully.

"I wouldn't think of doing anything like that," he vowed. "I just find you interesting and I'd like to get to know you better."

"If you wish to endear yourself to me you will see that I receive all the goods I've ordered so far as promptly as possible."

"Tomorrow is Sunday, but I'll work on it," said Ambrose, highly mindful of how many of Mr. Newton's thousands had been scattered about the various departments of his high-end emporium by Cassandra that day.

"In return I will offer you a bonus. As the girls come out to me from Boston and New York to interview about working at the club, you may be placed on the short list of locals who will be offered the opportunity to give them their introductory sessions. Frankly, it's only fair to guarantee them some allowance for coming out to interview and I think you'd find it piquant."

"I absolutely love that idea," Bartlett said. "But I'm not giving up on winning you over either."

"Why? I'm not even young," said Cassandra, reaching the bottom of her glass and finally stammering out the sentence that had been hovering around her consciousness ever since Anthony Newton unexpectedly took her up.

"You should be spanked for saying that," Bartlett observed. "I think you have the prettiest figure."

"Thank you. And damn you for knowing how to get around a woman," Cassandra smiled ruefully, knowing she should never have given voice to her insecurities. But what did it matter if she said such things to Bartlett? He was handsome, but cruelty repelled her and he had shown cruelty to Amanda. He had striven to make up for it since with kindness and generosity and even a much-softened manner. But that he had even hurt Amanda a little, would ever color her emotions towards Bartlett. A person who could willfully inflict hurt could never be trusted.

Chapter Eleven

Tidings of Cassandra Reach Venice and Paris

After checking into their hotel on the Rialto canal in Venice on a hot and sunny afternoon, Amanda slipped into the message center and read two puzzling notes from Pamela regarding her mother. The first was a brief and cryptic message, advising Amanda to warn Cassandra about Ambrose. The second was just as brief and merely read: "I can't believe you have the slightest idea of what your mother is up to in Random Point."

Colby came up behind Amanda in time to read a third note over her shoulder. This one was from Susan Ross and read: "Do you still plan to be in Paris the day after tomorrow? I'm traveling with my friend Diana Stratton Currie. We're staying at the Hotel Relais St. Germain. Let's hook up!"

"Who is Diana Currie?" Colby asked.

"A beautiful young matron who is married to Susan's boss. I've wanted to meet her."

"Is she in the scene?" he asked.

"Yes, but more into bondage," Amanda replied, following Colby into the dining room to order lunch. The room they had been given was tiny but delightful, with a view of the Grand Canal. But they had many palaces and bridges to visit before retiring to it in the early evening. Now they ordered pasta and Colby tried the local beer as they discussed Pamela's curious emails as well as the prospect of meeting Susan and Diana. Colby had met Susan Ross a few times and thought her adorable, for an older woman. Susan was at this time about twenty-six.

"Are you going to say anything to Susan about your mother being taken up by Anthony Newton?" asked Colby, for he knew that Susan was Anthony's protégée as well.

"No!"

"Okay, just checking," said Colby. "Am I going to get to spank Susan?"

"What an outrageous question. Maybe Diana," smiled Amanda, remembering Susan telling her that Diana was a small powerhouse of polymorphous perversity. "She on vacation from her baby for the first time ever and I would imagine she'll be packing every drop of excitement she can find into it."

Meanwhile, in Random Point, it was Sunday afternoon and Cassandra had borrowed Dennis and an SUV from Anthony's garage to go shopping for household goods, tools, cleaning items and labor saving devices with which to stock the club. She had a long list of items from paper to metal to wood and a separate one for groceries. As they went about the package store loading their palate with large sizes of paper items and bottled water, Cassandra asked Dennis many questions about his life with Anthony Newton. That Dennis was devoted to his employer was obvious and that Newton was fond of his assistant equally so. But Dennis didn't fully grasp what the house he was helping to stock was really all about. The English boy's fetish, ladies' feet, was not one that crossed with his master's fetish or those of his masters' women. He had been allowed to worship Susan's feet and those of her closest girlfriends in the scene. And Susan Ross had even introduced him to spanking. But if he had a particular taste in BDSM, it was for mistresses, preferably in very high heeled, thigh high boots.

They dropped their supplies off at the house but Cassandra didn't pause to put anything away, knowing she would be returning the next day to await cable technicians and the furniture deliveries.

When they returned to the mansion it was almost seven. Anthony had gotten home from his matinee performance and was at his computer in his study.

"Hi," he said, waving her in. "I've been ordering you some Macs and software for your office at the house. We're getting overnight delivery on everything and I don't have anything scheduled for the beginning of the week so I can get you set up."

"How nice of you," she said, for she had been wondering just that morning whether she ought to purchase the computer equipment herself.

"I ordered a TV for the lounge too," he said. "Maybe on Tuesday we'll go to Boston and buy mirrors."

"I would love to go to Boston with you!"

"Come upstairs, there's something I want to show you," he said, leading her up the back stairs to the antique furnished medical consulting room where he had seduced Susan a number of years before and where more recently, Colby and Amanda had ravished Pamela together.

"It took me years to collect all this stuff," he said, gesturing to the invasive medical and quasi-medical equipment that filled the several decorative cabinets. The room also boasted a large examining table and a number of strategically placed mirrors. "This time, we'll give the job to Susan's friend Diana Currie, the young lady she's traveling with. I'll pay her to spend the time hunting down a whole new set of this stuff and we'll trust her to get the best office fittings for the exam room. She's totally into it and she's a decorator. I don't think we should go as baroque as this room. The new house is modern and minimalist, and so should the various playrooms be. One perfect exam table, but the objects should be stored behind the doors of a cabinet you have to open to see into. The less extraneous objects, the easier it will be to organize the house, keep it clean and shoot in."

Cassandra said, "I haven't been completely idle either. I've already arranged with both Michael Flagg and Mr. Bartlett to session with the first few girls who come out for interviews so as to defer their traveling expenses. They're thrilled."

"That's excellent. Have you thought of what rates you're going to charge yet?" he asked.

"What do you think?"

"Offer locals the lowest rates on sessions and renting space and skip the membership fees. A non-local or anyone we don't know should be paying a thousand dollar yearly membership and at least five an hour for the type of girls we'll have. Give the girls all a sixty-forty split with the house so you can deduct out their withholdings without them feeling it. I'll have my accountant work up a rough estimate of what you should be putting aside for our - let's call them 'activities coordinators'."

"And what do the locals get charged?"

"Maybe two bills an hour and request at least a twenty per cent tip for each girl."

"What about for just renting dungeon space?"

"For out of towners, a couple of hundred, for locals, half that."

"Sounds fair."

"The girls who come from out of town can stay overnight as a perk, but no customers except bondagers who really need supervision should be accommodated overnight and if you ever do book an all-nighter, be sure to charge a couple of grand."

"You sound like you've really studied this," she laughed.

"I told you, my girl Isabel Bruno has been running a club in Manhattan for years. She tells me these things."

"When we go to Boston, we should visit my sister Carola's little dungeon and ask her who she can send us right away," suggested Cassandra.

"Good idea!" he agreed.

"I don't know if you're going to like her. She's somewhat brittle and rather a snob. Gets her corsets from Paris and her leather from Amsterdam. Her favorite tribute is Louboutin shoes."

"Speaking of Paris and Amsterdam, I must send Susan a letter catching her up on what's been going on," said Anthony.

"Tell me again how I'm supposed to behave with you in front of Susan," said Cassandra. Anthony leaned back in his chair and looked at her with a half smile.

"Why, what do you mean?"

Cassandra blushed. They had slept together again last night, after a great deal of foreplay in his attic dungeon. She felt warm all over just thinking about it. He had bent her over a spanking horse for the first time at her insistence.

"I can't take the suspense any more, we have to do this," she had said. She hadn't had a proper spanking since Hugo had come to see her the previous Autumn to remonstrate with her for keeping their daughter a secret from him for the first eighteen years of her life. And Cassandra had always enjoyed this type of thing. She hadn't explored anything of the kind with her erstwhile life partner, Eddie. He hadn't the temperament for it. She had missed this aphrodisiac for almost twenty years. Of course Anthony played as he did everything else, beautifully. And that was what made her blush.

"What I mean is, won't she sense what's going on between us?" Cassandra asked.

"If you're going to go around blushing every time I look at you of course she'll figure it out," Anthony replied.

"I'm sorry. Maybe I'll be past the initial phases of my infatuation with you before Susan returns and we have to meet," said Cassandra hopefully. Anthony smiled at her.

Amanda and Colby took the train from Venice through Switzerland to Paris that afternoon. They had abandoned Don Quixote in their Venice hotel room, taking with them instead the complete Casanova, which they read to each other on the train as long as they were alone in their first class carriage.

"I looked up the hotel Susan and Diana are staying at," said Amanda as they shared rustic sandwiches they'd bought in the train station. "It's said the building has been there for seven hundred years. Each room is named after a prominent French writer."

"How am I supposed to act around them?" Colby asked politely.

"What do you mean?"

"Is Diana similar to Pamela?" he asked.

"As far as I understand, yes, she is very decadent by inclination. But she's been in maternal harness for the last several years, so her extracurricular amatory adventures have been few."

"Does that mean she's going to be -" he was going to say 'horny' but that sounded crude, so instead he said, "-easy?"

"Well, the girl *is* on vacation," Amanda replied serenely sipping a Pellegrino.

"Well, how am I supposed to react if … if…"

"If you get a hard-on?"

"Oh never mind, I guess I'll just play it by ear, like I always do with you."

"Colby, don't give any of this a second thought. I trust you to behave well and always love me best. Just like I hope you trust me."

"But, I don't. Not at all," he protested, before going back to the club car to buy a few cold bottled beers. Amanda looked out the window at the soft green hills of the Italian countryside rolling past on the hot and sunny day. She looked down at the Casanova. She didn't like where things were going with the two sisters. It sounded too much like a standard porn video. When Colby came back he offered her one of the beers but she declined and he grinned, delighted to keep them both.

"I want to skip to Volume 3," said Amanda, "we can always come back to the beginning later. I'm bored with Giacomo as a callow youth."

"All right then, we'll pick it up with his escape from the Leads, the story that always took him exactly two hours to tell," said Colby, opening their book, "and our narrator is just about thirty years of age."

They arrived in Paris at around three p.m. and took a cab from the station to Susan's hotel in a light, misty rain that steamed away the intense heat of the day. Colby looked casual but presentable in khaki shorts and a white t-shirt. Amanda was in a short, form fitting green and lilac print sundress and green ankle strap espadrille sandals. Colby shouldered his large pack back and wheeled her large suitcase. Amanda carried a small green shoulder bag. Susan had told them to come up to the Rousseau suite. They took the birdcage elevator up to the third floor and found the placard bearing the famous philosopher's name at the end of a carpeted hall. Amanda knocked lightly at the door, which was opened almost immediately by Susan Ross, who pulled them in and whisked it shut in an instant.

Colby could see why Susan was so cautious. For a beautiful small brunette was curled up on the canopied bed, scantily dressed in a white jacquard baby doll halter dress, with her wrists bound behind her back and a white handkerchief gag in her mouth and tied around her head. The front of the dress had many buttons and some of them had been undone to allow one perfect, peach like breast to be glimpsed and the back of the dress had been hiked up to Diana's hip to reveal a pair of white, frilled, lace tiered panties. The petite bondager's legs were bare and her tiny feet were in champagne colored lacing ankle booties with 5" heels. Her ankles had been firmly lashed together with a medium gauge white nylon rope. The girl's long dark brown bob was silky, parted to one side and held back with a pearl clip. Her eyes were large and dark and full of pleasant mischief as she gazed into Colby's wide blue ones. Susan Ross came to each of them and hugged them in turn. She was a petite blonde in her middle twenties with long hair almost down to her waist pulled back in a high ponytail. She was dressed in a black cotton tunic over beige Capri leggings and on her little feet she wore black, high-laced platform sandals that added three inches to her height. Her face was delightfully pretty and full of fun and she gazed at them with excitement.

"Thank goodness, you brought us a man!" Susan said to Amanda, looking at Diana with exasperation, then saying to Colby and Amanda, "I can't handle her any longer on my own."

"Why not?" Amanda asked, unable to remove her eyes from the adorable image of the luscious, brown haired nymph on the quilted champagne satin counterpane.

"She's too much of a slut," said Susan sadly. "I thought she'd be content with me photographing her at Notre Dame with her hands bound under her summer cape, then flipped up all of a sudden, when no one was looking, allowing me to get the shot. And then we went to the Louvre and I got her up against an Egyptian pillar, with her wrists dead center in the shot. But she's not satisfied. Now she wants me to play with her and put toys in her and make her orgasm. And we don't even have a Hitachi wand with us. Or we do, but we forgot to get an adaptor. You see why we need a man?"

"Oh my god, are you saying that this lady needs a spanking?" asked Amanda, approaching Diana on the bed and smiling at her. "I'm Amanda," said the vacationing student.

"Hugo Sands' secret daughter who I told you about," said Susan to her friend, whose eyes widened. She made a noise behind her gag and looked at Susan appealingly. Susan sat beside her on the bed and began to untie the gag that had been knotted behind Diana's head.

"Diana has fond memories of Hugo," Susan explained to Amanda as she pulled the wadded handkerchief end out of her friend's mouth.

"Hello," said Diana to Amanda and then glanced back at Colby.

"This is Colby Hodge, my boyfriend. At your service, of course," said Amanda.

"Hi," said Colby to Diana.

"Oh, she needs a lot more than a spanking," said Susan. "You can see what a state she's in. I told her I'm not up to it. I've never been up to her demands. She's insisted all these years that I'm her top while all I ever do is hand her over to men."

"Why don't we leave Colby here with her for a couple of hours and we can go shopping?" Amanda suggested. "Is that okay with you, Colby?" Amanda asked him. "You hate to wait for me in stores and it's Paris after all."

"What a fantastic idea," said Susan. "Aren't you excited about being left with this beautiful, dominant spanker?" she asked Diana.

Diana nodded vigorously, never taking her eyes from Colby's gaze.

"So you're saying you're leaving me with her, alone?" asked Colby, forcing Amanda to look at him so he could fully understand her intentions.

"Yes. Clearly, your special abilities are needed in this instance," Amanda fondly replied, stretching her hand out to Susan and saying, "Now, let's go shopping!"

While Amanda was making sure she had everything she needed and no more for a several hour outing in Paris, Colby came and sat on the bed next to Diana. "Do you want to be untied before they go?" he asked softly, brushing a tendril of hair off her brow. She shook her head wordlessly, her medium sized and well-rounded bosom heaving with excitement at his nearness, his boyish, masculine scent, and the narrowness of his waist in contrast to the thickness of his thighs.

"I'd retie her hands in front of her," said Susan on their way out the door.

Out in the hall Susan paused with her hand on Amanda's arm, whispering, "Do you think he'll know what to do?"

"He knew what to do with me and I'm only about a tenth as

submissive as Diana," returned Amanda and took Susan's hand in her own to proceed towards the narrow wooden staircase down.

"Thank you for allowing us to annex your boyfriend," said Susan. "It's very generous of you."

"The gift will only further enslave him to me and make him ever more grateful for the glorious benefits he continues to receive as my lover," Amanda observed.

"Oh, by the way, speaking of gifts and benefits, do you have any idea of what your mother is doing at this very moment in Random Point?" Susan demanded as they emerged onto the street, which was still being lightly sprinkled with rain.

"No, what? Shall we go this way?" Amanda turned towards the closest boulevard.

"Yes, there's a boutique at the end of this block. I saw it earlier."

"I had a feeling you didn't know. Nobody knew, not even Hugo," said Susan. "I've just been emailing with him about it."

"About what? The last I heard from mother, Anthony was being kind to her," said Amanda.

"I should say he's being kind," said Susan. "I've had a long letter from him this morning telling me about what's going on."

"Is it this store?" Amanda said, looking into a window display of skinny jeans and skimpy tee's on mannequins.

"Yes, let's go in," said Susan.

"Well?" Amanda asked, going straight to the one rack of dresses she saw. They were short, tight and with the darts in all the right places.

"Your mother is opening a club in Random Point and Anthony is financing the whole thing. William Random has already sold him a house and your mom's been shopping at Bartlett's for furniture and linen. On top of all that, they're stealing Hope Lawrence from Sloan and Marguerite to put her in as co-manager."

"A club?"

"An exclusive B&D club. On the same road as Michael Flagg's house," Susan added, knowing that Amanda had received one of her first Random Point spankings there from the tavern owner. "There's going to be studio space set up for shoots that we'll all have access to.

And get this; part of the function of the club will be to provide rental space for couples to play in. After you told your mother what you heard at the Venus Club dinner, she figured out that all the scene couples in the village need a cool place in which to meet and regularly cheat on each other. She thought that alone might head off the next round of divorces."

"I always suspected my mother had the ability to do amazing things," said Amanda, serenely picking out several dresses to try on.

"She's staying at the house with Anthony," said Susan. "Just how pretty is she?"

"Susan, be yourself, she's old enough to be your mother."

"And Anthony's old enough to be my father."

"She's pretty cute," said Amanda with a grin. Susan sighed.

Chapter Twelve

Colby and Diana

Taking Susan's advice, Colby sat on the bed beside Diana, rolled her towards him and pulled open the simple knot that bound her wrists behind her back. Then he gently pulled her up to a sitting position beside him. She put her wrists together in front of her for him to retie them. He looked at them for a moment then made her stand up before him. She put her wrists out. He looked into her large brown eyes and saw that she was lost in the rapture of the moment.

"I can't believe I have to do this," he said, "a girl should have enough self-control to hold still for a spanking." She smiled slightly, blushed and looked down at her dainty boots, still bound at the ankle.

He doubled the short length of rope and wrapping it around her slender wrists pulled one cord through for the simplest possible tie, then, with the loose ends, of which Diana disapproved caught in one hand, pulled her firmly face down across his lap. She gasped with excitement and looked back over her shoulder towards him, suddenly realizing that she could watch him spanking her in the mirror set into the wardrobe facing the bed. He noticed the mirror at the same time and received a similar thrill at the sight of himself with the stunning, doll-like brunette disposed across his thighs with her short dress only half covering her frilly panties. Her shapely legs were bare, extremely fair and smooth.

"They tell me you're married. Does your husband spank you?" Colby asked, running both hands over the mounds of her bottom over her bikini panty, squeezing them and stroking them with passionate admiration.

"Not often enough. He's treated me like a china doll since I had my baby a few years ago," she confided. "I wish he would get this hard just looking at me," she added, grinding down against the large erection that had been Colby's accessory since entering the room.

"He's old though, isn't he?" Colby asked, with the candor of a nineteen year old.

"Yes, he's forty. But he's very handsome and I adore him."

"Do you think he would mind if he knew what you were doing now?" Colby asked, slowly rolling her panties down to expose her perfect bottom.

"He'd understand, but I won't tell him in case he's looking around for an excuse to tie me up for four hours," Diana replied.

"Oh my god, he's done that?"

"Bondagers tend to push it sometimes. It's okay. I'm an escape artist. I could have gotten free if I'd wanted to."

"I can't believe you've had a baby. You have the cutest body," said Colby, caressing her smooth oval cheeks with his large, sensitive hands. She wriggled across his lap. "I'm not sure about this bondage thing, though," he said, spanking her on either cheek six times. "It looks pretty, but I'd rather see your legs apart." He slapped her another six times, smartly on alternate cheeks. "And as for your wrists, I'd rather hold on to your waist under my hand." Colby dispensed more spanking, rapidly and rhythmically, holding her around her small waist, close to his own body.

Diana felt wildly aroused by his rock hard torso against her side and the way he was holding her set her aflame.

"All right, untie me!" she cried, wriggling away from his increasingly severe hand.

"Good!" he said and adjusting her position squarely across his lap bent her knees up and began to unlace the cord that bound her ankles together. That done he reached out in the other direction to recapture the end of the simple knot he had tied around her wrists and soon freed them. The ropes discarded, he once again grabbed firm hold of Diana and recommenced the spanking. Now he found the small panties continued to impede his unobstructed view of Diana's charms and pulled them off. Parting her satiny thighs, he inspected her minutely, intoxicated by her womanly scent.

"Maybe I won't spank you so hard if you let me touch you," he said, close to her ear, which he then lightly bit the lobe of just by her pearl stud earring. She shivered in pleasure and spread her legs wider.

"Spank me hard *and* touch me," she encouraged him, looking at him again over her shoulder, but then once again noticing how they looked in the mirror together. This time her legs were entirely free and he'd taken one wrist and pinned it back to her waist as he'd said he wanted to. To be physically restrained by a handsome man or sexy woman was as thrilling to Diana as being put in rope bondage and pre-orgasmic spasms of excitement darted between the pit of her stomach and her heart center. Now he began spanking her nearly as hard as he spanked Amanda. Diana kicked her little feet and squirmed across his lap, consciously grinding her belly against his rigid penis.

Having stained her alabaster skin magenta pink with the palm of his hand, Colby delicately spread her open and inserted a middle finger into her vagina, very slowly. He found her to be wet and so introduced a second finger as she wriggled on his lap and ground against him even harder.

"Stand up, young lady," said Colby, suddenly putting her off his lap and standing her before him. He reached into one of the pockets of his cargo shorts and retrieved a condom. "Open this and get ready to put it on me," he directed her, unzipping his shorts and allowing his large, throbbing cock to emerge and wag at her with the insolence of a Jack in the Box.

Diana looked at Colby's attractively circumcised and rose-colored penis with wide eyes. She tore open the condom and kneeling before him, carefully slid the sheath over his knob and shaft.

"Get it wet with your mouth," he instructed. She obediently began to give him head, but not like a girl who did this sort of thing very often.

"No, come lie back down so I can play with you while you do that," he said, taking her half way back across his lap. She once more began to moisten his cock with her tongue while he now began to finger fuck her pussy until she got much wetter.

"I have lube too," she said, lifting her head to indicate a dresser drawer by the bed.

"Oh, good! Because I want to spend a long time fucking you," he said happily, putting her aside to find the lube. "Now get up on all fours," he told her.

"Will you go slowly at first?" she asked, once again arrested by the sight of the two of them together in the mirror. He was pulling off all of his clothes now and she saw how lean and muscular he was.

"Yes, of course I will," he promised, putting her in position and entering her with infinite care. He hadn't watched five hundred porn videos without learning something. Diana was going to give a minute report of his behavior to Susan and Susan would tell Amanda, so it was important to impress his adorable damsel in distress with his technique in all that he did to her that day. He also suspected that this was the only time in his life this particular opportunity would be offered to him, so he was determined get it right the first time.

Once he was in well and truly, he worked on plunging deeper and very soon, he hit a wall. She cried out and pulled back and he backed off accordingly. "It's all right, we'll stay here," he said, adding a few drops of lubricant to his shaft while beginning to work it lightly and quickly in and out. The more she relaxed, the deeper and slower he went, adding a drop of lube now and then. Pretty soon, the small girl was both slippery and relaxed and she began to push back against him, encouraging him to plunge in deeper still. Once more, he hit the back wall and she cried out. Once more he pulled back a bit and continued filling and refilling her vagina.

"Let me sodomize you," he suggested. She caught her breath.

"No, you're too big!"

"I'm too big for your pussy too. Let me put it in your bottom. I know how to do it so it won't hurt. I promise."

"All right, if that's the case, you can take away the condom," she said.

"You trust me?"

"Why, is there any chance you have an STD?"

"No, I always use condoms."

"Even with Amanda."

"Yes, she insists."

"Even anally?"

"Yes, the one time she let me."

"You sound extremely safe," said Diana.

"But you sound like a little slut. I'll leave it on."

Colby happily pulled her onto the bed with him. Lying on his side, he put her in front of him to enter her from behind. Now he liberally anointed his sheathed penis and her anus with lubricant and pulled her back up against him, so that his shaft rested between her cheeks.

"I'm not going to do it right away. You tell me when," he said, slipping his arm around her waist to press his palm against her Venus Mound and insert a finger back into her vagina. Much more experienced at being taken in this manner than giving head to a teenaged boy's huge hard-on, Diana rubbed up against him and allowed a whole minute to elapse before she decided that everyone was slick enough and properly positioning for entry.

"All right, now!" she cried at last. Even so, she cried out the moment he entered her bottom, pulling back.

"Oh, no you don't, get back here," he said, pushing in an inch. With one hand firmly pressed to her abdomen, he pulled her closer to him and forced a little more of his cock through her ring.

"That's enough!" she cried. "It's too big."

"I told you to relax, baby," he said, massaging her stomach and holding her closer still. Finally she began to move back against him and clench his shaft with her sphincter.

"Okay, good!" she panted. "Just no deeper, please!"

"You can take it. Just push back against it and sort of open up, I'll go right in," he told her, feeling her obey and instantly plunging into her bottom to the hilt. After that it was over in a minute. He had never felt so aroused in his life and had already held off on coming for what seemed an hour. They had actually only been playing for twenty minutes. She came seconds later, just as his spasms began to fall away. The pulsing of his cock, the palpable heat of his spasmodic effusions inside her, felt even through the protection, his fingers relentlessly drumming against her clit, all converged to send her plunging into her own climax before he released her from his arms.

Diana fled to the elegant bathroom, covered in blushes, to refresh herself with the bidet, and then it was Colby's turn to shower off the sweat of the travel day and the funk of the naughty sex with Diana.

When he returned to his new mini goddess, he found her freshly clad in a full skirted fifties style sundress, covered with a small rose print on a white background, with a pair of dusty rose sandals on her tiny feet.

"Let's go out and get some food!" she suggested.

"Do you always say the perfect thing?" he asked, putting his arms around her and kissing her full, red lips.

Chapter Thirteen

Ronnie Van Horn Joins the Travelers

Sitting in an outdoor café sipping coffee, Susan and Amanda were unfolding and inspecting the dresses they had just bought.

"I can't believe I paid ninety five dollars for this," said Amanda of the nicely tailored stretch jersey sheath, "I could have gotten the same thing at the Guess outlet store for thirty five. But it does have a Paris label."

"I was just thinking," said Susan, "if Anthony is investing this much energy in your mother, he must be making love to her."

"Do you think so?" Amanda was shocked to hear Susan speak so casually of this possibility.

"I know what kind of women interest him. The deeper in the scene they are, the more fascinated he becomes. All of his girlfriends on the side are pro subs or switches or perform in videos or do erotic art. If your mom came to him with this proposition and she looks even half as good as you do, he's coming onto her. And I guarantee you; she's not resisting him either. You know how agreeable he can be."

"It doesn't upset you, does it, Susan?" Amanda asked with concern. The blonde girl shook her ponytailed head vigorously.

"No. I know I'm still his princess. But I feel like I should give him some space when he develops these interests. I suspect he's been having a little affair with Phoebe Robbins. I've haven't confronted him about it, but I can tell when he's crazy about a girl."

"Her husband is very jealous," said Amanda. "And she gave him a weapon when she told him she was in the scene. I know him. If he catches her cheating on him, he'll thrash her."

"That's sexy. He's a hot man. Maybe I should check him out myself," Susan smiled.

"He is hot. I've done it with him once," Amanda confessed. "Out in the summer house on the path by the Random Point brook."

"How did he get you to give in?"

"He battered away at me relentlessly until I finally did. You know, he's photographed me at least five times now. The last time I let him do nude shots. That drove him nearly mad with longing and I couldn't torture him any longer. I'm kind like that."

"Where are you two heading from here?" Susan asked, refolding her own new frock and putting it back into its bag.

"Amsterdam and then on to Scandinavia."

"May we join you?" Susan asked.

"Of course, but we'll have to pick up another boy to come with us. I can't lend Colby out every day."

"That sounds good!" Susan grinned. "Where shall we find him?"

"I just had an idea," said Amanda, taking out her phone and sending a text to an old boyfriend from freshman year currently studying in Paris. It read:

"In Paris with 2 hot girls. 1 in need of a spanking. Yes, U R being objectified again. Man up and call me now. Amanda."

She chuckled to herself as she pressed send. "There's a good chance he's in town."

Ten seconds later Amanda received the following text back, "R U nutz? I have a jealous girlfriend now who would castrate me. Where can I meet you, crazy bitch?"

Amanda laughed aloud. "He's in town and he's game!" she told Susan. Amanda texted Ronnie Van Horn their location and the girls ordered more coffee.

Twenty two minutes later a lean, good looking black boy of twenty, with short hair, horn rimmed glasses, black cargo shorts and a sleeveless white tee that displayed his broad shoulders and sculpted chest to advantage, zoomed up on a small motorbike and joined them at their table.

"Wow, Ronnie, you're a lot more muscular than I remember you," Amanda said, kissing him. "This is Susan Ross, one of my best friends in the scene."

"Hello," he said, intrigued by the look of the small blonde who was smiling at him with such interest. Ronnie sat down and a waiter came over to take his order.

"I'm so glad we found you here," said Amanda. "Do you have a summer gig going?"

"Not really, but I didn't want to give up the apartment. It's so close to the university. I have three roommates," he explained. "I've been making little movies with my friends all summer and getting a head start on my reading for next year."

"Look, Ronnie, I'll get right to the point," said Amanda. "I'm traveling with Colby Hodge. You know him, right?"

"Yes. Your new boyfriend."

"Yes. And Susan is traveling with Diana Currie, a young married lady from New York who she knows from Vassar."

"Oh, a Vassar girl," said Ronnie with interest.

"My friend Diana is on vacation from her older husband and toddler," said Susan, "and she's very eager to, how shall I put this, cram as much fun as she can into her time away from home."

"I just left her alone with Colby. But I will be wanting him back presently," explained Amanda. "That's where you come in. Need I add this girl is a little beauty? Or explain that this is a gift? I think not."

"See for yourself," said Susan, showing Ronnie a photo of Diana, taken moments before Colby and Amanda joined them in the suite. Ronnie took the phone out of Susan's hand to study the picture.

"She reminds me of Natalie Wood," said Ronnie.

"She's absolutely submissive," said Amanda.

Ronnie sighed and said, "If my girlfriend found out, she would probably break up with me," he said. "She's a highly politicized feminist," he added. "She doesn't look anything like you girls either," he went on.

"Is it the same black girl you were dating when you left?" Amanda asked.

"No, an English girl majoring in French at the University. She wears moth eaten jumpers and doesn't care about her hair. But she's a scholar. I enjoy that."

"I guess you haven't played with anyone since you broke up with me?" Amanda asked.

"You mean…"

"I mean, dominated," Amanda said.

"No, I haven't. My last girlfriend would have broken the arm of any black man who dared to raise it to her, and I think rightly so. And Caroline just wouldn't get it. She would think I had turned against her and didn't love her anymore."

"Sounds like you need us as much as we need you," said Susan.

And that was how, on the following day, Amanda's ex-boyfriend found himself seated opposite her current beau, Colby Hodge, in a first class train compartment, on the way to Holland. Next to Colby sat Amanda and next to Ronnie, sat Susan and Diana.

"Ronnie worked the camera for the videos we shot at Bartlett's last Christmas," Amanda told Susan.

"I've seen them," said Diana. "They were wonderful."

"You really liked them?" asked Ronnie, surprised and gratified. Unlike Colby, he had yet to be initiated into the very exclusive club of boys that Amanda Sands had hooked up with her uninhibited girlfriends on a whim. He would have thought that such things only happened to other people if it had been proposed to him even the minute before Amanda had texted him the previous day. He had felt badly about the way he had abruptly broken up with Amanda. She hadn't deserved to be broken up with in the slightest, but the twin opportunities of Paris and a radical, intellectual black girlfriend had been too tempting to resist, even for the sake of remaining with the blonde junior goddess he had so enjoyed spanking. Not that she had let even a week go by before selecting a new lover, nor did he suspect she would, so that was all right. Still, he'd felt badly. Now he had a chance to make it up to her. He still wasn't sure what he was expected to do with or to the adorable Diana, but he liked the way she was looking at him and found himself getting lost in her big, brown eyes.

"Susan and I went out to L.A. to do a bondage video shoot once," said Diana, breaking the spell, "but the video turned out so badly that Anthony wound up buying the master back from the producer for us."

"Seriously?" Ronnie was fascinated.

"It wasn't that bad," said Susan, "but the studio was tacky and the production standards really poor and on top of that, they brought in a poser femdom type top we didn't connect with. I think he either destroyed the master or locked it up."

"How much did he have to pay to get the master back?"

"Fifteen grand."

"You can be in a video I shoot next time we're all in Random Point," said Amanda to Diana. "We'll have a whole new studio to use."

"Really? Which one?" Colby asked. And Amanda realized she hadn't yet told him about the Venus Club.

"I mentioned my mother has returned to Random Point, right?" Amanda asked.

"Yes," said Colby.

"Well, nobody saw this coming, but I just found out she's opening up a BDSM club there," said Amanda. Both Colby and Ronnie found this equally interesting.

"It's just the sort of place that submissive lady Marion, who enlisted you for stud service in Boston last semester might enjoy working at part time," said Amanda to Colby.

"You know who else?" asked Ronnie, "Barbara, the other model." Barbara was an attractive and vivacious young black girl with whom Ronnie had conducted a brief but passionate affair, post video shoot. She was now a full time nursing student in Boston but had formerly been a video actress and occasional B&D call girl.

"Don't forget our Thalia," said Amanda. "She'll jump at any excuse to get back to Random Point and see Hugo again."

"Your... mother?" Ronnie asked.

"She's not that old. And she's in the scene. She co-edited some of the first New Rod Quarterlies that Hugo put out twenty years ago. You've seen those vintage mags. Look her up. Her name is Cassandra," said Amanda.

"What do you do for a living?" Ronnie asked Diana.

"I'm an interior designer," the brunette replied, "but I've been devoting most of the last three years to having a baby and nursing it. Now that she's finally weaned I'll go back to working full time."

"That reminds me," said Susan, "Anthony said we're to look for anything unique or interesting furnishing-wise that might fit in the club and to buy some leather boots and dresses for the wardrobe at Da Mask."

"So, there's going to be a spanking salon in Random Point?" Colby asked with trepidation, suddenly afraid that Amanda would want to work there. "Is it even zoned for that sort of thing?"

"It's going to be private and exclusive, no walk-ins," said Susan, "according to Anthony's letter. I suppose as long as no one disturbs the peace in the neighborhood, only members will ever know it exists. The closest house is Michael Flagg's a half mile down the road."

"Who's Michael Flagg?" asked Ronnie.

"He owns that tavern we stopped into for beers one night,"

"This all sounds crazy," Colby protested. "One day your mom's husband dumps her and she's coming out to the Cape to console her broken heart and the next day she's running a B&D club? How did that happen so fast?"

"Anthony is making it happen," said Susan. "She came up with a project that genuinely interests him and he's in Random Point for the summer anyway. I guess this proves beyond any doubt that he has more money than he knows what to do with."

"And you remember Hope Spencer Lawrence, the girl who runs the coffee bar at the bookstore?" Amanda asked Ronnie and Colby, who had both met and been charmed by that latte-dispensing Lorelei. The boys nodded, remembering the lithe body, perpetually garbed in jeans, a white shirt and red apron, persistently arresting their attention. "Anthony and Cassandra are stealing her from Marguerite for their club."

Anthony Newton invited Hope to lunch on her day off. Cassandra had gone to Woodbridge to make more purchases for the house and the composer was waiting for the bewitching blonde girl in the dining room alone. Again, he took delight in dazzling a luncheon guest with the culinary perfection his new team of cooks were capable of producing, especially when the guest was one of his favorite girls. A curve-hugging white sundress graced Hope's lovely form and her dark blue eyes were all for Anthony, her deliver from the one millionth soggy sack of coffee grounds she was coming up on, as a barista going on four years.

"Hope, I need you to start as soon as possible," Anthony said as the girl with the black cropped hair brought in the first course of cream of pumpkin soup with sautéed wild mushrooms. "Cassandra needs help organizing the house. She's begun the shopping but I can sense she's beginning to feel overwhelmed. She's not used to spending someone else's money liberally," he added.

"Nor am I," Hope replied, tasting her soup and beaming at him. "This is delicious!"

"I know. These kids have made me realize I need a cook in New York," said Anthony cheerfully.

"I'd love to come and help her as soon as possible, but I feel horrible about leaving Marguerite. I must find a proper manager for the coffee bar for her," said Hope.

"I understand you put some money into the bookstore to become a partner," said Anthony.

"Yes, twenty grand. We used it to build the patio. I thought I was buying into a somewhat more lucrative business, but I soon discovered that it's difficult to turn a profit in that way. I'm content to let Marguerite and Sloan have the patio with my love."

"Nonsense. I'll replace that money for you today. And any month you don't make at least four grand, I'll make up the difference," said he.

"Really? That's wonderful!" she cried. They fell to eating their soup with contentment. The next course was a roasted chicken dish, brought in by the black haired boy, James.

"James," said Anthony, "this is Hope Lawrence, she's been running the coffee bar at the local bookstore for years."

"Hello," James said politely, blushing.

"I love your food," she replied.

"James, do you or Josette have any friends at the Culinary Institute who might like to take over that coffee bar in a managerial capacity? It wouldn't pay much, but it would be a good start to a professional resume. Hope needs a highly competent self-starter who can be ready as early as, let's say, tomorrow?" Anthony looked at Hope as he said this.

James thought a moment of all the friends of his who were working as sous chefs for the summer around the commonwealth and there was no end of them. Running a coffee bar in a fashionable bookstore would no doubt be easier than say cleaning fish or grilling meat all day. "I can think of any number of people who would jump at the job. Let me makes some calls tonight," said James.

"Make them this afternoon, right after lunch," Anthony advised.

When the boy had gone back to the kitchen she got up and kissed her new patron.

"So can you tell me exactly why I'm here?" Ronnie asked Diana as they waited at the bar in the club car for drinks to bring back to the compartment.

"Well, Susan had suggested that you might video us when we visit Club Doma. I'll underwrite your room and meals in exchange for some sexy footage I can send back to my husband. Up until now, Susan's been taking photos of me in bondage, but a video would be so much more exciting to Plastridge."

"Plastridge? That's your husband's name?" Ronnie asked.

"Yes. And he looks like Rod La Rocque. You might know who that is because you're a film buff. Amanda told me. I love that. Though I don't know how you can bear to watch any American films pre-1960's, being black."

"I do know who Rod La Rocque is because I've seen that spanking clip from the 1936 B movie, Taming the Wild. It was remarkable for all the conversations about spanking that went on prior to the grand finale act, but you're absolutely right, it's hard to be a classic film buff and black at the same time."

"Well, my husband is just as handsome and an ardent bondager. He adores photos of me in bondage."

"I'd love to video you girls," said Ronnie. "But Amanda led me to believe that this was more about play than work," he added.

"Do you want to play with me?" asked Diana softly, against his ear. He shook his head yes.

"Oh, I'm so glad!" she cried.

Back in the first class compartment, Colby had fallen fast asleep with his head in Amanda's lap while Susan sat opposite them. "He's awfully cute," said Susan. "And so is Ronnie."

"It occurs to me, this party is short one man," said Amanda. Susan sighed.

"What?" asked Amanda.

"How can I think about anything like that when I know what's going on in Random Point?" Susan asked.

"What do you mean?"

"Between your mother and Anthony. I can't think about anything else."

"Oh!" Amanda felt a dart of pain in her heart at the thought that her beloved mother should give her dear friend a moment's unease. Susan noticed Amanda's stricken look and smiled reassuringly.

"It's going to be okay. I'm just momentarily obsessed. But you can see why I can't even consider flirting with a new man at this moment."

"Don't you think a handsome distraction would take your mind off whatever it is that may or may not being going on?" suggested Amanda.

"I'd rather just brood quietly," Susan replied.

Deciding to visit the Hague on the following day, the party debarked at Amsterdam and proceeded to the Sofitel, where Diana had already booked them rooms on the same floor. For herself and Susan she had chosen a suite, perfect for filming clips of herself in bondage to send back to her husband. But first they all went out into Dam Square and from thence made their way into the heart of the "green" district. The laws had recently changed in the city, making possible for residents only to enjoy the marijuana clubs. But Diana had the best connection in the world, a pair of gay interior decorators who owned an apartment in the old town and a furniture company in the suburbs. She had called ahead to her friends and in a couple of minutes they were all climbing a narrow staircase up to the third story of a fully modernized seventeenth century building. Joop and Juergen greeted them warmly and invited them into their beautifully furnished, modern style sitting room. They were pleasant, middle aged men, one with blond, and the other with gray hair, well dressed in a casual fashion and fluent in English.

"We're not only here to use you for your drugs," said Diana, accepting a pipe and lighting it. "I have a long shopping list of furniture I need to order from you while I'm here." The two partners beamed at Diana, who had ordered from them in the past and never tried to barter down their prices.

"We'll take you to the showroom tomorrow," said Joop, wrapping up a package of fragrant bud for them to take with them. Diana took her assignment from Anthony Newton seriously and planned to make thoughtful choices for the new Venus Club on the following day. Colby said to Ronnie on the way out, "We should go drink beer while they do that tomorrow." He hadn't liked the way Joop had smiled at him, with all his teeth. He didn't mind hanging out with men old enough to be his father, as long as they were into sports or politics, but those two things did not seem to be uppermost in the minds of the Dutch decorators. And the things that were, Colby wasn't interested in.

That evening, after the five friends had pub and club crawled to excess and felt ready to retire, Diana liberally bribed the desk clerk, the floor maid and the busboys for their floor not to report any scent of weed that might be traced to their suite that night as she was well aware that the Dutch were as draconian about rules as their German neighbors. After a final smoke and agreeing when they would all meet for breakfast, Amanda and Colby retired to their room, Ronnie went to his and Susan and Diana remained in the big suite. But as soon as Ronnie had done brushing his teeth and watching a few headlines from the BBC, he heard a soft knock on his door. He opened it to admit Diana, now clad in a cranberry velvet robe and slippers. She closed and locked the door behind her and the next thing he knew, her arms were around his neck while she stood on tiptoe to brush his lips with her own. When he took her to the bed to undress her, she pulled the velvet belt from its loops and doubling it, handed it to him, saying, "Tie my wrists?"

That morning, Anthony Newton awoke, as usual, to the sound of waves and gulls outside his bedroom window. He was alone, but the pillow next to his still bore the indent of Cassandra's head and the faint scent of her light, floral perfume. He reached for his tablet and stroked it on, seeing that his first email was from Susan. She had sent a photograph of herself, seated on a bed in the room at the hotel in Paris, regarding critically, and over folded arms, the specter of Diana Currie, in white lingerie and a hog tie, her mouth handkerchief gagged, casting a wide eyed and winsome gaze towards the camera. To this photo was attached the following lines: "You see how she makes me treat her? Happily, we hooked up with Amanda and Colby in Paris and they are helping me manage Little Mrs. Incorrigible." The next few attached photos were from Joop and Juergen's furniture show room and pictured several modern, sculptural sofas and deep arms chairs in gunmetal blue leather, with the caption, "Diana recommends we order these shipped to Random Point for the club."

Anthony immediately wrote back okaying the purchase and then signed off with his love. He lay back on his pillows with his fingers laced behind his head, smiling with pleasure at the agreeable independence of his lover, Susan Ross. Knowing that she was enjoying herself to the full with her friends while still keeping his interests uppermost on her agenda was pleasantly gratifying. At that point, Cassandra came in bearing a tray with fresh coffee and a few croissants. She was clad in a white silk robe and slippers.

"Thanks, honey. Amanda and Colby are now with Susan and Diana," he reported, taking the coffee and sipping it. "They're buying beautiful furniture for the club." He showed her the floor models of the sofas and chairs. Cassandra thoughtfully nibbled a croissant, wondering if Susan Ross could sense exactly what had been going on in the Cliff House so far. She had never met Susan but Amanda had been talking of her for the last year. Cassandra had no window at this point into Susan's mind regarding their mutual patron but hoped the European trip was proving sufficiently distracting to the 26 year old illustrator to prevent that young lady from dwelling on her older lover's undeniable new obsession with Cassandra herself.

That afternoon, Anthony accompanied Cassandra to the house in the woods and began setting up a computer system for her and Hope in the room they had decided would serve as the girls' office. Michael

Flagg arrived shortly after to begin installing a security system. And then Hope Lawrence showed up, in a glow of happiness, for having successfully speed trained her new temporary manager at the coffee bar and thus being able to walk away from Marguerite and Sloan without inconveniencing them.

That afternoon, a Bartlett's truck arrived and was unloaded by a team of three deliverymen, who also went to work assembling the bedroom sets. As the house was abuzz with workers all afternoon, Dennis was kept busy handing out sandwiches, prepared that morning by Josette and James, along with cold beers, coffees and teas. The deliverymen were well fed and well tipped before they departed in the late afternoon.

Just as the Bartlett's truck was pulling away, Laura arrived. She wanted to look at the rooms that had been designated as play spaces in order to plan her murals. Anthony went with her and gave his opinions. "Let's have a rocky coast in here, with a slate blue sky and white sand," he said, in the furthest corner playroom. He led her across a small hall to a larger room, opening the door. "This is the room that's getting the gunmetal blue furniture from Holland," he told her, in the terra cotta tiled salon, luxuriously painted with faux marbled apricot walls. They left that room and crossed another hall where he opened the door to a large navy blue salon with creamy crown molding and burgundy furniture. "We'll get a lot of gilt edged mirrors for this one," he informed her.

"I see, you're going for the opposite of a dungeon atmosphere," Laura observed, making notes in a small book.

"I never liked dungeons," he admitted. "I mean, apart from the equipment."

He continued to lead her through the house. The proceeded into the west front corner room, the library. There were cartons of books on the heavy planked wooden floor and fresh, empty shelves to put them on. The spacious room had a fireplace and was papered in dark green veined with gold and wainscoted in oak. Across the hall from this room was a small sitting room that also contained a fireplace. The furniture had not as yet arrived for this room, which was papered in dusky rose and accented with cream crown molding and a cream mantelpiece.

Now Anthony conducted Laura across another small hall into a room in the center of the house with a skylight to compensate for the lack of windows. "This is going to be the schoolroom," Anthony said. "There's a black board and a few school desks and chairs on order. What I think would look arresting in here would be a tromp l'oeil painting on one of the walls of maybe a window onto a 19th century European street. Something that a student would find irresistible to gaze at." Laura made a note, nodding her head with a smile.

"This isn't going to be like any dungeon ever seen," she said.

"I know, look at this," he said, opening a door to a connecting bathroom, colorfully tiled and beautifully fitted with state of the art fixtures. "Haven't you always hated the arrangements for freshening up in clubs? There's usually one little bathroom downstairs and another one upstairs, where who the hell knows what's just gone on in the tub. This house has seven bathrooms. It'll actually have eight plus a steam room, Jacuzzi and sauna once William finishes modifying the loft. "

"Stunning," said Laura, admiring the high arched Italian faucet and gleaming porcelain sink.

Anthony took her through two spacious bedrooms, richly painted in Tuscan colors, each with a private bath and each but scantily furnished as yet. "Girls can stay overnight if they've come in from out of town," he told Laura.

"Or if a client fancies an overnight bondage session?" she asked.

"Exactly. Or, if a couple just wants to come and play in a bedroom," he said, leading her across yet another small hall to show her the final designated play space, of the house, a small room at the back with pearl gray walls and nothing whatever in it. "This is going to be the exam room," he explained, "but we have to order all the furniture and equipment for it."

"What's it going to be like?"

"Not antique like mine at the house. No medical books or glass cases with objects on view. There will be an exam chair and table, a few leather chairs, a sofa and a few cabinets for implements and toy kits, preferably in multiples and factory sealed. The clients can buy them and take them with them when they're done. Oh and by the way, there's another bathroom right through that door."

"These are all great ideas," said Laura, amazed that he had already worked out so many details.

Now Anthony conducted her to the east wing of the house to show her the large master suite which Cassandra would command, the kitchen, laundry and pantry, the dining room, large office and at the front of the house, a large room that Anthony said would be the lounge. It was already equipped with a wet bar. There would soon be a pool table and piano. There was already a giant screen TV in place on one wall, opposite a few capacious chestnut leather armchairs.

"I'll start tomorrow," she promised, happy to observe that her sister's lover seemed more fixated on the perfections of the club that was coming into being than the attractions of its proprietor. And when all was said and done, as a creature of the scene herself, she felt that Newton could not have chosen a more felicitous hobbyhorse.

Chapter Fourteen

Club Doma

Ronnie and Diana talked about old movies for hours, lying in each other's arms, she with her hands tied in front of her, and her back and bottom pressed up against him, until neither of them could ignore his persistent erection any longer. She gratified him beyond joy by easily slipping out of her wrist tie and placing her head in his lap, while lying across one of his thighs, to take him in her mouth as deeply and completely as any girl had ever done. It was all he could do not to explode against the back of her throat, but he wanted to be inside her even more and pulled her off his cock.

She slipped a rubber on him, lay back and looked up at him. He buried his face between her legs for a few minutes, gently probing her with his tongue, tasting her and breathing her in. She was already wet with excitement. There was no making their first event last longer than three minutes, not with the hours of mental foreplay that had gone on before, and Ronnie being just twenty. But the second time did last longer and Diana felt herself well satisfied by the time she fell asleep to a clock in nearby Dam Square chiming three times.

The next day, Ronnie and Diana couldn't get enough of each other. They were lost in each other. Even Amanda was startled at how well her idea had worked as the five friends started on the train for The Hague. Colby was buried in a copy of the New York Times he had bought at the Central Station and Susan seemed a little subdued. Now that Diana had an eagerly attentive male companion, Susan was beginning to feel a little beside the point. The thought of her boyfriend with Amanda's mother had been preoccupying her for the last forty-eight hours. She stared out the window as the city gave way to the suburbs and a light rain began to fall.

Even the novelty of visiting the legendary Dutch BDSM club could not fully engage Susan's interest that afternoon, though with the best will in the world, she tied Diana to various pieces of bondage furniture in various ways while Ronnie videoed their antics. Colby was as determined as ever not to be filmed or photographed playing, but asked Amanda to pose for one or two shots bending over a bondage bed for his own personal album.

They all sat through an hour of live theatre in the playhouse, watching a mistress tie and flog a female submissive on a post, but found the performance lackluster. The boys did, however, enjoy the rounds of free beer that kept coming.

Colby insisted on being allowed to spank Amanda in Club Doma before they left but Amanda blushed with embarrassment at the idea of being spanked by Colby in front of Ronnie, Diana and Susan. So Ronnie, Diana and Susan went down to the bar and left Amanda and Colby alone in the big dungeon upstairs.

"Don't you think people get tired of you arranging things and bossing everyone around?" he asked her, turning her over his knee in front of a mirror.

"No."

"You're probably right," he admitted. "What would we do without you?"

"Masturbate a lot," Amanda said.

Meanwhile, at the bar, Susan was studying Diana with the younger man and concluding that they had fallen instantly in love. Her friend had so few days left to her allotted vacation, four or five. Then Diana would return to New York and resume being a mother and wife. After that it might be another year before she was permitted to indulge in any adventure to speak of. "I think I'll go back a little early," said Susan. "You'll stay with Diana, won't you, Ronnie? And take pictures of her for P.C.?" P.C. was Diana's husband's initials. "You'll like that," she said to Diana.

Diana looked at Susan wonderingly.

"You plan to leave me alone with Ronnie, Colby and Amanda?" Diana asked.

"Yes."

"You're going back early because you're worried about Anthony and Amanda's mother, aren't you?" Diana posited. Susan nodded.

"I can't help it, I always get lovesick for Anthony when he's having an affair."

"You don't know that for certain," Diana pointed out. "He may be showering her with patronage for Amanda's sake. Or attempting to distract her from getting in between Hugo and Laura."

"Diana, be yourself. I just have to see this up close."

"Well, thank you," said Diana, hugging her.

Anthony, Cassandra and Pamela were lunching together for the first time. They met at Bartlett's Café, on the second floor of the department store. As usual when meeting a very attractive woman, Pamela couldn't immediately decide whether to fear or fall in love with her. She saw Amanda all over Cassandra, though their body types and complexions were not the same. It was all about sensibility.

"I'm obsessed with Amanda," said Pamela to Cassandra frankly. "I let her tell me what to do."

Anthony laughed, noting that he had yet to see Amanda's bossy side. Cassandra blushed, realizing that she was being complimented on having done such a good job.

"I never dreamed I'd be best friends with a girl ten years younger than me, no less let her arrange my sex life," added Pamela.

"Does she?" Cassandra asked.

"She treats me like a doll she can play with or hand over to someone else to play with," Pamela admitted without resentment. "And as a result I find myself with a boyfriend on the side, who is also ten years younger than me."

"Really? You're cheating on Ambrose?" Anthony asked with interest.

"He's cheating on me too," Pamela returned. "He's never not cheating on someone."

"You say you know a local boy?" Cassandra asked.

"Yes, Dru Baxter, he's home for the summer. Works part time at the coffee bar," said Pamela.

"I was thinking, Hope and I could use a boy to help us get

organized at the house," said Cassandra.

"I know Dru," said Anthony. "He and his girlfriend crashed one of Hugo's parties while they were still in high school."

"That's him," said Pamela. "You want him to carry and unload things?"

"I'll pay him ten bucks an hour," said Cassandra.

"Cash," added Anthony.

After lunch, Anthony took Cassandra down to the jewelry department and bought her a black pearl necklace and drop earrings. Then they met Pamela upstairs in her recently remodeled design studio on the top floor of the building. In addition to a sleek workspace, Pamela had been given a private lounge with a sumptuous bed and accompanying Italian furniture, large, well upholstered pieces that invited one to stretch out or bend over on. This feature was not lost on Anthony as they made the tour.

"So how often do you actually relax in here?" he asked the dress designer as she showed them her wet bar and kitchenette.

"I grab a twenty minute nap in here a few times a week," said Pamela, whose phone vibrated in her pocket. "Excuse me, I have to take this," she said, strolling purposefully out of the room on her five inch stack heeled ankle booties.

Alone in the inviting studio boudoir, surrounded by mirrors, polished teak and Italian leather, Anthony felt relaxed enough to pull Cassandra onto his lap and kiss her throat and ears, his arms locked around her small waist.

"That phone call will last fifteen minutes," Anthony predicted. "Let's check out her dressing room." Knowing it would be breath taking, Anthony led Cassandra by the hand. This room too smelled like expensive leather, but this was from the hundreds of shoes in their own custom made pigeonholes. A three-way mirror faced a red leather ottoman six feet across. The perfect staging area to place a woman on all fours and fold back her fit and flare skirt. Anthony took the precaution of locking the door, trusting Pamela would use her discretion if she were to return early, and came back to Cassandra with a smile.

Pamela did not return for twenty two minutes, at which point she found them sitting together in a leather window seat looking down at the main street of tiny Woodbridge village five stories below.

"Strangely enough, that was a call from Amanda," said Pamela. "Among other things, she said that Susan's coming back early."

Almost unconsciously, Anthony and Cassandra sprang apart, both jumping to their feet, looking at each other, as much as to say, "I'm glad we did that while we could!"

That evening, right after dinner, Cassandra told Anthony that she would have to leave the Cliff House. "I'll go and stay at the house on Pine Tar," she added.

"If the house is to be a club," said Anthony, "I don't know if it's proper for you to also live there."

"But I'm agog to try out all those new beds and linens, the kitchen, and everything you've bought."

"Good point, it doesn't make sense not to enjoy all of that. You're not leaving tonight though, are you?"

"Yes. Susan could be here by tomorrow morning. I don't want it to be awkward for her."

"What makes you so sure she knows?"

"She knows you. She's figured everything out. That's why she decided to come back early."

"I'm sure you two will like each other," Anthony said. "Eventually."

"I like her very much. But I wouldn't blame her for feeling suspicious of me," said Cassandra.

"Once she knows you, she'll be your new little sister," he predicted.

Anthony had his chefs pack them a hamper, with sandwiches and wine, and then went with Cassandra to the house in the woods. He said that he would spend the night and have Dennis come pick him up in the morning. The following day not only contained the promise of Susan's abrupt return, but began the performance cycle of Anthony's week. This was the last day he would have in that week to completely relax with Cassandra.

They spent an hour preparing the bedroom with the new linen and expensive bedclothes that had to be unwrapped and put on the bed. It was a humble, domestic activity that made Anthony smile. But when the velvet counterpane was perfectly disposed, she sighed.

"What's wrong?" he asked.

"I suddenly feel guilty," she admitted.

"About what?" he asked.

"About Susan," Cassandra said.

"Oh!" Anthony replied. "Well, maybe you should feel guilty. You did move in on her man while she was away."

Cassandra saw that he was teasing her but continued to express her unease. "I didn't mean to. I don't think I meant to," she said.

"And yet, that's exactly what happened," he said.

"I never expected you to be attracted to me," she admitted.

"No?" he grinned.

"No, how could I?"

"You know you're cute," Anthony said.

"This must be a case of transference. You all adore Amanda and I've been sprinkled with her pixie dust."

"And what about what Hugo means to us? You being his first Random Point girl, it's significant. I still have those magazines from 20 years ago with those couple of photo sets you were in," Anthony admitted.

"In other words, I'm a ghost walking out of the past."

"More like someone who has been lost to us but has come back to where she's supposed to be."

"That's what Hugo said."

"Did I see a horse in one of the playrooms already?" he asked.

"Yes, in the room we're calling Cape Cod," she said, taking him back into the playroom in the northwest corner. This was the room where Anthony had suggested an abstract New England seascape be painted on the wall. There was indeed, one object within the room, an upholstered leather horse.

"When we go to Boston to get the mirrors," he told her, "we'll go to my favorite corset shop as well and get some wardrobe for the girls."

"You have a favorite corset shop?"

"Ever try on a real waist cinch?"

"Not since I left Random Point years ago."

"Come over here. Let's try this out," he said, gesturing her over to the horse. "Since you feel guilty anyway..." he bent her over and pinned her under one arm. She had on a white tank top and a rose and white flowered cotton skirt along with rose embellished platform sandals. He pulled one of her wrists back up to her small waist. "Shouldn't you be punished for pretending that you haven't tried to seduce me," he said, smacking her smartly through her skirt.

He pulled her head up by her earlobe. "Well?"

"Yes, I should!" she cried.

He let her ear go and pulled up her skirt to reveal the seat of her rose-colored cotton string bikini panties.

"Let's be honest Cassandra," he said, spanking her over her panties a half dozen times. "You *have* moved in on Susan's man. I'm already planning secret rendezvous in Boston and New York with you."

"Is it terribly wrong?" Cassandra asked, turning her head to try and catch a glimpse of him out of the corner of her eye.

He shrugged and said, "I've never persecuted Susan for giving into temptation," he said, pulling down her panties to mid-thigh.

He went on spanking her. She turned to him and said, "Maybe a little harder?"

"Really?" he said, stopping.

"I mean, remind me of what people expect in a session. I don't even know if I can really take it anymore."

"Could you ever?" Anthony asked, looking around for an implement. "And by the way, where are your paddles?"

Cassandra jumped up and said she would get one.

"Why stop at one?" he called after her. He didn't know if she could take it either, but it wouldn't do to test her limits with hands that had to play an entire libretto the next three nights in a row. She came back with a small rectangular wooden paddle and an oval leather one.

"Back over you go," he said, and began to smarten her up with the leather paddle in a quick, rhythmic fashion, one swat on each cheek, to the count of twelve, through three or four rotations.

"I'm really feeling that," she cried at last.

"I could tell the way you're wriggling around. And remember, if I just walked in, we'd only be ten minutes into the session."

"I think I like the wooden paddle better," she said.

"What makes you think that?" he asked, picking the wooden paddle up and pressing it against her warm, rosy flesh.

"I distantly remember, I don't like the sting of leather as much as I do the thud of wood."

He began paddling her, at a slower pace, letting every swat sink in. She did seem to like it better. With one hand on her waist, he continued paddling her, doling out harder smacks as he noticed her bottom rise to the paddle. Her bottom was becoming very red and she was breathing hard, but not crying out for him to stop.

"You'd be lucky to get someone as moderate as me wanting to spank you," he advised her, pulling her up to her feet and pulling off her dress and lacy bra. "It would more likely be someone fiendish, like Ambrose Bartlett. Be a smart girl and play the top at the club. You'll save yourself a lot of tears."

"I don't know if I have it in me to be a top," she admitted.

"Just channel your bossy daughter," he suggested taking her by the hand to lead her back to the bedroom.

They both awoke before seven the next morning. Cassandra brewed coffee in the new kitchen and they took it out to the loft playroom. The maple floor gleamed, the sky lights in the ceiling filled the duplex apartment with light, the wood paneling lining the walls contributed to the rustic ambiance and a sturdy wooden staircase led invitingly up to the open second floor landing.

"Don't they work fast!" Anthony marveled at the post and lintel structure of heavy oak had just been erected to accommodate suspension bondage and harnesses. "Maybe you can open in two weeks instead of two months."

"Two weeks?" Cassandra replied, startled.

"Well, I only have five weeks left before I have to go back to New York for the season," said Anthony, "and I'd like to see the locals enjoying the club before I go."

"We'll be ready in two weeks," Cassandra promised.

"And let's think in terms of having a big party at the end of the summer. I'll have the kids cater it," he added.

"Amanda's birthday is at the end of the summer. She turns 19 on September 1st."

"That's perfect. It'll be a double party for the club opening and her birthday."

Dennis came to pick Anthony up and Cassandra was showered and dressed by the time Hope arrived at nine. They sat together in the office command post, making lists of what had to be done, while Cassandra tried to suppress her panic at the responsibility of getting everything organized for a play party in one month's time. At ten the bell rang and she opened it to an immaculately dressed Pamela Bartlett, with the fresh, blond, blue-eyed Dru Baxter in tow.

"Hello. I've brought the boy you asked for," said Pamela, strolling into the house. Hope came out into the hall to greet them.

"I think you already met Dru at Marguerite's," Pamela said to Cassandra, who did indeed remembered being introduced to him at the bookshop.

"It's very nice to see you again," said Cassandra, extending her hand. Dru shook Cassandra's hand and smiled a greeting at Hope.

"I've been missing you at the coffee bar," Dru said to Hope, his former supervisor at the bookshop café. "I couldn't believe you'd quit."

"Yes, I'll be working here now, with Cassandra," said Hope.

"Working?" Dru asked, puzzled.

"Yes, please elaborate on that," Pamela said, clicking around the luxe new floors on her smart, gray, five inch heeled, bootie sandals. Her tall, willowy frame was becomingly clad in an outfit of her own design, a pink cotton blouse with three quarter sleeves and a full gray skirt with a broad, gray leather belt encircling her tiny waist.

"Is it time to tell all?" Hope wondered, smiling at the nineteen-year-old boy who was as much in the scene as they all were.

"This is going to be a private B&D club," Cassandra explained. Pamela began walking through the house and inspecting every room, with the others following.

As Dru Baxter walked along the planked wooden floor of the hall and peeked into the rooms they passed on either side, his heart pounded with excitement and butterflies tickled his stomach. It was turning into the most unbelievably wonderful summer of his life.

"And so these rooms will be for rent, by the hour, for scene couples to play in?" Pamela asked boldly, looking back over her shoulder at her younger lover.

"Yes, that's one of the prime reasons for the club being here in Random Point, there are so many scene people in town," said Cassandra.

"Yes, aren't there?" Pamela asked, "Especially my horrible husband. I'm sure he's going to be your first customer. You'd better pick out a heavy sub to go in the dungeon with him. Not weight wise though. She needs to be particularly slim."

It seemed to Cassandra that this was the second or third time she had been warned about Ambrose Bartlett, though she saw that Pamela's exasperation with her husband was tinged with affection.

"The first time Mr. Bartlett rents a dungeon it will be to play with me," said Hope confidently. "Because we've played before and when I give him the tour, it's what he will think of."

"Well, yes, you are probably right," Pamela agreed. "And on his second visit he'll bring Herren Guzman," Pamela observed, walking around the semi furnished rooms quickly and taking everything in. Then the brunette consulted her watch and decided she had lingered long enough. "I leave you in good hands, my love," she said to Dru; "One of you can give him a ride home when you're done with him?"

"Of course," said Cassandra, seeing Pamela to the door, at which point Pamela turned to her and said, "He's a very sweet boy. I'm sure you'll make good use of him."

"Thank you!" said Cassandra.

"I'll tell you what I think we should do first," said Hope, as soon as Cassandra rejoined them in the kitchen. "We should make sure each of the play spaces has a place to lie, a place to sit, a thing to be bent over and another thing to be tied to. Dru, you take a pad and make a list of what each of the play rooms lacks in these categories," said Hope, handing Dru a thick white pad and a razor point felt tipped pen.

"Right away," said Dru, turning back momentarily to ask, "Which were the playrooms?"

"I'll show you," said Cassandra, leading the boy from one room to another, allowing him time to makes notes, and then returning to Hope.

"Now let's start unpacking all these boxes of things," said Hope, regarding a stack of cardboard boxes and crates. "What are in these boxes, anyway?"

"Some of them have toys and bondage equipment I ordered on line," said Cassandra, "and the others have things for the house."

"Don't you think we'll need a big peg board to hang the toys on?" asked Hope. "I can send William a text about that," she said, getting out her phone. "It should probably go in the hall."

"I don't think Anthony would want it to be that obvious," said Cassandra instinctively. "He told me to order as many cabinets and armoires as I wanted. We'll store the toys and the other equipment in those, neatly arrayed and discreetly out of sight of the casual visitor."

Hope grinned at Cassandra and said, "I can see why Anthony made you the boss. You put my taste level to shame. I bow to my mistress." And she did make a little bow.

Cassandra found work gloves and they began opening boxes. Within the hour, William's crew arrived, bringing with them a few leather padded benches and horses that had been finished the previous day. The sound of hammering filled the air for the rest of the day. It was mid-afternoon before all of the boxes had been emptied and their inventory bestowed around the new house. Cassandra decided they should go to the Ball and Feather for lunch and then drive to the nearest mall with their lists and buy the rest of the small accouterments necessary to make each bed and bath and playroom civilized and habitable. Along with their lunches, they ordered a bottle of white wine and the three new friends shared their first drink together.

Always somewhat shy with Hope, whom he adored, Dru was even more intimidated by Amanda's mother, whom he thought quite lovely. She smiled at him from time to time but asked him no personal questions; loathe to intrude on a private life that had somehow intertwined with her daughter's the previous season. Without going

119

into all of the sensational details, Amanda had intimated to Cassandra, that Dru Baxter was a particularly close friend of herself and Pamela and that they all played in Boston together at Hugo's apartment. He was a very handsome young man, but Cassandra was not attracted to extremely young men and never guessed that such persons would be drawn to a woman of her own age. But Dru had always been fascinated by older women and whenever he met one he found pretty, wondered what it would be like to be over her knee. Cassandra was so soft spoken and delicately feminine, he could hardly picture her as a dominant, and yet it appeared she was to run an entire house.

"What are you going to go by?" Hope asked Cassandra.

"Go by?"

"What name will you use at the club?" Hope asked.

"I hadn't thought of that," Cassandra admitted. "I'll just use my own name, I guess."

"You can't do that," said Hope. "Nobody uses their own name in a dungeon."

"Well, it's okay because Cassandra isn't exactly my real name. My legal name is Sandra; I only unofficially changed it to Cassandra when I started doing astrological readings twenty-five years ago. Corny, right? Carola's real name is Carol. The additional "a" at the end is just an affectation she adopted when she started doing B&D."

"Mistress Cassandra, then," said Hope. "My stage name is Hope," she added.

"But you just said no one uses their real name in a dungeon," said Cassandra.

"Well, no one should," Hope conceded.

"Mistress means you're dominant?" asked Dru shyly.

When Cassandra hesitated to answer, Hope helpfully offered, "She's still sorting that out. At any rate, she's the mistress of the house. And I will be second in command. Which means that as always, I get to boss you around."

Chapter Fifteen

Susan Returns to Random Point

Contrary to Anthony's paranoid expectations, Susan was not back in Random Point in twenty-four hours. After the long flight back from Europe and tedious domestic connecting flight, Susan was delighted to sleep the night in Anthony's Greenwich Village townhouse and take the train to the Cape on the following day. In transit Susan had thought much of what situation she might be returning to, tortured by jealous anxiety at the notion of Cassandra being Anthony's new lover. In her mental distress she forgot that as soon as the summer was over, he was to return to New York to mount his next original musical. She would return to work at the Chipper Knight ad agency and go to bed with him every night after his long day was done. All would certainly be well. And yet she felt her heart was breaking.

Susan thought about Amanda's mother, who had seemed such a charming person while located on the opposite coast. But this close, she seemed only to be a formidable rival.

Exhausted from worrying, she slept in the train and emerged on the platform in the golden warmth of a July sunset. Dennis was waiting for her with the car as she had called ahead with her arrival time. He took her luggage and opened the door to the back seat.

"I'll sit in front with you," she said. The handsome English boy gave a little shiver. That meant she was going to try and pump him for information about Mr. Newton. He'd been down this road with Susan Ross before.

"Great!" he said cheerfully.

"Everything okay at the house?" Susan asked casually.

"It's very good, there are two culinary students in the kitchen. They've reduced my workload by 30%."

"That's nice. So this club, what's it like?"

"It's the next property down from Michael Flagg's on Pine Tar Road. They're filling it up with posh furniture and there's a lot of dungeon pieces on order, being made by William's crew."

"But, why would a respectable celebrity with a reputation to protect want to get anywhere near such an endeavor?" Susan wondered aloud.

"I expect he'll be as discreet as ever he can be about his involvement."

"I suppose you're right. I just wonder why all of a sudden he has a burning need to build a BDSM club."

"Would you..." he hesitated to finish his sentence, looking sideways at her as they began to drive up the hill to the Cliff House.

"Would I what, Dennis?"

"Would you ever work there?"

"Dennis, why in the world would I want to do that? Do I look like I need money that badly? Not to mention, how you think Anthony would feel about it?"

"I remember a time when you and Diana went to California specifically to work in a club."

"How dare you remember that so well?" she cried. "But that was years ago. And it was an appropriately naughty thing to do. Anyway, why do you ask such a thing?"

"Well, obviously, I'd want to come do a shoe session with you."

"Dennis!"

"You used to be so nice to me when you were just 19. You'd let me take care of your feet and shoes to my heart's content," he said, but not with any seriousness.

"I know. I was a wild child. Now I'm a mature workingwoman. I don't have time for such frivolity," she told him severely. He smiled at her.

"You know Hope is going to be helping Cassandra run it."

"So she got Hope away from Marguerite, did she?" Susan pretended surprise, but Anthony had already mentioned his desire to include Hope in the new enterprise when he had sent his long email to her several days before.

"Mr. Newton suggested it. It was all his idea."

"How did Marguerite take it?"

"Mr. Newton had the culinary students recruit their friends to re-staff her coffee shop."

"Now Marguerite, I can see her stopping in for a fly by session now and then," said Susan. "She would be the one to serve."

"I've adored her feet for years," Dennis admitted. "She wears magnificent heels and those insteps. So elegant."

They were at the house and Susan didn't hesitate to run inside and look for Anthony immediately. She wore an apricot cotton sundress that clung to her small curves like a velvety peel and terra cotta leather sandals on her tiny feet. Her long blonde hair was in its usual high ponytail and the color on her cheeks was high too as she ran upstairs. He was just emerging from his dressing room in a buff colored suit, when she ran into his arms.

"What in the world brought you back so soon?" he demanded bluntly, while affectionately squeezing her waist. "I thought you were going to be Diana's duenna for ten days," he said, adding, "By the way, that dress is very becoming to you. Let's go down to the dining room and get a little bite before I have to leave. These kids I have working for me are brilliant."

He led her downstairs by the hand as Susan explained, "Diana really needed the attentions of a male. Amanda happened to be able to hook her up with one of her Harvard boyfriends and the chemistry was instantaneous. I was just in the way, so I decided to come home."

"Why didn't you continue on with Colby and Amanda for a while? I would have thought they'd be fun to travel with."

"They were. But I missed you," said Susan honestly.

"Really? You got home sick?"

"Lovesick," she said, wrapping her arms around his waist and laying his head against his chest. He hugged her hard and laughed at her seriousness.

"Come on, let's eat," he said. In the end, she was too pretty to be peeved at, just because she came back a little sooner than expected. And he found her concern both reassuring and touching. The fact that he was still able to inspire sensations of passion in his much younger lover was undeniable. He could see her anxiety in her blue eyes, though her lips smiled at him.

"Will you come see the play?" he asked.

"Of course! I've been dreaming about seeing the play ever since you began rehearsals."

"By the way, good job picking out that furniture in Amsterdam. That's just what I wanted. I hope it gets here soon. Wait until you see this excellent house William found for us. I want you to do some custom artwork on the walls, murals. Laura is already starting in one room."

"Sure. I'll take a week or so more of vacation and stick around to do that," she said.

"I know it seems like a crazy whim," he agreed. "I honestly wasn't thinking about creating a club until Cassandra showed up and presented the idea to me. Then it seemed like the perfect project. I mean, think of all the clubs you've ever been in and how you would improve them. This will be a club you'll want to play in. And so will some of the locals, with each other. Plus we're setting aside parts of it for photography and filming."

Susan said, "This is the maddest thing you've ever done. But why shouldn't you be whimsical? You can afford it."

"Exactly!"

Chapter Sixteen

Carola, Lydia and Tai

On the following Tuesday, Anthony and Cassandra did rendezvous in Boston, setting up a base of operations at a boutique hotel in Back Bay. They spent the morning choosing mirrors and Anthony took her, as promised, to the little corset shop, where together they picked out waist cinches and corselets in a range of sizes and colors to keep for the girls' wardrobe at the club.

Then they went out to Allston to visit Cassandra's sister Carola, at the house she rented and called her photography studio. Carola, a tall, slender, strikingly attractive woman, who looked to be in her early thirties, but was in fact, forty, came to the door in a form fitting black and white gingham sundress, with a black apron cinching her remarkably small waist and fantastically high, shiny black spectator pumps. Her long, straight, jet-black hair was parted on the side and swept back from behind one ear to display an onyx earring that matched a circlet around Carola's white throat. Her lipstick and nail polish was dark red and her wide eyes as black as a tarn.

She led them into a well-furnished sitting room where a traditional tea of cucumber sandwiches, fruit cups and petit fours had been laid out beside a silver coffee and tea service. Anthony saw how determined Carola was to be formal and perfect and decided to seem to take her very seriously.

"I have some young ladies coming to meet you," said Carola, pouring coffee for her guests. "In fact, they should be here within ten minutes."

"You found some girls for Anthony to interview?" Cassandra was delighted. She remembered that Carola had long been a mistress of logistics and was too shrewd to pass up the opportunity to impress

Anthony sooner than later.

"I've worked with them both. Here are their photos," said Carola, placing an album in the composer's hands. "They are the first two girls in the book."

Anthony and Cassandra looked at the photos of Lydia, a graceful brunette in her mid-twenties with hair to her waist and Tai, a petite blonde with chin length hair. Both girls had blue eyes, natural bosoms and curvy hips and both were extremely pretty.

"Yes," said Anthony. "Perfect."

"Lovely," Cassandra agreed. Then there was a knock at the door and Carola went to admit the girls.

"She's very efficient," said Anthony, eating one of the cucumber sandwiches. "And these are good too."

"She's always been perfect." Cassandra explained. Then the girls were upon them and there was a flurry of introductions and shaking hands. The girls were seated on a wide leather sofa opposite Anthony and Cassandra. Carola poured the tea as she perched on the seat of a straight-backed armchair.

"So girls," said Cassandra. "I'm Carola's sister. And although I've been out of the scene for quite a few years, I'm just about to open a new club, out on the Cape."

"Yes, we want to work there!" said Lydia.

"How often could you girls come out?" asked Cassandra.

"We're freelance models, so whenever you need us," said Tai. "We'll work around the days we have gigs."

"Do you want to come out together all the time?" asked Cassandra.

"When possible," said Lydia and it was obvious to all that the girls were best friends.

"Tell Anthony a little about your backgrounds," said Carola. She had previously checked with Cassandra about what to refer to their patron as in front of others. It wouldn't do to call him by his real sir name, certainly. But he didn't wish to be addressed as master or sir. Cassandra had asked him and he had said just to use his first name, for simplicity's sake, but that the girls would surely learn soon enough who he was, if they didn't already know. He tended to invite scene girls to visit him both in New York and Random Point, once he knew and liked them.

"Well," began Lydia. "I've always known I was submissive. I read the Beauty books when I was twelve and started dreaming about living that life right away. I was a history major at Boston University and I'm working on a historical novel."

"What was your thesis on?" he asked.

"Rousseau's erotic obsessions."

"Do you have a boyfriend in the scene?" asked Cassandra.

"I'm owned by a man," Lydia admitted with a blush.

"But he's okay with you doing sessions in a club?" Anthony asked, organically opposed to hiring any girl with either a jealous boyfriend or pimp.

Lydia smiled and her nose crinkled, "He lets me do whatever I want. Honestly, he's more of a bondager and doesn't quite get spanking. Therefore, I don't get spanked much at home. But he is happy to let me have my adventures."

"I'm sure he's very handsome," Cassandra guessed, with a smile. Lydia nodded, pleased with herself.

"What about you, young lady?" Anthony asked Tai.

"I've always been into spanking," she said. "Ever since I was four or five. I don't know why."

"How old are you?" Cassandra asked them both.

"26," said Lydia.

"22," said Tai. "But I've hunted for spanking material since I was little. And then, when I was in high school, I found my older sister's spank porn collection. It had Hugo's magazine, videos and books. I spent the entire summer of sophomore year in a state of near constant orgasm, just being so turned on by the erotica. Luckily, I had a boyfriend to help me explore. But I've been working in pro B&D since I turned 18."

"Wow," said Anthony. "That's great."

"Girls, go and make sure the dungeon looks nice. I want to show it to Anthony and my sister," said Carola. The two girls had hesitated to do more than nibble on a small sandwich each. Now he realized why. Once they had left the room Carola raised her thin, dark brows at him.

"Do you want to see what we can do together?" she asked.

127

"Yes! And I especially want to see what Cassandra can do with those naughty girls," he said, looking at Cassandra expectantly. "It'll be good practice for you."

Cassandra looked doubtful but nodded in assent. "I agree. It's time to see if I can pull this off on any level."

"You'd better start channeling your inner 50's housewife, like your sister," Anthony recommended.

They joined the two girls in a small playroom equipped with a few key pieces of furniture. Carola told Lydia summarily to undress and when the shapely brunette had taken off and neatly folded every garment, Carola led the beauty to the whipping post and turning her to face it, fastened her wrists above her head with a short length of white nylon rope passed through a iron loop. A dainty waist offset Lydia's small, saucy breasts and wide, womanly hips. Her skin was a uniform, creamy rose white and everything about her was natural. The brunette's bottom was particularly curvaceous and smooth, classic in shape, hue and texture.

Carola took up a leather crop and used it like a cane across that perfect bottom, hard, fast and with cruelty, leaving a dozen evenly spaced red weals behind. Lydia cried out in great pain, but didn't protest the treatment, bearing it bravely, as an ardent young submissive is taught to. Anthony was more shocked than aroused by Carola's ferocious iciness. Cassandra's younger sister indeed seemed completely unmoved by the pain she had inflicted. She did notice a tear run down Lydia's cheek.

"Look at how she reacts," said Carola, turning Lydia's face towards them between her long, graceful, beautifully manicured fingers. Lydia looked timidly at Anthony.

"That's enough," he said, which stopped Carola from raising the crop again.

"Do you feel sorry for her?" Carola asked in disbelief. She released Lydia's wrists from the above head tie but keeping them together in the loop of rope, pulled the brunette over to a spanking bench and bent her over it. "I just want you to see something," said Carola, pushing Lydia's thighs apart and spreading the girl open with shiny dark red polished fingertips. Anthony and Cassandra duly noticed how wet the submissive girl was but Cassandra sensed her new lover's disapproval of her sister's unkindly manner.

Anthony said, "Very pretty but I'd rather see you take Lydia in your arms, caress her and ask her forgiveness."

Cassandra looked at him in surprise, her lips curving into a smile. How like her sister it was to bring out the perversity in even the most affable of men. Carola at first frowned deeply at this unexpected and uncongenial command, then amended her expression to one of robotic compliance. She had every reason to believe that she and the girls would be generously rewarded for their time that afternoon and provided with regular work thereafter as her sister's new club came into being. Not only were all her bills due the following week, but business in Boston had been slow the whole previous month, everyone having left town for the summer. But the Cape was a summer destination and she could see numerous opportunities arising from her spending a few days in the week there during the warmest months.

Carola did turn Lydia right side up, put her arms around the girl's waist and pushing Lydia's silky curtain of brown hair back behind one gold pierced ear, fastened her lips to her victim's throat, then to Lydia's bare shoulder, where she bit her lightly. Carola bit Lydia's earlobe and then reached up to cup the girl's small but full breasts firmly in her hands.

"Carola," Anthony said rather sharply, "I said to ask her forgiveness, not devour her."

Carola let go of Lydia, who caught her breath and dared to look up at Anthony. "All right, never mind. I may want a word with you later about this. Meanwhile, the both of you can leave us now. I want to be alone with Cassandra and Tai for a bit."

Carola had the grace to lead Lydia out by the hand, bowing her head to Anthony for an instant just before she left.

"Now, show me how you give a spanking," he encouraged Cassandra. "Tai is just about Susan's height and build. Imagine that you're spanking that naughty Susan for returning home so soon."

Cassandra took the small, well-rounded blonde girl over her lap and pulled her in close to her own torso. Tai had a small waist and jutting buttocks, now set off to perfection under the neat folds of a short, beige, pleated skirt. A white short sleeved blouse, white knee socks and black stack heeled oxfords completed Tai's outfit and naturally, under the skirt, the girl's panties were full seated and white. Cassandra displayed all the care and respect common to a spanking connoisseur in her treatment of Tai, stroking, smoothing, gazing at and admiring the lovely girl's bottom before striking it for the first time. The measured, slow building up of heat and sensation, the ritual unveiling of the target area, layer by layer, the attitude of quiet control mixed with amused affection, all defined Cassandra's careful and sensitive approach. In the end, Tai's exposed bottom had been gradually tinged magenta, from the repeated applications of Cassandra's surprisingly firm hand. Anthony nodded at Cassandra approvingly after her job was done.

Anthony then sent Cassandra and Tai out to tell Carola that if she came to him he would give her everyone's allowance.

Cassandra looked back at him quizzically as she went out of the dungeon with her new friend, Tai, who had been a pleasant, girlish weight across her lap. She expected many a client to engage her to spank either Tai or Lydia, for their voyeuristic pleasure.

When Carola came to him a flush crept across her high cheekbones. He looked at her over folded arms and said, "I don't like show offs."

"I don't know what you mean," she protested, but weakly.

"After watching you abuse Lydia I didn't feel like spanking her, I felt like spanking you," he said, gratified to see her flinch.

"Men like me to be strict with the girls," she defended herself with a bit more spirit. But when he met her eyes she quickly dropped hers. And well he knew why. She realized that he was the wealthiest and most influential client she was likely to meet in the scene and that he had already bestowed untold largesse upon her sister. And now it was clear that Newton was a whimsical top, not cast from the classic mold.

"I don't want you setting that kind of bad example for tops who come into the club to play with our girls. I don't want those girls leaving marked after every session. What if they want to model? It's not fair. Those marks you left on Lydia will last five days."

"She likes having marks. She's submissive," Carola replied

defiantly.

"And masochistic?"

"A little."

"How do you know she just doesn't do it to please you?"

"Well, that's part of it," Carola laughed. "She romanticizes incidents like the one that just occurred."

"Is that so? I'll have to study her closely one of these days to see if you're telling the truth," he promised, handing her fifteen hundred dollars. "Split that three ways," he said.

Carola smiled up at him, relieved that she wasn't going to be spanked.

A few minutes later, as he and Cassandra left the house he said to her, "How come your sister is such a crazy bitch?"

"She's always been an OCD perfectionist. When she gets out of bed, it's practically made. I think BDSM has brought out the worst in her."

"I hope she comes out soon. I'll book a session with her," said Anthony.

"I don't think she likes doing sub sessions," said Cassandra, trying not to smile at the thought of her sister screaming in pain.

"I don't care what she likes. I'll give her enough money so she'll have to take it," he said airily.

"It really bothered you how she treated Lydia, didn't it? Do you really have the stomach for what goes on in a B&D club?" Cassandra wondered.

"I'm not going to be in those dungeons. The girls can choose their own levels. But you're right, it rankled me to see her abuse her power. I would punish her for that. Do you mind?"

"Let me think about that for a second," Cassandra pondered. "I've never liked my sister all that much and I love you. She's always been cold and critical towards me whereas you have taken me to your bosom. No, I don't mind. Beat the hell out of her. She'll take it for a grand."

"I hoped you'd feel that way."

"Are you kidding? My little sister is a condescending bitch. She didn't bother to hide her astonishment when I told her you'd become my patron. I could almost hear her thinking, 'But what could he possibly see in her?' I'm sure she felt your vibe just now. It's going to puzzle her." Just then Cassandra's phone vibrated in her pocket and she looked at it and grinned. "Look Anthony, she just sent me a text: "Why doesn't Mr. Newton like me? Did I not look good today?"

"What are you going to write back?" he asked.

"Whatever you tell me to," said Cassandra.

"Invite her to come visit early next week. And tell her I like her well enough to want to beat that skinny ass."

"Okay, but I'll put it more nicely. She's not used to bluntness from me."

"All right. Be as diplomatic as you always are. I'll be content to express my disappointment with her character with a hair brush."

Chapter Seventeen

Anthony and Susan

The day after returning from Boston Anthony began the day with a swim and had his coffee and breakfast rolls poolside. Susan joined him, dressed in a nautical playsuit and high-heeled white sandals with ribbon ties around the ankles. She looked heavenly, sitting there naughtily smoking a joint, with her high blonde ponytail reaching half way down her back and her full red lips curved into a lazy, summer day smile. She poured his coffee and put in just the right amount of milk. She had gotten home late the previous night, having closed Michael's bar with Michael, Marguerite and some other friends and had joined a sleepy Anthony in bed without discussing his adventures in Boston earlier that day.

"Did you meet Carola?" she now asked.

"Yes and she's a horrible woman," said Anthony.

"Not beautiful?" Susan was surprised.

"Oh, she's pretty enough," he conceded, "but she has a terrible personality. She made me want to beat her. I do want to beat her. And I'm going to beat her as soon as she comes out. I've had Cassandra tell her so. Maybe you could help me."

"Me?" Susan stared at him.

"Yes. You could do the rigging."

"The rigging?"

"You could tie her down for me. You know I could never be bothered to learn bondage."

"You want me to go in a dungeon with you and a lady?"

"Yes, you need to come and help me with this bitch."

Anthony hadn't participated in a scene with Susan and another woman since she had first brought Diana Stratton home to the Greenwich Village townhouse when the girls were in college.

"I can't believe Cassandra's sister is so bad," said Susan, coloring a little at the idea of assisting Anthony in a dungeon.

"She's a sadist. She was so mean to this pretty girl in front of us. By the way, we met two cute subs. They're coming to work at the club. You'll want to draw them, a brunette and a blonde. And she's been awful to Cassandra in the past. She puts her down and disrespects her. I'm glad you know bondage. I want her in the most inescapable and embarrassing position you can invent."

"Will she go for that, me tying her? I understood she was a top."

"She'll be anything we want her to be," Anthony replied serenely.

"You mean she's available for a price?"

"Of course," he replied.

"Anthony, you sound like you've gone over to the dark side," Susan accused him.

"I know," he readily agreed, "that terrible woman has brought it out in me. As soon as you meet her you'll agree that she needs a thrashing. But I know how you can't stand to see another lady get a really good beating, even if she does deserve it, so don't worry, you can leave us after you tie her up."

"That would probably be best," Susan agreed, buttering a bit of roll to nibble on, "but it's nice to be included. And if this woman is as much of a gorgon as you say she is, I'll be happy to have my position in the harem clearly delineated from the get go."

"Susan, everybody knows you're the mistress of my house and my heart," he said gallantly. Now Susan knew without a doubt that he was having an affair with Cassandra. He never displayed flowery or sentimental emotions to Susan unless he was cheating on her. She was a little surprised he had redirected his passions so quickly from Phoebe Casper, whom he'd been courting only the previous month, to this lithe newcomer and idly wondered who he'd be in love with in the Autumn, when he returned to Manhattan. At any rate, to be the acknowledged Queen was good and Susan was content. In Europe, she had been fearful. But now at home again, with the new woman tucked away under a different roof on the other side of the village, her fears had been calmed.

Meanwhile, Cassandra had spent her first night alone at the house. She had stayed up very late putting things away. At about two am, it began to rain. She smoked a pipe in her front garden and then pulled back into the shadows of the porch when she saw a car cruise slowly by the house. She recognized Michael Flagg's SUV. He stopped the car and waved to her from the curb. She waved back at him and motioned him over.

"You're up late," he said.

"You too. Did you just close up the bar?"

"What are you doing, smoking weed?"

"I thought you quit being a cop," she admonished her tall, handsome, judgmental neighbor.

"You girls," he said in exasperation.

"What girls?"

"Every girl I've ever been involved with has been a degenerate stoner," he complained.

"Didn't you just come from the bar that you own where it's practically your duty to get your patrons wasted? Even conservatively speaking, three to five poor tourists will be waking up with a hangover tomorrow simply because they crossed your threshold."

"All right, I yield," he laughed, for it had indeed been a busy night of just barely legal kids on vacation drinking themselves sick on cheap pitchers of beer at his tavern. "Hey listen, I have a favor to ask you."

"Sure, whatever I can do," she said eagerly.

"I might come by in a day or two with a lady," he began confidentially.

"Oh?"

"And want to rent a dungeon, or at least a play space, let's say a room, preferably with a bed."

"Really!" she grinned.

"Since the lady will not be my wife, the utmost discretion will be required."

"Oh, absolutely. Give me an hour's notice and I'll have everything ready for you. Will this be one of the degenerate stoners?"

"No actually," he smiled. "And just about the only one who isn't."

Then, for some reason he barely understood himself, he took the pipe out of Cassandra's hand and taking the lighter out of her other hand, expertly relit the pipe and took a hit. She stared at him in disbelief. But he had watched his wife go through this ritual often enough to have memorized the gestures. He suddenly coughed and looked surprised.

"What are you doing?" she asked.

"I don't know," he said, feeling a dimensional shift in his mood and perceptions as he gazed at Amanda's pretty mother. "I can't tell you how many times Marguerite has begged me to get stoned with her. But I never do. I never do with anyone," he confided.

"You'd better come in and tuck me in," said Cassandra helpfully.

Michael looked at his watch, everything around him blurring and vibrating as a sudden head rush overcame him. "2:10," he said aloud. "Don't let me linger more than twenty minutes," he ordered as he followed her into the new wood scented house.

When they got to her bedroom, Cassandra made Michael sit in a big upholstered chair while she looked in the large, elegant walnut chest of drawers that had arrived from Bartlett's the day before. She looked over her shoulder at him, deciding what to change into.

"Tell me about the mysterious lady you are meeting here," Cassandra asked.

"You'll find out sooner or later, so I might as well. But say not a word of this to Marguerite. It's my old girlfriend Jane Eliot. She's been stalking me for sex lately and well, let's just say she's gotten a lot prettier and a lot kinkier than she ever was when we were engaged."

"I take it you left her for Marguerite?"

"Yes. We came to Random Point to go antiquing and I happened to walk into the bookstore and see Marguerite. It was love at first sight. Though I wound up married to Damaris for a year or so first."

"So you broke up with Damaris because of Marguerite as well?"

"Yes. I couldn't keep away from Marguerite and Damaris isn't the kind of wife who tolerates that kind of thing. I respect her for that."

"But Marguerite is?"

"Well, she is more broad minded, but the longer I can put off her finding out about this insane thing I'm doing with Jane, the better."

Cassandra had gone behind a painted screen to change from her summer dress into a thin sleeveless cotton nightgown with a fitted bodice that emphasized the fullness of her bottom, the slenderness of her torso and small, sculpted roundness of her bosom.

"Turn around," he said from the chair. She turned and looked at him over her smooth shoulder, noticing his gaze going to her bottom.

"You'd better tuck me in now," she said, going to the bed and pulling back the comforter and sheet. He came to her, sat on the bed, pulled her down on his lap and put his arms around her tightly. She put her arms around his neck and said into his ear, "All the girls talk about you. So how could I not be curious?" Meanwhile, as she settled herself down on his lap, she felt his sudden erection. "Ten minutes left," she said, looking at a clock on the bed stand.

"I feel like I've gone through the looking glass," he said, gently laying her on her back and pulling her gown up to her chin. While gazing at her, he pulled his zipper down and reached down with the other hand to cup one of her creamy white, pink tipped breasts. She parted her thighs and he reached down to touch her, exploring her with his long fingers.

"Wait a minute," she said, turning and getting up on her hands and knees. "There's no time for fancy foreplay," she said, "but there's always time for a spanking."

Michael smiled and applied his palm to her up thrust bottom in a couple of stinging volleys. She smiled and arched back towards him, inviting him to spank her again. Moving to her side, he took her around her small waist and gave her a proper spanking under his arm as she knelt on the bed. After sixty or seventy medium hard swats she groaned, "Okay, good!" She reached in her bedside drawer for a condom, which she began to unwrap but he snatched it from her and did the job much faster than she could have done.

"Is it okay to do it from this angle?" he asked, putting her back into the doggy position. "Yes. Just take your time. You're huge," she said.

"Flatterer," he laughed. Then he remembered time management and refocused his floating, fuzzy, funny attention on Cassandra and made sure she was wet before positioning his cock against her parted labia. Then, even as stoned as he was, and with only seven minutes left, he stopped to extract a tube of lube from her bed stand and thoroughly slicked down his long shaft as well as her tiny pink aperture, before invading her snug inner precincts with his formidable cock. With the help of ujai breathing, her sudden excitement at the turn of the night and the excellent lubricant, full penetration was achieved almost painlessly and it felt deeply good.

"What does it take to make you orgasm?" he asked, plying her slowly.

"I don't think I could orgasm in eight minutes," she said.

"I'll stay a little longer then," he decided, "and tell her I had to drive a drunk home to P. Town. I do that all the time."

"You really want to make me come?" she asked, reaching between her legs to lightly cup his balls.

"God, yes!" he replied, in response to the pressure of her deft fingertips.

"Okay, let's switch positions. Get on your back and let me get on top," she said, pulling away and letting him pull out of her. He lay back on the bed and she mounted him, straddling his thighs with her flexible legs and taking him back inside her. She eased all the way down on his shaft until her groin was flush with his and she was sitting on his cock. "Now," she said, taking his hands and placing one on each of her cheeks. "Touch me," she encouraged him, nudging his hand toward her bottom crack. He needed no further instructions to begin fingering her bottom and pulling her even more tightly to him while she ground down on his pelvis.

With this happening to her, and then suddenly gazing down into his impossibly handsome face, Cassandra felt her crisis approaching momentarily.

"Okay," she panted, "about to come!" And then she did come, throbbing and tingling as she rode the crest of sensation for ten seconds before expiring against his chest.

He flipped them over so that he was on top again and began fucking her hard and fast. Pulling her gown up again to completely expose her torso, he suddenly pulled out of her, pulled his condom off and taking his cock in his hand, pumped it to a effusive explosion that rained creamy fluid down on her perky bosom, concave belly and small, neat triangle of brown pubic curls. Cassandra hadn't seen a male come that long and hard since high school days and laughed with appreciation.

"Careful, don't let any get on that beautiful gown." he said, pulling her nightie up and over her head then tossing it to one side. He looked at her lying under him and smiled. "You're so pretty," he said. "Thank you."

"Don't mention it. It never happened," she said, slipping out of bed to make repairs in the adjoining master bathroom.

Michael redid his trousers, stretched and joined her to wash his hands. He looked at her in the mirror. She was now fully nude while he was fully dressed in a light plaid short-sleeved shirt and light colored pants, a thin leather belt encircling his trim waist. He was a good foot taller than she with an impressive shoulder expanse.

"You're larger than life, aren't you?" she asked, leaning back against the vanity and smiling up at him. He bent to kiss her lightly on the lips. "I wish you had time to take your clothes off. I'd like to really see that body," she said.

It had begun to rain hard and they could hear it pounding on the roof.

"I'd love to stay and cuddle with you for a while," he said, walking back into the bedroom and casting a longing look at the bed.

"I don't think that's a good idea," she said, pulling on a wrapper. "It's been a long day and after what we just did, you could fall fast asleep. And then I wouldn't want to wake you."

"Okay, I'd better go. It's really starting to come down," he said; "Take care and lock everything up tight before you turn in. Always put the security system on. Promise me you'll do that."

"I will," she said. Michael drove off and Cassandra obediently locked everything up before retiring to her bedroom. As the rain began pelting the windows hard she got completely undressed and climbed between the twelve hundred count sheets fresh from Bartlett's luxury linens department. She had slatted the wide wooden venetian blinds and could see the raindrops splashing against the windowpanes of her back garden and woods facing bedroom.

"What a beautiful man," she thought, lacing her fingers behind her head and looking out the windows. "That's the second beautiful man I've temporarily annexed from a local woman. I should work on finding a beautiful man of my own." Since returning to Random Point, she'd now had a man in his forties, Anthony, and tonight a man in his thirties, Michael. Should she try it with a man in his twenties next? Raphael Price from the art gallery came to mind. She grabbed her phone off the table and began to send a text to Amanda, "Is it okay if I go after Raphael Price?" But before she hit send she realized that Colby Hodge could be looking over her daughter's shoulder when the text came in. And she suspected that Amanda hadn't mentioned anything about Raphael Price being one of her lovers to Colby. She aborted the text and settled back in bed. And then perhaps she could complete her summer rampage through the warm and leafy back roads of Random Point with a man still in his teens, just for the sake of symmetry; that adorable Dru Baxter for example, he who craved a spanking so badly. No, she shook her head on the pillow, to sleep with a boy that her own daughter had slept with was unthinkably perverse.

Cassandra's last thought before drifting off to sleep with a smile was, "I did Michael Flagg!"

Meanwhile Michael pulled away from the house, thinking, "What the hell did I just do and why?" Had he really broken a twenty-year spell of not getting high and within minutes of doing so, made love to a woman who wasn't his wife? So far he was confident that Marguerite knew nothing about his resumption of relations with Jane Eliot. But this would not be the case for long. Someone would see him at one of his rendezvous with his former fiancée and report to his wife. And that gave him pause. Marguerite was a temperamental creature who had broken up with her first husband at the first sign of crankiness. She was too passionate about Michael not to be fiercely jealous of his affections and he feared that this could lead to an unappeasable anger in his redheaded goddess if she were to discover even a tenth part of what he had been up to that summer. The unfair thing was that he hadn't gone looking for these adventures. They had more or less coming looking for him. At least Jane had. Jane had in fact been completely self-determined in her stalking and seduction of him. She had made up some story about a biological clock, but Michael was beginning to agree with Hugo Sands that this was nothing more than a righteous fib the novice thrill seeker Jane had made up to somehow justify what was a simple case of lust. Michael was a known quantity, he was convenient, she had once loved him and he her. It was natural that she turn to him the first time true sexual restlessness began to preoccupy her otherwise serious and socially committed consciousness. The fact that she had only grown prettier as well as much less inhibited since they'd been engaged, made her impossible to resist. All she really had to do was ask him to play with her while looking attractive and he found himself aroused. At the same time, he was still enthralled with his wife, who had only really been his for the last couple of years. It was delightful to actually have Marguerite at home with the added bonus of the beautiful baby that was theirs and of Marguerite being his wife now. Was he suddenly putting it all at risk for a whimsical Jane and whatever had just happened with Cassandra, which he couldn't even begin to understand? The rain pelted down on his windshield as a text came in from Marguerite. He stopped the car and pulled over to look at his phone. "Just fed baby. Meet me at the house." His heart lurched. The house Marguerite meant was his property, a little further down Pine Tar Road. He sniffed at his shirt. Would Marguerite detect Cassandra's perfume? There was a faint wisp of a floral scent that his wife might notice.

In a moment or two he was pulling into the driveway of the house, his heart pounding at an unaccustomed rate. He wasn't used to feeling guilty. It was an awkward and alarming sensation.

Marguerite appeared in the timbered living room in a smoky blue lace nightgown that displayed her hourglass figure handsomely, the creamy peach tones of her skin adding texture to the clinging ensemble. Her beautiful face, framed by a gleaming of curtain of light red hair, beamed on seeing him. She came to hug him, the warmth of her skin and absence of eyeglasses indicating that she had jumped out of bed when she'd heard his key in the door.

"Let me take a quick shower," he told her, abbreviating their hug. "It's been a long, hot day."

There was nothing odd in this. After a fourteen-hour shift in his own bar, it was reasonable to take a shower and Marguerite didn't question it. She climbed back into bed and awaited him. A few minutes later he emerged from the master bath with a towel wrapped around his trim waist, which he tossed aside before getting into bed beside his voluptuous but equally small-waisted wife and drawing her to him.

She turned her back to him and fitted her body against his as he lay on his side, arranging his arm around her waist. As always, being in such close proximity to her magnificent bottom caused his penis to jump to attention and it nestled as a hard bar against her lace wrapped cheeks.

"Do you have a little energy left?" she asked, pulling up her gown behind and grinding back against him.

"Always," he said, wondering if he actually did. But instead of continuing in this manner, he sat up and said, "But let me ask you something."

"Okay," she replied agreeably, sitting up herself.

"Do you really love me?"

"What? How can you ask that?" she asked. "Didn't I have your baby? And didn't I marry you?"

"And you definitely plan to stay with me?"

"Of course I plan to stay with you, why wouldn't I?"

"Having a baby together is a huge commitment," he pointed out. "But you didn't even tell me about it until you were months along. And then you insisted on staying in Europe until baby was born. Why so independent? That's what alarms me. That you could so cheerfully do that all on your own."

"Oh, Michael, it was all for vanity. I didn't want to parade around the village with a big stomach. It would have been so awkward. You said you weren't mad at me for that anymore."

"I'm not mad. But how can I trust you not to dump me over the littlest thing and take Felina away in the same way you brought her?"

"I'd never do that. I can see you're very fond of her. Everything worked out perfectly in that respect, just as I knew it would. What little thing are you talking about?" Marguerite asked.

"What if you found out I'd cheated on you," he said. Marguerite's light green eyes narrowed at him.

"Well, that was fast!" she cried with vexation.

"Remember what you promised," he said.

"I will, but who is she?"

"When I tell you you'll understand that this isn't my fault."

"That's very interesting. I'm all agog," said Marguerite, jumping out of bed and pacing, her plumper than usual bosom heaving with indignation. She caught sight of herself in a full-length mirror and added, "I knew it was time to stop nursing."

"Honey, don't say that, it's so good for baby."

"Baby is twenty months old. She's already walking and talking She's practically legal to drink. No, it's long past time!" Marguerite folded her arms and glared at him. "Well? What local slut is it? Tell me!"

"Jane."

"Jane Eliot?" Marguerite cried incredulously. "But, why? How?"

"This isn't my fault," Michael reiterated. "Someone invited her to that Venus Club dinner and it reawakened all sorts of memories of the hot sex we did have and the kinky sex we never got around to because she was an uptight bitch in those days. She stalked me and propositioned me just days after that dinner. And then she doubled down on how it was only fair I help her have a baby."

"A what????"

"She said she wants a baby but she's with a female partner. She said I owed her one because we were supposed to have gotten married and had a family."

"And because of that you've been having sex with Jane again?"

Michael shrugged. "That and she's been looking really good lately. And said she wanted that spanking I never got around to giving her while we were together. How could I resist, Marguerite? I did jilt her. Because you turned my head."

"Yes, I see. It all makes perfect sense. Do you believe this story of wanting a baby? And have you been trying very hard to give her one, dearest?"

"I did believe it at first, but not anymore. Now I think she's just bored with being gay."

"So, she's not pregnant yet, as far as you know?" Marguerite asked.

"No."

"Well, did you spank her?"

"Yes."

"You're a horrid man!" Marguerite said, stamping her foot at him.

"Please, Marguerite, help me solve this problem?"

Chapter Eighteen

First Official Business at the House

The storm wore itself out overnight and was just a light mist as the sun rose. Cassandra awoke early, started the coffee and showered as though in a dream. Mixed emotions about her previous night's adventure flooded her mind. That she'd broken down the reserve of a handsome, stubborn, upright, heroic character like Michael Flagg so effortlessly, had seduced him so easily, curved her pretty mouth into a smile. But that expression faded when she visualized his beautiful, proud wife, still carefully wet nursing their thriving baby. Marguerite was the Queen Bee of Random Point's inner BDSM clique and had been a pet of Hugo Sands and Anthony Newton for many years. No one would be okay with the notion of some outsider from the ancient past suddenly appearing in the village to bewitch the men of the resident belles. It was bad enough to have temporarily tempted Anthony away from Susan, but Marguerite had an even greater and more dignified hold on her man, Michael, who was hard won to her after a very long and frustrating courtship, interrupted by imprudent first marriages on both sides. And for that matter, how would Anthony feel about Cassandra making love to other men at the house? Knowing Anthony even as little as she did, she suspected he would be relieved, for he had had to abandon her to all intents and purposes as a lover as soon as Susan returned to Random Point and that would be bothering him. And yet, mightn't he still be jealous? She was extremely cognizant of her responsibilities as mistress of the house, the foremost of which was to get it opened for business as soon as possible. Or at the very least, make sure a number of subs were booked to visit while Anthony was still in residence for the summer. Cassandra sensed the best she could do to justify his investment would be to provide him with an ever-varying supply of interesting new lady-girls to play with and show off to his scene friends in the village. He would be thrilled to hear that Michael Flagg was already planning a rendezvous there. But wait, should she be revealing the details of sessions in the house even to Anthony? Would that not violate Michael's privacy and that of whatever lady he was bringing? That everyone knew each other so well challenged discretion.

Cassandra longed to confide in someone about all of this, and that person was Amanda. Cassandra laughed to herself as she pictured Amanda's face hearing of all she had done. She had always been Amanda's confidante. All through high school, as well as through her first year at the university, Amanda had shared her adventures with her mother. But Cassandra had never had any amusing anecdotes to beguile her daughter with. She had led a staid and well behaved life with darling Eddie, never straying until the previous fall day when Hugo had come to find her and make her give an account of why she had concealed Amanda's existence from him for eighteen years. Now she had two escapades with which to regale her daughter, the wildly successful Anthony Newton campaign and the subsequent madcap antic of seducing Michael Flagg. The latter confession would be doubly delicious because she knew that Flagg had spanked Amanda, during her first visit to Random Point the previous autumn. She never dreamed that she and her daughter would share a play partner but knew that Amanda would find the entire situation fascinating.

Cassandra found Hope already at her command post in the office, answering email. The blonde beauty had her hair in one long, careless braid and was clad collegiately in a maroon and gray plaid skirt, a maroon polo sweater top, oxblood red penny loafers and ankle sox.

"What a cute outfit," said Cassandra, coming in with her coffee.

"I have my first session today," said Hope, looking up at her new boss with a smile. "Mr. Bartlett is coming in this afternoon. I just hope the school room furniture gets delivered this morning."

"Mr. Bartlett is certainly eager," said Cassandra. "I've heard he's a hard session, though," she added.

Hope grimaced, nodding, "That's true! But he's a big tipper." She sighed. "I knew he'd be my first session. Didn't I tell you he would?"

"What's our dungeon situation? How many spaces are ready?"

"Look, I have it all here on the blueprint," said Hope, getting a graphic file open on her computer. "The white spaces are the rooms that haven't been finished yet, the gray ones are partially furnished but usable and the pink ones are complete."

"That's nice. Anthony will be impressed with this," said Cassandra, noticing that there were only a few white spaces. One was for the exam room to come. Special furniture and equipment were to be ordered for that room after careful consideration.

"Dru is unpacking the library and arranging the books right now," said Hope.

The noise of a large truck arriving outside brought them out to the front of the house. It was the modern gunmetal blue leather furniture from the Dutch firm, drop shipped from New York.

"I'm so happy," said Hope to Cassandra as the deliveryman began unloading. "Now we can set up the terra cotta parlor!"

Cassandra went back to Hope's computer to study the blueprint of the house again. As of that afternoon they would have many private spaces available for playing in. A parlor and the schoolroom were about to come together. The classic whipping post and stocks had been placed in Cape Cod, the airy corner room with windows on two sides, where Laura had painted an abstract beach on the walls. The remodeled loft was ready to play in. And two of the plushly decorated bedrooms were also fully squared away. Suddenly a text message appeared on Cassandra's phone from Michael Flagg. "A lady will visit at noon. Put her in a room to wait."

"Copy that," Cassandra wrote back immediately, her heart jumping with excitement to hear from her new lover so soon.

In the next half hour the second furniture delivery arrived. Hope supervised the unloading and Cassandra was well pleased at the speed with which the club was being filled up with pleasant and comfortable things.

Jane Eliot arrived at the stroke of noon in a russet skirt and white sleeveless blouse, pumps and dark glasses, her medium length brown hair parted on the side and brushed back from her brow. She wore almost no make-up but looked very pretty and polished. Hope greeted her cheerfully from her command station, inwardly overjoyed that the first official customer of the club should be a lady.

"Hi Hope," said Jane, quietly, as though she was afraid of being overheard. "I'm supposed to meet Michael here."

"Someone is waiting for you, but it's not Michael," Hope disclosed.

"Not Michael?"

"No, it's Marguerite'" said Hope in an undertone.

"You're kidding, right?" Jane pulled off her sunglasses to stare at Hope, her chest contracting in a sudden rush of guilty anxiety.

Hope rose to conduct Jane to the newly furnished terra cotta salon. She opened the door for Jane then discreetly disappeared. Jane walked in to see Marguerite lightly perched on the arm of a blue leather sofa, smartly clad in a cream suit with a nipped waist, white shirt and beige on black four-inch stack heeled oxfords. As soon as Jane appeared, Marguerite folded her arms across her remarkable bosom and tossed her smooth, shiny light red hair back from her brow.

"Hello," said Marguerite, in a not unfriendly manner, smiling faintly as though at an amusing situation.

"Hi," said Jane, with a pounding heart, the blood rushing to her cheeks.

"Michael's girl called in sick today last minute and he had to go open the tavern," explained Marguerite, pleasantly, "so he asked me to meet you and take you to lunch in his place."

"Oh!" Jane murmured. "Oh, great."

"He told me he was going to show you around the club because he thought it might interest you. So I offered to come and look it over with you. Hope says a great deal of furniture has just been delivered, including these pieces," said Marguerite, gesturing to the loveseats, sofas and deep chairs that filled the spacious, handsomely crown molded room. Jane looked about her.

"Beautiful," said Jane, breathing in the leather-scented air.

"Come, let's look at the dungeons," said Marguerite, leading the way out of the room and down the hall. They looked into and walked around the rooms that already had play furniture in them. When they reached the one called Cape Cod, Marguerite closed the door behind them and leaned her back against it.

"It's a lovely club, isn't it?" Marguerite asked Jane.

"Oh, yes!"

"Anthony Newton saw fit to endow Random Point with this space, mainly so he and his friends would have an interesting new environment to come and play in, both with their partners and if they were being naughty, others," said Marguerite.

"Really?" Jane said, looking with interest at the spanking bench and whipping post, set against the pale blues and sands of the shoreline on the walls.

"This would be a fun room to play in, wouldn't it?" asked Marguerite.

"With the stocks, this room reminds me of the Scarlet Letter," Jane agreed.

"It's funny you should mention adultery," said Marguerite.

"I didn't mention adultery," said Jane.

"You mentioned The Scarlet Letter."

"Oh, that's right."

"No, that's wrong."

"I think I see where you're going with this," Jane replied uncomfortably. Marguerite folded her arms. "But, how did you find out?"

"Michael told me himself."

"That surprises me," said Jane.

"I know, it does seem unusual, but he was distraught and confused. Because you seem to have left him with the impression that he owes you a baby."

"We'll, we were engaged to be married and I was kind of counting on him to be the father of my children at one time."

"Yes, but that was a long time ago, Jane, as you well know. Why did you not express this intense desire you now seem to have to procreate with him at any time during all those years?"

Jane didn't have a good answer and hung her head.

"I'm not buying this biological clock fairy tale, Jane," said

Marguerite. "You're making this mischief out of sexual boredom and for no other reason."

"Well you can blame yourself for that," said Jane, her nerve returning a little as she realized Marguerite didn't plan to slap her.

"Oh?"

"Yes, if you hadn't invited me to the Venus Club dinner I wouldn't have been so vividly reminded of what I've been missing."

"You didn't seem to want him very badly when you had him," Marguerite observed, "as I recall you gave him up to me, Damaris and the scene at the time without so much as a fight."

"Of course I wanted him, he was my man. I enjoyed sex with him. He could never deny that. But I was up against the glamor of the scene that you were offering him. And I was too stubborn to find out what it was really all about."

"And then Hugo Sands enlightened you," Marguerite recalled.

"Yes, and by that time it was or seemed too late to get Michael back," said Jane.

"But now it doesn't?"

"I'm not trying to get him back," Jane protested, "I'm just having a little fun."

"Fun, is it? Let me show you something," said Marguerite, pulling a phone from an envelope purse she had been carrying under her arm and tapping it until a brutally adorable photo of she and Michael cuddling their baby girl appeared. This the redhead forced before Jane's gaze.

Jane laughed, "Marguerite, don't."

"Listen, Jane, you have to stop this nonsense with Michael at once. The time is not right for that. I'm far too recently married to be comfortable sharing my husband."

"I will," said Jane sincerely.

"But there is a new piece of nonsense you ought to start at once. You need to start working at this club."

"Work here? Me?"

"Yes, my love. And you *will* be my love from now on."

"But what would I do here? And why?"

"What you'd do would be to play. Why? Because you're restless."

"But what about Marnie?"

"I'm sure she'd be happier with you working here than having a passionate love affair with your ex."

As this conversation between Marguerite and Jane was taking place, Hope Lawrence happened to wander out the kitchen door into the back garden with its own beaten path leading into the woods. It was a warm afternoon beneath a cloudless blue sky and the trees were alive with soft summer sounds. Hope was about to light a joint before addressing the rather large task of making sure each of the playrooms and bedrooms were amply supplied with a set of paddles, straps, floggers and restraints when she noticed a bit of movement at the back of the house and espied young Dru Baxter standing at the very northwest corner, under one of the windows of the Cape Cod room, where the two visiting women happened to be. Hope put away her joint without lighting it and crept a little closer, observing with surprise that her trusted bus boy from the coffee shop, whom she had known, liked and respected for several years, appeared to be actually watching Marguerite and Jane, with his hand stuck down his jeans.

Going quickly and silently into the house again, Hope came back out just seconds later, leading Cassandra behind her by the hand, both taking care not to make a sound. They approached Dru so stealthily and quickly that he was surprised in his peeping before having time to even pull his hands from his pants. The women were upon him and he stood speechless and flushing with embarrassment before them. They spoke softly and firmly to him, Hope taking him by the arm and pulling him away from the window, back towards the garden, well out of earshot of their guests.

"Dru, what the hell?" asked Hope angrily.

"We're you spying on Marguerite and Jane?" Asked Cassandra.

"I was curious," Dru admitted, for within the room, Marguerite had begun to show Jane how the various pieces of furniture could work in a spanking scene and the tall, voluptuous redhead's gestures were fascinating to the young man who had once had such a large crush on the book store owner and was favored with her exquisite attentions on several occasions. Her employee had charmed Marguerite, for he had

151

worked at the bookstore for several years and was well known to her for his cheerful affability and worshipful devotion. Marguerite had rewarded him one season by making his submissive dreams come true, giving him a wonderful strapping and then, because she was in just the right mood, allowing him to possess her physically. The result had been bliss for Dru and perplexity for Marguerite, when she realized that she was subsequently pregnant and that the father could have been Dru, Michael Flagg or Anthony Newton. It had been rather a busy month for Marguerite, the month after splitting up with her first husband, Malcolm Branwell. Subsequently, Michael had taken a stray strand of hair from baby Felina's pillow and had it tested to prove beyond a doubt that she was his daughter. But this hadn't stopped Anthony Newton from generously endowing Marguerite with a nanny for the duration of Felina's toddlerhood. No one argued with this. The addition of Belinda Cowper to the household had allowed both Michael and Marguerite to tend their respective businesses as usual. Belinda was the sister of Anthony's English driver and personal assistant Dennis and she was every bit as pleasant and efficient an employee.

"This cannot go unpunished," declared Hope. Cassandra strove to conceal her surprise at her assistant's remark, thinking, "I guess I can't put off the man spanking thing indefinitely. Might as well get a little practice in."

"We should take him in the woods and give him a good switching!" Hope suggested, her wide blue eyes full of excitement.

"We'll each take a hand so he doesn't get away," said Cassandra, taking Dru by his wrist. Hope got on his other side, grabbed his pleasantly muscular upper arm and they began to pull the blond boy into the woods.

"I got a switching once from Hugo," confided Cassandra to Hope, as though Dru wasn't even there. "I hated it. It made me cry. It was in the woods too."

"I had exactly the same experience with David the year we moved here. It was outside the cottage and three strokes had me in tears," said Hope.

Both women noticed that Dru had not said a word more, though he was blushing furiously. Hope's eyes and Cassandra's eyes traveled down to Dru's jeans, just below his belt and at the same time noticed his burgeoning erection.

"You're lucky Miss Cassandra doesn't fire you," said Hope. Dru lowered his eyes and murmured, "I know."

"My only concern is that he might enjoy it. And then we'd be rewarding instead of punishing bad form," said Cassandra.

"Oh, he may think he'll enjoy it, but he won't," promised Hope, stopping them before a fallen tree trunk.

"Put your hands on the tree, lean forward and stick your bottom out," Cassandra instructed, "while we go find a switch." Dru obeyed without question and the pretty women began to search the ground.

"I suppose it should be me?" Cassandra said softly to Hope.

"Yes," Hope replied. "But then me. We'll each give him three swats."

"Oh look," said Hope, kneeling on the forest floor to gather long, thin twigs, "here's a bunch all around the same size. If you had something to tie them with we could make a version of a birch rod."

Cassandra spied a length of mulberry velvet ribbon threaded through Hope's braid and deftly extracted it, saying, "Tie it with this. Birch rods I like!"

"Me too," Hope agreed, "as long as whoever is using it isn't too hard. Which reminds me, we'd better make this quick. Mr. Bartlett will be here soon and if I'm not ready he'll make me suffer for it."

They returned to Dru, who was half leaning over the log and half looking nervously back over his shoulder.

"Of course, we should make him take his jeans down but I don't want to see his rude boy hard-on, do you, Miss Cassandra?" asked Hope, pushing Dru back down over the tree trunk and holding him down by his trim waist.

"No, I can do without that," the mistress of the house agreed, taking up the makeshift rod and aiming carefully to swat the nineteen year old soon to be college sophomore directly across the middle of his jeans clad seat. Dru cried out in surprise at the sharp, stinging, penetrating stroke that imparted such a painful kiss to his denim covered bottom. It was a trim, muscular, somewhat jutting backside and Cassandra had no doubt the downy skin beneath the pants was lily white with a tinge of pink coming up quickly in the wake of the lash.

"Good," Hope observed Dru's shudder, "he felt that, you can tell." Dru groaned in fearful anticipation of the next two swats, for he had overheard that each of his adorable persecutors planned to administer three. The next two strokes fell quickly and harder. Cassandra did not think herself capable of real cruelty to the handsome boy, but his respect for her as the head of the club was at stake and besides, she knew very well that most boys in the scene could take and indeed wanted sterner punishments than their female counterparts might. This time Dru strove to manfully muffle his cries. Cassandra handed the rod to Hope and they switched positions.

Now Hope got behind Dru and took aim just slightly below the strokes that Cassandra had placed crosswise upon Dru's backside.

"How dare you peep at our clients at play?" Hope demanded, laying down the first swat, twice as severely as Cassandra had done. This much stricter assault summoned forth a heavy grunt of pain from the no longer stoic Dru, who looked back at Hope reproachfully over one shoulder.

"Back in position, young man!" ordered Hope, raising her slender arm once more. "We reposed our trust in you and you betrayed it," continued Hope, striking once more with the same enthusiasm. Dru flinched but didn't cry out. "You're lucky we don't drag you back before Marguerite and Jane to let them express their indignation as well," said Hope, "but it would be bad policy to reveal such inexcusably indiscreet behavior to our very first customers ever."

"I'm so sorry," Dru moaned, then tensed for the final swat. Hope raised her arm and let go with full force, this final stroke eliciting a full-throated cry from the fair-haired miscreant.

"All right, then," said Cassandra, pulling Dru up, "run back to the house and return to your tasks and we'll mention this no more."

Dru looked at them both shyly, rubbing his hurt bottom through his jeans then impulsively seized Cassandra's hand, kissed it and then ran away back to the house.

Hope grinned at Cassandra and said, "You did well, my goddess. Shall we return now?" They walked back to the kitchen garden arm in arm.

Chapter Nineteen

Carola Arrives in the Village

Ambrose Bartlett arrived at the appointed hour and gave Hope and her schoolgirl style outfit a nod of approval. She led him into the library, where the bookshelves had been well stocked and several canes, paddles and straps placed in easy reach within a cabinet.

Having seen Marguerite and Jane out, Cassandra left the house for the railroad station, where her sister's train from Boston was about to arrive.

Carola disembarked in a pale gray suit, white shirt and black spectator pumps, carrying a small gray tweed suitcase and a black envelope purse. Her long, straight, glossy black hair fell forward over one brow a la Veronica Lake. Her lips were dark red, to match her fingernails and her usually pale face today held a delicate blush of embarrassment at needing to avail herself of the assistance of her older sister's new patron. It was a strikingly attractive face that defied the years and suggested that its owner was thirty rather than forty. Carola's willowy, size two figure contributed to the illusion. The eye was drawn to her tiny waist, sharply accented by the trim cut suit, then traveled down to the long, sheer hosed legs, which were strong and shapely after decades of scientific weight training. Cassandra's younger sister's expression, was, as always, nearly unreadable, as that lady hated to give anything away, even to a sister who had always meant her well.

"Well," said Carola's, once settled beside her sister in the sedan, "tell me what I can expect."

"You can expect me to get you thoroughly stoned as soon as we get to the house," Cassandra grinned, throwing the car in gear. Finally Carola smiled.

"That sounds delightful but I meant from Mr. Newton," said the

156

elegant brunette.

"I'm not exactly sure," Cassandra replied, "but I don't think you need worry too much. Anthony isn't sadistic. He just got peeved at the way you treated those girls."

"Why do these tops always want to spank mistresses?" Carola wondered, looking out the window as the familiar leafy foliage fringing the quaint village streets flashing by.

"Probably because they find them attractive," Cassandra smiled. "But mainly because they're not interested in subbing."

"All high powered men are secret subs," Carola said with finality.

"I think most men are switches, but there are still some hardcore tops and subs at either end of the spectrum. Do you really hate going sub?"

"No," Carola smiled, and Cassandra, "not if the man is good looking and rich!"

"That's what I thought. I'm actually jealous," said Cassandra.

"Why? What do you mean," said Carola with a start.

Cassandra confided candidly, "Well, I'm madly in love with him and we've only played a few times. Now that Susan is back, I doubt he'll stop by to be with me again in the near future. He'll be going back to New York at the end of the summer and I won't see him again for ever so long."

Carola understood why her sister was madly in love with her patron as soon as she entered the house. It all seemed very new, and everything within had been chosen in expensive good taste. As they walked through the various rooms and lounges Carola mentally ticked off how much had been spent on the furniture, the floors, the custom paint, the fixtures, the Ray Caesar prints and so on. In the corridor Dru Baxter was assisting William Random to install a network of spotlights to illuminate the framed portraits. William hadn't seen Carola in many years and they embraced warmly and duly admired how well the other had worn after all this time. Dru blushed, slightly bowed to Carola, whom he recognized instantly as a mistress, and gratefully obeyed Cassandra's command to go and make sure a guest bedroom was ready for her sister to occupy.

The girls continued on through the house, avoiding only one room, the library, from which cries and whimpers, punctuated by slapping sounds, had issued from the moment they had entered the west wing.

"My number one girl Hope is in there with the owner of Bartlett's," said Cassandra. Finally they went out to the garden, where Cassandra offered her sister a pipe.

"He'll never make the money that he spent on the place back in a hundred years," said Carola.

"I don't think he cares. This is his hobbyhorse. You wouldn't expect someone like Anthony Newton to want to come play regularly in a house that was anything less than beautiful, would you?"

"Who else is going to work for you?" asked Carola, her shoulders finally untensing for the first time since she'd gotten off the train.

"Well, the village is full of scene girls. There must be as many scene people per square foot in Random Point as there are in the San Fernando Valley. Most of them are hooked up with nice men. But the thing is, they've all dated each other's guys in the past and they all like each other enough to want to keep playing on the side. So, I expect the local players will use the club as a private make out mansion. Then, Anthony knows a lot of pros he's going to invite to visit. You know a mistress named Isabel Bruno?"

"Of course, she's from New York. She's a pain in the butt," said Carola, because Isabel Bruno was popular and exciting.

"Anthony's been seeing her for years. She'll be coming out. And that B&D model Teresa Clifford, she's another one he said he'll be flying in."

"She'll book sessions," said Carola sagely, for this was true of any young lady who had appeared in scores of videos over the years.

"Then there's a Boston business woman who needs an outlet for her perversity, I think her name is Marion. She'll be a once a week whipping girl for sure."

"You need to give her a sexier name," said Carola, passing the pipe back with a sudden sense of calm enjoyment. She was almost disposed to be grateful to her sister for letting her into this new world of opportunity.

"What are you going to do about Amanda?" Carola wondered.

Cassandra had more or less kept Carola's niece away from her aunt these many years, for fear that Carola would urge Amanda to adopt extreme diets in order to remain razor thin. Amanda had met her aunt, but not often. When Amanda returned to Random Point to spend the last month before sophomore year in the village, that would certainly change. The niece would know the aunt and the aunt the niece. Cassandra didn't think it would be a good match up. Her sister would be fiercely and intensely jealous of Amanda's beauty.

"Luckily, her formidable boyfriend keeps her occupied most of the time. Also, she did a few sessions last year; with that same man you hear beating the hell out of my lieutenant. I think that satisfied her curiosity about sessions."

Late in the afternoon, Susan Ross arrived at the house with a basket of food from Anthony's kitchen for his little club staff to share. Susan was introduced to Carola, who closely scrutinized the petite blonde in the khaki shorts, cropped white cotton shirt, high collared urban walkers and crew socks. Still in her 20's, Susan had nothing to hide. Her goldenrod hair, bound in a high ponytail almost reached her waist and figure was near perfect.

"Oh, he's so thoughtful," said Cassandra, passing out the Bahn Mei sandwiches to Hope, Dru, Susan and Carola, who now sat around the large wooden kitchen table with her.

"There's a coconut chili salad and cucumber soup too," said Susan, turning to Carola and explaining, "He's never had even one cook let alone two and he's really enjoying showing them off." Making every effort to appear carelessly casual, Susan was surveying Carola every bit as minutely as the older woman had done her. The commercial illustrator immediately noticed large differences between the warm, supple, relaxed Cassandra and her brittle, icy sister. The similarity was their prettiness.

On arriving home about five p.m., Susan began looking around the house for Anthony. She found him in the music room at the piano, working on his new score. She curled up on the closest love seat and waited for him to look up. When he did she said, "I met Carola."

"What did you think of her?"

"She could give ice lessons on being cold."

"Ha!"

"Yeah, you can count me out of that scenario where I'm supposed to tie her."

He grinned, "Don't tell me she intimidated you."

"Hell yes, she did."

"Well, never mind. I'll take care of her myself," he replied.

"Tonight?"

"Maybe tomorrow, after she's worked herself up into a state of nervous anxiety about it."

The next day Pamela Bartlett invited Hope Lawrence to her studio atelier on the top floor of her husband's department store. This suite had been designed especially for Ambrose Bartlett's latest wife and reflected her smart, modern tastes. The girls ate at Pamela's long table desk. The sleek brunette hostess had ordered up a large Caesar salad and two modest portions of Parmesan flat bread from the excellent in-store cafe. Pamela herself made the former barista an espresso in her own well-equipped pantry and the girls fell to nibbling.

"Your workspace is divine," said Hope, having eaten enough, getting up to wander around the studio, which even included its own bedroom lounge.

"Hope," said Pamela, "I know I've always been awful to you. The Betty and Veronica thing. You understand, I'm sure. So I have no right to ask you for a favor."

"Oh, you haven't been that awful," Hope laughed, "I do get the Betty and Veronica thing. And we *are* both in the Venus Club, aren't we? What can I do for you?"

"Well, it has to do with Ambrose, of course. I know he's going to be using the new club as his personal bordello from now on."

"A lot of our close friends will," Hope predicted.

'I know, but between his new mistress, you being here and all those new subs he wants to test drive, he's gonna be there a lot," said Pamela.

"Ambrose has a mistress?"

"Yes, Polyxena Guzman. I predict she'll be the first guest slut he brings in."

"You don't seem particularly distressed," Hope observed, thinking that she herself would be greatly alarmed to discover that David had been running after the platinum blonde Dutch woman. Pamela shrugged, then actually flashed Hope the first mischievous grin that Hope had ever seen on the face of the fashion designer.

"I've been seeing someone on the side as well," said Pamela. "He's very nice and no trouble at all, Dru Baxter."

"Aw, how nice for him," said Hope, "he's such a cute boy."

"Is he behaving himself at the house?"

"No, not at all. But what do you expect, throwing him into that environment? And furthermore, are you sure it was wise to put him at the command of several women? He could easily become a subbed out little bitch."

"Oh, I know. He already is one. Didn't you see how I boss him around? But he's also nineteen, with all the riotous virility that implies. I'm using him for pure, vanilla sex."

"I get that. What can I do to help?"

"Well, I don't want you to tell me whenever Ambrose has been there. That would be betraying a scene confidence and also, if he found out you'd informed on him, he'd book a special session with you just to thrash you."

"Yeah, I agree. You know your husband well."

"What I'd appreciate once in a while is an all clear," said Pamela. "You let me know at what point in a particular week he's done all the playing he's likely to do. And then I might breeze by for a quick meet with my boy Dru."

"I can do that without fail, Pamela," promised Hope.

On returning to the club, Hope found Cassandra and Carola in the office, each at one of the desks, checking their mail.

"You know ladies, I was thinking," said Hope, "if Mr. Newton isn't going to be coming by until this evening, we ought to work on getting Carola a few local sessions today."

"Did you have someone in mind?" Cassandra asked.

"Well, I can certainly propose it to Dru," Hope said, with a grin. "He only got a little taste of it in the woods with us. He's probably burning up for a proper session."

"You're talking about that cute boy who helps out around here?" Carola asked.

"Yes," said Hope, "he needs a spanking."

"What are the house rates, by the way?" Carola asked.

Cassandra and Hope looked at each other.

"They're going to be on a sliding scale," said Hope.

"With special consideration for locals," Cassandra added.

"Except for millionaires like Ambrose Bartlett," said Hope; "We charged him six for the hour with me. He didn't question it, especially after Mr. Newton spent a couple of hundred grand at his store furnishing this place. But he wouldn't anyway. That's what he expects to have to pay. Plus he tipped me a hundred."

"What do you think Dru could comfortably pay?" Carola asked.

"Two hundred," said Cassandra. "But for a half hour."

"50/50 split?" asked Carola.

"60/40 your favor but the house will do your tax withholdings on that," said her sister. "Anthony's accountant is going to let us know how much that should be."

"Bless that man!" said Hope. The two fortunate women beamed at each other. Then the infinitely practical blonde said, "We have to be smart when new talent is in town and make the most of our time. Now I just remembered someone else I could call!"

Hope took her phone out to the garden and called Braemar Prep, where her husband was a teacher and an amiable young man named Freddie Johansen managed its computer networks. Hope remembered that at the Venus Club dinner, Freddie's girlfriend, Alison Albrecht, had stated that her lover was a switch. She had known Freddie, as David's co-worker and a perpetual guest at Hugo's parties, for several years and this being the case, didn't feel he would resent a call of this nature. But when she connected with him on the phone, for the sake of discretion she pretended they needed some help at the new house with their computer cabling and asked if he could come by after the close of the school day. Freddie didn't know what house she was talking about and Hope quickly explained that she had a new job full time managing a social club with several computers on the same network and his expertise was required in hooking them up. Freddie didn't question this, as his friends were always asking him to help them with their systems. He took down the address and promised he would be there at four. Hope went back inside and explained what she had done.

"Now, him we'll charge three for the hour," said Hope.

"You're pretty sure he'll agree?" Carola asked.

"I am," Hope said serenely.

She found Dru arranging furniture in the schoolroom. He had worked the previous afternoon putting together the school desks and chairs that had been delivered.

"Did you know that Cassandra's sister Carola, a famous mistress from Boston, is staying here for a few days?" Hope asked.

"I did get introduced but they never mentioned the mistress part," Dru admitted. "She does look terrifying dominant," he added with a grin.

"She's going to be here until tomorrow morning. Why don't you go to your ATM, take out two hundred dollars and present yourself to Mistress Carola for a session?"

"I could do that?" he flushed with excitement, there being no part of the suggestion he didn't like. He was living at home with his parents this summer between freshman and sophomore year and had no expenses besides gas.

"Yes, but do it at once. She's going to be booked at four and then again this evening, so the sooner the better. She'll be waiting for you in the library."

Cheerful Freddie Johanson was a big, squarely built yet youthfully attractive man in his late 30's, who behaved impeccably enough to satisfy the requirements of his demanding girlfriend, a very pretty but somewhat neurotic submissive he had found right in Random Point. Freddie and Alison were invited to scene parties and were acknowledged players. Even so, Hope felt some trepidation when Freddie arrived at the house at the appointed hour.

She met him at the front door and led him straight back to her office. He looked around him as he followed her, saying, "What a beautiful house. You don't work at the bookstore anymore?"

"No, I work here." Now they were in the office and she shut the door behind them. "This is a spanking club and there's nothing wrong with our computers. I just made that up in case that line we were talking on wasn't private," Hope explained.

"Did you say it's a spanking club?" Freddie asked.

"Yes. It's a club for doing sessions, deluxe, with all the frills. We haven't officially opened yet. Come to that, we may never officially open. For now you can think of it as your local BDSM social club with visiting pro tops and subs, rentable dungeon space for couples and deep discounts for locals."

"A club right here in Random Point, that's a dream come true," said Freddie appreciatively.

"I thought you'd feel that way, though I hardly know you," Hope admitted. "The thing is, we've got a beautiful spanking mistress from Boston here for just one day and I thought you might like to take advantage of this opportunity to play with her in this fine new facility. We just finished putting together the schoolroom."

"That sounds so interesting," said Freddie, "but I don't have much cash on me. How much would it be?"

"For you, three hundred an hour. You can bring us the allowance tomorrow," said Hope.

"That's very nice of you. And it was smart not to mention this on the phone," he said.

"I hope I'm not putting you on the spot. You don't have to do this now. Carola will be back. I mean, if you want to think it over," Hope suggested.

"No, I'm completely up for this. You were absolutely correct to think of me. And the schoolroom would be perfect," he assured her.

Anthony Newton had called to say that he would see Carola that evening at eight. At seven Cassandra joined her sister in her bedroom to see what she was wearing. Carola had just gotten out of the shower and was wrapped in a light cotton robe.

"I was going to wear those," Carola gestured to the garments she had laid out on the bed. Cassandra looked at the white leather dress and long line open bottomed girdle for a moment.

"It's a very cool dress," said Cassandra. "But are you sure you want to make him work that hard to uncover you?"

"What do you mean?" asked Carola tensely, "I thought he was way into retro."

"I'm just saying, you've got a heavy leather skirt going on and then the girdle is another form of body armor. Seems like he'd have to start with a hairbrush or cane just for you to feel anything at all."

"Well, what do you suggest?" asked Carola.

"Let me see what else you brought," said the older sister, looking into the armoire. "Oh, Carola, this is stunning," said Cassandra; pulling out a raspberry waist cinch corselet with the classic eight garter straps and a fichu of cream tulle edging the cleavage. "And so much sexier than that huge girdle. Wait here a minute, I have the perfect dress to go over it," said Cassandra, going into her suite for a minute. She returned with a smoky blue and rose print sundress over her arm. "I got it for Amanda but she won't mind you wearing it first. It's a Betsy Johnson. And look, it has a darling pink crinoline slip sewn in," said Cassandra, spreading the full skirted dress out on the bed. "He loved that you wore a crinoline under your dress the day we visited you at your studio," Cassandra added.

"You won his heart and I pissed him off," said Carola, "so I guess I'll take your advice."

"Need help getting into the corset?" asked Cassandra. Carola looked at her, as much as to say, "Be yourself." Slipping off her wrapper and taking up the fitted, boned garment, she easily snapped the six front hooks into place in front, then caught up the back laces behind her and pulled them snugly in, tying them in a back bow. Next Carola stepped into a scrap of raspberry G-string and then sat on an upholstered chair to carefully pull on her sheer, beige nylon seamed stockings. Cassandra hadn't seen her sister undressed in years and was relieved to see that in spite of Carola's thinness, she still had a curvy bottom that was prettily revealed and framed by the hem of the corset, which girded her hips and the tops of the stockings encasing her shapely upper thighs. Together they selected a medium high pair of black patent leather pumps from the collection of heels the Boston mistress had brought. Then the dainty, torso-hugging dress was slipped on and zipped up the back. The fit was very good and looking at her reflection in a mirror, Carola thanked her sister.

"Where will I be seeing him?" Carola asked. Cassandra led her sister to the room Anthony had requested, the navy blue chamber which had been fitted that day with tall, gold framed mirrors that handsomely accented the burgundy velvet upholstered furniture. The predominant piece was a long, deep, high backed tufted sofa, set against one wall. There were a few high backed, armless chairs in the same material and a spanking horse and whipping post covered in burgundy leather. Carola immediately became pleasurably transfixed by her image in the mirrors that decorated two walls of the playroom.

"Now how can we soften him up?" asked Carola, "does he get high?"

"Not very often," said Cassandra, "but I'll bring some wine. And meanwhile, you can smoke a little weed and relax."

"I guess I might as well," Carola sighed, following her sister out of the room.

As Cassandra serenely busied herself opening a bottle of Pinot Noir and filling a crystal carafe with water, then delivering these with glasses to the velveteen dungeon, her heart had begun to pound with excitement at the eminent arrival of her patron.

Anthony arrived at eight sharp, immaculately groomed, clad in a light summer suit and carrying a small briefcase. When Cassandra opened the door to admit him he embraced her warmly, locking his arms around her waist.

"Is she waiting?" he asked.

"Yes," Cassandra replied.

"Is she apprehensive?"

"Yes, very. I put her in a frou-frou dress for you."

"Nice!" He looked at Cassandra closely, brushing the hair back from her brow before kissing her there. "Oh, honey, I'm sorry we had to stop seeing each other so abruptly, but you understand that with Susan in town, I can't do that so much."

Cassandra smiled up at him mildly, her heart once again pounding hard.

"I'll be here for you when you want me," she promised, bringing his hand to her lips and kissing it.

"You're a sweet girl. I'm so glad you came back to us. Okay, take me to her."

Carola had been perched demurely on the edge of a chair, but she sprang to her feet when the door opened and Anthony strode in.

"Hello," he said, closing the door behind him. He cast his gaze over her up and down without smiling, but ended by looking penetratingly into her eyes. She instantly dropped her own gaze, a delicate blush spreading across her high cheekbones in her handsome, lightly olive toned face. He put the briefcase down on a table and seeing the open bottle of wine and glasses, went and poured a half glass for each of them. He handed her one, saying, "You know why you're here, right?"

She sipped her wine, raising her large, dark eyes to him in some confusion. It had been ages since she had done a submissive session and never with a client this powerful. Her mind blanked as she tried to remember what they wanted the submissive to say.

"Because of how I treated Lydia when you visited my dungeon," she finally decided to say.

"Yes," he nodded, downing his wine in two gulps and putting the glass down.

"But if you only knew what that girl is really like," Carola protested suddenly. "Let me show you her Fetlife page. There are pictures of her at The Armory in the most severe breast bondage. And others of her hooked up to monstrous machines. And several with a corrugated bucket on her head!"

"That would only distress me without mitigating your own bad behavior in the slightest," he replied. "That girl is obviously too submissive for her own good and people like you are taking advantage of her."

Carola stubbornly folded her arms, saying, "I disagree!"

"You have a great look," he said, "but I don't care for the haughty mistress persona. It's fake."

"Submissive men seem to enjoy it," she retorted.

"If that's the case, why are you broke?"

All mistresses are broke," she sighed. "It seems to go with the territory. Maybe we spend too much on corsets."

"Is that what you have on under that pretty dress?"

"Yes."

"You begin to interest me," he admitted, smiling at her for the first time.

"What's in the briefcase?" she asked.

"A pair of stainless steel dildos, six inches long and linked on a chain."

Carola looked so surprised that he laughed, "Don't tell me you have a problem being penetrated."

"I... just didn't realize that's where this was going," she admitted. "A pair, did you say?"

"Don't worry, I'll double your allowance," he assured her. "But I never met a girl who needed to be forced to orgasm more than you do." Carola not only found nothing to object to in his statements, but the reference to doubling her allowance caused her lips to curve into a smile that she herself was unconscious of.

"Come here," said Anthony, suddenly taking her by the hand and pulling her towards the long sofa. Unbuttoning his jacket, he sat down and drew her across his lap. "Give me your wrist," he said, taking it and pulling her arm back to her waist. She turned to look over her shoulder at him but instead became arrested by their image reflected in the large, gilt-edged mirror opposite. Anthony followed her gaze and not letting go of her wrist, with his other hand brushed her smooth, straight, shiny black hair behind one ear, to fully reveal her face.

"I love this mirror effect, don't you?" he asked. "We look like an A-list couple in one of the better spanking videos." He patted her through the skirt and crinoline. "I like this," he said, folding back her skirt and then the stiff, multi layered petticoat. Carola watched with fascination. "Oh, look at that, a corset with no panties on," he said, running his sensitive pianist's fingers across her velvety bottom.

"G-string with this type of corset," she murmured, pillowing her head on her free hand with her face turned to the mirror, enjoying the illusion of still being in her 20's, that being over his knee created.

"Are you ready?" he asked.

"Not really, but go ahead, the suspense is killing me."

Anthony reached under the hem of the corset to pull down her G-string to her stocking tops.

"How long has it been since anyone spanked you?"

"A very long time," she replied.

"Can you even remember if you ever could take a good spanking?"

"Of course I can."

"Well, you know you can always say mercy," he noted.

"At these rates?" she replied in surprise.

"You're the dungeon dragon, not me," he pointed out.

"I just thought..." she hesitated.

"What?"

"Oh, since you considered me so cruel that you planned to beat the hell out of me to teach me a lesson."

"I'll admit that was my plan," he sighed, "but what with the dress and the corset and you acting human, I'm feeling less hostile and more sympathetic."

He felt Carola untense across his lap as she finally looked away from the mirror and down at the dark, polished wooden floor. Then he did begin spanking her small but very nicely rounded bottom, no differently than he would have spanked her sister or Susan Ross. For in spite of his fleeting fantasy of inflicting a severe punishment on a lady he perceived to be heartless, he could not be other than himself and so ended by charming instead of devastating her. Once she was properly warmed up, which she expressed by lying inertly across his lap, he made her get up and got her out of her dress.

"I don't mind passive girls," he said, running his hands over the incurving sides of the glove tight waist cinch. "I take it as a sign that they're relaxed." Carola didn't know if she was being complimented or mildly criticized. She made no reply but turned to face him, showing off the bodice top that lifted and thrust her small cleavage forward. "Normally, I love this kind of thing," he said, turning her around again and beginning to expertly unlace her by pulling on the bow at her waist and beginning to loosen it; "but you're so slender, all

169

these garments are overwhelming you. I want you out of them all. Then maybe you'll be less constrained." As soon as the corset was slightly loosened, Carola was able to pop the front clasps and shed it in one motion, though she held it up against her body until Anthony had unfastened all eight garters.

He smiled at her, "Feels good when you take that off, doesn't it? Don't deny it, all my girls corset and they all tell me it feels really good when you take it off."

Now the corset was laid aside and he made her sit fully nude beside him and put her legs in his lap so he could roll down her stockings and take them off along with her heels.

"There isn't much to you, is there?" he teased, caressing her waist. "Why do you even bother corseting? It's beside the point." He stood her up before him and led her to the spanking bench. There was a level to kneel on and one to bend over. He bent her over now. "You look so much prettier and so much younger without all that gear on," he said, petting her like a favorite cat. "I can't believe you're getting to me like this."

Carola flashed him a look over her shoulder that showed his kindness confused her. Yet she began to relax just a little more.

"Don't move," said Anthony, going to a large, highly polished walnut bureau and smoothly sliding open the middle drawer. "Oh good, it's here," he said, removing the sole implement that had occupied that new, cedar scented space, a fresh, nicely trimmed birch rod. "They were selling these as novelties at the Boston Corners trading post the other day when Susan drove in from New York. She cleaned them out of their stock. We had them sent over to the house today and your sister has put one in each playroom. Do you like the birch?"

"Yes."

"Since you're sufficiently warmed up, this will be real. Are you ready?" he asked, swooshing the birch and placing his hand on the small of her back. She caught her breath at the sound but she now glimpsed her side reflection in another mirror and watched mesmerized as he raised his hand and let go with the first swat of the multi twigged rod against her out thrust bottom. Again he struck her smartly, raising a bouquet of pink roses across her slim cheeks each time he let fly. As she didn't cry out in distress he began to swat rapidly, whipping the fragile and ephemeral instrument against her firm, muscular buttocks hard and fast, until tiny pieces of the twigs began to flake off. Finally Carola began to react, not by screaming, but by panting. She gripped the bench with both hands and rode the pleasurably stimulating yet painful sensations delivered by her glamorous client with something amounting to abandon by the unemotional brunette.

"Isn't there anything you want me to do for you?" she softly asked, turning her large dark eyes towards him.

"What could you do for me?" he asked with interest, laying down the birch and going to open the briefcase.

"I could pleasure you with my mouth,' she suggested. "I'm very good at that."

"Are you trying to distract me from forcing you to have an orgasm with these? Or just trying to be honorable?" he brought the shiny stainless steel phalluses back for her to examine, showing her the small bottle of sheer lubricant he had also placed in the briefcase.

"Neither," she replied, "I just know I would come faster if you filled my mouth with your cock at the same time you were masturbating me. That would focus me completely and it would be hot."

"It's a good idea," he agreed, "filling you in every possible way." He was also relieved that she had come up with a way for them to enjoy each other completely while avoiding classic sex. He didn't think it right to cheat on Susan with any more ladies at the moment and he didn't want Carola to be able to tell Cassandra that he had made love to her too. Opening the bottle of lube, he began to coat the shiny toys. Carola continued gazing at her own reflection until he blocked her view.

The balmy morning after her sister's scene with Anthony, Cassandra drove Carola back to the station to catch her Boston train. They left plenty of time to stop in the nearby patisserie to enjoy espressos and croissants. Carola seemed pleased and more at ease than

Cassandra had yet seen her since coming back east.

"Did it go okay?" Cassandra asked tentatively.

"Yeah, yeah, it went great. Thanks for the hook up," Carola said, the blood rushing to her normally pale face. Cassandra's heart contracted with vicarious excitement as she inferred from her sister's embarrassed yet happy expression that she had been intimate in some way with the composer. "He's a dreamboat. It wasn't only the best paid session I've ever had, it was the best session content wise."

Cassandra smiled but was glad that Carola was going back to town.

Chapter Twenty

Colby and Amanda Head Toward the Midnight Sun

Amanda and Colby parted company with Diana Currie and Ronnie Van Horn in the Central Station on the morning of their third day in Amsterdam. The small married brunette and her college boy had decided to travel south to Spain while Amanda and Colby were bound north to Scandinavia, each couple to continue on their summer rambles, though Diana would have to cut her own tour short in the space of a week to return home to her husband and toddler in Manhattan.

En route to Copenhagen, Amanda and Colby fell in with a small party of Cambridge students whose beer drinking capacities made Colby's consumption appear modest. Amanda didn't like beer and disapproved of the effect enormous amounts of it had on her boy, but determined to bear with these excesses pleasantly until they had shaken loose their companions. Upon reaching the Danish capital she and Colby would repair to the nice little hotel into which she had booked them, while their rowdy new friends would stumble into the cleanest hostel they could find and they would likely not run into each other for the rest of their stay. What Amanda didn't reckon with was the fact that at this point in the summer, virtually every hotel in Scandinavia with less than four stars would be packed solid with drunken students from every nation in the world eagerly seeking the midnight sun, as much spontaneous sex as possible and of course, ever more beer.

They managed to detach from the group one afternoon, taking the train to a village several hours from the city with a small, sixteenth century castle, which Amanda estimated could comfortably accommodate no more than a few dozen souls, though it had its own playhouse. Had Hamlet been staged there? It made sense. They took a long walk through the nearby town, ending up at a beach, where a few small groups of young people were sunbathing and of course, drinking beer. It made Colby thirsty to see this and conversations were soon struck up, leading to the sharing of beer.

Colby had never been happier. He loved trying new beers and it tasted even better with Amanda beside him. Of course, all the ale in Europe couldn't compare with the rarified thrills he had enjoyed in the Paris hotel with Diana, Amanda and Susan's gift to him, but he couldn't expect his girlfriend to spend her whole summer placing other pretty women over his lap.

By the time they got to Stockholm Amanda's patience with her bar hopping boyfriend began to wear razor thin. The affable English students had been replaced by even harder drinking Germans. They had all gone in a group to view the original Viking ships and the raucous hilarity of that group embarrassed Amanda in a way that being naked in a dungeon never could. After watching Colby pass out blind drunk three nights in a row, Amanda staged a revolt. They had just boarded the night train to Oslo and had been able to book a sleeper car.

"You'd better take a few nights off drinking," Amanda recommended to her slightly hung over traveling companion.

"Fine," he agreed.

"And let's not travel in a pack anymore," she pressed her obvious morning-after advantage to propose. "Those boys were all looking at me. And not with the pure, disinterested intentions of spankers. They all wanted to rape me."

"Well, you do put it out there," said Colby objectively. "That dress you have on, for example, it's way too short and clearly you aren't wearing a bra."

Amanda knew her halter sundress was too short and blushed.

"Do you want me to change?" she asked, half defiantly.

"No. In fact, thank you for giving me a good excuse to spank you on the train. If my head ever stops pounding."

"Why is it that the blonder men get the drunker they get?" Amanda wondered.

"Japanese men drink hard too, like that kid from yesterday."

"That's true, he's the one who said he wanted to *lape* me," Amanda remembered.

When they discovered that the door had a lock they considered spanking and sex in the train.

"Like in that Milo Manara book," said Amanda.

"I like the way he draws women. But his men look like girls too," Colby pointed out. "And there wasn't nearly enough spanking in a book he called The Art of Spanking."

"But there was sex in a train with a skinny girl with short hair, like me," said Amanda.

They fell silent, each listening to the rhythmic sound of the train as it chugged along.

The conductor came to the door and knocked to check their tickets. They asked how long before the next stop and he said ninety minutes. They locked the door.

Colby pulled her across his lap and waited to start smacking her bottom through the skirt that barely covered it, determined to sync his smacks with the pistoning of the train. Always in complete agreement about not drawing attention to themselves, Colby kept the swats as quiet as he could and Amanda made no sound. Both were half on edge, wondering if the train clacking really masked the smacks. But the motion and sounds of the train were hypnotic and Amanda soon fell into a sensual swoon across her lover's muscular thighs.

Presently he pulled her panties off and unzipped his jeans. She straddled his lap facing him and he took her smooth oval cheeks, still warm from his hand, back into them, squeezing them hard as pulled her against him. She deftly reached into his back pocket for a condom and unsheathed it for him. He let go of her momentarily to put it on then reached into his nearby pack for lube. They matched their thrusts to the rhythm of the train for an extra sensory boost, relishing the novelty of the tryst for a quarter of an hour.

That night it rained but although the skies were heavy with clouds, it never seemed to darken at all. They finally pulled the shades in order to sleep.

They arrived in Oslo in the early morning and were able to check their bags at their hotel, but their room would not be available to them until three. Meanwhile they repaired to the dining room for a smorgasbord breakfast, which Colby had been declaring was the best feature of these northern countries. Amanda helped herself to poached eggs, toast and half honeydew. Colby piled his plate high with cured meats, pickled herring and other items that Amanda found revolting. Then they boarded a tram for Frogner Park, where they spent hours viewing the eccentric and erotic statues and fountains. Amanda found the expensive fur shops opposite the park both fascinating and horrid and expressed her aversion to that industry while admiring the beauty of the full-length sables displayed in the windows.

Next they traveled by tram to the city center and visited the museum, then went for a comfortable lunch of roasted chicken and dumplings in the small cafe beside it. On the waterfront, they looked at the ships and boats in the harbor. They had been reading Hunger by Knut Hamsun in the train the previous night. Many of the stone and brick apartment buildings they strolled by in downtown Oslo had stood cold, hard and bitter from Hamsun's time. They discussed the unthinkable, that which had never happened to them, having to walk about hungry, without money to buy food.

"Did you ever read The House of Mirth?" Amanda asked Colby.

"Edith Wharton, right? I've seen it on my mother's bookshelf, but haven't read it."

"There's a scene at the end of that that's the twin of the one we just read in Hunger. Only the heroine is starving on the streets of New York in the 1890's. She has a little room, works as a hat trimmer, but she doesn't have enough money to eat. She winds up committing suicide, cold and hungry in her little room, clutching a doll."

"I remember seeing the movie with Gillian Anderson," said Colby. "Didn't she gamble her small inheritance away and then was too proud to ask her boyfriend for help, even though he was a successful society lawyer?"

"That was the perversely novelistic part of the story. But the hunger part seemed very real to me," said Amanda, reaching into her pocket for a chocolate covered marzipan bar, which she divided in half and shared with Colby.

Walking through the less upscale Oslo neighborhoods, they speculated at how inhospitable these streets might seem when darkness fell at four pm amid wintry winds and thick falling snow. Then they marveled at how many natives went for a walk with their cats on their shoulders. "I can't get over it," said Colby. "What if a cat sees a rat? Will it ever return to its owner?"

"First of all, cats own people, not vice versa. And the answer is that the cat would follow their trail back to their original starting point, which would presumably be their house."

That night they saw a production of A Doll's House in Norwegian with English subtitles scrolling on a crawler above the stage. In the intermission, Amanda ate ice cream profiteroles while Colby downed two pints of local ale. After the subtle production of what Amanda considered to be one of the best plays in the world, they repaired to the closest pub for a late supper of lamb chops and roasted potatoes. Colby was charmed to find the pub an adjunct to a local microbrewery he had been hearing about but had yet to try. Amanda didn't care for alcohol in the same way that Colby did, but she could enjoy a glass of wine with a meal. This time, to keep him company in his mirth and continue the animated discussion they were having about Norah and Torvald, she drank two glasses of wine. Presently, Amanda became quite drunk and noticed herself weaving when she went to the bathroom. While she was washing her hands, and admiring the excellent Scandinavian design of the faucets and sinks, the room began to spin around her. "Why does anyone like this?" she wondered.

Normally competent at getting them on the right form of transport at the right time and pointed in the right direction, Colby fumbled on the way home and they wound up on a train going out to the suburbs instead of back to the neighborhood where their hotel was. Waiting for the return train Amanda began to sober up.

"Next time I go to Europe I'll take someone who can actually read a map," she said.

"Anyone can make a mistake," he said, looking down the empty tracks.

"It's my fault too. I wanted to see what you find so attractive about being in a drunken stupor and I drank too much to think straight."

It was almost midnight and the skies were only just being transformed by an extended twilight. Colby sat down on the bench and Amanda sat on his lap, winding her arms around his neck and burying her face in his shoulder. He put his arms around her waist and they waited quietly for the train.

The next day they took the spectacular train route to Bergen, which sped past forests, alpine lakes and a wide range of lush pastoral landscapes. They reached their picture postcard destination, a charming little seaside city, which looked as though it had been built by trolls, in the late afternoon.

After checking into their attractive small hotel, refreshing themselves with coffee and sandwiches at a nearby cafe, visiting a chemist's shop to replenish Colby's store of condoms and buying Amanda a set of blue and pink haired trolls at a tourist shop, they went into an Internet cafe and checked their email. Since they had entered Scandinavia all connections had functioned at maximum efficiency and Colby suggested that Amanda might want to call her mother. Amanda agreed and sent Cassandra their number at the hotel, asking her to call if she could within the hour. They went back to their room and tried having sex with the new condoms. But the Swedish condom proved too small and broke on being slid down over Colby's massive column. They agreed to rely on the pull out and shoot method until they were able to locate better condoms. Colby was just as eager to switch to anal sex, but Amanda was determined to dole that pleasure out to him only once in a while, due to the inconvenience. Colby was just as happy with the new method as he liked to ejaculate porno star style, upon or against her smooth, firm bottom cheeks.

While they were dozing in each other's arms after this satisfying act, their room phone rang. It was Cassandra, delighted to speak to her daughter for the first time since she had left for Europe.

"Oh darling," said Cassandra, "I'm so glad you're over eighteen! You are so going to love my new house."

"Are you really well and truly settled in?" Amanda asked. "I mean, what is it like? Will there be room for me to stay there when we get back in August?"

"Yes, there are two extra bedrooms. Everything is beautiful, sleek and new. I ordered most of the furniture from your friend, Ambrose Bartlett and it's all top of the line. The house is right on the edge of the woods, right down the road from Michael Flagg's place. You can just hear the brook if you go out in the back garden. And we've already started hosting sessions. Your aunt Carola has already come in from Boston and Mr. Newton spoiled her rotten. Oh, I let her borrow that Betsy Johnson dress I got for you. It looked so cute on her."

"I can't believe all this has happened in so short a time," said Amanda.

"Everything has happened," Cassandra agreed.

"Have you talked to Eddie lately?"

"Eddie? Oh, Eddie! You know, I haven't thought about him since I got back here. I ought to send him a thank you note. Can we get Colby's family to send him a case of wine?"

"Mother, are you seriously not hurt by what Eddie did?"

"Amanda, my sex life has improved by five hundred percent since I've come back to Random Point without even involving Hugo. Oh and I hope you can wrap your head around the fact that we're practically having sex with the same set of people."

"Mother, what on earth do you mean?"

"Don't tell anyone, but I did Michael Flagg."

"What?"

"And not only that, I got him stoned."

"Why Michael?"

"He stopped in one night on his way home from the bar to check on me. And things just happened."

"And who else?"

"Mr. Newton."

"Does Susan know?"

"She sensed something and that made her come home sooner. She's being angelic about it though. But don't tell her what I told you. Hope knows, of course. She's my new best friend. She works here with me every day. She did the first session of the club, with Mr. Bartlett. I adore her."

179

"But what's it all about? Is it a real BDSM club, like Doma?'

"More like Mr. Newton's clubhouse that he's sharing with his friends and letting his favorite girls work out of. I came to him with some vague idea about having a little club and he created a luxurious environment that won't ever earn enough to pay for even its own maintenance."

"Is it going to be alright if I bring Colby home with me?"

"Yes, I'm sure it will."

"What did she say about me staying?" Colby asked when Amanda put down the phone a few minutes later.

"She said it was fine."

"What were you expressing so much amazement at?" Colby asked.

"It's really a club. My aunt sessioned there the other night."

"You have an aunt in the scene?"

"Yes. She's very beautiful. I've only met her a few times."

"A dignified top lady or a crazy slut like her niece?"

"An icy dominatrix," Amanda said.

"Your mom is full of surprises, or has she always been this way?"

"No, you met her. At any other time she would have been barraging me with questions about the trip, as any mom would. But suddenly her own life has gotten even more interesting."

The following morning, they wandered through the riotously colorful harbor market, which was wonderful to look at but stank too much of fish to please Amanda altogether. They noticed ferries departing for day tours of the fjords and found they were just in time to buy tickets for the last boat leaving that day.

They began the epic cruise in the middling dining room where Colby ate heartily of everything offered from sausage to herring, while Amanda made a simple meal of eggs and toast. Then they hung on the rail for hours, gliding through Norway's lush waterways, awed by breathtaking cliffs rising and falling on either side of the ferry as they went. They talked about Led Zeppelin's Immigrant Song, Scandinavian films they had seen and Norway's enviable economy. Colby counseled Amanda to continue taking economics classes with him at Harvard, opining that unadorned liberal arts degrees were now completely worthless. In spite of it being summer, the breeze was brisk and Amanda was glad of her thick sweater and the added warmth of Colby's arms around her as she leaned back against him and they watched the waterfowl wheel overhead.

The boat docked at a small village with an unpronounceable name and one rudimentary cafe where they ordered cheese sandwiches and coffee. After a short stroll, all the passengers returned to the ferry for the final leg of the water cruise. Then they once again debarked and boarded a bus that navigated a narrow Forrest road that seemed to climb a mountain before descending again and carrying them back to Bergen. When they finally returned to their hotel, exhausted and ready for bed, it was after ten p.m., but still light, a fact at which the young travelers never ceased to marvel. On the following day they would board a new train and penetrate even deeper into Norway.

Nibbling her third petit four in the Trondheim konditeri that drizzly afternoon, Amanda said to Colby, "Punish me severely if I eat one more chocolate covered thing today." She'd been idly leafing through a local newspaper and skimming the articles in English while Colby demolished an enormous Napoleon across from her in the wooden booth overlooking the busy Prinsens Gate thoroughfare. The next page she turned over revealed a crudely designed double truck black and white ad that drew her interest at once. "Oh my god, Colby, we have to go to Hammerfest, there's a metal festival on right now and look who's there," she pushed the paper across to him.

"I've never heard of any of those bands," Colby said, though not without interest.

"Neither have I, except for Kreator. But what does that matter? This is ground zero for black metal. Can you imagine the coolness of the people who would go to the edge of the world to see metal?"

"That might mean the hotels are booked solid," said Colby, taking out his mini tablet and doing a search.

"Don't be silly, those kids will be sleeping in tents or their cars," Amanda said with confidence.

"Looks like there are about four hotels in town," Colby said. "Let me put in tomorrow's date." He played with his device for a few minutes before delivering the crushing news that all the hotels in Hammerfest were booked for the rest of the week.

"We can't let ourselves be so easily defeated," said Amanda. "Look up B and B's."

"Okay, we're in," said Colby triumphantly, "there are two or three available. One says they have a loft for five hundred kroners a night."

"That's less than a hundred bucks," said Amanda, "so it'll be pretty basic and broken down but I think we should go for it."

"Okay, I'm booking us now," said Colby. Amanda jumped up and down in her seat, clapping her hands. "It's an island and it's pretty far from here," said Colby, further consulting his pad. "We'll have to fly in."

"You might as well book us return flights to London, if you're doing that," said Amanda.

Their B&B hosts in Hammerfest were Axl and Bettina Petersson, who owned a modest wooden house about a half-mile from the city center and within view of the coast. He was a civil engineer in his late 30's, tall and spare, with a short, pointed, red beard and straight red hair to match. She was English, in her middle 30's, plump and rosy with strawberry blonde hair and blue eyes. Bettina was a cake decorator who said she got up very early in the morning to go to work at a nearby bakery. And indeed, the entire small, neat house smelled like baked goods enrobed in fondant. They showed Amanda and Colby the loft, which was clean and pleasantly rustic, with a pitched roof and private bathroom with a claw footed tub. As was usual in all of the European accommodations they had had so far, except the luxury suites they had seen in company with Diana and Susan in Paris and Amsterdam, the single beds were extremely narrow.

Their hosts offered them coffee and told them of the local sites and also a bit if their own personal history. They had met five years before in London during the intermission at a chamber music recital and had been together ever since. Axl was not unpleasant but seemed dour. Amanda could picture him in a 19th century frock coat terrorizing school children with a cane. Her insight into the character of her host proved uncanny as she later noticed a shelf in the couple's sitting room, right beside their new flat screen TV, that held a collection of about two dozen vintage British caning videos, with titles like *4 O'clock Report* and *Half Term Punishments*, in VHS format. Amanda got Colby's attention and quietly directed his gaze to what she had just found. Colby's brows shot up in surprise.

Amanda waited to speak to her lover about their discovery until they had left the house to make their way into the village. The festival was already in progress and being held in a large outdoor space in view of the harbor. Deciding to have a bite of lunch before entering the concert venue, they found a small cafe and ordered sandwiches.

"So which of them do you think is into it?" Amanda asked.

"It's hard to tell," said Colby. "It could be both of them. She is English."

"Should we tell them?"

"Do you want to tell them?" he asked.

"Maybe I should tell her, privately, when he's not around."

"It would be more interesting staying with them if they knew," said Colby.

"She's cute but I'm not into him," Amanda said.

"You don't usually mind old geezers," said Colby.

"But I don't like beards," said Amanda. "And he looks like a ball buster."

They walked around the town and located the bakery where Bettina worked, though she was off that day. The window was filled with beautiful, delicate confections. Colby observed that Bettina appeared to enjoy her own products. Amanda asked him if he could be attracted to a chubby girl. Colby said that he liked them, as long as they had some sort of waist, which Bettina certainly did.

Again, Amanda promised to get their hostess alone at the first opportunity to discuss her interest in the scene. Then they spent the rest of the afternoon absorbing violent metal vibrations as a lineup of Scandinavian, American and English bands went on in succession. Going out into the colorfully tatted, pierced and t-shirted crowd of metal heads, Amanda was able to exchange a hundred kroners for a couple of fat spiffs, which she showed Colby in her hand triumphantly.

They decided to go back to the house, smoking one of the joints on the way. The bands would go on all day and through to around midnight, so they had no fear of missing much by leaving for a few hours.

Luckily, when they returned to the Petersson house, they found that Axl had departed to lay in some groceries while Bettina was in the backyard, in sight of the sea, hanging up wet laundry on a line. Colby told Amanda he would take a quick bath and left her alone with Bettina. Amanda immediately began to help her pretty blonde hostess with her wash, expertly shaking out each garment before hanging it on the clothesline.

"Bettina, Colby and I couldn't help notice you have some very interesting English videos on your shelf."

"Oh my god," Bettina rejoined in her London accent, "you noticed them? I told Axl he should put those out of sight!"

"Maybe he wanted them to be noticed," Amanda suggested, her smile and easy manner relieving Bettina's fear that the sight of the videos had offended their guests.

"Would you tell me, if it's not too rude a question on this short acquaintance, is it you or your husband who likes that sort of thing?"

"He likes the caning," Bettina explained, and then seemed reticent to continue.

"And you, do you like the caning?" Amanda asked softly.

"Well, you'd think that being English, I would," said Bettina confidentially, "but I would prefer it be spanking."

"Oh, is that so? How interesting," said Amanda. "But who got who into what?"

"It's something we've always both thought about. That came out on the night that we met," said Bettina.

"So when you play, he canes you?"

"Oh, yes."

"But doesn't spank you?"

"No."

"That's a shame," Amanda sympathized.

"Do you mean to say you're into it as well?"

"Oh, yes!" Amanda admitted without hesitation.

"At your age?"

"Oh, I've been playing since high school. You and Axl should come out to dinner with us tonight and we can have a jolly discussion about these things." Amanda suggested. Bettina agreed at once, quite excited at the prospect. But almost immediately her brow wrinkled with doubt and the shy, older woman felt bound to say, "We've never gone out or done anything with another couple into this, it might give Axl wrong ideas."

"You mean like he might want to cane me?" Amanda asked with a grin.

"Actually, yes!" said Bettina, amazed at Amanda's penetration.

"But you're not afraid that Colby might want to spank you?" Amanda asked teasingly.

"Oh, he never would. Would he?" Bettina asked, flushing to the roots again.

"He would," said Amanda with certainty.

"Oh, that would be lovely!" Bettina confided.

"Don't worry about me and Axl, I can handle him," said Amanda, with a cheerful smile. She was about to reenter the house when she abruptly turned back and rejoined her hostess. "I just realized the perfect way to handle this, Bettina," she said. "Don't mention to Axl about us being in the scene at all. We'll go out to dinner together and then, after we come back, I'll contrive to get Axl to come out with me again on some pretext. You'll be alone with Colby and you can have a proper over the knee spanking. I'll bring Axl back within an hour, and he'll be none the wiser."

Bettina blushed deeply but smiled back at her lovely houseguest with deep appreciation of the good deed Amanda was doing in lending her her good looking boyfriend in this manner. If it was obvious to Bettina that Amanda did not find her husband equally desirable as a playmate, Bettina scarcely cared. That was Axl's problem, not her own. For Bettina never got just what she wanted from her husband as foreplay, but rather only what he wanted, and she was coming to resent this.

Amanda and Colby spent the rest of the afternoon hiking in the local hills and met Bettina and Axl in the city center at around seven.

There were many restaurants to choose from and Amanda made it clear that she did not eat fish. Axl led them into one of his favorite bistros, specializing in seafood. When Amanda protested he advised her that there were plenty of items on the menu other than fish. On consulting the menu, they found the only dishes available to Amanda were salads. Amanda saw that Colby was excited at the prospect of eating oysters and other similar oceanic nightmares and declared affably that she would have a Cesar salad. All the while she sat in the restaurant, Amanda felt oppressed by the smell of seafood, until she asked if they could move to the outdoor patio where the fresh ocean breezes made it a bit too chilly to sit still. However, the view of the harbor was beautiful and eventually Colby volunteered his own sweater to be pulled on over Amanda's, and she felt she could tolerate yet a little more of Axl's pomposity. She could not, however, fail to narrow her eyes at him when he airily suggested that she eat whatever was put in front of her and not be so fussy. Colby laughed and advised their host that Amanda was practically a vegetarian. Amanda felt gratified at her lover coming to her defense so naturally. It occurred to her that her training of him was paying off; Colby was becoming subtler and less jocular every day. And so he would be rewarded, with this blushing English rose of a virgin spankee across his muscular thighs.

Taking everything of value out of her mini back pack and transferring these small items to the pockets of her jeans, Amanda managed to forget the backpack behind her in the ladies' room of the restaurant, not to discover the loss until they had returned to the cottage on the seaside road. Quite naturally, just as she had predicted, Axl offered to walk back to the village with Amanda to retrieve her property. Colby was left alone with Bettina and Amanda marked the time as she went out the door as nine pm.

The sun would never set that night and the wooded path to the town was bathed in golden light as Amanda and Axl proceeded hence. After claiming her backpack from the restaurant, Amanda insisted that Axl conduct her to the nearest grocery store so that she could buy chocolate. He told her that their fridge was full of cakes and cookies from Bettina's bakery and that she could eat her fill of them as soon as they got back. But Amanda was adamant about needing to replenish her chocolate bar stock before departing on the train the following day. Not to mention that she and Colby were going back to see the closing bands at the Metal festival that night and would need the portable energy of candy bars.

As they were walking back again along the forest path, Axl began to complain about how spoiled she was.

"Are you attempting to initiate a scene?" Amanda abruptly demanded of her lanky escort.

"What do you mean?" he asked in surprise.

"You called me spoiled, that's spank-flirting."

"What?" he rejoined, even more astonished at the turn their conversation had taken.

"Don't pretend you don't understand, Humbert Humbert," she said coolly, "I saw your collection of vintage caning videos."

"Oh!" he almost smiled and that almost made him bearably attractive to Amanda. However, the man's arrogance evoked an uncharacteristic cruelty in her. She remembered the terribleness of her first scene with Ambrose Bartlett, the wealthy storeowner who had bestowed so many gifts upon her after making her cry. While playing disciplinarian, this Axl could be as bad or worse than Mr. Bartlett, who at least was handsome, meticulously groomed and properly generous.

"By the way, there's a new thing around called DVD's "

"Why were you looking at my videos?"

"I wasn't looking at them, don't try to make this about me. I saw them because you left them out to be seen," Amanda charged vigorously, this last thrust leaving him momentarily speechless. "And you have your nerve calling me spoiled after insisting we go to that smelly fish shack after I told you I don't eat fish. You can eat there every day of the week. I'm only in your city for two days. How dare you ruin dinner for me? And now you presume to put me in the subordinate position to you. Well let me tell you something, Mr. Petersson, the only caning action that's ever going to happen between you and me will have you doing the bending over!" She ended this speech in her haughtiest tone, realizing that Colby and Bettina were going to need a lot more time to enjoy themselves. As she expected, reading her man correctly, Axl looked instantly intrigued.

"You're being rather severe with me," he said at last as they continued to stride along the path. They were now coming up on an old stone bench that they both took note of. Amanda stopped and looked at him with her hands on her hips. Then she said, "Find me a suitable switch." He immediately walked off the path to search for a long, supple twig. She smiled and sat down on the bench to await his return. She almost laughed aloud. How grateful Colby and Bettina would be. The next instant, he was before her, handing her a selection of switches. She got to her feet.

"Drop your pants and put your hands on the bench," she told him coldly. "And I mean all the pants you have on." Down came jeans and boxers revealing a pair of fairly muscular buttocks and thighs. No doubt he hiked the hills often and Amanda approved of that. "Well, so far so good. You've obeyed me and your lower proportions are not unattractive. But there is still the problem of your horrible, overbearing personality to address." Amanda drew back and struck him dead center cross wise with her first switch, leaving a red mark and drawing a cry from Axl. "Stick your bottom out more and arch your back," she told him sternly. "No, not that way, dip down and thrust your bottom out. And hold perfectly still," she said, taking aim above her first stroke to leave her second mark a little high. "Perfectly even," she said, admiring her own work. "And stop making noise," she warned. "Someone could come by at any minute and see you. If you're quiet, we'll have time to hear an approaching step. Understand?"

"Yes, Ma'am," he replied submissively.

"While I whip you, you're going to think about what perfect little cafe you're going to take me straight back to in the village where there's something I can actually eat." And then she began to switch him as hard as she could, breaking the first twig, the second and the third across his increasingly marked bottom. He held his position and stifled his cries, but she could read his breaking point coming in his trembling body language as the switching progressed. After about two dozen strokes she paused and said, "I'm going to enjoy seeing you squirm on your seat while I eat." And to make sure that this was true, she came in close behind him and laying aside the switch for a moment, used her hand to spank his upper thighs dark pink. "This is the area you actually sit on," she told him, "but I'm kindly not using the switch on it, lest I whack your horrible boy parts by mistake. Am I not generous?"

"Yes, Mistress!" he cried. She smiled at her promotion.

"Well? Where are we going for dinner?" she asked, taking up the last unbroken switch and lashing him with it four more times.

"I'll take you to the Indian restaurant," he gasped, jumping to his feet and pulling up his pants as both of them had heard a footfall on the path.

Casually turning and beginning on the path back to the village, Amanda quickened her stride, passed the pair of metal heads who were walking in the woods to get stoned, and merrily proceeded towards her well-earned meal.

While enjoying a plate of paneer mattar, dahl, saag, aloo gobi and basmati rice, Amanda encouraged Axl to recite the history of his life in the scene, which largely amounted to being caned at the religious boarding school he had attended and then later convincing any woman he dated to submit to a caning from him. He had never gotten a single one to take a second caning until he met Bettina in the U.K.

Probing further, Amanda got Axl to admit that he had seen mistresses in Stockholm, Amsterdam, Hamburg, London and New York to satisfy his urge to experience being on the receiving end. "So, you think Bettina truly enjoys being caned?" Amanda

So far she had kept the conversation entirely focused on Axl and in doing so, had manipulated him into doing exactly as she wished, therefore she saw no reason to reveal any interesting fact about herself relevant to the scene.

"Not so much as I do," he admitted.

"Maybe as a lady, she'd appreciate a kinder, more friendly form of corporal punishment, like over the knee spanking," Amanda suggested. "Maybe I'll teach you how to do that properly on the way back. On that particular bench where we stopped before."

"You mean I can practice on you?" he grinned.

"No," she said. "I'm sure you're a horrible spanker."

Axl hung his head in tacit agreement. Then he looked at her and asked her how she came to know so much about men at her age. She gave her standard reply, that she was from San Francisco and he nodded as though that made perfect sense.

Good as her word, when they passed by the bench on the way back, while the woods remained bathed in what might have been afternoon sunlight, though it was almost ten, she sat down and without letting him think, pulled him by the hand down and across her lap.

"You're a bossy one, aren't you?" Axl observed with a chuckle at finding himself in the unexpected position.

"Yeah, well, this bossy girl is still the first woman you ever met who was willing to cane you for free," she sagely reminded him before proceeding to administer as detailed a lesson in spanking the opposite sex as she could compress into the nine minutes that elapsed before they heard an approaching footfall on the path.

Axl was agreeably silent on the walk back to the cottage, which allowed Amanda to mentally review all of the points on which she had touched, lest she had omitted any crucial advice there was still time left to add. "Let's see," she thought, "I went over positioning, holding, advocated wrist pinning, nixed leg locking, showed him how to hair pull painlessly, made him aware of earlobe and nipple pinching, went into layer removal and warm-ups, discoursed on rubbing, warned against scratching, against repeatedly striking the same spot, discussed productive vs. hurtful scolding, and I had just gotten to the area of intimate caresses. Yes, I think I've covered all the bases."

When they arrived at the cottage they found Colby and Bettina in the kitchen placidly eating chocolate cake and drinking milk. In fact, the two homebodies had only ceased to play ten minutes before Axl and Amanda's return. Amanda was given a large slice of torte, which she happily consumed, giving Colby the smallest wink. Axl poured himself a genever and stared out the kitchen window at the bit of shore visible from the house.

After restoring themselves with cake, Amanda and Colby departed once more to bang heads for the rest of the night in the metal arena in the town, not arriving back at the cottage to fall into bed until two a.m.

The following morning, they ate a hearty breakfast with their hosts, who charmed them by refusing to accept any payment for their food and lodging. Then they dashed back to the city center to catch an express bus to the airport, where they would board a small plane for the six hour flight to London, the final destination city of their tour. Both Amanda and Colby had carefully copied Bettina's email address into their devices for future correspondence with the charming young woman.

Chapter Twenty-One

David Takes Advice from Michael Flagg

David Lawrence sat at the bar in Michael Flagg's tavern with something of an air of defeat and a shot of Irish whiskey before him. School was out at Braemar Prep, but David taught a number of summer school classes at the local community college and tended to make Michael's his last stop on the way home from work. It was the late afternoon and the bar was very quiet.

"Little early in the day for whiskey, isn't it?" asked Michael, who was used to serving David beer at this hour.

"I'm in a terrible mood so I might as well make it worse," confided David, swallowing his first shot in a couple of gulps. "Another."

Michael poured, asking, "Still steamed about Hope working at the new club?" David's exasperated expression confirmed the former detective's suspicion.

"I thought when B&D club girls got married, the last thing they'd ever want to do would be to spend more time in a club," said David, contemplating his second shot for a long moment before disposing of it. "I mean, I met her in a club," the English teacher added.

"I know the one. My ex-wife ran away to work there once. I had to go and get her."

"So you wouldn't want your wife working in a club either!" David declared.

"Maybe not a club like The Keep, two blocks from Hollywood Blvd., where anyone can walk in off a newspaper ad. This isn't like that. It's more like a private clubhouse for people in the local scene, and maybe friends of friends. And it's not run like any other club I've ever seen. They have a real cleaning crew twice a week and everything is so new you can smell it."

"So you would let Marguerite work there?"

"If she ever gets a yen, I won't try to stop her."

"Seriously?"

"Well, she's been understanding about certain recent lapses of mine," Michael admitted.

"Come to that, Hope is very understanding as well, but that doesn't justify what she's up to. Not by my lights."

"If it makes you so unhappy, tell her you won't put up with it."

David sighed, "Believe me, that's my natural inclination, but every time I try to pull rank as her top she starts whining about how her feet hurt from running around filling coffee cups eight hours a day, six days a week for bad tips. And then I feel guilty."

"She won't have to work nearly as hard now, but her feet will probably still hurt from wearing five inch heels," observed Michael.

"Those richies, Anthony Newton and Ambrose Bartlett, they've never stopped courting Hope ever since we came here. Bartlett's always sending her clothes and shoes and Newton insisted that Hope be the second in command at this new local den of inequity. How can I demand that she give up the extra attention, no less the luxuries? You know how vain she is."

"Why don't you let her have her way for a while? By and by you'll be making enough to support her and by then she'll probably be tired of sessioning anyway."

"I can support her right now. She just doesn't think it's enough. And of course, she wants to work in the club."

"Marguerite hated like hell to lose her," said Michael. "But Anthony is Felina's godfather and she'd never interfere with his plans."

"Have you noticed Random Point resembling a feudal village in that respect?"

"Ready for another?" asked Michael cheerfully. "I'll get Carmen to drive you home."

"Why not?" asked David, pushing forward his glass.

"You know, you ought to go play at that club," Michael suggested; "At the very least, you can blow off some steam."

At first the idea seemed absurd, but after finishing another drink, it began to make good sense. And instead of having Carmen drive him home, David had Michael's bargirl drive him to Tar Pine Road.

Cassandra answered the door and remembering David from a brief introduction one morning in the bookstore coffee shop, the mistress of the house informed him with a smile that Hope had left early and would no doubt be home by now.

David said, "May I come in? I got dropped off. I've been at Michael's and he insisted I wasn't fit to drive."

"Come in!" Cassandra said cheerfully. "Let's go into the lounge. Do you want me to get someone to drive you home? Dru's still around here somewhere."

"Oh, by and by," said David, looking around the piano bar salon with interest. "I have to admit, this isn't like any club I've ever been in," he generously allowed.

"Do you want another drink or are you good?" she asked.

"I'm good."

"Did you want to talk to me?" asked Cassandra, inviting him to sit opposite her on a firm tweed sofa.

"I came to do a session."

"You want to play with a sub?" Cassandra asked, wondering whom she could call on such short notice.

"Yes."

"I could call Jane Eliot. She wanted to come and start working here now and then. Do you think you'd like to play with her?"

"I want to do my session with you," David said, looking at her so seriously that her heart jumped.

"Me?" Cassandra laughed, thinking he had to be a good twelve years her junior, to say nothing of being married to the fairest of the fair.

"I wish to spank you and you alone."

"Oh!" Cassandra felt her face begin to go hot. "Well, are you a hard spanker?" she asked casually.

"Yes, I suppose I am," he replied, just as nonchalantly. "Aren't we all? Hope says we are."

"I don't know that I can take it that hard," she admitted.

"Sounds like you need some toughening up. I can help you with that."

"I envisioned myself more as the dispenser of discipline than the receiver here," Cassandra said, pulling back a little from him, while remembering that tops who have been drinking can be dangerous.

"Oh, don't tell me you're a wimpy little scaredy cat? You're going to expect your girls to take hard spankings, aren't you?"

"The ones who are into it."

"Oh, I see, a humanitarian, are you?"

"Yes, of course. And so is my patron," Cassandra said firmly.

"Patron," David snorted, "don't you mean the village whore master?"

"I would slap you face for that if you weren't about to spank me," said Cassandra.

"But I am, so don't."

"I wouldn't anyway, it's not my style."

"Fine, your indignation on behalf of your benevolent and disinterested master has been duly noted," said David. "Nor does it surprise me. He spoils all of you girls."

"Thank you for calling me a girl. For that chivalry alone, I will accept your challenge and prove I'm not afraid."

"Great, how much is a half hour?"

"With your academic discount, let's say two."

"Seems fair," he said, producing two of the newly minted golden inkpot embossed hundred dollar bills from his wallet. She put the money in a drawer and asked him if he wanted her to change her clothes. He liked her flowered, close fitting sundress and flat sandals and gave her his hand to lead him to a playroom. She showed him every room and he decided on the library.

"You know, I spanked Amanda last year," he said, locking the door behind them, "and she didn't whine about not too hard. She took a great spanking. Did she tell you?"

"She said you were dreamy," said Cassandra.

"I've never spanked the mother of a daughter that I'd spanked," said David, glancing at the wide selection of erotica on the shelves of the library.

"Sounds like a letter to Janus magazine," Cassandra observed, standing with her hands clasped in front of her and gazing mildly up at him, for he was quite tall and a pleasant man to gaze upon.

"Except I have a much more legitimate reason to punish the mistress of this house than any husband in a piece of fiction ever had," David maintained, sitting on an oversized and armless straight-backed leather chair and motioning her to him.

"Look," Cassandra protested, "it wasn't my idea to recruit Hope, though I admit I couldn't live without her now."

"It was your idea to open this place and you were shrewd enough to somehow pry a fortune out of Anthony to make it happen. Say what you will, you're largely to blame for disturbing my domestic tranquility."

She began to stammer an apology but he pulled her across his lap and silenced her with a few experimental swats.

"Don't you realize," David said, "that I married Hope and took her all the way across the country to this cold place, just to get her away from working in a club?"

"She did take three or four years off," said Cassandra, putting back one hand to shield her bottom, but having it instantly pinned to her waist.

"Yes," David agreed, "and it's been lovely. I haven't had to go to work every day thinking about strange men manhandling my wife and Hope has enjoyed a respectable reputation in this town, suitable to the wife of a school teacher."

To this statement there was no reply and Cassandra subsided across his strong thighs, steeling herself for the coming ordeal. The problem was that his resentment was not inappropriate in proportion to the changes that Cassandra's moving to Random Point had actuated.

"So, first I'll do this," he said, carefully folding her skirt up to her waist; "and then, this," he added, hooking his fingers into the sides of her skimpy blush silk bikinis and pulling the panties down to the backs of her knees, revealing her small, smooth bottom, its complexion warm and peachy in the golden late afternoon light spilling into the room through the half curtained windows. "Then," he said, "we'll get right to it."

He started to spank her hard and fast, delivering an assault with the very hard palm of his hand too robust to stoically withstand. In seconds, Cassandra was kicking, screaming and struggling against his restraining arm, pleading for him to let her go and offering to return the allowance. He was determined to make someone feel his indignation and had chosen herself. So this was what it felt like when the play was bad, she thought, deciding instantly that she would never accept a submissive session with a stranger again.

"Oh no," he said, pausing only momentarily. "You're not getting out of it that easily." And then he went on spanking her. In response to which, she began to loudly cry. Of course, after she began to cry, he could no longer ignore her distress and ceased belaboring her backside. She tried to scramble off his lap but he held her in place. "Where do you think you're going?"

"Let me go, you're not nice!" she whimpered, her hand to her streaming eyes.

"I'm not letting you go anywhere," he said, neatly rolling her face up on his lap and slipping an arm under her shoulders. He looked at her tear-streaked eyes and then his gaze dropped to her parted mouth. "What are you making such a fuss about? I barely touched you," he said reproachfully, before brushing his lips against hers. In the next instant she felt him tightening his arms around her and then he kissed her harder. She abruptly stopped crying and stared at him wide-eyed. "What?" he asked; "You obviously can't take a good spanking. Maybe there's something else you can do for me."

Cassandra was amazed at the turn the strange session had taken, but rather than take any more spanking from David, she was ready to distract him in any way he deemed acceptable. She didn't even question it, for such odd occurrences had almost become commonplace to her since returning home to Random Point.

"What do you want me to do?" she asked.

"Bend over the desk for me," he said encouragingly.

"I can take more spanking," she said helpfully, "now that I've had a break."

"But I want to do this now."

"Do what?"

"You'll see what," he promised her, bending her over the edge of the large desk. Then he once again folded back her skirt and this time, pulled her panties off altogether.

"Spread your legs," he ordered.

"Why? What are you going to do? Do you have a condom?" she asked, looking back over her shoulder at him.

"Of course," he assured her, producing one to show her.

"Are you sure you want to do this?" she asked, watching him pull his zipper down and allow a penis, which looked both formidable and highly likely to insist upon itself, to escape from between its teeth. "Oh my god," she cried, "how could you get so excited so fast?"

"Just from spanking a pretty lady to tears? I wonder," he said, expertly rolling a condom down over his erection and then experimentally probing her with the tip of one long middle finger. "Oh, good," he said, "we won't need to get any lube."

Cassandra was shocked to find that his rough treatment had left her wet but moved back against his finger, immediately deciding to make the most of this new experience. He fingered her for several minutes together, admiring the pinkness his hard hand had imparted to her cheeks.

"I'm ready now, I think," she murmured, beginning to long for the sensation of something larger than two fingers inside her.

"Go and get some lube anyway," he told her, helping her up and pulling down her dress. She ran off to her bedroom and returned as quickly as she could, a small bottle concealed in her pocket. Now he put her back in position and applied a few drops of the clear liquid to his shaft and her labia. And with every precaution taken to insure a safe, secure and easy passage, David began to enjoy the first woman he had made love to outside his marriage in years. There had been the few encounters with the ladies at the school, Paula Rohan before her first marriage and Alison Albrecht before she had begun dating Freddie. And the tiniest transgression had taken place, but once, between himself and one of his more determined student female stalkers, Lupe Freeman. And then there was Gigi, Dru's former girlfriend, and also a student of David's, who was madly infatuated with him. He'd given each girl a spanking or caning and perhaps one intimate caress. But he'd done nothing of the kind in several years.

The most recent erotic contact he had had with any lady other than Hope had been the admonitory spanking he'd given Amanda the previous Autumn.

Thus this afternoon was an exciting new adventure. He liked the submissiveness displayed by the mistress of the house. He'd been able to bully her into subbing to him very easily and now he was taking every liberty without even being questioned about it. It made him feel as though Cassandra were either genuinely attracted to him or that his B&D had gotten very good. Either way, it was gratifying to be obeyed without question for a change. Hope seemed to be fighting him for control in their marriage of late and because she was winning, he felt battle fatigue. Victory over Cassandra had been easy and complete. Hope had taught him multiple ways to make a woman climax and in this case, g-spot massage joined to vigorous intercourse proved instantly efficacious and David could feel Cassandra's spasms when she came. Without saying a word, both felt that this moment would bond them forever as something like lovers. That he would orgasm shortly thereafter, there was never any question.

A few minutes later, they were setting their clothes to rights.

"That was pleasant and soothing," said David, adjusting his tie in a mirror.

"You see, even you can get something out of the club on a personal level," observed Cassandra, with amusement.

"Just do me a personal favor and discourage Hope from doing what we just did, in a dungeon," David asked, brushing a tendril of brown hair back behind Cassandra's ear and giving her ear lobe an affectionate pinch. Cassandra shivered and felt a thrill in her stomach.

"Shall I offer myself up for all such sessions?" Cassandra asked helpfully, ready to giggle at the absurdity of what had just happened.

"No, and don't be smart, young lady. You want to discourage such things from happening in the club altogether."

"Right. No sex in the club," said Cassandra, as if rewriting a mental note. "Ever. Except for just this one time," Cassandra said, not adding that probably there was that other time, involving Anthony and her sister.

"Oh, who am I kidding?" he asked his own reflection.

"No, no, you're absolutely right!" she assured him, impulsively throwing her arms around him and laying her head on his chest. "I should be running this place like a convent for the girls."

"No, I said, less sex, not more."

"But seriously, David," she said, looking up at him, "I will absolutely steer the amorous tops well away from Hope and I'll tell them that Mr. Newton has strictly forbidden such goings on at the club."

"He hasn't, has he, though?"

"No. He's letting me figure things out as I go."

"Have you played with Ambrose Bartlett yet?" David asked.

"No. And I don't intend to. I hear nothing but bad things about him."

"Hope plays with him all the time."

"She's very brave."

"Do you think she's giving him sex? She'll never tell me the truth about him."

"No, he gets plenty of sex from Pamela and from what I understand, Polyxena Guzman now. David, don't you realize that your wife adores you and you alone?"

"Oh, I don't question her devotion. But you don't understand her personality. Working at the coffee shop brought her down to earth. Now she's some sort of BDSM goddess again and no one can tell her anything."

"Oh David, I'm so happy to have Hope as my companion. Please don't say you still disapprove," Cassandra appealed to him.

"Well, we'll have to wait and see," he grumbled, but nonetheless, bestowed a kiss on the top of her head before departing into the summer night.

Part Two: August

Chapter One

Before the Party

At five p.m. on one of the last days of August, Amanda knelt on a sofa under the front facing window of the lounge, her face almost pressed against the window pane as a torrential summer rain poured down from gray skies and soaked the woods behind her mother's new house.

"What if this rain stops people from coming?" she asked her companion, Anthony Newton, who sat behind the grand piano he had furnished the club with, looking over a list of songs.

"Don't be silly, Amanda, if nothing else they'll want to try the food," he chuckled, having just visited the kitchen, where his little cooks, James and Josette, plus Dennis and Michael's bar girl, Carmen, were setting out fascinating trays of hors d'oeuvres and creating spicy garnishes to surround them. "I must say, you have unusual taste in music for a teenage," he added, having promised her the birthday present of playing her favorite songs as they waited for their guests to arrive. "Harold Arlen, Jerome Kern, Richard Rodgers, Kurt Weill, wait a minute, I'm seeing a pattern here," he said, recognizing his own repertoire from the various tribute albums he had recorded.

"My mother had all of your albums and I listened to them over and over again all during high school."

"Well, we know that Tai, Lydia, your Aunt Carola and Marion Craig are all coming down on the train from Boston. Haven't Colby and Dru gone to pick them up?"

"That's true. So I'll be meeting Colby's older woman for the first time," Amanda said, catching her reflection in a side mirror and critically studying the image of herself in the short, shiny, dark red PVC slip dress that was so tight as to seem painted on and so marvelously enhanced the curves of her generous bosom, shapely bottom and tiny waist.

"I trust you'll be gentle," said Anthony, also noticing the remarkable spectacle of Amanda's modelesque body displayed to such shiny advantage.

"I was going to ask her to be my surrogate for the birthday spankings," Amanda said, more than half seriously. She had been truly honored when she had been told that Anthony's club initiation party at the end of the summer would, as its theme, celebrate her 19th birthday. Her official birthday was the first day of September, which coincided with the first day of class, therefore, the party had been arranged for a few days earlier allowing Colby and Amanda ample time to return to Boston, move into their new dorm and register for classes.

Amanda and Colby had not spend the whole of August in Random Point, but upon returning from London, had, along with Cassandra, gone to Northern California for a couple of weeks, so the mother and daughter could pack their possessions and have them shipped to their new home. Eddie had offered to pack everything meticulously for them and take care of the shipping, but neither Cassandra nor Amanda felt comfortable at the idea of Eddie and possibly Eddie's new wife, going through their things, especially when they remembered their diaries, photos and collections of love letters. After consulting with Anthony as to the propriety of bringing all of their belongings out to the house on Pine Tar Road, he encouraged her to use the property in any way she chose, reminding her that the house was very large, and full of storage space. He recommended making one of the bedrooms Amanda's permanent room and furnishing her with a locking armoire so as to feel safe leaving all of her things there. Now that he saw how deeply attached to the house Cassandra had become, he didn't try to discourage her from living there at all times. As long as the club was extremely exclusive, all would be well.

Amanda was touched and delighted by Anthony's concern for and devotion to her mother. She had been quietly worried that the loss of her life partner would be a crushing blow to her mother's ego, but the whole incident of being walked out on by Eddie seemed to cause barely a ripple in Cassandra's emotions. On the contrary, the relocation back to Random Point had suddenly injected her mother's life with a glamor and excitement she hadn't known in twenty years. Suddenly her mother, like Hope Spencer Lawrence, was out from behind a counter and being eyed in sexy outfits by men with (acceptably) bad intentions. When she had first seen Cassandra upon her return from Europe, she barely recognized her mother, who seemed to look ten years younger. Her hair had been trimmed to a sleek, long bob, and she was wearing a figure hugging summer dress. And the first thing Cassandra told Amanda when she got her alone was that she had most recently been made love to by David Lawrence! Cassandra confided this secret with so much delight that Amanda could not allow herself to be shocked.

"It was entirely his notion, not mine," Cassandra explained. "He came here all fussed at me for taking Hope away from her straight job and said he wanted to do a session with me to blow off some steam. I balked and resisted but he baited me, or flattered me or somehow made me overcome my better judgment and I agreed to let him spank me. Well, he wasn't dreamy at all. He gave me an angry spanking that was too hard, or too fast, or too angry and it made me cry right away. Then he said I was useless, then he kissed me. And the next thing you know, he was bending me over the desk, in that way English teachers have perfected."

"Ah! Nice!" said Amanda; "I think he was suddenly attracted to your vulnerability, going from angry to aroused the second you started to cry. He never got aroused when he was spanking me. At least if he did, he had the good taste to not draw attention to it."

"You mustn't tell Hope," Cassandra cautioned her daughter. "Or Marguerite about that Michael incident."

"No, no, of course, I would never!" Amanda promised.

When it was decided that Cassandra and Amanda would return to California to get their things organized, Colby seemed extremely reluctant to leave them and offered to come and help them pack and ship. Cassandra was grateful for the physical and moral support her daughter's young champion provided and Amanda was impressed with her lover's devotion, though she was somewhat suspicious that a lack of trust in her fidelity accounted for his unwillingness to leave her in San Francisco without him.

During most of the time they were gone, Diana Currie, her husband Plastridge, their baby daughter and nanny, occupied the Pine Tar house. Plastridge and Diana, ardent bondagers, who had indeed met for the first time by chance in the lobby of a New York BDSM club, were going to look over the house and equip it with any additional pieces they knew would be beloved to fellow bondagers. They were also going to finish decorating the examining room. In the daytime, the nanny and toddler were sent off to visit with Damaris' baby and nanny and/or Marguerite's baby and nanny. Pretty soon, all the babies and nannies were spending their sunny afternoons on the beach together, while Diana and her husband played undisturbed at the house. Diana was especially grateful to Susan Ross and Amanda for introducing her to her beloved Ronnie in Paris. They had traveled together from Holland to Spain and spent three idyllic days in a coastal town, eating the best food of their lives and making love in every way they could think of. It had been a revitalizing experience and had touched Diana's heart. She and Ronnie Van Horn would be friends all their lives, crossing paths now and then and locking hotel room doors behind them.

That night they had sent the nanny and baby back to New York and had themselves relocated from the Pine Tar Road house to Anthony's house on the cliff. They would arrive back at about seven-thirty.

Carola would be occupying the other guest bedroom that night, while Tai and Lydia would be taken to Susan's house, across from the graveyard. That would appeal to the Goth influenced Lydia, Susan thought. Marion Craig would be initially checked in at the Ball and Feather, where she had booked a room.

Thalia, who had been doing summer theatre in Rhode Island, was driving out, with an E.T.A. of eight p.m. She would also be staying at Susan's house, as she had done on her previous visits. Thalia, Amanda's jolly friend from B.U. and the Boston scene, still had rather a large crush on Hugo Sands and looked forward to claiming his attention for at least a small part of the evening. She had already been out once to work at the club, as had Lydia and Tai. Hope had faithfully reported every day's activity to Cassandra and some auspicious patterns were already beginning to develop. Ambrose Bartlett was their most frequent visitor, coming in every Friday and Tuesday late afternoon. If one girl was on, he would play with one. If two happened to be present, he played with two. As a very frequent client, they decided to lower his hourly rate to five hundred, and offer a further discount for doubles, though he always tipped each girl generously. Certainly it was evident that Bartlett intended to kick back a good deal of what had been spent in his store on furnishing the bulk of the house in sessions.

When Cassandra returned from California, even she was recruited for one of Bartlett's double sessions. She had been going to resist, but he had taken to bringing over dresses and other outfits from the store, and leaving them with the girls as presents. She happened to be on with Hope the afternoon he brought two size small flare skirted lace over tulle halter dresses, one in pale pink and the other in pale green, along with strappy sandals to match. Just looking at the cut of the expensive dresses, Cassandra knew she would look divine in the green, therefore, she agreed to be the second submissive. Nor had it been so bad.

Hope watched Bartlett narrowly, ready to jump in and interpose her own bottom between that of her largely inexperienced mistress and his hard paddle or strap. But she found it wasn't necessary. Ambrose kept himself well in check during that first session with his Amanda's darling mother. As a lifelong enthusiast, he naturally loved the idea of spanking both a daughter and her mother and would never have passed on this rare opportunity. Beyond that, Bartlett had been attracted to Cassandra's lithe body since first seeing her register at the inn, then later at the gym. He had even taken a yoga class to get a better look at her. She knew he was there and smiled to herself. She had heard of Bartlett's fickleness from Hope, who got it from Pamela, Bartlett's second wife, that he'd made Polyxena Guzman his mistress, though he hadn't brought her to play in the club, as yet. Hope had not exactly kept Pamela informed as to the regularity of her husband's visits to the club, but she did give Pamela to understand that on any given week, the best time to sneak over for a fly by with Dru in one of the bedrooms, was any day other than Friday or Tuesday.

Pamela did drop by to play with her boy. She usually stayed forty-five minutes and left the better part of a hundred dollars at the front desk for the room rental. Hope and Cassandra tried to discourage Pamela from paying for the room, but Pamela insisted that they had to become better businesswomen about the club and be content at the generous discount she had given herself as a regular customer. At any rate, Dru would be going back to school at the beginning of September and after that she doubted she would ever visit the club again. Cassandra and Hope waited to laugh at that until after Pamela was out the door.

Other locals began to become regulars, including Freddie Johanson, who had begun appearing every other week and Dieter Brandt, the masseur and Polyxena's partner in the gym, who had taken to showing up every Saturday morning for a quiet little foot session with whichever lady was available. The first time Jane Eliot was especially invited to visit the club, it was to play top during one of these easy Dieter sessions, which the novice couldn't begin to understand, but quite enjoyed.

Hugo had come in to do photo shoots whenever a new girl came into town. He paid the girls modeling fees and a little over for the house.

Dru had so far paid to see Carola twice. Dennis had seen her once. Both had gone submissive to her. And the next time she came out, she was scheduled to introduce Raphael Price to the confusing world of BDSM, to which he felt somehow drawn, but groped to understand. Carola would help him to define his character as a player and he was eagerly anticipating the journey.

Marguerite's still single ex-husband, Malcolm, had come in to play with Lydia, Tai and Thalia, on successive weeks. The next time he came in, Jane would be up and perhaps the irony would not be lost on him, as Jane was the original lover of Marguerite's current spouse, Michael Flagg.

Pascal Robbins had paid model fees to Lydia and Tai and merely photographed them. He didn't quite understand what the house was all about, but he was interested in keeping close tabs on it, lest his own wife try to sneak off to it and rendezvous with her glamorous erstwhile lover, Anthony Newton, who was the club's financier.

Even Michael had been over once, to play with the uninhibited college girl Thalia, whom he had met on the occasion of a photo shoot held at his tavern the previous winter. Michael had discussed supporting the club in this manner with Marguerite and she had concurred that it was the right and proper thing to do now and then.

David's visit to the club was to remain off the books, a secret Cassandra was pleased to keep from everyone but Amanda, whom she felt compelled to confess everything to these days. But even not counting his visit, the business was quietly growing.

Now Anthony Newton was playing That Old Black Magic for Amanda, who thrilled in every fiber at the way the vigorous, original piano arrangement filled the large, posh lounge. They spoke only when he paused between songs.

"What did you think of my aunt Carola?" Amanda asked. "She frightens me a bit."

"She's scary but we're in the process of taming her," he disclosed.

"My mother has always been afraid of exposing me to her too much."

"I think you can handle her," said Anthony. "Like most bullies, she will yield to a more dominant force."

As he played Where or When for her, she gazed at him, misty-eyed, never remembering having been so happy.

"By the way," he said, "I don't think you could look any better if you tried. That dress looks like it was made for you."

"Colby thought it was outrageous."

"But he didn't tell you to take it off."

"He will later," she laughed.

"What country did you like best of your trip?" Anthony asked before playing Speak Low.

Amanda replied without hesitation, "The scenery was best in

Norway, the food best in Italy, the drugs best in Holland, but England felt like our spiritual home."

"Did you get down to Old Compton St.?"

"The Janus bookstore? Yes, but we didn't go in. There was no one in there except two very old men behind the counters. Colby and I suddenly realized we didn't want to have to explain why we were bringing an English spanking magazine back into the states in our luggage. So we passed on the whole Janus experience."

Before Anthony had a chance to comment, Susan Ross entered the room, her trim-waisted, small breasted, round bottomed body beautifully arrayed in a double breasted white leather vest, a glove tight black hobble skirt and a five inch heeled stiletto booties that took her from petite to medium high with edgy elegance. Her hair was pulled back in its usual long, high, blonde ponytail and dark red lipstick drew the eye to her agreeable mouth.

"Hello," she said, "the girls are settled in so I thought I'd come right over." She embraced Amanda and spun around so Anthony could admire the curve of her bottom in the shiny black skirt. Hugo and Laura came in a moment later, he in a faultless suit and she in an evening gown.

"I'm glad you came early," said Anthony. "Let's go and get some champagne." He led them into the dining room and sent Susan into the kitchen to tell Dennis to open a bottle for them. Amanda was sent to fetch Cassandra. Dennis came out with the tray and began to fill some of the glasses that had been set out on the sideboard and handed them around. Cassandra came back with Amanda, dressed in a dark blue leather club dress that Damaris and Pamela had sent her for good luck.

When they all had a glass in their hands Anthony said, "Let's drink a toast to our darling Amanda on her birthday." They all clicked glasses and sipped. "And let me say something more, while it's just us here," he continued. "You all mean so much to me. Hugo, if it wasn't for you, I'd never have met Susan, Laura or anyone else who will enter this house tonight and my life would have been immeasurably duller. Amanda and Cassandra are new additions to my scene family, but already very dear to me. So I propose that we all meet back here at Thanksgiving and spend it together."

Amanda looked at Hugo with a deeply affectionate smile, relishing the thought of her first holiday season spent with both her parents. But Cassandra smiled at Anthony. How like him to think of a charming way for her to enjoy Thanksgiving with her daughter and her daughter's father, without excluding her daughter's father's new wife.

"And when we do come back to Random Point in November, Susan and I will be married," Anthony added, in his most matter of fact tone. Susan looked at him and flushed to the eyes. "Yes," he said, looking back at her, "and I won't let you wriggle out of it this time."

"But, why?" she stammered.

He took her about the waist and kissed her, saying, "Because it's disrespectful to date a girl for eight years without marrying her. Don't argue because you know I'm right."

Cassandra smiled at Anthony again; impressed by this strategic maneuver calculated to remove any doubt from Susan's mind as to where his main loyalty lay.

"Finally, I have a birthday present for you," Anthony said, reaching into a breast pocket for an envelope and handing it to Amanda. Now it was her turn to blush. A present didn't fit into an envelope unless it was a check.

"Should I open it now?" she asked.

"Why not?" he encouraged her.

It wasn't a check, but a card, with an etching of an ivy covered building on the cover. Inside Anthony had written: "Three years hence, graduate school's on me. Anthony Newton"

Amanda was hugging Anthony when Dennis returned with two more bottles of champagne. Anthony noticed a troubled expression on his assistant's usually composed face and putting Amanda from him, took one of the bottles and began refilling glasses while saying to Dennis, "Everything okay in the kitchen?"

"Actually, there's a bit of a situation developing," Dennis disclosed softly.

"What kind of situation?" Anthony asked, taking Dennis aside while handing him a glass of champagne. "Here, you have some too. You need to be fortified for the long night ahead."

"Thank you," Dennis said, delighted to sip the expensive golden white libation. "It's Josette."

"What about Josette?"

"She says she's ruined the cake. She's devastated and she's crying in the pantry."

"Did she really ruin the cake?" Anthony asked with interest, excusing himself to the others and leading Dennis back to the kitchen as they talked.

"The middle looks a bit caved in," Dennis admitted, "but I don't say it's entirely ruined."

They entered the kitchen, where James was preparing trays of beggar's purse pasties. Michael's bargirl Carmen stood cutting limes behind a granite island in the middle of the large room, where she had set up blenders for complex mixed drinks and a variety of liquors and liqueurs for cocktails. She was an attractive blonde in her late twenties with a pixie cut in a white halter dress and white sandals, a young woman who appreciated her job, adored her boss, never spoke much, did her work well and quietly charmed everyone.

Anthony scanned the surfaces of all the countertops and quickly located the cake, inspected it and then went to knock on the pantry door. "Josette, it's me, Mr. Newton. Let me in," he said softly. The door opened immediately, he entered and closed it behind him. Josette looked up at him with a tear-streaked face and trembling lips. The room was large for a pantry, but no place to talk. Rather than take her back out through the kitchen, Anthony opened the other door, which led out to a screened porch that ran the length of the east side of the house. He motioned her to follow him outside and closed the door behind them. It was still raining hard but the porch was dry and dusk was still several hours away.

"Honey, I can understand you being upset about the cake, but James can't complete this service without you."

"I've failed you," she sobbed, wiping her eyes with her apron.

"Oh, Josette, you think these skinny bitches coming to the party tonight are going to miss another five hundred calories of pure sugar? Anyway, I saw trays of marzipan petit fours out there and as for the cake, you can cut the middle out and call it a ring cake."

She looked at him with wide eyes, saying, "Yes, I could do that!"

"Have a cigarette and compose yourself," he suggested, remembering seeing her out in his own kitchen garden smoking. She looked at him gratefully and lit up. He noticed her tiny hands, innocent of polish and with several fingers bandaged from small knife accidents.

"You know, I've been wondering all summer if and when you'd ever make a mistake and how I'd react," he commented. "Up until now, you've been perfect."

"I'm so sorry!" she cried, ready to burst into tears once again.

"Josette, I don't fault you for the cake, but these dramatics surprise me." Josette blushed deeply. "I hope this whole cake fiasco wasn't just a bid for attention."

"Oh no! Of course not!" she protested.

"Really? Are you sure about that? You didn't somehow figure out that this is an exclusive spanking party and decide you'd earn yourself a pass into the library with me?"

Josette's blush increased in intensity to dangerous Celtic levels under the accusation.

"I didn't do it on purpose," she exclaimed, "but, I would like to…to…go submissive to you!"

"And where did you hear that expression?" he asked her over folded arms.

Josette stubbed out her cigarette in an ashtray stand and pulling aside her white shirt, showed him a tiny black Triskelion tattoo on her shoulder. Newton recognized the international symbol of BDSM.

"So it's like that, is it?" he asked. She nodded vigorously.

"Since age 13!" she then admitted.

"I hate ink. I should spank you just for that. But now is not the time. You need to get right back to the kitchen and do your job for the next three hours. When all the food is out and everyone's been fed, you can go and ask Cassandra to lend you a party dress and you and I will play."

"Really?" she asked with delight.

"And Josette," said Anthony, "don't give the cake another thought. You've fed us beautifully all summer. Anyone can have a bad day. When will you graduate the C.I.A.?"

"In January," Josette replied.

"What about James, is he graduating in January too?"

"Yes, but he's going to France after that to continue his studies," she said.

"Well, as soon as you graduate you can come to me in Manhattan and be my cook."

"Really, Mr. Newton?" Josette's pretty little face lit up.

"Yes, of course, now give me a hug and off you go," he said, pressing her to him briefly.

"Thank you, Mr. Newton," she said before rushing back inside, her cheeks aflame. Anthony reentered the house through the door to the lounge where he resumed his seat behind the piano.

Meanwhile, Colby Hodge, looking more like twenty-five than nineteen in a gray suit, was settling Marion Craig in her room at the Bone and Feather. They hadn't spoken much during the short drive from the train station and Marion seemed to be in her usual tense mood, though as attractive as usual in her trademark black suit and heels. While Colby helpfully hung her hanging bag in the closet Marion snapped open a small travel case and extracted a silver hip flask of vodka.

"Get me some ice?" she asked Colby, who located a small bucket on the desk and disappeared into the hall. Since the building was a very old one, the halls and landings were too small to accommodate an ice machine, so Colby ran down the three flights of narrow stairs to the utility room behind the lobby and got his very occasional lover some ice. When he ran back upstairs and reentered the room, Marion had already changed from her suit into a white silk robe, discarding her shoes, hose and plain black bra and panty set all together. She had two glasses ready, added some ice cubes and poured them what Colby knew to be Grey Goose or Belvedere. His own expertise lay in identifying beers, but he knew Marion's taste ran to high-end labels. Tossing back the generous drink she poured him in two gulps, he winced at the flavor, put the glass down and allowed the warmth to wash through him. Marion sipped her drink, got a joint out of her case, lit it and walked around the room, eyeing him.

Colby went into the bathroom and came out with a towel, which he waded up and lined the crack under the door with. Then he opened both the double mullioned windows wide and sat in one of the windowsills. This upper floor room had a view of the woods behind the inn. She came to him, held the joint to his lips and he inhaled. The next moment he had slipped his arms around her slender waist and drawn her onto his lap. He opened her robe and pulled it away from her thin shoulders, exposing her small yet elegant breasts. She was lean and they suited her body. He began to pinch her nipples, remembering her preference for painful stimulation. She threw head back, exposing her beautiful, long white throat. He kissed her throat then bit her lightly on the shoulders and neck.

Without speaking, he picked her up in his arms, carried her to the antique four-poster bed and tossed her on it. Looking at her all the while, he began to methodically remove his clothes, laying them neatly on a chair. Ordinarily, he would have torn them off and tossed them on the floor, but he was expected back at his girlfriend's birthday party shortly and wanted to make the best possible impression upon his arrival there. Marion untied her belt, shrugged out of her robe, pulled back the counterpane and lay naked on the crisp, sweet smelling white linen. Coming to her nude, Colby straddled her and allowed her to heft, admire and orally worship his lengthy and substantial organ for several minutes before tearing open a condom, rolling it down over his erection, capturing both her wrists under one hand and using the other to guide himself into her.

Finally he broke the companionable silence by saying, "None of your usual screaming. I don't want everyone at the inn knowing what's going on here."

"Then you'd better turn me over, so I can bury my head in a pillow," she said, with one of her rare grins.

After dropping Tai and Lydia off at Susan's house, Dru Baxter began driving back to Pine Tar Road with Carola in the back seat of his parents' new SUV. But Carola stopped him before he turned at the corner of the graveyard that faced Susan's Victorian.

"Where are you taking me?" she asked.

"Back to your sister's house," Dru said, startled and all a thrill to be spoken to in that preemptory tone by the beautiful dominatrix who had already disciplined him several times that summer. "Why? Was there somewhere else you wanted to go?"

"Yes, several places," she said, contemplating getting into the front with Dru but reluctant to expose her high heeled spectator pumps to the rain any more than was necessary. "I need to get Amanda a birthday present. Drive me to Bartlett's. They'll be open a few hours yet."

"Right away," he said and took the fastest way he knew to Woodbridge, via the back roads of Random Point as the rain continued to pour down. He looked in the rear view mirror at her now and then, finding her even more attractive this visit than the first. She was wearing a gold colored summer dress with a white collar and full skirt, a broad black belt girding her tiny waist. The moment he had seen her in the skirt he had thought how easy it would be to gain complete access to her charms without removing any clothes besides her panties. When he saw her touch up her glistening dark red lipstick with the tip of a small brush, he thought of how much he wanted to apply the tip of his tongue to her nether lips, while inhaling all of her mingled perfumes. He shook his head and concentrated on the wet road. He looked at her again and saw her combing out her silky, jet-black hair.

"You look beautiful, Mistress," he said, without self-consciousness, as they were alone. She smiled.

"Thank you," she said, without adding her thoughts on his own thoroughly pleasing appearance. Most of her customers were not tall, handsome, muscular Ivy League college boys and she was enjoying the difference. "Were you thinking of playing with me this weekend?" she asked casually.

"Oh yes, please!" he replied. "But, if I could ask one favor?"

"What's that, Dru?"

"Can we do it tomorrow?"

"Of course we can. I have nothing planned," Carola replied pleasantly.

Dru didn't speak again until they had pulled into the large parking lot behind Bartlett's department store. Dru got an umbrella out of the trunk and opened it for Carola. Then he noticed her heels again. "Should I drop you at the door?" he asked.

"It's all right," she smiled, taking the umbrella from him.

"Mistress?" he began as they began to walk toward the back entrance of the store.

"What is it, Dru?"

"Well, there are going to be some people at the party tonight who I'd rather not know I was subbing to you."

"What people?"

"Pamela Bartlett."

"Bartlett, you say? Any relation to this Bartlett?" Carola asked, looking up at the large, imposing, and elegant building that dominated the busiest corner on the Main Street of Woodbridge village.

"Yes, she's his wife. And she and I have been seeing each other a little this summer."

"And Pamela doesn't know you're submissive?"

"She knows I'm a switch and bosses me around of course, all women do. But when we play, she prefers for me to spank her and then we have sex."

"How nice for you," said Carola with a smile. "And I fully understand what you're saying. You're turning her on just the way you are, why put visions of you squirming across another lady's lap into her head?"

"Exactly," he agreed, enjoying the way Carola was taking control even of this conversation. "But besides her, there's Amanda."

"My niece and the beautiful birthday girl?" Carola said.

"Yes. She's been very nice to me."

"Oh? How nice has she been?"

"Very. Though only once," he said, adding optimistically, "So far."

"So my new submissive is a live wire, is he?" Carola asked.

"I've just been lucky enough to be in the right place at the right time," he admitted, holding the back door open for Carola, who put up her umbrella and preceded him in.

"Dru, darling, put your mind at rest. I won't discuss what happened or will ever happen between us with anyone who doesn't already know, meaning Hope and Cassandra, who set up our first

215

appointment."

"Thank you!" Dru said, beaming at his leggy companion as she strode into the basement of the store, past one of the many security cameras with a feed into Ambrose Bartlett's large bank of monitors, an array that dominated one whole wall of his executive office on an upper floor.

Bartlett happened to still be in his office, though it was past six, changing and getting ready for the party. Pamela was one story up, in her design studio, also dressing. But the wasp-waisted brunette in the perfect cotton sateen dress caught the connoisseur's eye. Shifting his gaze to another camera, he saw Carola stroll into home furnishings, with Dru Baxter following obediently behind her. He recognized that lad well enough, but the woman, who was a beauty of indeterminate age, was new to him. Ambrose thought, "Gotta be a guest for the party tonight. But who is she?" He sat down behind his desk and shifted his gaze from monitor to monitor as Carola and Dru made their way from department to department, up the escalator to the second floor and came to a halt in the BCBG boutique. "She must be buying a present for Amanda," he thought, as Carola began to quickly scan the dress racks, inspecting various garments and hanging a number of selections over Dru's arm. At one point, when she thought that no one was observing her, Carola reached under Dru's medium blue suit jacket and it seemed to Bartlett, pinched Dru's nipple. "Ah ha, so she's a top and he's a bottom," Ambrose thought, delighted to have discovered a bit of scandal about his young rival. He pondered calling Pamela down to see how her squire behaved around a dominant woman, but thought it best to reserve the information for the moment. It would be beneath his dignity to show too much interest in Pamela's cub; still it was interesting to him. Now Ambrose remembered Cassandra mentioning that her sister, a dominatrix, was coming into the party that night. "Wonder what her price to go submissive would be?" he thought to himself, unable to tear his eyes from Carola's lily waist, the part of a woman's body he found most fascinating, after her bottom.

Just then Pamela teetered into the office to get her husband's opinion of her outfit, a two piece blush pink silk knit dress composed of a close fitting, sleeveless midriff and a long, straight skirt, slit up the side to the thigh, set off to advantage by a pair of latticed, open-toed stiletto booties.

"Don't look, unless you want to be disillusioned about your boyfriend," he said, drawing Pamela's attention to the proper monitor by momentarily shielding it from her view with a file folder.

"Why? Who's in the store?" she asked with quick and lively curiosity, coming closer to the bank of screens. He pulled the file aside to reveal Dru leaning on the wall outside one of the fitting rooms.

"Oh, it's Dru," said Pamela, with interest. "Who's he waiting for?"

"I don't know if you know her, but I'm pretty sure it's a Cassandra's sister from Boston. She fits the description Hope gave," said Bartlett, directing Pamela's attention to the fitting room that Carola had just entered with three size 2 dresses.

"Oh, Ambrose, you're not going to watch her undress, are you?" Pamela said reproachfully, her eyes immediately drawn to the shopper's waist. "What a figure."

"That's what I was thinking," said Ambrose. Then they both noticed Carola turn to the door of the fitting room and say something.

"She's calling him to help her with a zipper," Ambrose speculated.

"She wouldn't!" Pamela declared with certainty.

"Look!" Ambrose pointed to the first camera, where Dru, sitting standing outside the ladies fitting room had just started, as he had heard his name called from within.

"Oh no, he's not going in!" Pamela gnawed on her knuckle in embarrassment for Dru, were he to be caught by a saleswoman on the floor and thrown out.

"Why not? She called him, didn't she?" Ambrose chuckled, delighted to have his rival revealed to be the small lapdog that he was. In the next instant Dru was entering the changing cubicle in obedience to Carola's summons.

"He shouldn't be in there. He should tell her so!" said Pamela.

"He's clearly intoxicated with the new mistress in town to the extent that reason has deserted him."

Then both Pamela and Ambrose quietly watched the seasoned model slip in and out of the dresses she was contemplating giving her niece as quickly as it was possible to do so, using Dru only to zip and unzip her.

"I've been timing her, she got each dress on and off in less than twelve seconds," said Pamela, consulting her new diamond watch, "that's professionalism."

"Uh oh, hide your eyes," said Bartlett, as Carola's hand went under Dru's jacket once more to reward him for his assistance with a hard nipple tweak. The security camera wasn't sharp enough to show his blush, so Pamela blushed for him as she witnessed the little pantomime of possession going on in the fitting room. Ambrose said, "Tsk, tsk," as though in sympathy for her misplaced affections.

"Oh, never mind Dru and the new witch in town, tell me if you like this outfit," Pamela said, turning completely around slowly before him.

"It's wonderful. It is one of your new designs for your show next week?" he asked, taking her in his arms to encircle her own willowy waist with his hands.

"Yes!"

He sat down on the edge of his desk and pulled her to him and then across his knee. Smoothing down her clinging skirt he said, "Let's see how it stands up to a spanking," and applied six or eight resounding swats to her small, gym pampered bottom, firm enough to bounce his palm off after each smack. "Do you have anything at all on under this?" he asked, without attempting to disarrange her evening dress by pulling up her skirt.

"Of course I do, some sheer, silk bikini panties. This fabric is cleverly lined," she explained proudly.

He stood her up and they both inspected the back of her skirt in a full-length mirror.

"The fabric doesn't wrinkle," he observed. "Smart choice."

Chapter Two

Early Arrivals

Both the type of people who tended to arrive early, Jane Eliot and Malcolm Branwell knocked on Carola's door at seven sharp. They were admitted by Dennis, who directed them to the schoolroom, which contained a large cloakroom for their raincoats and umbrellas. Jane and Malcolm knew each other only slightly, but each of them had the sensation that was about to change. They walked through the first hall slowly, stopping to look at some of the illuminated Ray Caesar prints that lined the walls. When they got to the schoolroom they paused to admire the finished trompe l'oeil painting of a window looking out into what appeared to be a fashionable Edwardian era London street. Malcolm took her raincoat and hung it up. They placed their umbrellas in a stand. Jane looked slim and lovely in a pearl pink raw silk V-neck cocktail dress and black high-heeled pumps. Malcolm, a tall, handsome and athletic man in his late thirties, was dressed in a light gray suit over a darker gray shirt, with no tie.

They walked around the room, looking at its appointments. Jane tried sitting at one of the school desks. Malcolm sat on the edge of the teacher's desk, looking at her.

"So, what's this I hear about you working here?" he asked, as her name had been suggested to him by Hope as a possible play partner on a future visit to the club.

Jane shrugged and smiled, casually replying, "I've dropped in a few times."

"I thought you had a regular job?"

"I do."

"And aren't you part of a lesbian couple?" he asked bluntly.

"Yes and no," she replied with another smile.

"Marnie Price, right?"

"Yes."

"Is she going to be here tonight?"

"No, fortunately, she's traveling. She's not in the scene and she doesn't really know about my new secret life. I'd prefer to keep it that way for the time being," Jane disclosed.

"You know, you were suggested to me as someone I could possibly play with," he said.

"I know," she said serenely.

"What do you think about that?"

"I don't know. What do you think?" she riposted mischievously.

"I think you're very pretty."

"Thank you. You're pretty too. Why did Marguerite divorce you again?"

Malcolm sighed, "Because I wasn't enough fun."

"That's interesting. I think that's part of the reason Michael Flagg dumped me."

"And now they're together," Malcolm observed.

"In what ways were you not enough fun?" she asked.

"Marguerite's frivolity didn't sit well with me. When we went to Vegas for William and Damaris' wedding, I blew up at her for gambling. My business was on the rocks at the time and it seemed like such a waste. I was wrong because it wasn't even my money she was gambling; it was Anthony Newton's. The whole trip was on him. But I flipped out and went home. I'm afraid I behaved so badly that it actually caused Susan to cancel out of marrying Anthony that same weekend. It gave her a bad impression of husbands. After that it was all over with Marguerite and me."

"I'm not frivolous at all. I'm a social worker," said Jane, still smiling. "I don't gamble or even smoke weed. My only vice is kinky sex."

Now it was Malcolm who smiled, for it seemed to him he might have just found his second wife.

Phoebe and Pascal Robbins were the next couple to arrive, he in a dark suit, she in a navy embroidered lace gown with a sheer, cap sleeved yoke and slim, banded waist. Her light brown hair was down on her creamy shoulders and a large pearl on a gold chain drew the eye to Phoebe's lush cleavage. She was a petite and curvaceous young woman in her late twenties with an arrestingly pretty face and charmingly composed demeanor. She was in higher color than usual in anticipation of attending her first scene party and spending at least part of the evening singing while Anthony Newton played piano. Pascal was less enchanted to be attending an event hosted by the powerful man he perceived as his rival for Phoebe's affections, in that man's posh bordello, while all of Newton's decadent friends eyed his wife. And yet, the idea of being at Amanda Sands' birthday part, and of possibly being alone with the nymph he secretly idolized, excited the photographer.

Within the previous year Pascal had not only shot Amanda for Damaris clothing ads and his own photo archives, but he had sex with her in the summer house on the wooded path that ran alongside the village brook. He knew that he had only achieved this conquest because Amanda had felt sorry for him after he had lost his wife's affections, at least temporarily, to Anthony Newton. He'd been pursuing her for months and she'd been steadfastly resisting. Then one afternoon, she simply gave in and a quick, nearly zipless sex act had been achieved with her straddling him and concealing what they were about by the clever arrangement of her skirt.

Not that he had hopes of lightning striking twice. Not this year. But he'd be in Boston in the fall, as he always was, and she'd be at the university for three more years. Someday Amanda might want him again and he would be there for her. Meanwhile, she took him straight back to the bar that Carmen had set up in the kitchen, to get him the whiskey she remembered he liked. Phoebe joined Anthony, Hugo, Susan and Laura in the lounge. The beautiful contralto was glad enough of her husband's agreeable departure, for at the sight of Anthony at the piano, a blush spread from her throat to her brow in moments. She hadn't seen him since the Kiss Me Kate revival she had starred in had closed several weeks before and the embers of her love for the composer needed very little fanning to glow again. She hoped that Pascal would amuse himself for quite some time in other rooms of the house, even if that meant running after Amanda.

It was getting on towards seven and Amanda was beginning to wonder why Colby had not returned. Each time the doorbell rang, she jumped up to admit the new guests, taking their coats to the cloakroom and directing them to follow the hall to the dining room where many of the hors d'oeuvres were already laid out on the long table and Dennis had set up a wine bar. David and Hope arrived next, he in a lightweight suit and she in a smartly tailored dark blue leather dress with elbow length sleeves, an open collar and short flared skirt, paired with matching over the knee boots in butter soft dark blue Italian leather.

"That's the coolest outfit I've ever seen," said Amanda to Hope, after directing David to Carmen's kitchen cocktail bar.

"I love yours as well," said Hope, accepting a glass of red wine from Dennis.

"Come with me a second," said Amanda, drawing Hope by the hand into the large and well-furnished bedroom that Cassandra had said she might think of as her own from now on.

Hope said, "Are we getting high?"

"I probably should. I'm feeling very agitated," Amanda confided, getting out a pipe and stuffing it from a small tin of weed Hugo had given her for her birthday when he first came in.

"Why, what's up?" asked Hope, catching the reflection of her smart outfit in a cheval mirror with satisfaction.

"Colby went to pick up Marion Craig from the station over two hours ago."

"Marion? Do I know her?"

"No. I don't think so. She's from Boston, 30 something, has a high-powered real world job, but underneath the suit she's a subbed out slut. She got hold of Colby earlier in the summer and he slept with her a couple of times. At least, that's what he told me. I've kept pretty good tabs on him since then, but men are such liars, so who knows."

"Was he dropping her at the inn?"

"Yes."

"Hm," said Hope, smoking, putting down the pipe and strolling around the room. "The color of this room is beautiful, isn't it?"

"Yes, it's called Amalfi Red," said Amanda, smiling in spite of her anxiety. "I can't believe this is going to be my room. It's ever so much nicer than my room at Eddie's house. But don't you agree that Colby's been gone a very long time with that skinny bitch?"

"Is she skinny?"

"Very."

"She must be attractive," said Hope.

"You'll see. The whole plan was that she was going to come here tonight and see if she might want to visit and work here from time to time. Just to get rid of some excess energy. So she would leave Colby alone."

"Why, was she stalking him?"

"It was about to come to that."

"She sounds like someone Mr. Bartlett would be happy to engage for a session," said Hope.

"Exactly. And he'd fuck her brains out too, which is what she really wants," said Amanda.

"Hey, don't say things like that," Hope laughed. "We're supposed to be playing pure B&D in here."

"Is that what Anthony said?" Amanda asked.

"No, it's what I say," said Hope, out of force of habit, for she'd never worked in a club where the mention of sex was not strictly discouraged. It might be practiced, but it wasn't mentioned.

"Anyway, I'm sure that's what Colby is doing to her right now. I know him. There's all sorts of micro brewery beer here, not to mention the food that's coming out. He was already starving when he left for the station. If he hadn't been yanked into her room for sex, he'd be back here eating and drinking."

"You're probably right, Amanda," Hope agreed. "Does she smoke weed?"

"Yes. And pours gallons of vodka down her scrawny neck weekly, as far as I know," Amanda exaggerated based on the description Colby had given her of Marion Craig's habits.

"Then, without a doubt, they stopped to party in her room," Hope concluded.

223

"I don't know why it should bother me so much, but it does," Amanda cried, picking up a brush and running it through her short blonde hair.

"Why don't you wear this?" Hope asked, espying a red leather headband on the marble bureau top.

"I was going to, but you don't think it's too dorky looking with the sexy dress?" asked Amanda, sliding the headband on.

"It's cute and retro. Older men love that. Speaking of which, what do you think Mr. Bartlett will give you for your birthday?"

"Oh, I hope its boots," said Amanda, knowing Ambrose Bartlett well enough by now to expect something of that exact nature on the present occasion.

"Did you hear we did a session together, Mr. Bartlett, Cassandra and me?"

"I heard it but I didn't believe it. He was well behaved though, wasn't he?"

"He was as nice as I've ever known him to be. And he left us with beautiful dresses."

"Bless his metrosexual soul," said Amanda. "He seems to have undergone some sort of metamorphosis since last winter. I don't know how to describe it, but it's almost like he's human now."

"Mr. Bartlett likes variety. So this club has been an amusement park for him. Then, on top of having Pamela for a wife, he's made Polyxena Guzman his mistress. He's just been having more fun lately."

"Hope, I know I'm not going to be able to handle seeing Colby with Marion," Amanda said, suddenly remembering to worry again.

"Amanda, you'll be surrounded by attractive men tonight. Just divide your attention between them and you won't have a chance to think about Colby."

"But Colby is all I can think about at the moment," Amanda protested. "It's gotten to the point where I'm finding it most agreeable to focus all my sexual energy on him and him alone. It took me months to train him, but now he really is almost perfectly trained."

"Except for this sleeping with the older woman thing," Hope said.

"Yes, except for that," Amanda agreed. "I mean, I got him to stop guzzling beer every night in Europe. All I had to do was ask. Several times. Maybe five. But then he really did behave beautifully."

"Well, better he fuck a slut now and then than have a beer belly," said Hope.

"You're very wise," Amanda said. "All right. You've calmed me down. We can go back now."

A stirring in the room next to Amanda's signaled the return of Dru and Carola. Departing to refresh herself with food and wine, Hope left Amanda to knock on her Aunt's door. Carola called for Amanda to come in and Amanda saw that Dru was still with her aunt, now obediently hanging Carola's dresses in the wardrobe. Carola embraced her niece, looking her critically up and down. Dru murmured something about going to pick up Lydia and Tai before discreetly slipping away.

"Since autumn's almost here, I thought sweater dresses," said Carola, watching Amanda eagerly untying the thick ribbons and peeling back the tissue still provided by the elegant department store where her aunt had bought her gifts and been exposed to the interested gaze of Ambrose Bartlett as he observed her shopping.

"They're perfect," said Amanda, holding a russet wool mini dress up to her body in a mirror. "Thank you!"

"With you at school in Boston and me living there, we really should become better friends," Carola said. "We should meet for lunch now and then and go shopping together. Don't you think?"

"Oh yes!" Amanda cried. "I would love to!"

As she left her aunt to return to the guests, Amanda ran into Pascal Robbins in the hall with a slim red leather album under his arm.

"I was just coming to find you," he said, handing her the book. "I didn't know if you had one of these yet."

"What is it?" she asked.

"A book of your best photos. You can take it around to go-sees," he said.

"Ooooh, how nice you are. Let's go and look at it," she said, leading the way down the hall past the dining room and into her mother's deserted office. They sat side by side in a deep, upholstered window seat and Amanda opened the book of photos. As it happened, Pascal had been the photographer on the three major shoots she had done that year, and had access to all of her best shots.

Amanda leafed through the eight by tens with a smile, remarking of the fashion shoot in Boston, "I didn't enjoy that one! Five a.m. thirty degrees, no coat, mini skirts, hours outside."

"That's what modeling is like," he reminded her.

"I know. That's why I'm at the university."

"You're right, of course. All the same, I may be able to dig up a gig or two for you this fall," said Pascal.

"I'd like that," she said, "but I won't be able to accept any jobs that conflict with classes or hard deadlines."

"I'll keep that in mind. Though you're the only model I ever met who played hard to get with clients."

"Are many of your other models at ivy league schools?"

"None of them are at any schools at all," he smiled.

"Mr. Robbins," she began.

"You're still calling me by my sir name, after what we did?" he protested.

"Pascal," she corrected herself, "I hope you're only trying to promote my modeling career as a friend and not as a wolf in friend's clothing."

"If you're asking me have I gotten you out of my system yet, the answer is no," he replied honestly.

"That could be a problem if we work together again. For one thing, I'm more emotionally attached to my boyfriend than ever. When it comes to sex, he's the only one I'm thinking of right now."

"You weakened once. It could happen again," Pascal rejoined opportunistically.

When Diana and Plastridge Currie arrived, the husband was again dispatched to the bar and the pretty wife pulled into Amanda's room for a private conference. It was the first time they had found themselves alone together since they had parted company in the Central Station of Amsterdam and Amanda was full of questions about the remainder of Diana's trip with Ronnie Van Horn. Diana looked over her shoulder and put her finger to her lips, saying, "Never mention that while Plastridge is in the house. He has ears like radar receivers."

"Just tell me this, did you part happily or grumpily?" Amanda asked.

"Oh, so happily. That is, sadly to part, but happy to have been together," Diana disclosed, taking Amanda's hands, carrying them to her lips and kissing them. "Thank you, fair Princess of Spanking Land." Amanda grinned and hugged her new friend.

"Speaking of glorious hook-ups, where is the handsome young jock of my dreams?"

"Oh, you mean Colby?" Amanda sat on the edge of a table and swung her shiny black platform heels. "I honestly don't know where he is. What time is it?"

"About seven-forty-five, I think."

"He went to pick up a sub he knows from Boston at the train station. That was almost three hours ago."

"A girl from school?"

"No an older woman, one of Hugo's subscribers. We did some editorial work for Hugo while he and Laura were on their honeymoon. Colby took over the letters to the editor column and immediately collected his first groupie, this lady Marion. Did I say lady? She isn't quite that. She's such a nympho she's having an interview with my mother tonight about coming to work here part time."

"Amanda, you don't sound happy about this development," said Diana. "In Paris you seemed so lassaiz faire about Colby. You and Susan treated him like a sex robot you could just pass around."

"Well, it's different when you're in control and know exactly what's going on. I was happy to lend him to Pamela a few times this summer as well. Remind me to tell you about an incredibly hot "e" scene we did with her in Doctor and Nurse uniforms one time."

"I wish that had been me," said Diana. "What's this woman from Boston like? And you shouldn't say nympho, it isn't P.C. and by your definition, I may also be one."

"I'm sorry. I'm just becoming irritated with him at this point," said Amanda over crossed arms. Then there was a knock at the door.

Amanda opened it to admit Hugo.

"Oh, hi, Diana," he said as Diana jumped up to hug him. Then she stepped back to show him the full effect of her pale cream satin strapless evening gown. "Do you like this dress?"

"I love it. You look divine," he assured her before turning his attention to Amanda. "Colby just called. He had to fix a flat as they were leaving the Inn and he isn't fit to be seen. He asked if I could lend him a suit. I'm going over to meet him at my house now."

"A flat, was it? For the last three hours?" Amanda asked over folded arms. "Is she with him?"

"Yes. I'll bring her back with me directly while he showers and changes," Hugo told her.

"Huh!" said Amanda judgmentally. Hugo waved goodbye and departed.

"I saw him fix a flat once," said Amanda to Diana. "It took him seven minutes."

Chapter Three

The House Fills Up

Amanda stood next to David solemnly watching Carmen shake a martini for him.

"I want to drink something, but I don't normally drink;" she said, "what would you suggest?"

"Have Carmen mix you a series of peach champagne Bellinis," David replied, adding, "but don't actually finish any of them."

"Carmen, would you make me a peach champagne Bellini?" Amanda asked.

"I'll fix you a classic Bellini, with fresh white peaches, Prosecco and a dash of cherry juice," said the agreeable bartender, who had met Amanda before, at Michael's tavern.

At that moment, Hugo and Marion Craig walked in. Amanda had seen the attractive Marion's photo and was expecting a sophisticated brunette in her early 30's, leggy, slim and minimalistically chic. But it gave her a jolt and a pain in the pit of her stomach to see how much more attractive Marion was in person. There was nothing remarkable about her plain black cocktail dress and heels, yet the outfit was exactly right for her.

Hugo introduced Marion to David and Amanda. Marion and Amanda shook hands, but Amanda was at a loss for any words beyond a faint hello. Looking at the confident older woman, Amanda felt choked with jealousy. Why was it so easy for her to not care about Colby with Pamela, Colby with Diana or even Colby with Bettina in Hammerfest, but so impossible to be indifferent to the concept of Colby with Marion Craig?

"It's so nice to meet you, Amanda," said Marion. "I've wanted to thank you for that introduction to Marty for some time."

"Oh, Marty! I forgot I gave him your number. That did work out well?" Amanda cried. "He never did let me know. But men don't kiss and tell, do they?"

"It went beautifully for a couple of weeks. Then he got a job offer on the West Coast and left Boston."

"Oh, I see," said Amanda.

"Is that where you live?" asked David, as he had finished his first martini and ordered another to be mixed.

Marion said she did, looking David up and down in the shamelessly appraising way that she had first regarded Colby when she took him for an escort. He told her she had better take the martini that was being made for him and said that he'd wait for the next one. She agreed. David didn't have to ask or guess her orientation.

"So, I asked Colby but he didn't seem to know, is this going to be a play party?" Marion asked.

"I'll play with you," said David, handing her a drink.

"Really? Are you a top?"

"What do you think?" he asked.

"Do you play flawlessly?"

"Yes," said Amanda, helpfully, "he does. He's an actual schoolteacher. And we have an actual schoolroom in the house."

"What are we waiting for, then?" she said. Amanda smiled at David as he led Marion out of the room. Then she told Carmen she would take the Bellini now.

Carefully sipping the fruity drink, Amanda hurried towards the front door to open it at the most recent knock. At first she didn't realize that it was Raphael Price standing before her, for his long hair had been cut short and his clean cut face, which had formerly appeared perhaps a bit too refined, now featured a rugged mustache and short trimmed beard. He wore black pants and boots and a dove gray tucked out shirt that clung to his broad shouldered V-shaped torso. His smile was sweeter and more ingenuous than ever and she remembered it, before she did him.

"Raphael, I didn't know you were coming!" she cried, finally realizing who her new guest was and drawing him inside.

"Why would I not come to your birthday party?"

"Oh, it's only ostensibly my birthday party. It's really a party for the opening of the club."

"Well, I plan to become a denizen of the club any week now," he told her, presenting her with a small, beautifully wrapped package.

"Oh, that's right, under the tutelage of my glamorous aunt," she laughed, sitting down on a hall bench and bidding him to sit beside her. Pulling open the ribbons on the small box, Amanda lifted the lid to reveal a small pair of white gold hoop earrings.

"How kind you are!" she said, hugging him.

"Is your boyfriend here?" he asked in an undertone.

"Not at the moment," she disclosed as softly. Then she mischievously allowed her hand to fall on his thigh and momentarily creep towards his crotch. But just as abruptly, as they heard someone stir at the end of the hall, she pulled her hand back. The gesture was not lost on Raphael, who turned up her chin and lightly brushed her lips with a kiss as soon as they were once again alone.

"You know I'm at your service any time," he promised her.

"I shouldn't have touched you like that," she said, jumping up. "But your new look is so attractive. I forgot myself."

Just then, Carola emerged from her bedroom in a skin tight black leather cat suit with a mock turtle neck, short sleeves, gloves and boots and strode up to them.

"Oh, what a wonderful cat suit," said Amanda. "It'll cause a sensation because everyone else is wearing a dress," Amanda hugged Carola affectionately. "What a waist she has, don't you think, Raphael?" Amanda said, placing her hands around her aunt's tiny waist.

"Exquisite," he agreed.

"I'd better go check on things in the kitchen," said Amanda abruptly, relieved to be able to detach herself from the dangerous Raphael so gracefully. Though she couldn't resist looking back at him once over her shoulder to again marvel at his new and much more masculine look. "Hot enough for a fireman calendar," thought Amanda with a smile, as she went to order another Prosecco Bellini.

But the doorbell rang and now Amanda ran to admit Marguerite.

The bookstore owner's flame-colored hair was down on her shoulders and her magnificent curves were set off to advantage in a metallic gold gown. Right behind the redhead on the doorstep was the white blonde Polyxena Guzman, also splendidly clad, in a platinum halter gown with a diamond pendant necklace accenting her cleavage. After depositing the two glittering sirens in the lounge and promising to bring them back dishes of dainties and champagne, Amanda ran back to the dining room.

Before she was finished loading up two plates for the new arrivals, Dru ushered Tai and Lydia, Carola's submissive staff from Boston, into the room. Quick introductions were made and as Tai and Lydia admired Amanda's shiny red dress; she in turn, made a fuss over their matching blue and green tartan, stretch cotton cocktail dresses, each with a short pleated skirt. Then she made use of them by handing each a plate to bring out to Marguerite and Polyxena in the lounge, while she promised to follow with champagne.

Bringing four glasses and Dru carrying a champagne bottle, Amanda returned to the lounge and saw Lydia and Tai immediately rewarded for doing her bidding with flutes of champagne.

"I'm sorry to say that Michael won't be able to leave the bar and come over until ten," Marguerite reported. "Oh, and by the way, in case you're looking for your boyfriend, he's over at the bar watching the baseball game."

Now William, Damaris, Ambrose and Pamela walked into the lounge. Anthony waved from the piano. Amanda ran to embrace Pamela. Marguerite eyed Damaris' black leather crop top and pencil skirt outfit, which echoed the longer blush silk version that Pamela wore. Marguerite would always think of Michael's first wife as her archrival and Damaris was in very good looks that night.

Taking Pamela with her to fetch the new group drinks, Amanda interlaced arms with her friend as they walked down the hall.

"So you're going back to school in two days," said Pamela. "I'll miss you, my love!"

"I'll text you every day," Amanda promised. "And come back here as often as I can."

"With you and Dru gone, it'll be terribly quiet around here," said

Pamela.

"But you're showing at Fashion Week. That won't be quiet."

"No, that will be a gigantic stress headache."

"Will you have any time in New York to be naughty?" Amanda asked.

"Ambrose is coming with me, so I'm going to be naughty with him," smiled Pamela.

"Speaking of the top that never rests, how are you dealing with the hottie from the Hague?" asked Amanda.

"She is something tonight," said Pamela, "I'll give her that. She looks like she stepped out of an MGM blockbuster from the 1950's."

"Oh, I agree, she's channeling Maria Schell," said Amanda. "But doesn't that worry you?"

"No. She's got her gig, the gym. She's not going to try and move in on mine. And anyway, look at those hips. In five years she'll be a chubby forty-year-old. And you know Ambrose's taste in waists. She's pushing it at a size eight."

"Oh, speaking of waists, have you met my Aunt Carola?"

"Ambrose and I saw her shopping in the store today with Dru."

"Did he notice what a skinny bitch she is?"

"Of course, he was instantly intrigued. And then, she being your aunt makes her even more exciting."

"We'll go and find her in a little while. Right now she's mesmerizing Raphael Price."

"And where's our darling Colby?" Pamela asked.

"He's more like Michael Flagg's darling at the moment. He's at his bar right now."

"Why?"

"Baseball game. And maybe he had to collect himself after spending the last two hours fucking Marion Craig."

"Do you want me to go and get him?" Pamela asked.

"All the way over there in the rain? You'll get the bottom of your dress wet."

"I don't mind. I want to put off that moment when I'll inevitably run into Sloan and Paula anyway."

"Are you serious? That's going to bother you?"

"I get such a terrible pain when I see them together," confided Pamela.

"It's no use. If he's watching the game, he won't leave until it's over. You'd better stay here," said Amanda, "and have a Bellini with me."

Chapter Four

The Shank of the Evening

William Random was conducting his first wife, Laura, to various parts of the house where his crew had installed extra upgrades, when they found themselves alone in the Rose parlor. The velvety textured walls were the perfect backdrop to Laura's cherry red halter evening dress; side slit to the knee and set off by a heavy gold necklace.

"I've never seen you with your hair up," he remarked; "It's very becoming."

"Thank you. You look good as well. I like your suit," said Laura, though not perfectly at ease.

"What would you think about meeting me here to play one of these days?" he shocked her by casually suggesting.

"Who, me?" she stammered.

"Yes. Why not? Getting this place ready was a labor of love and I wouldn't mind spending some time here with my adorable first wife."

"That's crazy, William. I just got married and Damaris would never go for that."

"Yes, she would. I've already discussed it with her."

"What? I don't believe it."

"Damaris has changed. She's not naughty and flawed anymore. She's the hard working, high earning, mother of my child. I find her hotter than ever, but if I'm honest, I can't be paternalistic with her anymore."

"She has become a paragon of virtue and industry," Laura agreed.

"Whereas you have remained the same lazy, spoiled, fritter the day away brat you ever were," William blithely observed. Laura started guiltily, for she had just that day been thinking how seldom she ever volunteered to help Hugo man the shop. Even so, she folded her slim arms and raised her chin defiantly.

"Luckily," she said, "my new husband is fine with that!"

"So you won't ever meet me?" he asked, disappointed.

"I didn't say never. But I have to think about it. And then, you're such a hard spanker. Couldn't we, I mean, for old time's sake, just have sex again?"

William grinned.

Ambrose Bartlett was keeping the newly arrived Thalia company on the enclosed porch as the Boston University girl smoked a joint. They were about to go into the Cape Cod playroom, where there was a stocks, and Thalia thought it wise to fortify herself before the ordeal to come. This would be her first session with Bartlett and she knew from Amanda that he was always harsh and severe the first time. Thalia was a tall, bosomy twenty year old with light brown hair and a humorous, animated face. She looked young and fresh in a cream chiffon cocktail dress with butterfly sleeves and an empire waist. She had chosen it for the ease with which the skirt might be pushed up.

Thalia had happily visited Random Point on several previous occasions, during which she had met, worked for and become deeply infatuated with Hugo Sands. Hugo did nothing to encourage the crush beyond emailing with her regularly, giving her modeling work whenever he could and making love to her whenever she suggested it. Meanwhile, the new club represented a nice little side income for the occasional call girl, along with a safe route to erotic adventures. She had no fear of the stocks or Mr. Bartlett's cane, having just washed down a Xanax with champagne. Mr. Bartlett was conquerable. Amanda had conquered him just by letting him spank her to tears once. Thalia was prepared not only to cry, but to let herself be put into the stocks and afterwards give Mr. Bartlett head. There wasn't a chance that he would leave her untipped that night.

Pamela joined them on the porch momentarily, taking possession of the joint, hugging Thalia and declaring pointedly to her husband, "She's here, and looking drop dead gorgeous."

Ambrose smiled and said, "Is she wearing a dark blue, bateau neck, liquid crepe gown, slit to the thigh?"

"Oh my god," said Pamela, "did you actually help your ex-wife choose a dress for the party?"

Ambrose shrugged, "What could I do? She came to me for advice. She said she wanted to make you sick with envy but needed secret weapons. I merely helped her pick a dress."

"You're making it up."

"You're right. I saw her leaving the store the other day and asked the girl on the floor what dress she bought."

"I'm even more distressed to hear that she's developed such good taste," said Pamela.

"Go run along and get the dungeon ready," Ambrose said to Thalia. When the younger woman had gone, he said to Pamela, "I don't think you're distressed on my account, though."

"Why? What do you mean?" Pamela was glad night had fallen and the porch lights were dim or her husband would have seen the color rush to her normally pale face.

"I mean that when we switched partners, Paula got your ex."

"We didn't deliberately switch partners. I don't think. Did we?" Pamela remembered back to a certain fateful New Year's Eve party.

"No, but as soon as Sloan realized you were marginally more into me than you were into him, he refocused his considerable charms on my then discontented wife. And immediately won her. Does it annoy you that he let you go so easily? It shouldn't make you feel badly. Paula also cut me loose on the tiniest whim. Their love for us was but anemic."

"Here," Pamela said, handing her husband the joint. "Maybe if you get a little stoned, you won't feel the need to beat the hell out of Thalia."

He took a hit and handed it back to her. "We're really a lot better suited to each other than we were to either of them, you know," he told her.

"Because we're both shallow, brittle people?"

"I don't think we're either of those things, Pamela. We're generous and loyal to our friends and employees. Doesn't that count for something?"

Pamela smiled at him. "Go and play. I will ponder your kindly advice."

Susan was helping Dennis hand pieces of cake to the guests in the lounge when Anthony motioned to her to follow him out of the room. In the hall she said, "What's up?"

"I think I'm about to give a girl who's never played before her first scene. Don't you think I should get stoned?"

"Hell yes, I do!" Susan grinned. "Where do you want to do this thing?"

"Go find some weed in Cassandra's room and meet me in the library," he told her. A minute later Susan was locking the library door behind them and preparing a pipe for her lover.

"I haven't seen you take a hit in years. Who is this innocent babe?"

"Josette, our little cook. Turns out she's submissive."

"Aw! Really?" Susan smiled, and then suddenly looked serious. "Uh oh, is she already in love with you?"

"No. I don't know. But I asked her to come be our cook when she graduates culinary school in four months." Anthony took a hit and immediately felt the good of it. "Does that make sense?"

"It makes very good sense," said Susan, who loved food. But she looked worried as she thought of the adorable tiny moppet who was about to be expertly abused by Anthony. If she weren't already in love with her boss, after he administered her first spanking induced orgasm, she surely would be.

"I'll tell her that you need to interview her as well, before we make a final decision."

"Me? Why?"

"Did you forget I just told you we'd be married by the holidays? You'll be the lady of the house. Josette will answer to Dennis, you and me, in that order. You should be sure you can stand her."

"But didn't you already tell her she had the job?"

"Yes. But I was thinking of my stomach when I said that without talking to you first."

"Since when did you ever have to talk to me about what goes on in your house?"

"Since never before, but everything's going to change now. You'll be my wife and have authority in the house."

Susan laughed. Then she looked serious again. "I suppose you're going to offer Josette Dennis' old room?"

"That was my first thought. But then I had an even better one. We'll ask Dennis if he wouldn't mind letting her stay in his spare bedroom across the street for a while. Say, until I'm able to locate another small condo in the neighborhood or Dennis and Josette fall in love."

"Dennis and Josette?"

"It's time he settled down, don't you think? He's been single forever. He must be over thirty by now. He needs someone to come home to."

"It'll be more than that if they're working together every day."

"Yes, well, I'm counting on her sweet affability and his inner grouchy Englishman to gel nicely. He actually needs someone as meek as Josette to bring out the latent top in him, don't you think?"

"Oh, there's nothing latent about the top in that boy," said Susan, remembering the spontaneous spanking Dennis once gave her when he got fed up with her casual treatment of him. "You know, the more I think about it, the more brilliant your idea is," she said. "Josette is hard working, humble, shy, she already looks up to him, you can see that."

"And it would balance the house out much more evenly. You'd have your girl to oversee and I'd have my boy. They'll work together to take care of us and we'll see that they have everything they need to be happy. A neat little household of compatible souls."

"But what if she's already madly and deeply in love with her master?" Susan asked.

"If she's smart enough to stay on the right side of her mistress, all should be well."

At around 9 p.m., when the last tray of cake slices had been delivered to the dining room, James, Josette, Dennis and Carmen sat down around the kitchen table to finally partake of the choice foods they had so lovingly prepared for Anthony's guests. Cassandra poured wine out for them, relaying the words of praise for the kitchen she had heard from all the guests. Josette bolted her food and a full glass of wine, eager to be unencumbered as soon as possible, in case Mr. Newton remembered what he had said about playing with her. Noticing that Josette had finished her meal, Cassandra took her aside, saying, "Come with me, I have something for you."

Cassandra led the little cook out to the porch and then across the long driveway to the loft, the door of which she opened with a key and then locked behind her when they had entered. Josette barely had time to take in the large, lodge like room before Cassandra led her through a door to a Scandinavian bath suite done in milky tile, frosted glass and dark wood.

"Take a shower or bath and relax for a bit. There's a Jacuzzi, a steam room and a sauna down the hall," said Cassandra. "I've left an outfit for you in the armoire in the loft. Anthony will be over in about a half hour."

Josette vibrated with pleasure. She had been inwardly fretting over how hot and sweaty she felt after cooking all day and night. "Thank you," she said shyly.

"I'll leave you locked in and Anthony will be the only one with the key, so you don't have to worry about being surprised by any of the other guests."

"Oh, how nice," said Josette. And then Cassandra was gone.

Yearning to bathe in the gleaming tub, Josette sensibly took a quick shower instead, allowing herself only moments in the fragrant sauna to warm up as she dried off. Wrapping her small form in an enormous bath towel, she ran up the wooden staircase to the loft, where a steady rain still beat against the skylights. Opening the armoire, Josette saw a dark blue stretch cotton sundress sprinkled with white flowers, a pair of chunky, gleaming black platform sandals and a pair of white, frilled rumba panties. As she slipped the dress on she noticed its Saks 5th Avenue label and felt a little thrill. The best day of her life was getting better by the minute. The little bodice hugging dress had a halter-top and a full skirt that became the young cook better than any she had ever chosen for herself. Not that she often bought dresses.

Taking a brush from the dresser, she ran it through her short, straight black hair. Finding a lipstick in the top drawer, she touched up her rosebud mouth in the vanity mirror. Then she heard a key turn in the door below.

Josette ran down to meet Anthony, who came in with a bottle of wine and two glasses.

"Tired?" he asked, pouring her a half glass of Merlot and handing it to her.

"No!" she replied, with glowing eyes and a racing pulse. He poured himself some wine and strolled around the room, sipping it.

He found a CD player and stack of discs on a shelf and flipping through them quickly, selected Sticky Fingers and started the Stray Cat Blues track. "I haven't heard this song since college, but I love it," he said.

"Me too!" she agreed.

"I'm glad because it's about you."

"I'm not fifteen."

"Close enough. I wonder what's hiding behind this," he said, regarding a large, black leather screen on wheels riveted with silver studs. He pushed the screen to one side to reveal a St. Andrew's Cross affixed to the wall in a circle and covered in the same black studded leather. Josette knew exactly what it was and her heart skipped a beat. Anthony contemplated the X-frame and looked at Josette.

"You'd have to be pretty much nude before that would make sense," he said. "Otherwise your little skirt would wind up over your head."

"I would get nude to try that!" Josette said without hesitation, adding, "I'm not as innocent as I look."

"Oh? How so?"

"I mean, I've never played before, no less, in a dungeon. Not that this pretty place looks anything like a dungeon. But I've had lots of boyfriends. So I'm not opposed to getting nude."

"That's good to know!" he grinned. "But when you say you've never played before, do you mean that all those boyfriends never spanked you?"

"They never thought of it," said Josette.

"Even when you had that tatt done?"

"They were never BDSM types. I just pretended it was a design I picked out for no reason."

"I don't get it. You went so far as to have that done, but you couldn't bring yourself to ask your boyfriends to play with you?"

"I didn't trust any of them to understand me or get this right," said Josette.

"When did you first realize you were in the scene?" Anthony asked, sitting down on a leather sofa and motioning for her to join him.

"I found Marguerite Alexander's books in a Barnes and Noble when I was thirteen and read them incessantly all through high school. But even before that, I was always attracted to spanking scenes on TV, spanking references in music and magazines. I was fascinated and fantasized about being spanked all the time. I still do. But it's never happened yet. Not once."

"What about when you were little?"

"I was raised by a single working mom in a one bedroom walk-up in lower Manhattan. We worked together as a team from the start. She never had to ask me twice to do anything, so that was never an issue."

"I wonder why you became fixated on spanking then," said Anthony.

"I know why. The Super's girls, who lived in the basement, were my best friends. They were third generation Italians and always getting spanked and strapped by their father. I spent my whole childhood in their kitchen, helping their mother cook. In return, I got to eat with them while my mother worked the late shift at the bar. I witnessed many spankings and heard even more. I think that's what did it for me."

"Ah, I love Italian food," said Anthony.

Josette beamed.

"So, what are you looking for?" Anthony asked.

"A master, of course," she replied.

"Why a master? Why can't it just be a nice boy into spanking who spanks you?"

"Sure. That would be fine," said Josette. "But a master would be hotter."

"Why?"

"Because they take control more."

"But how much control do you want to give up?"

"I don't know. I've never played, no less been in a relationship."

"You know, Josette, if you do commit to a master, you'll be expected to obey him and never lie to him."

"I would do that, willingly!"

"Really? If I were your master, would you get that ink removed from your flawless shoulder and promise me on your word of honor never to get another tattoo for the rest of your life?'

"Yes!" she cried with excitement.

"Really?" he asked in surprise. "Okay, that takes care of the obedience part and I'll hold you to it. Now for the lie you told me."

"What lie, Mr. Newton?" she looked confused.

"About not letting the cake fall on purpose to get my attention."

Josette lowered her eyes and murmured, "How did you know?"

"Because I remember you telling me when I interviewed you that baking is your specialty. Also, you produced dozens of flawless baked desserts all summer."

"I'm very sorry," she said, looking up at him.

"Good you admitted it," he said. "And I am going to spank you for that shortly. But we still have to refine a few details of this master-submissive contract we're working out."

Josette blushed deeply.

"I plan to marry Susan Ross this Autumn and that will make her your mistress when you come to us in the New Year. It should be your study to please her. In addition, Dennis will also be over you, just as he has been all summer at the house. Both Dennis and Susan have been with me for upwards of eight years. They constitute my household. Winning them over will be key to your success."

"They already both like my food," said Josette helpfully.

"That's your secret weapon. That wins hearts," he agreed. "Now promise me you'll never spoil the food again just to get my attention."

"I promise!"

"All right," he said, gently taking her by the arm and pulling her over his lap. Hearing that familiar gasp of excitement, he smiled. Being chosen to give a girl her first scene was not a responsibility he took lightly. She would compare all subsequent scenes to this one. He had to give her a high standard of excellence to use as a measure of future experiences. "By the way," he said, smoothing down her skirt, "you look very pretty in that dress."

"Thank you," she said softly.

"I'm very fond of smaller women," he said, caressing the bare backs of her knees under the cotton skirt. "But I don't suppose it's very easy being a little cook. Those cast iron pots are heavy. When you come and work for me, ask Dennis for help lifting things, won't you?"

"You're so thoughtful!" she turned to say. He gently pushed her back down.

"So are you," he said, stroking her through her skirt. "I could feel the love you put into the food that you made us all summer."

She turned to look at him, touched. He gently pushed her back down, ruffling the back of her short black hair and caressing her bare neck. "According to every P.G. Wodehouse book I've ever read, the man who doesn't do everything in his power to hold onto a very good cook is a fool."

Then he proceeded to spank her. She was a small but sturdy and somewhat bottom and thigh heavy girl, with the sort of lily skin that turns rose pink from the first smack. By now he had pushed up her skirt and tugged her panties down. Though she hardly moved at first, the little noises that she made, her small intakes of breath and tiny pants, all told him that Josette was deeply engaged in the moment. He pulled her close to him and took her by the waist, a youthful, supple waist that might all but disappear if she indulged too much in her own cooking over the next few years.

"The food you cook is very rich," he said, pausing to caress her, "don't you think, Josette?"

"Is it too rich?" she asked.

"Well, I don't want to have to spend two hours at the gym every day working off my dinner."

Josette sighed.

"What's the matter?"

"It's so hard to cook delicious food that isn't fattening," she admitted.

"Well, anyway, you can make the portions smaller. And save the desserts for holidays," he compromised, not terribly anxious to entirely forego the creamy marvels that had come from the small girl's hands to his table all summer.

"I will."

"You seem to have a pretty high pain tolerance," he said, putting her on her feet. "Let's go upstairs and try out the spanking bench with a strap or two."

Josette kicked off her panties and obediently followed Anthony up to the loft, where the cupboard was filled with wooden and leather implements that they looked at together. She picked up, hefted and smelled every item before handing them back to him.

"Which do you want to try, honey?" he asked.

"Can we try them all?"

"Yes," he said, gently arranging her face down over the spanking bench, so that she was kneeling on the lower step and the bench was under her stomach, "and I'm glad that you asked. Because as soon as you start playing in the scene, strangers will want to use these straps and paddles on you. You should know what constitutes normal usage. And we should review your safe word etiquette."

He arranged the half dozen straps to start with them.

"I know about that," she said. "I went to a seminar. My safe word is 'mercy' and I'll say it if I'm ever in genuine distress."

"Good girl," said Anthony, and then began dispensing a series of six strokes with each strap to Josette's exposed bottom draped over the bench. She took each swat with a little grunt of resolve. The straps striking her bottom stung sharply and rung resoundingly. But she was waiting breathlessly for the wood. And in fact, she only began to truly cry out when repeatedly struck by the flat of a maple hairbrush, and yet it was the thudding sensation of wood she found the most provocative aspect about the toy cabinet.

Between spates of smacks with the little wooden paddle, the bigger wooden paddle, the thick wooden hair brush and the broad wooden hairbrush, Anthony caressed and soothed her deeply reddened and radiant bottom, weaving a fascinating tale of her future life as a small sized BDSM playgirl in Manhattan. He promised to fit her up in becoming yet protective leather outfits that would keep people guessing as to her orientation before turning her loose in the clubs. He counseled her not to wear her submissiveness on her sleeve but to reserve it only for those who had earned her trust and respect. Finally, he melted her heart by promising to send Dennis along to discreetly guard and watch over her on her first subterranean adventures, which to Josette implied the finest sensibility on her new master's part.

"Please," she said, when she saw he had done with the entire collection of disciplinary toys, "I want to be spanked to tears."

"That might happen someday, but not tonight," he said, gently helping her up and hugging her to him. "You have way too high a pain tolerance and your tender bottom is already this close to bruising or the skin tearing. I've been walloping you for a half hour."

"Of course it hurt," she reasoned, "but I almost felt too excited to feel the pain."

"You got numb from being whacked so repeatedly. That happens."

She hugged him back hard, saying, "I won't let you down, I won't make you fat and I will make both Susan and Dennis like me!"

Anthony smiled down at the smart little girl who had carved herself a comfortable place in his household beginning with the new year.

Chapter Five

Hope's Glory

Hope Lawrence was in an extremely good mood when she sat down with Amanda in the lounge to watch the continuously looping promo video for the club that Amanda had shot her in the previous week. This five-minute clip had no dialog, but simply featured Hope walking through the club from room to room, her outfit changing as she went through each door, as she wordlessly indicated the features of special interest to the prospective member. The video was shot in the provocative style of a high end Vegas hotel ad, with Hope in five inch pumps and a black leather dress as she walked down the halls, then in various costumes appropriate to the specific playrooms. She walked slowly through the lounge in an evening gown and elbow gloves, pausing behind the bar to shake a cocktail. But when she came through the office door, her hair was pulled back in a clip, she had on glasses, was wearing a tight pencil skirt, heels and an even tighter white blouse and immediately sat down at a keyboard and started to type. She looked up over her glasses, as if startled at being seen at work. Next, Hope went into the dining room, carrying a tray of tea things, dressed in a formal gray maid's uniform with a white apron and black heels, put the tray down and straightened her apron strings in a mirror, looking back over her shoulder at the camera.

The business with the apron struck Hope as ironic, as this was the summer she had hung up her red barista's apron for good with great joy. The girls sat hugging each other with elation at how smart the promo video looked. Anthony Newton had taken the time to record particular piano music to go with each room and mood change and he watched the video over the girls' shoulders from a perch on a stool at the bar with great satisfaction.

They continued to watch as Hope appeared in the school room in a plaid prep school skirt and dark blazer, fearfully revealing the inner cloakroom, with its trestle bench for caning and its cabinet full of rulers, pointers, birches, paddles and school straps. Then she went and sat at one of the school desks, put her chin on her hand and stared out the trompe l'oeil window at the illusion of the 19th century Mayfair street. The next room Hope was seen in was the library, where she wore an autumnal wool sweater, tweed skirt and riding boots and picked out a book from a shelf to read by the fire. In the dusky rose front sitting room, Hope appeared in a tightly laced dark green velvet Victorian riding habit, accurate in many details and exceedingly dainty. In the burgundy salon, she wore a sheer, gold latex sheath and six inch heels as she knelt on a spanking bench and bent over it to demonstrate its functionality. But in the terra cotta salon, she strode in dressed in the dark blue leather outfit she was wearing that evening, with a matching blue leather paddle tucked under her arm. This time when she pointed out the spanking bench, she indicated that the viewer might be invited to bend over the bench him or herself, while she, Hope, would administer the discipline. Staying in dominant mode for the Exam room segment, Hope transformed herself into a white uniformed nurse, circa 1959 and guided the viewer around the elegant pearl gray exam room, with the rich leather furniture that Diana and Plastridge Currie had chosen for it. Hope showed all the positions the exam chair could be put into and also the table, managing to combine naughtiness with determination in putting over her nurse persona.

The tour continued with Hope in Cape Cod, unbuttoning a dark wool dress to reveal a white bra and panty combination and then showing the viewer the whipping post and stocks before turning to unhook her bra. The final interior scene showed Hope entering the loft, in riding pants and shirt and riding boots, pushing aside the screen to reveal the St. Andrew's Cross, then taking the viewer up the stairs to the bedroom under the skylights, with its own spanking bench and cupboard full of toys. Nor was the bath and spa neglected. Hope led the viewer through these wrapped in a white bath towel.

The video tour of the club and its amenities concluded with Hope, now dressed in jeans and a cropped vest, leading the viewer into the woods with her, in search of a switch.

The girls eagerly watched it through a second time, completely mesmerized. But even though she was mostly paying attention to the video, Amanda couldn't help but hear a whispered remark that Anthony made to Phoebe Casper behind them. She was the wife of the photographer Pascal Robbins, who had given Amanda the book of her photographs earlier in the evening. She had also been Anthony's leading lady in the Kiss Me Kate revival earlier that summer. And she was a member of the Venus Club, that interesting sorority of local scene girls and women who had agreed to be each other's particular friends at a dinner back in June. Amanda knew that Phoebe struggled with her passion for Anthony Newton, mainly because it ran so contrary to being a faithful wife. She knew this because Pascal had told her about Phoebe's affair with Newton, which had also taken place at the beginning of the summer. So now, it made perfect sense when she overheard the quickly whispered, "Do you think you can get away for a bit and play with me tonight?" from Anthony and Phoebe's quick reply, "I would dearly love to. But what about Pascal?"

Slipping away from Hope, who would happily stare at her own entrancing image for the next hour, never stirring from the sofa, Amanda presented herself to Phoebe and Anthony and said, "Maybe I can help."

Phoebe gave a start. But Anthony grinned. Back in June, the sight of Pascal merely talking to Amanda had given Phoebe a pain in her stomach, but tonight her desire for her maestro was at an all-time high and trumped even her jealousy of her husband's teenaged muse.

"What are you thinking of, Amanda?" Anthony asked.

"I'll tell him we need to hunt down every lady in the house who's going to visit the club for a group photo," said Amanda. "That will take no less than an hour, I guarantee." For Amanda knew from experience how Pascal liked to shoot and how long he took to pose his models. Phoebe's beautiful shoulders relaxed in relief as she realized that she wouldn't be ceding her husband to Amanda alone as the price of an illicit interlude with Anthony in one of the playrooms.

"I love that idea," said Anthony. "And make sure you invite Marguerite, Susan and Laura to be in the picture as well," he added.

"As our muses."

"I'll take Hope with me and we'll round up Pascal," Amanda promised. "When I've got him in hand with me, I'll text you," she said to Anthony, for he had long since given her his phone number.

"Where do you expect to wind up with all the girls?" Anthony asked.

"The terra cotta salon. The faux marble walls will look divine as a backdrop," Amanda said.

"Good, we'll go play in the loft at the opposite side of the house," Anthony told Phoebe, who clapped her hands softly.

Amanda took Hope by the hand and pulled her friend from the room.

"Where are we going?" Hope asked, reluctant to walk away from the screen where her own alluring image was parading about the house in the many flattering outfits.

"To find Pascal and all the girls who are going to be visiting here for a group portrait," explained Amanda.

They stopped when they encountered Alison Albrecht, dressed in a pleated camel skirt, blazer and white blouse, sitting on a bench in the hall outside the schoolroom.

"Hello," said Amanda.

"Hi," said Hope. "Are you waiting for someone who's playing in there?"

"Yes," said the pretty brunette, "your husband."

The girls all listened for a moment to the rhythmic sound of slaps being administered within.

"Oh, he's still playing with Marion?" Hope wondered aloud.

"Yes," said Alison. "But he handed me this 'See me!' note yesterday when I told him I would be at the party." Alison was the assistant comptroller at Braemar Prep, where David taught English.

At any other time or in any other place, Hope might have felt disturbed and uneasy by the notion of two pretty brunettes fighting for her husband's attentions, but here and now the situation seemed the perfect sop to his previous antipathy toward the club. Tonight he would surely realize what a benefit the Venus Club could be to them both.

"We may need Marion," said Amanda to Hope. "She may start coming to the club to session."

"Go and get David a martini and then knock on the door," Hope told Alison. "Tell them Marion is needed for a photo now."

Alison was growing tired of waiting and agreed at once. Hope grinned at Amanda, "Yay, this is perfect timing. While there's still smacking sounds coming through the door, there's no way they've had a chance to have sex yet."

"Do you really think she'd be doing that right after fucking Colby?" Amanda asked.

"Yes, of course. That's how thirty-something-sluts operate."

Hope and Amanda found Pascal Robbins already busily posing Polyxena Guzman and Marguerite Flagg in the terra cotta salon. Neither lady had officially decided to visit the club in a professional capacity, but each was considering the option. Meanwhile, the very fact that they had both appeared in evening gowns was excuse enough for cameras to come out. Amanda texted Anthony: "P. Robbins corralled for next hour."

Chapter Six

Pamela and Sloan

Pamela Bartlett and Sloan Taylor had been looking at each other all night across rooms and hallways, then turning quickly away. Then came a moment in the evening when each realized that their mates were fully engaged elsewhere in the house and unlikely to surprise them. Half the female guests had disappeared into the Tuscan parlor to be in the group photograph, which had considerably thinned the assemblies of guests in each of the open rooms. By a quick process of elimination, Pamela had come to the conclusion that Ambrose had corralled his ex-wife behind one of the doors that were closed and locked and was now playing with and/or making love to her there. Catching up with Sloan in the hallway right outside the vacant Cape Cod playroom, Pamela touched his hand and said, "Come in here for a second, would you?"

Sloan followed her into the still sparsely furnished, white washed room with the seashore scene painted on two walls.

"Do you have any idea of where Paula might be at this moment?" Pamela asked.

"I know exactly where she is, she just went into the schoolroom with David Lawrence and I distinctly heard them locking the door," he replied.

"And now this door is locked," said Pamela, bolting the wooden door of Cape Cod and putting her back against it.

"Why did you do that?"

"I want to be alone with you," she admitted. "Is that all right?"

"I suppose so," he replied indifferently.

"Oh, I see you're still peeved at me. Well, never mind then," said Pamela, throwing back the bolt and starting to pull it open.

"Wait!" he said, going over to the door and relocking it. "Of course I want to be alone with you." He took her in his arms and kissed her on the mouth in the way that he knew melted her. When he finally let her go she looked at him with wide, dark eyes.

"Sloan, you still love me," she declared in her softest voice.

"How could I not? You're more beautiful than ever."

"And you look more camera ready than ever," Pamela said. "You always were a sharp dresser. I love that about you."

"I know. I was perfect for you except for not having any money or influence," he sighed.

"But hasn't it all turned out for the best?" she asked, wandering around the room and looking at the play furniture. "What do you think of this whipping post?"

"We never played on a whipping post," he said.

"Do you want to?" she asked.

"I take it the stocks don't interest you?"

"Sloan, we've both read enough 18th century history to know how deadly the stocks can be," Pamela reminded him.

"At least that was one thing we had in common," he said, opening a cabinet to survey the available arsenal of implements.

"Oh look, the post already has leather cuffs attached at the top and center," Pamela pointed out. "It's all been very well thought out in the house, hasn't it?"

"I found something," he said, pulling out a fresh birch rod.

"Oh, a birch!" Pamela exclaimed.

"I can't believe you'd trust me with a birch after what you did to me," he marveled, but came over to examine the fittings of the post.

"Of course I trust you, Sloan. You're good and kind and thoughtful. You would never hurt me."

"Thank you," he said.

Sloan looked at Pamela's silk two-piece dress and said, "That outfit needs to come off. The birch would damage it."

"I know," she agreed, reaching back to unzip the top. She shrugged it off to reveal a nude strapless bra. Next she unzipped and stepped out of her skirt, laying both pieces carefully on a plain wooden table. Now she stood before him in just the bra and a pair of French bikinis in the same flesh tone as the bra. Her long, elegant feet were shod in elaborately latticed 5" blush stiletto bootie sandals that brought her almost up to standing eye level with her 6'2" ex-lover. Her dainty bosom had filled out ever so slightly and her slender bottom seemed marginally rounder since he'd last seen her like this and the few extra pounds became her. He beckoned her over to the post and turned her to face it. The base of the post featured a leg spreader plank with straps. Sloan knelt and began to fasten Pamela's slender ankles to the spreader bar, then remembering she still had panties on, reached up, pulled them down and then off before continuing with the ankle straps. She seemed to shiver from head to toe as he pulled her scrap of lingerie off. She looked over her shoulder at him. His hair was straight, black and shiny. He turned his face toward her. They had been perfect mirror reflections as a couple, each tall and slim, with their dramatically black hair and pale olive toned complexions. They had been quiet and reserved, fiercely attracted to each other, yet oddly dispassionate when the time came to part.

He got up, unhooked her bra, freed her small, peach shaped, high set bosom and caressed her satiny back and narrow rib cage with his fingertips, then traced her spine down to the jutting curve of her bottom.

"Thank you for bringing me in here," he said. "I'm not sure how or why I let you slip through my fingers so easily, but tonight you seem to want me again, so for the next half hour, let's just pretend that you and I belong to each other, as we once did."

"Gladly," she replied. "And go as hard as you like. I need to feel a cathartic emotion to wash away the anxiety of impending Fashion Week. Damaris and I are showing for the first time and I'm as tense as a wound spring."

Sloan fastened her wrists above her head around the post and only stepped away to arrange a plain wooden cheval mirror at an angle her turned head could gaze at, picturing her own nude profile from head to toe and himself behind her.

Sloan did use the birch hard and fast, but not from the outset. Light tapping gave way to firmer rapping and then ever faster lashing strokes, until the bouquet of bound, trimmed twigs was whizzing through the air and landing across Pamela's bottom in rapid, whippy volleys. Pamela began to wriggle, twist and cry.

He tossed away the birch, freed her from the post, turned her around and took her in his arms, asking, "Should we, Pamela?"

"That table looks sturdy," she said practically. He picked her up in his arms and carried her to it. "I could sit on it, facing you, and look into your eyes the entire time," she suggested.

"I used to be able to make you come like that," he said fondly.

"You can again," she said, leaning back and making herself completely accessible to him.

Chapter Seven

The Return of Colby Hodge

It was going on eleven when the rain finally ceased to fall. As Susan helped Dennis and Carmen restore some semblance of order to the kitchen, Anthony found Cassandra locking up the loft. The nearly full moon emerged between the parting clouds to illuminate the misty drive as Cassandra turned to smile up at her benefactor.

"The party went well, don't you think?" she asked as he stretched his hand out to her.

"Marvelously well," he agreed, leading her towards the sheltered side porch where they began to stroll up and down. "I couldn't be happier with what you've done here."

"Me?" she laughed. "You and your magical credit cards did it all."

"You made it all come together," he told her. "Just as I knew you would."

"I wish this summer didn't have to end," said Cassandra, stopping to lean against a post and look out into the dripping forest. "I'm going to miss you."

"Will you?" Anthony seemed pleased.

"So much!" she cried.

"Write me every day," he told her. "Tell me what you're doing and all about the club."

"Will you have time for that?"

"Of course I will. Don't you know how attached to you I've become?"

"Have you, really?"

"Can you doubt it?" he asked.

"I shouldn't, after all you've done for Amanda and me."

"Amanda is an adorable girl, but you're the one I love."

"I don't know why you should, but it makes me very happy."

"I've been obsessed with Random Point ever since I threw my first party up at the Cliff house years ago. It's my happy place."

"Not Broadway?"

"That's a different happy place. But coming back to you, the fact that you were Hugo's first Random Point girl fascinated me, especially when Amanda showed up. You were a romantic figure to me before, when you were a disappeared mystery, but when your girl arrived, it reawakened my interest in you and I had a Venus club ring made for you as the original member. I knew it would bring you to me."

Cassandra did not think of reminding him that Eddie leaving her had been her primary motivation for migrating back to the eastern seaboard. She too was romantic and more than cosmic and understood the meaning of rings as well as he did.

"And then you arrived," he continued, "and were just the kind of girl I like. That's why I went with your idea and bought this place right away. I want you to stay around and be in my life."

"Anthony," said Cassandra tentatively, "maybe it's presumptuous of me to even ask, I know how busy you're going to be as soon as you get back to the city, but would you ever want me to get in touch with you if I happened to be in New York this fall?"

His face lit up and he replied, "I would take it greatly amiss if you didn't, young lady. And you might make a note that Monday afternoons and evenings are when I'm most likely to be free."

"I might have to visit in October. It's my favorite month in New York."

"Let me know when you're coming and I'll book you into a close by hotel. We'll go play at my friend Isabel Bruno's club and line up some visiting talent to come out to Random Point. "

Cassandra's heart throbbed with gladness at not being invited to stay at his house, where Susan also lived. A hotel room promised a continuation of their erotic adventures.

"By the way," he said, as they reentered the house through the side porch, "I'd keep an eye on Amanda. She's looking a little unsteady on her feet. Might be time to put her to bed."

On the way through the east wing, Cassandra passed by the open door to Carola's bedroom and saw her sister touching up her lipstick in her bureau mirror. Since the photo shoot, Carola had changed into a black and white tulle hostess gown outfit with tight fitting satin pants.

"Are you good?" Cassandra asked her sister, joining her in front of the mirror and running a brush through her silky brown hair.

"I just saw poor Dru sighing and pining for Pamela Bartlett. Then she disappeared down the hall with that devastatingly handsome Sloan Taylor."

"Yes, he's been her plaything all summer and suddenly he's forced to see her on her husband's arm and then go off with her former lover," Cassandra said. "But after all, he's had a great summer and he'll be going back to college next week."

"If he's still at loose ends at the end of the night, I might let him stay with me," said Carola. Cassandra started with surprise. "Just to console him," Carola hastened to add. "He is my favorite new client. And a client like that, you keep for life."

"Have you ever slept with someone that much younger than you before?" Cassandra asked.

"Why? Do you think it wrong?" Carola asked casually.

"No, of course not. You're giving him a gift and he'll appreciate it to his dying day. He's a nice boy."

"A very nice boy," Carola laughed, fondly musing on her new admirer's youthful attributes. "And I thank you most sincerely for sharing him with me."

"Oh, you know I'm not really a top. What would I do with a boy like that?"

"You seem to have made pretty good use of him so far."

"Speaking of which, you know he's been with Amanda at least once, right?"

"I didn't know the exact details but he gave me to understand that he didn't want to be treated like a subbed out bad boy by me in front of her."

"I think it was on a double date with Colby and Pamela."

"Quite the decadent little niece I seem to have," Carola observed with a grin.

"She was the catalyst that made all of this possible," Cassandra indicated the fine house that surrounded them. "I mean her coming to Random Point last year to make herself known to Hugo and then bewitching everyone he introduced her to. That was what got Anthony thinking about me."

"Not many kids bring their parent a patron. You did a good job with her."

Cassandra found Amanda pacing back and forth on the front porch as the tapering raindrops turned to mist. Malcolm was leaving with Jane and Cassandra bade them both a fond good night.

"Eleven and he's still not here!" Amanda complained to her mother. At that moment, Colby and Michael Flagg drove up in Michael's pickup. Cassandra immediately took Michael inside to set him up with food and drink while Amanda confronted Colby with her hands on her slender hips.

"What kind of boyfriend are you?" she asked, in exasperation. "It's not enough that you fuck another woman but you miss the whole party for a baseball game and beers in a bar?"

"I thought you'd enjoy the party more without me standing between you and your long line of elderly admirers," he cheerfully rejoined.

"Oh, so you were just being unselfish and considerate?" she removed her arms from her hips to fold them across her bosom.

"Exactly!"

"Sending me through my first grown up scene party all by myself seemed like a good idea to you? And not just any scene party, my birthday party too! Do you really think a nineteen year old wants to be at that kind of party without her boyfriend?"

"I didn't think of it like that," Colby admitted.

"Of course not, you were too busy spending two hours with Marion Craig at the Ball and Feather Inn. Why two hours, Colby? You must have known I was waiting for you to come back. You obviously had to service her, but that could have been accomplished in twenty five minutes and still allowed for foreplay."

"You heard about the flat tire, though?" he asked.

"Yes. I've seen you fix a tire. Make it forty minutes with Marion, including sex and the tire. You could have been back to me within an hour of going to pick her up with very little harm done to my evening. Instead, you chose to be MIA the entire night."

"All right," he paced, "I'll admit, when the tire blew on top of me spending too much time with Marion, I was nerve shattered. Besides being a mess. After your Dad lent me the suit I figured I'd steel myself for the party with a couple of beers at Michael's."

"Why did you have to steel yourself for the party?" she demanded.

"Mingling with all those grown ups who want you is an unnerving prospect."

"Who? Who the hell wants me in there? People have been unbelievably respectful of my age tonight. No one so much as suggested a public birthday spanking. But if they had, you should have been there to administer it."

"That man you prostituted yourself to last spring is in there."

"Yes, but he hasn't come near me all night. He's far more interested in the new blood in the club tonight. Last time I saw him he was going into the exam room with Marion."

"Really?" Colby's face broke into a grin. "That's great!"

Amanda's face and stance softened as she realized how heartily Colby wished to be rid of the obligation of entertaining Marion.

"You're lucky you came back when you did," Amanda said, "I was about to give up on you entirely and pick out one of my not so elderly admirers to console me."

"That wolfish photographer?" Colby asked.

"No, someone even younger and more handsome. But you just reminded me of something; you weren't here for any of the pictures. As a penalty for being a horrid boyfriend, you have to come inside with me and pose for a photo."

"I will if you say you're not mad at me. I know it wasn't right to hang out at the bar, but I had a hundred bucks on the game."

"Did you win?"

"Yes!"

"Good, you can make this up to me by getting us a suite at the coolest hotel in Boston for my actual birthday night."

"Now you're talking!" he said, taking her hand.

Just as they were about to go inside, Raphael Price exited the front door.

"Oh, hi Raphael," said Amanda, "I don't know if you've ever met my boyfriend Colby. Colby, Raphael." The young men shook hands.

"I think we met once at the Dutch," said Raphael.

Colby asked, "Is the party ending?"

"Of course it's ending," said Amanda, "it's late!"

"No, it's still going, but nothing is going to top the scene I just had with Carola, so I'm going home," said Raphael.

"Will you take our picture first?" asked Amanda.

"Sure!" said Raphael.

"Colby, give Raphael your phone."

Colby produced his phone, the photo was posed and taken several times and Raphael bade them a fond goodnight.

"That's going to be a terrible picture," predicted Amanda; "You're completely rumpled from fucking other women and drinking in a bar all night and I'm wasted from drinking five Bellinis."

"He's the one, isn't he?" Colby asked Amanda as they entered the house.

"Which one?"

"The one you said was younger and more handsome than the camera wolf."

"Oh, yes, of course he's the one. But don't let talk about that now. I know you can't tell but I'm barely holding it together. I need you to get me out of this torturously tight dress and monstrous shoes and put me to bed, preferably in the next three minutes."

If there was a duty Colby could be relied upon to perform with alacrity, it was removing all garments from Amanda's body. Not even the intricacies of the glove tight PVC dress confounded him and he soon had his girl nude between the cool sheets of the large and luxurious bed in her assigned room and was serving her ice water, which Amanda sipped thoughtfully while sitting up, the bedclothes pulled up to her shoulders. Colby was about to turn off the lights and take off his own clothes when Amanda startled him by announcing that she was feeling a little better, and getting her second wind.

"Go and bring me some food from the kitchen while I put some clothes on," she said.

"Seriously?"

"If you see my mother there, she'll make a plate for me."

Cassandra was indeed in the kitchen, as was Josette, returned from her blissful scene in the loft and wandering about the big room performing small duties, as though in a trance. Cassandra had been informed by Susan of the little cook's adventure with their master that night and had been keeping a fond eye on Anthony's latest protégée since she had come back. But when she heard that a plate was required for the daughter of the house, Josette came out of her reverie and rushed to fill a dish with small sandwiches and deviled eggs. Cassandra added two petit fours to the edge of the plate, then remembering Colby was going back with her, added two more.

When Colby returned to Amanda he found her up and dressed in a short, form fitting hound's-tooth jumper, mahogany penny loafers and white anklets, sitting at her vanity and slipping a different headband onto her short, blonde hair.

Colby watched Amanda eat, surprised at her powers of recovery.

"You know, Colby, you're right. There are a hell of a lot of older individuals at this party."

Colby wasn't sure where she was going with this and let her continue without comment. At any rate, it didn't really matter what she was saying, the important thing was that her tone was friendly and non-confrontational. He felt he'd gotten off very easy that night, what with his blatant unfaithfulness and then missing her whole party. Even so, he wasn't prepared for the generosity of her next statement.

"We all know this party wasn't solely for my birthday, but my birthday was a definite part of the event. Well, I really didn't get to play at all so far, and neither did you. But listen to this, Colby, even though there are a lot of thirty somethings and up in the house, there are also a bunch of us kids. So I propose we round them up and take over the loft for the next hour or two and have a party of our own."

"Who did you have in mind?" he asked, his mini tablet and a stylus appearing in his hand.

"Okay, let's see, Thalia, Dru and those two young girls from my

Aunt's club, Tai and Lydia, Diana Currie, she's thrill-starved as you know, and she adores you; and Pamela needs to lose some stress before Fashion Week, so make sure you find her. I'll hunt down Susan Ross."

Colby liked the odds of two boys to seven girls very much and merrily went out to hunt down the group of guests on the list. Meanwhile, Amanda finished her midnight snack, fixed her lipstick and went looking for her mother.

"May we use the loft?" Amanda asked Cassandra, noticing a shudder pass through the small girl cook in the blue sundress when she said the word loft. Amanda explained her idea of a junior players' party where she and her younger friends could just be their version of kids.

"I'm so glad you're feeling better," said Cassandra. "I don't think anyone is in there. Go for it."

"Oh wonderful!" cried Amanda, hugging her mother. "Do you like this dress? It's one of the presents Mr. Bartlett brought me."

"Adorable," said Cassandra, and then noticing Josette returning to her neatening up, drew Amanda's attention to the pretty culinary student. "We just found out tonight that Josette is one of us, Amanda."

"Really?" Amanda turned to gaze at the small brunette, who blushed. "Oh, how cute is that! You have to come to our private party then. Meet us in the loft in five minutes!"

Amanda found Susan playing billiards with Pascal Robbins in the lounge. She explained her mission and apprised Susan of everyone else she was inviting to the loft. Susan was quite ready to accompany Amanda back to the party within the party when she heard that Josette had just been invited to attend. She hesitated for a moment, then shook her head and said, "I think I'll pass."

"But why?" Amanda cried.

"Josette is going to be working for us come the new year and I'm going to be her mistress. If we play together now, it might be awkward later, when I'm her boss."

"Not if you just come and play as a top," Amanda suggested.

"No, thanks," smiled Susan, "I think I'll just hang out here and try to seduce Mr. Robbins. I've been trying to catch his eye for years and I just might have a chance tonight." This little speech was made in Pascal's hearing, in order to make him smile. He knew he was being teased and suspected it was to keep him pleasantly occupied while his wife was engaged in some piece of forbidden behavior in a different part of the house, but it also occurred to him that it might serve them both right, his sometimes unfaithful wife and her sometimes lover, Anthony Newton, if he dragged that blonde girl Susan Ross off into a cedar scented walk in closet and ravished her in the way that he believed spanking girls fancied. Susan had been flirting with him for years and he had long admired her petite curves and waist length wheat gold ponytail.

"Well, if you happen to see Diana before Colby intercepts her," said Amanda, "send her straight to us in the loft."

Susan promised to deliver an enchanted Diana into the hands of Amanda and her friends directly and went off to find her closest girlfriend. She found the small brunette just leaving one of the powder rooms and made Amanda's invitation to her.

"Oh, isn't this good timing!" cried Diana, "P.C. has just gone into the room with the claret walls with Damaris, Carola and rope. He'll be an hour."

Meanwhile, Amanda found Pamela, who was still inwardly vibrating from her prolonged encounter with Sloan, surreptitiously nibbling on a piece of Josette's dark chocolate raspberry ring torte while studying one of the delicately moody Ray Caesar portraits in the hall.

"They're wonderful and then they're horrible, the way they morph into insect legs and limbs," said Pamela. "Why are they all mutants? And did you notice that they all have the tiniest waists?"

"Some of them are only barely deformed," said Amanda, "some just have large foreheads and translucent skin. I love their retro costumes."

"The costumes are everything. They're God," agreed Pamela.

"It doesn't bother me that they look teenaged. I'm teenaged and I enjoy being eroticized," admitted Amanda.

"They look younger than teenaged," Pamela felt bound to point out. "And they look like they are being prostituted, in a Storyville style bordello at the turn of the 20th century, with their deformities a selling point."

"I agree, displaying a little girl in an eight garter corset that shows when her tiny skirt is blow up by the wind is very perverse," said Amanda.

"I would like to see what Ray Caesar's bedroom looks like," said Pamela. "I'll bet he has kept all of his mother's vintage toys, from the 1950's."

"I'll bet his closet is even more interesting," chuckled Amanda, "where he keeps his own collection of 9" ballerina pumps."

"Where are you bound for?" asked Pamela, turning away from the mesmerizing print to regard Amanda's preppie outfit with interest.

"The loft and you're coming with me," said Amanda, linking arms with her same size but ten years senior friend. They had both cut their hair short at the beginning of the summer, Pamela choosing a Louise Brooks bob at Amanda's suggestion and Amanda electing the more radical Jean Seberg crop. Now Pamela's jet black hair was a smooth, sleek, collar length version of the Veronica Lake side part wave and Amanda's ash blonde bob was at last once again long enough to grab her by.

"Why? Who is in the loft? And where is Ambrose?" asked Pamela. She had only been married since the spring and this was the first scene party they had attended as a couple. During the last and only other scene party they had ever attended, on New Year's Eve at Anthony house the previous year, she had come as Sloan's fiancée and Ambrose had escorted his first wife, Paula, with the party acting as the catalyst to the dissolution of both relationships and the forming of the two new ones.

"He's locked in the exam room with Marion Craig. I doubt he'll be out anytime soon. Come along with me, I've got Colby, Dru, those cute club girls from Boston, Thalia and Diana waiting for us."

"Colby and Dru!" Pamela clapped her hands.

"And that adorable little cook, Josette, it turns out she's in the scene."

"Just two young boys for all those girls?"

"Two strapping young men can certainly handle a half dozen

girls."

"I count seven girls, with you," said Pamela.

"Oh, I'm going to be the mistress of ceremonies. I'll think up the games and make everyone obey me. It is my birthday."

"And I'll nominate you for a birthday spanking from every one of us in case no one else does," said Pamela helpfully.

"I don't mind," laughed Amanda, for she had selected a group of playmates too close to her own age and generation to feel embarrassed before. "I'd die if all the old guard were watching every smack that fell. And my father and his best friends would be even more squeamish about witnessing his own daughter bare-bottomed. It would confuse and distress us all."

When Pamela entered the loft and saw its occupants to be already fully engaged in making use of its unique appurtenances. Lydia and Tai were at work fastening Diana, clad only in a sheer black bra and panties, to the St. Andrews Cross, facing it, with her back to the room. When she was perfectly bound, the experienced club girls began to slowly rotate the wheel, a few inches at a time with the eventual object of completely inverting the bound girl. At some point in the evening, every girl in the room would take a ride on the wheel, facing the room with her back to the wheel, to be either nipple tweaked, breast spanked and pussy whipped or facing the wheel, with her bottom to the room, to be bottom smacked, caned or flogged. Colby and Dru divided up the dominant duties between them very quickly. Colby started downstairs, manning the St. Andrews Cross while Dru escorted Josette and Thalia up to the bedroom to dispense strappings to them as they lay face down across the bed or side by side over the large, tiered, leather spanking bench.

Pamela didn't know where to look first, it was all so interesting. She was no stranger to the talents and abilities of Colby and Dru, both of whom she had gone cheerfully submissive to at a word from her much younger friend, Amanda. Pamela's relationship with Dru had developed into a discreet but nonetheless continuous love affair all summer long, with Dru meeting her for trysts both in her old studio above the Damaris shop and here at the Pine Tar house.

In the end, Pamela decided to perch on the corner of a sofa and watch the St. Andrews Cross show as it progressed before her and then volunteer to take Diana's place and experience a flogging from Amanda's college sophomore boyfriend as soon as possible. Amanda stood behind Pamela, watching with all her attention as well, while gently massaging her friend's shoulders through the feathery silk of Pamela's cropped top.

"I so wish I could be with you at Fashion Week," Amanda sighed.

Pamela turned to her and said, "I'm not showing until Friday night. Even if your last class is that morning, you could catch a train and be in Manhattan with plenty of time to spare."

"Oh, that's perfect!" Amanda cried, hugging Pamela.

"You can stay with us overnight and we'll spend Saturday together in New York. Ambrose got us a suite at The Library for the whole week."

"Let me talk to Colby first. He might want to come with me."

"Damn right I'm coming with you," Colby turned from the cross and Diana to tell Amanda. "Think I'm letting you shack up with that sophisticated slut and her Back Bay bred Tiberius for a weekend if I can help it?"

Chapter Eight

An Account of Sundry Adventures

In other areas of the house too, water was seeking its own level. Amiable acquaintances who knew of each other's scene interests but had never played together, as well as a collection of friendly exes, began pairing up, forming three ways or quartets in every room in the house.

William Random lingered in the rose sitting room, somewhat melancholy after Laura left him without agreeing to a definite future play date. The insatiable Marion Craig happened past the open door on her way back from her adventure with Ambrose Bartlett in the exam room and paused to chat with William. Within three minutes, they were locking the door and Marion was going down on her knees to him. She had been on her knees a good deal that night, but they were strong, well exercised knees and she enjoyed nothing more than testing their limits in this manner.

Tonight Marion was finally getting what she had dreamed about for years, her own private Chateau Roissy, full of good looking, well-endowed men who were happy to thrash her and use her at the first invitation. She had been to many BDSM parties and support groups over the past dozen or so years, but they had always been painfully light on attractive male tops. These men were not only good looking, but they wore beautifully cut suits, a sight to gladden her sensibilities. And not one of them was asking her to spank them, which was a great relief to her, as she had no interest in playing mommy. Her fantasy was to be used as a sexual resource, by as many men as any particular evening could reasonably hold. She didn't need to go to this type of excess all the time. Once a month was sufficient, with a random Friday evening pick up to take the edge off the other three weeks. She did belong to swingers clubs in both Manhattan and Boston, and there were virile men to choose from, but not the spanking kind.

This had been the perfect party. She'd begun it with the satisfying scene in the Ball and Feather with college boy Colby. After the tire-changing incident, Hugo invited Colby to shower and change into clean clothes at his house while he escorted Marion to the party. It was the first time that Hugo and Marion had met. In June, while on his honeymoon with Laura in Italy, Hugo had left Amanda and Colby in charge of the New Rod magazine editorial office. They had divided up the duties and it fell to Colby to answer the reader correspondence. This happened to be the month Marion discovered The New Rod Quarterly and she wrote both as a new fan and a frustrated female submissive. She and Colby began emailing and soon a meeting was arranged. Marion frankly admitted to Hugo that at first she took Colby for a hustler and was ready to pay him for spanking and servicing her. That turned out not to be necessary but once she was hooked on a spanking man, it was difficult to think about anyone or thing else. So Amanda had suggested that Colby bring her into the Random Point circle. And most recently, there was talk of her working at the club. Just to burn off some of her surplus sexual energy. It wasn't about the money. She made sufficient money for her needs as an attorney. Though of course, she could always use more Louboutins.

Once she was in the car with Hugo, Marion confided that she had gotten every available back issue of his magazine and read them voraciously all summer. She was on fire to play with the editor of that publication, and the sooner the better. Being Hugo, he drove Marion to his shop in the village, took her back to his lounge and spanked her. He did not, however, accept her offer of oral sex. Marion was very attractive but Hugo was newly married to the woman he had been pursuing for years and in any case, blow jobs didn't make his world go round. He told Marion to behave and took her to the party.

At the party, Marion had first enjoyed a thorough schoolroom discipline scene with David Lawrence, which had in fact ended in her servicing the teacher. Then, after the smallest of snacks and a couple of flutes of champagne, she joined Ambrose Bartlett in the sexy exam room, where he strapped her, she gave him head and then let him sodomize her. Not only had it been a divine scene, but he had also given her allowance, being under the impression that she was already a club girl there. Marion had never been paid for going submissive to a man before and the sensation was thrilling.

At the very end of the evening, she walked by the open door of the rose parlor and saw William there. She never hesitated a moment in telling him her fantasy, which was to be thrashed for not giving good enough head. Nor did William hesitate a moment in accepting the offer. Up until then, he had been enjoying the evening, happy in the praise he was receiving from everyone on the job that he and his crew had done in restoring the house and making it club ready. But something had been missing. Some form of illicit excitement. He had sought to kindle it with his ex-wife, Laura, but she had put him off. Marion wasn't Laura, but she was an entirely new submissive girl and apparently her boundaries were non-existent. He could only see this small interlude as a gift to make up for the previous disappointment. And everyone likes a gift.

In her glittering metallic gown, platinum blonde Polyxena Guzman, owner of the Random Point gym and mistress of department store owner Ambrose Bartlett, strolled through the party with an ease and lack of self-consciousness that indicated how much at home she had come to feel amidst her new scene friends in her adopted country. The former Dutch mistress had made a pact with Ambrose regarding their mutual behavior during the evening. He would be escorting his new wife, Pamela and although Pamela was aware of and not hostile to the relationship that had recently developed between himself and Polyxena, Ambrose told Polyxena he would not be asking her to play that evening and Polyxena agreed to pretend that their romance did not exist. By now she knew Ambrose Bartlett well enough to know that he would be more interested in spending the bulk of the party with the new women who would be visiting for the evening only anyway. At any rate, this left her free to please herself. Feeling hyper alpha in the magnetic dress, Polyxena looked around for a pretty boy or man to dominate. She fixed on Anthony's man Friday, Dennis Cowper, as the young man passed her in the hall carrying a tray of wine and glasses into another room. She waited in the hall until he came out and quite consciously extended her extremely pretty foot, shod in a pair of bejeweled five inch stiletto pumps, ever so slightly, and then met his eyes. The English boy's blue eyes met the Dutch siren's blue eyes and he quivered all over. Polyxena knew her little village and all of its scene gossip by now. And she knew very well that Anthony Newton's man was a foot fetishist.

She led him back to the terra cotta salon, which was vacant, and locked the door behind them. They spent a half hour within, with Dennis down on his knees to Polyxena, taking her shoes off, touching her feet, adoring them and herself. She didn't give him permission to lick, kiss or suck her toes, but held these favors in reserve for their next meeting, when she said he was to book a proper session with her here at the club, the next time his master brought him back to the village. And then, paradoxically, because she was utterly charmed by the polite English boy, she bent over a console table and encouraged him to raise her skirt and now worship her bottom through the sheer panty hose she had on. Under the pantyhose Polyxena wore gold lace panties, which she allowed him to lower so that he might have full access to her fair charms.

Since Dennis was only slightly into his thirties, he was fully prepared for this type of adventure, and had a condom in his hand as soon as she made the sweetly breathless suggestion that he carry on now however it suited him to. He had primed her with his tongue and now he produced a strapping hard-on to continue pleasuring her with. He wanted it to be all for her, but the excitement was too much and he feared he came too soon. But Polyxena was pleased. It gave her control over him. She ended the scene then and there, promising that the next time would be even more delightful.

After having been paid homage to by the handsome Dennis, who left her flustered and covered in blushes, Polyxena refreshed herself with champagne, in the company of Marguerite Alexander Flagg, when the two ladies met in the lounge. Polyxena confided about what had just transpired between herself and Dennis and Marguerite confessed that she too had been thinking about topping someone that night, her golden gown being just too elegant to go over someone's lap in. And anyway, she had little desire to sub to anyone but her handsome, hard won husband, Michael Flagg. Polyxena suggested that Marguerite do a good deed and take advantage of Dieter being at the party. This was Polyxena's ex-lover and ex-slave but still the man who was her business partner at the gym and also the popular masseur who had used his strong, clever fingers to relieve the stress of half the women in the room in his professional guise.

Marguerite smiled with approval at the suggestion. She liked Dieter very much but had never played with him. It was an interesting idea. But what did he like? Polyxena told her that Dieter would like whatever she wanted him to like. The girls clicked glasses and Marguerite strode out of the room on her own five-inch heels to track down the Dutch immigrant sub. She found him pacing on the screened porch that faced the woods, smoking a cigarette and moodily contemplating the rain. Marguerite scolded her masseur for smoking a terrible cigarette when he could be smoking wonderful weed and produced a joint from a tiny golden purse. After each taking a few hits, she took him to the room called Cape Cod, at the northwest corner of the house, where there was a whipping post and floggers in a cabinet. She told him she would punish him for smoking tobacco, but it became a highly therapeutic session for the trim, fit and attractive gym owner. Dieter was accustomed to removing stress from his client's bodies through his fingertips. Marguerite, during her several adventures as a mistress, had learned to provide similar relief to her own submissive male clients through whipping. Every other fetish she also understood, but whipping was her specialty when topping men. She was sure that the European bred Dieter was accustomed to harder and much more explicit usage in a dungeon, but Marguerite liked to whip and that was what his session would consist of and not a jot more. Marguerite might move in close to her captive, to lightly stroke a hard pec topped with an even harder nipple, she might lightly nibble an ear lobe or squeeze a firm buttock, but even when Dieter was stark naked, she affected to barely notice his throbbing erection and touched it not at all. She did know he would have loved for her to have taken it in one of her graceful and capable hands, gloved to the elbow in gold satin, but this was much too good for a slave, even if that slave were the worthy Dieter Brandt. A whipping was what Marguerite was giving out that night and a whipping was all Dieter received, but it was a very good whipping, a cathartic whipping, a whipping that allowed him to feel cared for and appreciated.

Once Polyxena had gotten the toppiness out of her system for the evening, she looked around for something more in line with her current orientation and happily almost immediately locked gazes with Freddie Johanson, one of her first intimate acquaintances in Random Point, and the first American to spank her in her adopted land. Freddie had been looking around in vain for his girlfriend, Alison Albrecht. Polyxena was able to tell him that she had just seen Alison being led into the exam room by Ambrose Bartlett. Bartlett had staked out the exam room as his personal playroom all night. It suited him perfectly, with its adjustable exam table and chair, and cabinets full of new toys in boxes. Ambrose had seen Polyxena looking at him as he drew his latest prey by the hand with him down the hall to the exam room. He had winked at her and she had winked back. She would dine with him the following evening and he would stay with her in the lighthouse all night. For Pamela was leaving first thing tomorrow for Fashion Week in Manhattan and Ambrose was not to join her there for several days.

Freddie looked somewhat worried at the thought of Bartlett with Alison but also relieved to be able to talk freely to Polyxena without his lover in earshot. He was naturally bowled over seeing her in the glittering gown that clove to every inch of her shapely torso like metallic stardust. Polyxena was no sylph like Pamela or Amanda or even Alison, to whom thinness was a mantra. Polyxena was a luscious and voluptuous size 8, albeit slowly and surely being coaxed down to a six by Ambrose Bartlett, who was tiny waist obsessed. She had round arms, a full bosom, strong swimmer's legs and a firm, plump bottom. Of course her waist was small. She ran a gym and exercised every day. But she loved cream tarts and spaetzle. So she was slim and yet full, lithe and yet round, with more of a 1950's shape than that a 21st century one. Freddie loved Polyxena's figure. He was a tall, husky young man who wished his own girlfriend were just a bit juicier too. To Freddie, Polyxena was a goddess of love. She had been kind to him once and seemed inclined to repeat that kindness now. Re-commandeering the terra cotta salon, Polyxena took Freddie by the hand, led him inside and once again, locked the door. Telling him now that she craved a good, long, sound spanking over his monumental lap, she turned her back to him and told him to unzip her from the platinum gown, so as to save it from being destroyed through rough usage. When he had done this, she stood before him in only a tiny lace G-string and her wonderfully high, platinum heels. However, he still managed to be almost a half-foot taller than her and when over his lap, she felt a small girl again.

Meanwhile, back in the exam room, Ambrose Bartlett prepared to devastate his third girl of the night. His adventures had begun with the college coed B&D call girl, Thalia, one of Amanda's best friends in Boston. He had had his eye on the leggy rebel for some time, but tonight had afforded him his first opportunity to top her. Thalia was a charismatic twenty-year-old beauty, very irreverent and insolently proud of being a playful prostitute. Getting her to talk about herself, he soon discovered that she was nurturing an ongoing passion for Hugo Sands and was anxious for any chance to visit Random Point, either to shoot for his magazine or work at this new club. Ambrose promised to see her whenever she came to the village and gifted her generously for the beating he subsequently gave her. Amanda had told Thalia in detail what she could expect from her first session with Bartlett, who was always awful the first time. So Thalia had made sure to drink three champagne cocktails and smoke herself glassy eyed before going in the exam room with him. The encounter had been mutually satisfactory, with Thalia calling upon her histrionic abilities to temper Bartlett's severity and actually succeeding where others failed. She cried almost immediately and that worked in her favor.

Bartlett's next playmate had been the insatiable Marion Craig, whose appetite for corporal punishment and rough sex amazed even Ambrose. His harsh style of discipline enchanted Marion, who finally found what she was looking for when she initially wrote to the New Rod Quarterly and Colby answered her letter. When she told Ambrose Bartlett to treat her like a slut, he didn't question the gift. Wearing his belt out on her and then having her sink to her knees before him was like Christmas morning for the well-dressed sadist who had been kept in check more or less by the sensitive submissive girls of Random Point for years.

And then came the final gift of the night, Alison Albrecht, that slim and nervous girl who he had been watching as an interesting store patron her entire life. Initially he sat behind the consulting desk, with Alison in the patient's chair as they conversed.

"We've never formally met," he said, "but I've known of you and your family for years. In fact your father was the principal of my junior high school when you were born."

"Please don't hold that against me," said Alison with a faint smile. She was a slender brunette of medium height, well dressed in a pleated skirt, wool blazer and white shirt, her pretty feet shod in oxblood stack heeled brogues and her legs hosed to the knee in clocked stockings.

"I've been working at Bartlett's since I was a kid, sometimes part time, sometimes full time, during the summers. Your mother was a regular shopper. She would come in every other Saturday without fail. Your first ballet slippers, your first riding boots, your graduation and prom dresses, were all selected at my store, under your exacting mother's watchful eye. She was a very fashionable woman. Is she enjoying her retirement in Florida?"

"Yes, and thank you for remembering her," said Alison, greatly surprised by Bartlett's affability and warmth.

"My condolences on your father's passing," Bartlett adding.

She looked at him and said, "Thank you, but if he was your principal, you can probably figure out how I felt about him."

"Him being your father almost makes me want to spare you more punishment," Ambrose said.

"But not quite?"

"Well, seeing as you're so cute, with that little waist, no."

All his girls tonight had had small waists. Marion had been downright scrawny, which he found very attractive. Ambrose traced the origins of his fascination with delicate waists to his extreme childhood. From his toddlerhood, he was brought to Bartlett's, to play in the stock room of the lingerie department where his smart Aunt

Clary was the manager. Even though it was the late 1970's, foundation garments still had their own section of the elegant lingerie department and the very young Ambrose saw many a young matron come out into the hall of the dressing room to view her torso reflected in the biggest three way mirror. He was especially riveted by the ladies with the smallest waists. And then, one Christmas, before he was quite six years old, he witnessed a tiny scene before the lingerie department, where the loveliest new negligees were displayed on mannequins. This department was the jewel of Bartlett's, a perfumed bastion of silk, nylon, velvet and lace, edged with armoires full of challis, voile, cashmere and the finest embroidered Italian cotton sleepwear, and filled with every dainty garment designed to cling closely to or float about the bare skin of a woman or girl.

The scene that Ambrose witnessed was of a handsome young businessman, escorting a young beauty who was obviously his girlfriend or wife around the store. As they paused before a mannequin clad in a luxurious cashmere robe trimmed with fur, the pretty girl pressed closer to her man and expressed an interested in the expensive dressing gown. She insisted in trying the robe on. The young man scolded her roundly, telling her that she knew very well he couldn't afford to spend that much money on her. She pouted and seemed to refuse to take the becoming robe off. She looked at herself in the mirror and preened until he warned her that if she continued behaving like a brat he'd have to spank her. She stuck her tongue out at him and he responded by turning her under his arm, the cashmere robe snugly outlining the shape of her trim bottom, and administering five or six sharp but by no means severe spanks. She protested indignantly and when he allowed her to regain her footing, her face was pink with embarrassment. She took off the robe and stamped her foot at her boyfriend, who laughed at her and led her by the hand into the lingerie department to buy her a gown set for a hundred instead of nine hundred dollars.

From that day on, Ambrose Bartlett was not only fixated on women with dainty figures, but on spanking their bottoms. And he had also noticed how much the idea of wearing a cashmere robe had excited the spankable lady. After noticing this he began to be aware of the way in which shopping seemed to affect the moods of women, how they seemed to move in a dream world, yet hone in on exactly the colors and shapes that interested them the most and flush with pleasure as they did, as though they had unexpectedly met with a favorite lover. He studied those colors and shapes and remembered them years later, when he began to go on buying tours with the buyers for Bartlett's. The lessons he took away were multiple, that new clothes made girls happy, that when girls were happy, they were flirtatious and sexual susceptible, and that the clothes that made them the happiest were always the ones that made them look the smartest, sleekest and sexiest. Thus his fetishes entwined with his managerial career at the store, which came entirely under his control while he was still in his early thirties.

"Do you still work at Braemar?" Ambrose asked.

"Yes."

"Are you good friends with my ex-wife?

"Yes, Paula and I are best friends."

"Oh!" he was startled. "Best friends, is it?"

"Of course. Why wouldn't we be? We have lunch together every day."

"I suppose you'll be telling her about whatever we do in this room together tonight?" Ambrose asked.

"Should I not do that?" Alison replied.

"Do you usually confide your adventures to Paula?"

"I don't usually have adventures. This is the first big spanking party I've ever been to."

"Have you played with anyone so far?"

"Yes. David Lawrence."

"That's good. Hope has been trying to convince him that this is a nice place to work. So the more perks he gets off the club, the better."

Alison smiled to think of herself as a perk.

"Who are you seeing?" he asked.

"Freddie Johanson. He works at Braemar too."

"Good match for you?" Ambrose asked.

"Yes, he's a darling man."

"But tonight is for being crazy, right?"

"Sure, why not?" Alison replied, excited to be with the sophisticated Bartlett, in spite of his reputation as a severe spanker.

"Don't worry, it won't be anything bad. I have too much compassion for you being raised by Lionel Albrecht to want to punish you anymore. But have you ever been forced to orgasm?"

"Forced to orgasm, how?"

"We're in an exam room and that cabinet is full of anal probes, vibrators, dildos, lube, all factory sealed. You see where I'm going with this?"

"It sounds so very explicit," Alison reflected.

"I know. But what do you expect people to think of when you dress like that? Whenever I fantasize about playing doctor with a girl, she's dressed preppie."

"If you plan use all those things on me, don't worry, I'd be too embarrassed to tell anyone about it, ever. As far as the world is concerned, you will have merely spanked me tonight."

"It is going to be extreme. As I said, you may even climax. I think it would make you feel more relaxed about the whole thing if I bribed you to accept my proposal. I'm sure you could use a shopping spree at Bartlett's before the school year commences. Come in tomorrow and pick out a half dozen dresses on me."

"Seriously?" Alison grinned, delighted at the thought of being bribed to submit to the delicious indignities he was proposing.

"You barely know me, and I have a bad reputation. I want you to be completely at ease. I've discovered nothing calms a woman's anxieties like shopping."

"You seem so nice. Why did Paula leave you again?"

Ambrose sighed. "Because I pressured her to be skinny for me."

"Oh, right. I remember. Something about a Christmas torte," Alison said.

"Ironically, she slimmed down beautifully as soon as she moved in with Sloan," Ambrose said.

"With me, you'd be a terrible enabler," Alison said. "I already obsess about my weight. But Freddie couldn't care less."

"You know, if you were to submit to a purge tonight, you would probably find yourself a good two pounds lighter tomorrow for trying on clothes."

"You don't have to oversell it," said Alison, getting up to make sure the door was locked. "I'm the assistant comptroller at a high school. I don't get that much excitement in my life. Anyway, I know my boyfriend has already been bad and come here to play. So, why I shouldn't I? And it's okay to be perverse with me. As you say, I barely know you and I'm told these things are always better done with a stranger."

In one of the powder rooms, Marguerite asked Paula whether she and Sloan might fancy playing as a couple with herself and Michael. It was the end of the evening and Marguerite had drunk enough champagne and talked enough, now she was in the mood to play. She had played with her handsome partner in the bookstore once, years before, but not since. Marguerite took it for granted that Michael would very much enjoy playing with Paula Taylor. Who would not be interested in spanking a good looking, shapely, discreet and charming blonde? Paula grinned at the idea of being spanked by Michael Flagg. She was probably the only lady in the Venus Club who hadn't played with the tavern owner, but she had fantasized about it.

The girls found Michael and Sloan and put the idea to them. The husbands both nodded in agreement. All the rooms on that floor were currently occupied, but Michael knew the layout of the club well, having installed its security system, and led his wife and friends down to the large, semi-finished basement, currently partitioned into a series of shooting sets. Hugo had been shooting and filming all week there and each of the rooms contained key pieces of furniture and equipment.

Marguerite and Paula discovered an armoire full of leather and a trunk full of boots. They instantly decided to exchange their delicate gowns for snug fitting zip leather dresses with pleated gladiator skirts. Their bejeweled heels were changed for butter soft black leather thigh boots. Emerging from behind their dressing screen in their sexy but sturdy leather outfits, they looked much more playful than when they had gone behind it in their glittering gowns.

No one else came downstairs to intrude upon their private games and the two couples separated after trading up partners, putting whole sets between them, which created an even more private atmosphere at either end of the basement. Marguerite and Paula were both sensitive ladies who were at the moment unwilling to be observed playing. Marguerite loved to show off her own dominant skills in front of an audience, but wasn't the slightest bit inclined to be watched while slipping into subspace over Sloan Taylor's elegantly trousered lap. While that was happening, she planned to bury her face in her arms and simply enjoy the sensations rather than worry about playing to an audience. And Paula Taylor was similarly glad that she could give herself up to a sort of well-behaved physical ravishment by the muscular Michael Flagg, without her husband looking on. That would have distracted her to the point of the whole venture being a waste of all their time. Of course she wanted to play with Michael. Every girl did, but in private.

Chapter Nine

Susan's Bachelorette Party

Susan Ross knew very little about billiards, but she knew how good her bottom looked in the laced leather hobble skirt when she bent over the table to take a shot, and now, so did Pascal Robbins, who also approved of the front view, featuring the semi-exposure of Susan's small but lush cleavage, pushed together by the tight fitting white leather vest that clung so affectionately to her trim, dainty torso and up thrust bosom. She had returned to him to continue their game, and to continue flirting with him. She'd drunk almost nothing that night, had eaten but lightly and at midnight still looked clear-eyed, pink cheeked and fresh. She was stoned on Cassandra's weed of course, but Pascal knew nothing of that and nothing she did or said betrayed her ongoing state of euphoria as a result of the many pipe hits she had taken in the master bedroom throughout the evening. That private inner sanctum had welcomed a steady stream of kindred female spirits the whole night long, affording the best of friends multiple chances to update each other's grasp of the current match-ups in the house and share any subsequent scandals or near scandals.

Pamela, when she chanced into the room with the weed, was made much of by every other woman who entered. Everyone knew about her upcoming show and almost all the younger women at the club that night had played with her powerful, generous husband. But Pamela was most thrilled when Amanda was by her side, the gift of that wonderful summer to her, her new, her best friend. Carola had passed through the room and stopped to get high with her girls, Tai and Lydia. Cassandra and Hope appeared often but lingered only briefly before running back to the party. Laura, Marguerite, Damaris and Diana, had all made unceremonious visits to the room all night long, staying so long to talk to each other that their friends sent other friends to fetch them back. Even Marion and Alison made their way to the perfect and most inner salon of the house, Cassandra's private suite, and fortified themselves before their interviews with Ambrose Bartlett. But Pascal knew nothing of this and never would, for his wife Phoebe was among the naughty only to the extent of sometimes straying with Anthony Newton, never in pursuit of the greenest fairy. And he certainly didn't realize that Susan Ross came back to him in the lounge very stoned indeed and feeling in need of the same sort of relaxation she sensed her fiancé had enjoyed with Pascal's wife earlier in the loft, before it was taken over by the younger set.

"Do you want to go somewhere where we can be alone?" she asked Pascal at the conclusion of their game. He had just been about to pour himself a cognac but he put the glass and decanter down and looked at her.

"Why? What did you have in mind?"

"What do you think?"

"I don't know."

"Really?"

"Are you asking me to play with you?" he asked.

"Yes, but not in the way you're thinking."

"Take me somewhere where we can be alone, then," he said.

Susan led him down the hall to the library, which she knew to be empty. When they were within, she locked the door and pressed her back against it, looking at him.

"Anthony told me we're getting married soon. Before the holidays," Susan confided. "I don't know why he feels it's necessary all of a sudden."

"Does that mean he's going to stop sleeping with my wife?"

"Phoebe? She's so two months ago," Susan said.

"Why? You mean he's seeing someone else on the side now?"

"Of course he is. The mistress of this house was his mid-summer pet, he also played with her sister and tonight he's been breaking in the tiny girl chef."

"You really think he's over Phoebe?" Pascal asked eagerly.

"Of course he's over Phoebe. Phoebe is your girl. Nothing will ever change that," Susan said reassuringly.

"Doesn't it bother you?" Pascal asked.

"To be honest, I felt so threatened by Cassandra, I cut short a trip in Europe to come home and make sure she wasn't annexing him right out from under me. But this gesture he's making of marrying me, is his way of telling me to relax about everything."

"And are you becoming relaxed?" he asked.

"I could be more relaxed," said Susan, slowly unzipping her vest. "If I got out of these tight, confining clothes and off these incredibly high heeled booties." When the vest fell completely open, revealing her small, plump, charming breasts, Pascal was riveted with interest. She perched on the edge of the large desk and extended one small foot towards him. "Help me?" she asked. He bent to unbuckling the tiny buckles of her shoes and one by one took them off. She wiggled her crimson tipped toes with pleasure. As he relieved her of each shoe, he massaged each lily foot between his strong hands. Susan regretted having to give up the extremely sexy shoes at this point, but having been on the heels for hours, she needed relief that very moment. Now she slid off the desk, got back onto her now bare, pretty feet, and with one zip shed her long, glove tight hobble skirt, letting it drop to the ground. Shrugging off the vest, she now stood before him in only a pair of sheer black bikinis. Even her black velvet ponytail tie she undid, letting her long, wavy, blonde hair fall about her shoulders and almost down to her waist.

Susan turned slowly around to let him see her from every angle.

"You're really giving yourself to me?" he asked.

"Wouldn't that restore the balance to your marriage?"

"If we do something together now, are you going to tell him?"

"Not if you don't want me to."

"I think I do want you to."

"He isn't a wolf, you know. I'm sure he never consciously set out to cuckold you or cheat on me. Women just gravitate towards him and he can't resist them."

"On second thought, don't say anything about this to anyone. As unfaithful as she herself has been, Phoebe wouldn't be cool about me doing this with you."

"I guess you managed to keep your escapade with Amanda a secret from her?" Susan asked, reaching out to unbuckle his belt.

"Oh hell, yes!" he replied. "Amanda told you about that, did she?"

"She told me that you have a big cock," Susan said. "I remembered that when I was looking at you tonight and it made me even more interested."

Now he too began to shed clothing and soon stood before her as nude as she did before him. He was a tall, thin man in his late thirties, with some good natural upper body definition and surprisingly beefy thighs and calves.

"Oh, you have big legs, I like that," she told him.

"From squatting down all the time to take shots," said the photographer.

"And this is nice and big as well," she said, reaching out to touch his newly sprung erection. He hugged her to him for a few minutes, breathing in the scent of her hair and stroking her silken back, then he took her by the hand and led her to the wide, deep, tufted leather sofa facing the hearth. It was too early in the season for a fire, but it was still a wonderful setting for a love scene.

He lay down beside her, took her in his arms and began to caress her, softly squeeze her breasts, and entwine his fingers in her soft, blonde pubic curls. He kissed her throat, bit her earlobes and pressed his fingertips against her lower abdomen. But when he introduced a finger slowly in between her labia, he found that she was barely moist.

"I know you didn't plan for me to spank you, but you're a spanking girl, and spanking girls like spanking for foreplay. So let me spank you too," he said, not waiting for a reply, but rolling her over, and then deftly repositioning her over his lap, with his cock pressed up against her under her stomach. "It isn't like I don't know how to spank girls. I spank my wife, you know," he said. And when she didn't resist, he began to spank her, somewhat smartly, yet not extremely hard. She wriggled across his strong thighs, gave a little squeak now and then, kicked her small, bare legs, but not violently, and then, very sweetly, put her wrist back for him to hold fast to her waist as he continued smacking her seductively. With all of this going on, Susan soon became as wet and welcoming as any new swain might desire and he discovered this shortly.

Condoms were found in a desk drawer and Susan asked him to possess her in her favorite way, from behind, while she was on all fours on the couch.

"Is that how you can come?" he asked.

"No, there's another way to do that. I'll tell you just before you're ready to come as well," she said, assuming the all fours position. After several minutes of vigorous pile driving sex from behind, Pascal urged Susan to confide to him how he could make her climax.

"Lie on your back and I'll get on top," she told him; "And while I stare into your disturbingly handsome face, maybe you can finger me."

Loving the feel of the warm, responsive beauty grinding against him, absorbing him to the hilt, Pascal made her look into his eyes the whole time until she came, expiring against his lightly fuzzed chest and clinging to him hard for several minutes after. When she had recovered her senses a little, he put her beneath him and fucked her with long, rapid thrusts until his own moment of release was upon him.

After withdrawing, Pascal asked, "Where should I get rid of this?" he indicated the condom that sheathed his still semi erect penis.

"The closest bathroom is two steps down the hall," Susan said.

"Will you wait for me until I get back?" he asked, pulling his clothes on, socks and shoes on quickly.

"Of course, but I'll lock the door until you get back. You knock and let me know it's you," she said, following him to the door and then closing and locking it behind him. While she was waiting, she also regained her outfit, except for the torturously high-heeled booties. When Pascal returned, he took a seat in one of the large, leather armchairs and told her to come and sit on his lap, which she did, placing her face between his shoulder and throat.

"Are you glad we did it?" she asked.

"Very glad!" he said softly, grazing her cheek with his lips.

"You've been with us for a while, but this summer, you really became one of us," said Susan.

"I tried to fight it for a couple of years, but my wife is right, you people really are more interesting to hang around with than vanillas.

Of which I guess I am one."

"Not any more, you aren't. Not with those moves. You're a honey of a spanker and fuck as suavely as Tom Byron."

"Gee, thanks!" he chuckled. "But tell me, how often do you do something like this?"

"You mean cheat on Anthony?"

"Yes."

"Not often. I work in Manhattan, and it's full of hot men in suits. When I go out to a bar with my girlfriends after work, odds are a cute guy will try to pick me up. If I'm in the mood, I'll spend an hour or two with that stranger. But I never tell them what I'm into. So all the casual hook ups I've had in the city have been vanilla and I've never spent time with the same man twice."

"I hope it won't be that way with me, Susan," said Pascal. "I know part of why you came on to me tonight was to help me cope with Anthony seducing my wife. Amanda did the same thing. I could get used to these mercy fucks. But at the same time, I'm getting the distinct impression that you genuinely like me."

"Pascal, you should think of me as one of your closest friends from now on," she said, "as I will of you. We're very similar you and I. We are both artistic, but it's our partners who are the true artists and we have to realize that we can't be their only muses. Nor should they be ours."

"You probably won't believe this, but I never try to get over on my models," said Pascal.

"Of course not, you like cultured, educated women. Your wife is a classical actress, not an empty headed mannequin. I guarantee you that if Amanda was just any leggy, blonde size 2 model from the agency instead of a super smart Ivy League brat, you wouldn't have fallen for her at all, no less the way you did."

"Amanda who?" said Pascal, bestowing a final kiss on her little hand, "I'm madly in love with Susan Ross now."

Chapter Ten

Satisfactory Resolutions

When Pascal and Susan returned to the lounge, they found Hope behind the bar preparing individual espressos for those present who were about to drive home. Hugo, David and Dennis were already sipping the brews, which the former barista had so perfectly prepared, while Anthony, also behind the bar, poured Cassandra and Phoebe cordials. Pascal was about to ask Hope for a coffee when she said, "I remember, double shot, with cream, no sugar." She did in fact, remember how everyone in the room took their coffee, having served them at the bookstore for so many years.

Even though she had played with no one that evening, it had been a night of pure triumph for Hope Spencer Lawrence, who had the satisfaction of both a new position that she loved and a husband made freshly confident as a result of the attentions her several attractive girlfriends and others, had paid to him that night. For this one night, serving coffee to her friends was a pleasure she wouldn't have missed, because as they looked at her, in her cool, chic leather outfit, as lovely as she had ever looked, none of them regretted the absence of her perpetual jeans, white shirt and red apron any more. This was their Hope as she was always meant to be, a sleek and sexy fetish girl goddess, ruling gracefully and lightly in her own leather and wood scented environment.

The party in the loft was finally breaking up. Plastridge Currie came into the lounge with Diana and was given his own espresso, to wake him up for the drive back up the hill to the Cliff house, where he and Diana were staying one more night with Anthony and Susan.

Colby appeared with Thalia, Tai and Lydia, whom he was about to drive back to Susan's house opposite the graveyard, where the three visiting girls were spending the night. Dru did not appear any more that evening, having been summarily pulled into Carola's room as he walked down the hall several minutes before.

William and Damaris were leaving by the front door, with Marion Craig, whom they had offered to give a ride back to the Ball and Feather. That lady was completely exhausted by all the riotous playing and sex she had been engaging in since the late afternoon, and fell fast asleep in the Random's back seat on the way to the Inn. Damaris never had the slightest inkling that her husband had first thrashed and then received deep throat to conclusion from the skinny brunette in the back of their sedan, and chattered gaily the whole way back to their house at the end of the cul de sac of Shadow Lane about the fun she had had playing bound damsel to Plastridge Currie and Carola Campi.

Josette went and stood beside Dennis, who would be driving her home as well. It was the first night of many that she would be the front seat passenger while her master and mistress rode in the back of the Bentley. In the years to come, she would accompany Susan, Anthony and Dennis, on stateside vacations and visits abroad, fitting into the domestic scheme of the Newton household like a piece of the puzzle that had been missing until then. Meanwhile, for one more night, she was to reside in Anthony's Random Point mansion. Then this strange summer fairy tale would end and she would return to Dutchess County to finish her course at the Culinary Institute. And after that, she would come to Manhattan and begin her career as personal chef to Mr. Newton and his new wife. She looked up at Dennis, who smiled down at her. There was nothing about little Josette that Dennis didn't like.

One by one the various couples emerged from their play spaces and departed the house, fatigued to the bone but still inwardly humming with excitement from the evening. Alison and Freddie had both been so individually bad that they could barely look at each other and yet each couldn't help but laughing at the mad things they had just done.

Susan walked Laura back to the schoolroom to get their raincoats, confiding to her sister on the way that she had played with Pascal Robbins to their mutual satisfaction. Watching Laura slip on a black velvet cloak, Susan asked, "Did you play tonight?"

"No, but I got incredibly stoned with all those girls from Boston," laughed Laura.

"You didn't want to play?"

"I don't want to play with anyone but Hugo right now. After all, we've only been married a few months. I'm still enjoying new wife status," said Laura. Susan looked around to make sure they were completely alone, then whispered, "Keep an eye on that Cassandra. She's like catnip to these men."

"I know," said Laura softly. "It's okay. She's entitled to amuse herself after keeping herself contained for so many years. But she's not the type to steal another woman's man, even if he was hers to begin with."

"Still, I won't rest completely easy about her until we find her a boyfriend of her own," said Susan emphatically.

Laura laughed and hugged her sister, saying, "If I know Hugo, he's already working on that. Meanwhile, she's got Hope as her constant companion here at the house and you can see they adore each other."

"I know. Anthony did a good thing here. This has been the best night that our scene has ever had. Everyone left with a smile on their face."

Hugo came over at ten the following morning to see Amanda and Colby off. He gave Amanda money for her first term expenses and promised to drop off some furniture for her dorm room that week when he went into Boston.

"I'm so glad you're so much closer now," said Amanda fondly to her mother. "Come visit me as soon as you can."

"I'll give you a key to my apartment," said Hugo to Cassandra.

"I still have the key to that apartment," said Cassandra.

"Do you?" Hugo asked with a smile. "Does that mean you always meant to come back?"

"Well, something made me keep it," she replied lightly.

Amanda kissed both her parents. Colby shook Hugo's hand and hugged Cassandra rather warmly. Then the children got into Colby's car and drove off to begin their sophomore year.

Carola had not yet emerged from her room, though Cassandra was pretty sure she heard Dru creep out of that room shortly after the sun came up and then quietly slip out of the house. His stint as club houseboy was over for the summer and he too was on his way back to college that day.

The cleaning crew was already at work about the house, tidying it up post party. It was a fragrant, balmy, end of summer morning, the air fresh from the rain and the sky a deepening blue. Hugo asked Cassandra if she would walk in the woods with him. She invited him into her room while she put on walking booties, telling him to roll them a joint. He showed her that he had one and they both laughed, realizing how little they had changed since being together.

"I can't figure out if it's really a club or just a rich man's hobby horse," said Hugo at length, as they strolled and smoked.

"People have paid for sessions and ladies have come in to work, so it must be a club of some sort," said Cassandra.

"But will it ever make enough to pay for its own upkeep?"

"Anthony told me not to worry about that."

"Will a percentage of the sessions be enough for you to live on?"

"Yes, since I can live here rent free."

"Do you see yourself doing many sessions?"

"I didn't think I would initially but the locals are starting to figure out I'm a switch so, yes," Cassandra grinned.

"I knew of a girl who in Hollywood who used to bill herself as a metaphysical switch. You ought to annex that."

"I like it," she smiled.

"Carola and those girls are staying until later so we can do a little shoot," said Hugo. "Do you want to be the second top?"

"Why not?"

"So everything comes full circle for us," he said, "with you posing for one of my magazine spreads, just as you did twenty years ago."

"Yes and no," she said thoughtfully.

"You mean because of Laura?" Hugo asked.

"Exactly," said Cassandra.

"You notice that she isn't here with us now," he said.

"Where is she?"

"Actually she's making herself useful for a change opening the shop for me," he said.

"What does she do with herself most days?" Cassandra asked.

"Whatever she likes, plus a little cartooning over at the studio she and Susan have. Otherwise she takes walks, rides her bike, visits Marguerite, and goes shopping."

"Sounds like she has entirely too much time on her hands. Send her over here and I'll put her to work in a dungeon," said Cassandra.

"She's way too spoiled to pass herself off as a submissive," said Hugo.

"So, I'll call on her if I need a top," suggested Cassandra.

He thought it over and said, "That might be a nice gesture coming from you. Double domming a subbed out guy would allow you to get to know each other better. And all girls like making extra allowance."

"Is she still highly suspicious of my motives in coming back to live here?"

"She knows I'm still attracted to you," said Hugo. "She knows I was with you last year in San Francisco. She smelled your perfume on my suit. It made her cry and stamp her foot at me."

"I'm still attracted to you too," said Cassandra, extending her hand for him to take.

"The day will come when we find ourselves alone together in a dungeon," he said.

"I've been thinking about that since the day I moved in," she replied, squeezing his hand.

About the Author

Eve Howard has been writing, editing and creating spanking erotica since the 1980's. There are 11 previous volumes in the Shadow Lane series as well as a lush magazine called *Shadow Lane's The Art of Spanking*, all available from CCB Publishing and online retailers. Eve has also directed and produced 200 spanking videos, appearing as a performer in a number of her own productions. Designed to make people feel good, rather than guilty about being into spanking, Eve's books are romantic yet irreverent; portraying the battle of the sexes with a BDSM twist. Eve was the editor of the beautifully designed *Stand Corrected* magazine, which raised the bar for spanking publications in the 1990's. And for over 25 years, Eve's company Shadow Lane has been one of the primary social organs of the real-life spanking scene. Eve lives in Las Vegas with her husband, Tony Elka, and their calico cat. Follow Eve Howard's Spanking Blog at:

www.shadowlane.com

Reader Reviews about the Shadow Lane Series

"I've become addicted to the "Random Point" series so much that I can't wait until the next chapter. I've ordered the first two Shadow Lane volumes and have re-read them over and over. I never tire of them. Eve is the only person I know who can make an enema sexy."

"I discovered Shadow Lane about a month ago via AOL. Prior to that time I thought I could write excellent spanking erotica. Then I ordered, "The Problem with Laura." This is just a note to commend Eve Howard's spectacular talent and to say thanks for an incredible erotic experience."

"I have just completed "Return to Random Point" and decided that I had to write about how much I enjoyed it. I have not been so aroused since reading my first discipline novel many years ago, about a girl raised in England and "coming of age" as I believe they put it. More recently I have enjoyed reading Grant Andrews' My Darling Dominatrix and Ann Rice's "Beauty" series. It seems that women, though, have the right touch when it comes to writing about this subject. Eve, especially, knows how to touch that erotic nerve and bring it to a pure, raw sensuality until one feels that he/she is near bursting with lust."

"I, for one, have always loved (and by loved I mean devoured... breathlessly) Eve Howard's novelettes. To read them... especially when I was just 'coming out'... was to feel completely validated. I truly identified with each and every heroine; the feisty, sassy ones, the shy, demure ultra 'subby' ones... the young ones, and the more mature. I loved the gentle yet firm "taken in hand" nature of the romantic variety of spanking D's that Eve always incorporated into the stories. I loved that the plots were not complicated... but, feasible nonetheless. I loved the depictions of sexual escapades after many of the spanking interludes. I appreciated that the girls were cherished and adored by the affably rogue-ish gents... that the submitting was willing and desired... that it wasn't like 'rape.'

I like the settings... having grown up in New England and living here almost my whole life. I LOVED the idea of the bookstore (which I always find sexy). Then and now. I could cite many passages too, but I fear I've rambled enough. Eve was/is always my favorite spanking author."

www.ingramcontent.com/pod-product-compliance
Lightning Source LLC
Chambersburg PA
CBHW021957010726
47494CB00003B/771